SHE WILL RETURN

By
Mark G. Pennington

Copyright© 2023 Mark G. Pennington

ISBN: 978-81-19228-88-1

First Edition: 2023

Rs. 200/-

Cyberwit.net

HIG 45 Kaushambi Kunj, Kalindipuram

Allahabad - 211011 (U.P.) India

http://www.cyberwit.net

Tel: +(91) 9415091004

E-mail: info@cyberwit.net

Printed at Vcore.

PROLOGUE

1

The air inside the cabin smelled of pot roast and body odour. Clara woke, smelled the sickly perfume, felt her nerves shredding above the hum of the engine. Heard voices flood the sky as if they were songbirds keeping the stars company. She placed a hand to her stomach; it was still flat. Breathed easier knowing that it was just a dream. She'd been sleeping since Berlin.

Clara leant on Bill, still dozing a little. Placed her hands in between the crevice of his arms. The day before the flight she'd had the last telephone conversation with her mother – who had urged her, pleaded almost, to use the trip to get her marriage back on track. Clara never really heard that. All she could talk about was how exciting it was to be heading to San Francisco where Bill was going to break America.

Bill stroked her head and she began to stir. The captain announced their imminent landing, and the time at ten minutes past one. From the galley, a woman came down holding a basket in her hands. Clara took a piece of hard candy and sucked.

The plane touched down and Clara willed for her ears to react a little quicker to the changes in air pressure. She swallowed hard and it seemed to do the trick. Bill stood and grabbed the bags from the overhead bin.

'It must be the reason why you're such a successful writer,' said Clara.

Bill lifted the sunglasses from his eyes and gave her a tired look.

'Because you really understand the plight of us all,' she said with a huge grin. She took her holdall and they made their way to the front of the plane.

'I'm only looking out for my number one girl,' Bill said.

The heat was already clinging to the nape of her neck, as sultry as a midsummer night. They picked up Macdonald, their cat, from cargo. Clara held the camera she had borrowed from her father – the instant

Polaroid which was as vintage as his old boy scout badges he kept in a trinket box up in the loft – and snapped one of the cat as Bill loaded up the rental car.

'He must be starving,' said Bill, 'we'll get him some tuna or something when we arrive.'

They headed west on Lincoln Way. Carried on towards 26th Avenue. There were plenty of people milling around, tourists and wayward folk, she figured. The sunlight snaked its way through the window of the car. The buckeye trees of sun-soaked streets looked on. Eventually, they crossed Golden Gate Bridge. Clara took more pictures, seeing as they had a little time before their dinner plans. The street was fine in the streaming light. It was almost vertical as they drove upwards to a tall building with a flat roof and a yellow entrance. They threw the suitcases to a corner of the lounge, beside a shoe depot where a row of sunscreen bottles lay. One hour later they were sitting on the balcony of their apartment, the sun stewing lazily in their laps. It was not quite like home, where the dogwood and the pompoms in the garden grew sweetly in the Cumbrian rain. It rained most often at home. Now the afternoon sun was glorious and the traffic below seemed dreamier than it ever could be in Coniston. In the horizon Clara could see the lighthouse of Alcatraz, beaming out on its axis across the water. She hid behind the huge lens of the Polaroid, and rang off a few more instant pictures. Bill got up and went inside, almost slipped on the hard wood floor.

'You should be wearing those writing slippers I bought you,' said Clara. 'One of these days you're going to catch your death.' She took a picture of his white socks, just to remind him later.

The silence between Bill's dull thuds against the floor, the opening of the large refrigerator and then the piercing smash of glass made her put down the camera. But it was Bill's scream that really got her attention. Bill never ever screamed. At once she leapt out of her plastic chair, knocked over her glass of wine, panic setting in already. She didn't know what it was but it was something. Through the screen she saw Bill's body, slightly bent at the knee, but she could not see his face, or whatever had made him holler. Clara rushed in to the apartment and stopped. She cupped her mouth with her hands, stricken with fright. 'Stay back!' Bill shouted. Clara gasped, ignored him and ran bare foot over to the open refrigerator door, where just three feet to the side lay Macdonald, dead. She hardly noticed the blood on the soles of her feet where she had just trodden through the broken glass of a mason jar, knocked from the counter.

The cat had a plume of white foam dribbling from its open mouth. Its eyes were closed. The whiskers were thick with vomit, matted to the jaw. Clara's face was flushed; her eyes wet with the sting of tears. She let out an ungodly sound through her hands, which still clamped her creased face. Bill told her not to touch it as she began to edge closer, not caring about the sting of the broken glass in her heel. He picked up a small bottle from beside the still body and examined.

'Clara, when you gave Macdonald his lunch, did you perhaps touch this?' He said, holding up the bottle, which looked like the capsule of pills her father took every night before bed. Clara stammered out something that sounded like 'What on earth is it, Bill?'

'Xylitol,' he said. 'Maybe you knocked it down to the ground by accident.'

She started to weep, wished that she could turn back time, hated herself all at once.

'Of all the things that could have gone wrong on this trip,' Clara began, 'we end up losing the damn cat.' She suddenly felt the pain of the glass shards in her foot.

'You mustn't blame yourself, it was an accident,' said Bill. He clutched at his cross, the loop around the neck, and said a prayer. 'Through the mercy of God, rest in peace.'

Clara kissed its paw, moaned in agony – for the loss and for the throbbing ache in her feet.

'I loved that cat,' she said, feeling her jaw quiver. For the next two hours she refused to eat, and watched on as the skyline darkened.

The lighthouse flitted on and off in the dusk. The sound of gulls flared. Thunder bellowed in the dusky plum sky. She took off her sunglasses, which Bill had asked her to do a couple of hours ago, and felt the world again. She felt its vastness, its precariousness, its horror. She gazed down at the manic traffic building below them. Heard the honking of horns.

'It's a horrible way to go, poisoned like that. I'll never forgive myself,' Clara said. Her bandaged foot began to ache again.

'It was an accident,' repeated Bill. 'You never meant to hurt him; he knows that.' She couldn't bear to look back into the kitchenette, where a blanket covered over the small body, but at the same time she just had to look. Just like she had to look again at the pictures she had taken earlier that day. The view from the apartment roof, the airport, the buckeye trees on a sunlit street, the trams, the Fillmore lights of union street where the college kids leant against the brickwork, the view from Marina Green where it cuts across the city like a spiny wire, and poor Macdonald clawing at the bars on his carrier. They should have been wine drinking now in Cow Hallow, meeting the editor from Bill's US publisher. They should have been greeting the nightcrawlers fishing through the mill of fog city. But instead, they were sitting in the dark on the balcony, under a pin head of a moon, mourning a death.

She heard the crows perched on the roof above them, a caw so deranged that she felt sick again. She placed the photo of the cat inside her pocket and it felt at that moment, even though it was only the middle of July, that summer was finally over.

2

Bernadine thought then that if she had a knife, she would stick it right through him. Cut him the way he was cutting her in half. But maybe it was for these kinds of thoughts that she was being asked to take a leave of absence. Michael Rainford knew that she never liked being called Bernadine, but such was his level of frustration, he called her so.

'I'm not asking for the moon, Bernadine, in fact, I'm not asking anything at all. I'm telling you - don't come back to work until you've sobered up,' he said.

'I was on a story,' she said.

'It's being passed to Kristen.'

She scoffed at that and felt as if the whole world was against her, was watching her, waiting for this very moment. 'Michael, the paper needs my words, don't take them away.'

Now it was his turn to scoff. 'What the paper needs is a coherent reporter,' he said. 'Kristen will do a fine job on the Jetty closure.'

'What will I do?'

'Go home and get some sleep.'

She would have but she knew that it was one of those days. At least it wasn't pissing down. That was when it was the worst. When it rained, she could not escape the marching band that drilled at the window, ran down the pane in torrents, reminding her of that awful night. The one which made her reach for the bottle again. 'Look, if you take some time out and things are going well, then we can talk about you coming back to work,' Michael said.

'Oh right, and you'll stick me with the changes in bus routes or something even worse.'

Michael studied her, smiled warmly, which was not returned. 'You're lucky *The Herald* isn't firing you right now, Bernadine.'

There it was again, that name that only her mother used. The newspaper didn't owe her a damn thing and she knew it. But it was hard to take nonetheless. She thought about pleading for her job, getting down on her knees, but that might be construed as something else entirely. It was the last thing she needed – to be seen offering a blowjob. What she did need was this job, otherwise she had pretty much nothing. No boyfriend, no hobbies - besides drinking. No real friends to call on either. They were all shadows of the past.

They were what Bernie would have called *in the dead air*. Just like the wasp nest up in the attic all those years ago. 'If you fire me there'd be trouble.'

'Is that a threat – what does that even mean?' he said.

But as soon as he had spoken the words, they were ringing through the dead air again, and she could hear the drone buzzing in her ears. She was back as that scared little girl in the attic, sweating through its hot and stale breath. She could smell the cold, harsh damp breathing over her like a fungus. She could feel the darkness crawling on her bare arms. She could see the wasps coming out of the dark as they floated, screeched at her ears. Paralysed her with fear.

She was out of Michael's small office, back in that attic, and she watched as they crawled on her face. Then she began to pound the floor below her, at her sandals and white socks, at her ruddy knees. They kept coming and so she kept pounding. She screamed for her mother, she even screamed for her absent father, knowing that he was not going to show up and rescue her. It felt like an hour or so yet it couldn't have been that long, she would have been stung to death.

She spent a week off school following the ordeal. At night it haunted her, the air that kept coming too close to her, tied her like a noose. All things now had a place to go, a place where they remained hidden, where they were just sleeping. It was called the *dead air*.

'It's no threat,' Bernie said to Michael, who wondered where it was she had just gone to. He thought it was the booze that made her go off like that. Now she was back in the land of the living. He didn't care much to be spoken to this way, not some drunkard making idle threats, despite her protestations to the contrary.

'I think we may need to go our separate ways,' he said, the hypocrisy not lost on him in that he was making his own threats now. Bernie felt hot. She fanned herself with a copy of *The Herald* and pondered her next move. It would have to be a good one. She couldn't lose this job. Sure, there were other papers to write for in the area, but getting a reference from Michael Rainford would prove problematic, and she actually quite liked it here.

'Please, Michael, just hear me out,' she said. 'I'll take a little break, I'll do whatever you want, I'll clean your house for a month, I'll do your laundry.'

'My wife does all of that.'

Bernie ignored the chauvinistic pig. 'Just don't fire me today,' she said.

'I'll give you some time. Sure. If you promise to go home, get some rest and lay off the sauce.'

She didn't need to consider it for long, it was the olive branch she was hoping for.

'I'll do anything to keep my job, Michael.'

'Well, maybe you could do one more thing,' Michael said.

'Anything,' said Bernie.

'Find me a story. Get me something with heart, something with teeth. It's been too long since the old man and the millwright curse. Now that was a story. One of your finest pieces. Find me something like that, only better.'

Bernie was a little surprised by the sudden U-turn on her reporting. 'Any leads for me to follow?' Bernie casually asked.

'I don't know what I'm looking for yet. Why don't you use your contacts, seek something out and maybe we can talk about you staying on?'

Michael Rainford was now sitting on the edge of the desk, inches from Bernie, arms folded. His greying hair receding like the tide, and his scalp shining under the sunlight that pecked its way in to the square office. 'Thank you,' Bernie said, and she meant it.

'Just go and do your job, kiddo,' Michael said.

'You won't regret giving me a second chance.' Michael mouthed 'third' and held up three fingers. Bernie was at the door when she said, 'don't go giving my heart to Kristen.'

Michael crossed his chest with his fingers, simply shook his head when she was just out of the door.

Bernie started the car at the fourth attempt. It was her tank of junk, as she named the BMW – the one she pays a hundred and forty-four pounds a month on with its gleaming black hood, as black as fruit bats against an ornery sky, the one with the scuff on the rear wing. She knew that she would need to get a handle on the drinking. But right now, the most pertinent of thoughts was where she was going to find a good story. She had done field work all the time at *The Herald*, but she had always had direction. Rainford told her to use her contacts. It was then that she needed a drink most of all. Because it was then that she felt alone and helpless. Not quite like it was in the attic. But as alone as she did fourteen years ago, when she thought that it was the end of her reporting career. She thought of *him* then, of Francis, and what he was doing right now. She had thought of *him* when she walked the soaked streets alone, with a heavy heart and a bleeding conscience, one rainy night in Vienna. She always thought of *him*.

CHAPTER 1

1987

Waterside House looked like it needed a little more than a lick of paint. It was just a couple of years ago when it had its major revamp, but still it seemed run-down. The furniture had been ripped out of its main quarters and the north west annexe had been completely demolished. A thicket of trees and more wildflowers had been planted, snaking up to a large pond. The old building still remained about a quarter of a mile down the gravel path. Its ruins a relic of the past where shocks, steam cabinets and needles were used to quell patients of varying traumas. It was where the crows screamed. Anybody who ever ventured out that way always heard the crows. They also always felt that the mountains at any moment could topple down like an avalanche and crush everything down below.

At the side of the entrance, where the two huge oak trees stood like plinths, or beefeaters guarding the door, one of the decorators lost his footing. He fell from the middle rung of the ladder. Smashed his collarbone, broke two ribs and sprained his left hand badly. Tim Hindle saw the whole thing from the window. Tim Hindle was the manager of Brantwood ward – the high dependency men's unit catering for just over a dozen patients. He was visiting a former patient now on The Old Forge. The sun had been pouring down from a gorgeous sky all morning, even as the patients from the second floor of The Old Forge – a house where patients could prepare for an imminent release – twirled their umbrellas in the yard, and laughed at the mention of the shower room's graffiti. But even they heard the scream that shook the trees free of those sonorous crows.

Tim almost fell down the stairs himself, pushed past a couple of the men in the kitchen, and ran out to the wailing man, who had just taken a hard plunge to the ground. 'Don't move, for fuck's sake, just stay still. I've called an ambulance,' Tim said.

All he got in response was a low gravelly groan. He told some of the men who had heard the scream to get back inside. He took a look around to see who else was there but at first only saw only the cricket pitch over the short wire fence, lusting for some company in the bright sunlight. Until in the distance he saw a woman in a wheelchair. 'It's going to be alright,' he said, watching as they neared.

She was grey and frail. Her face was saggy and her eyes were pale as the moonlight. She was being moved somewhere but Tim had no idea where, patients come and go all the time. But he did recognise the languid gait of Denny Halford pushing the back of the wheelchair. Denny's face was a picture when she saw the man lying broken on the gravel. Tim raised his arms and shrugged. Denny knew that it meant: *another day, another fuck-up.*

After the paramedics had lifted the man onto a gurney and plied him with oxygen, Tim turned to the woman in the chair. She came across as 'distant' which Tim knew that in this place meant too far gone. 'Which ward?' asked Tim.

'Eastview,' said Denny, shielding the sun from her eyes. 'I'm supposed to be giving her a tour of the grounds first.'

'Just come in?'

'Late last night.'

'A nightcrawler?'

He bent so that he could be at eye level with her, but she did not move an inch, not one he thought quietly to himself. 'Don't you speak?' He asked her. She never moved. Her eyes were cast down to the gravel, where Tim's shadow stretched out behind him like a train. 'Alright,' he said, 'be on your way, Denny. I've got a fair bit of paperwork now that Humpty Dumpty has had his great fall.'

Denny laughed, said she wished him well, said she hoped the man would be fine, then grabbed the chair by the handles. They slowly moved across the gravel, eventually moved out of sight. Tim Hindle watched them all the way to the main entrance, via the grassy courtyard of The Octagon, which he supposed counted as 'showing her the grounds.'

The Octagon still made Tim shiver. It was a two-level room, and on the bottom floor there were offices and a row of treatment rooms specifically for EEG, where the brain is evaluated in terms of its electrical activity. On the second floor was where the real ghosts lay. It was where the lobotomy used to take place, the last one being in 1964 – a certain Ingrid Becker, now long gone. The building is now largely unused, say for a few meetings here and there between senior partners mostly, and potential investors. Even as desolate as it now is, it still had a power over Tim. When he looked up at the highest window of The Old Forge, he saw it was still open, and that was some serious shit to be dealt with, if anybody found out.

CHAPTER 2

Present day

1

It was the last Saturday in October and it was raining hard. So hard that there was hail fog rising up from the water. Coniston was alive that afternoon, alive in the pouring rain, right there in that moment – just as Clara was slipping away. Just as she was losing parts of herself. Since the death of Macdonald things had gone bad, and then worse.

Dr Francis Bird waited for Clara to sit. He noticed how pleasant she looked, dressed in one of those orange button jumpsuits. Clean hair, good figure. But he could also tell a lot from the way she cast her gaze to the window where the rain hammered incessantly. Avoiding eye contact like that only meant one thing: Clara was suffering and she would need his help. She hadn't known sun from moon these past weeks, her husband had said as much on the telephone.

'It's like those crows cawing up there,' Francis said. Clara looked at him through riled eyes, but they were quickly deadened by the sound of the rain. Bill was sat next to her, close enough to hear her throat closing, but not that close, not any more. 'It means that everybody has got their own story,' Francis added. 'I'm eager to hear yours.'

Bill was the one doing all the talking so far. Clara sat, fiddled with her buttons, and kept her mouth shut, hoping that the nightmare would go away. She hoped they would just send her back home and tell her to get a good therapist. She held one picture in her mind, that of the snow-capped Langdales high above the glistering water, the craggy peaks that were kissed with a fine rain. And of course, her two young children, who probably knew that something was deeply wrong. Children often did.

'My wife has been having some blackouts,' Bill said. 'I told you this on the phone.' Francis waved with his hand, encouraging more.

'We did have one or two serious episodes recently. Clara had placed, accidently I might add, some tacks in David's coat pocket. The teacher found them in the cloakroom. We were called in for a meeting.' Francis kept nodding, kept writing in his notebook. 'Then there was the boat incident.'

'The attempted suicide?' Francis asked.

'I'm afraid so,' Bill answered. 'There have just been too many.'

'Is there any history of mental disorder in the family?'

'Not that I know of,' said Bill.

'Do you hear any voices, Clara?' The doctor asked.

Clara took one look around the room, noticed the desk fan sitting atop long grey cabinets, unplugged, as it certainly wasn't needed in October. On the muddy walls there was a sign: IT'S BEEN A LONG TIME COMING.

There was a circular clock where the pendulum had stopped swinging. 'No, sir, I never have heard voices,' she said. Her voice was cracked, seemed to fall down as soon as the words escaped her dry lips. 'She has extreme bouts of anxiety, doctor,' said Bill. Then he looked at his wife in the eye and said, 'and the blackouts are becoming more serious.'

'And what occurs mainly during these blackouts?'

'She has a tendency towards violence. I don't believe that the children are safe anymore. Christ, it's not just the children, we need to get this sorted for the good of our marriage. It has just gotten that way.'

'And you said on the phone that you have tried a therapist.'

'Yes, a rather good one.'

Clara flinched at that. It was perhaps the first time she had ever heard Bill talking in praise of Dr Nicholls. He had been a crook and a smoothie and a useless bastard but he had never been a good therapist. 'Even the best therapists will seem unable to compute in the face of such severe mental problems,' said Francis Bird. 'Well, look, I'm satisfied at this point that your wife would be better off with us than in the community. In light of recent episodes, I think that it would be best if we sectioned her right now for a period of up to three months. This will form part of the assessment.'

'Assessment?'

We have her in one of the secure wards for three months, so we can decide on what the best course of treatment and, just as importantly, where she will reside during said treatment. All our wards are very different, catered according to a patient's needs.'

Clara felt the heat rising up her spine, on her neck, in her raddled cheeks. She wanted to scream but she felt too weak. She wondered whether this really was the best place to go, or whether she should just tell them it was all a mistake. Suddenly it didn't seem as voluntary as Bill had made out back home.

'Don't worry, we will have your wife as right as rain,' said Francis Bird.

Clara sat as calmly as she could, as calm as a summer breeze and eyed this strange man and her strange husband and felt the earth tumble at her feet. Bill stood from the shade underneath the window where the venetian blinds hung sadly and Francis did the same.

Francis Bird wasn't a very tall man, but he carried himself well, looked taller in his white coat and grey hair that swept over the tip of his scalp. His spectacles made him brooding, almost sinister.

'Doesn't that sound promising?' Bill said, watching his wife and hoping for a verbal response. She managed only a tilt of her head.

'I have to say, usually there is a fair amount of kicking and screaming, but this one seems to understand the better way to go. Nice and calm and we won't fall out,' said Francis Bird.

'You're here now and you should learn to accept that.'

Clara had to shake off the urge to kick them both.

'You're in the best possible place now,' Francis said. His voice was taut, each syllable carried with an acicular frame. He seemed to cast a shadow with his gaze. He covered Clara with the glint of his steely eyes.

'Most of our girls come from the prison, wrong side of the law, they get into trouble and are then transferred through the system. You'll be an unusual case. But one that is absolutely right.'

Bill shook the doctor's hand.

Clara wanted to beg him to stay, wanted to say how they could sort this out, find a better therapist. Bill told her he would bring the children at the earliest chance. He kissed her lightly on the side of her face. She held him tightly by the waist, closed her eyes and felt the shudder of tears rising, then they fell.

When the door shut, leaving her alone with Dr Bird, it felt as though the floor had just given way to an earthquake, and that rattling of crows, who were either scoping carrion or preparing to dive into the battlefield, seemed to come as a grave warning.

'They gather at the treetops,' said Francis Bird. 'In the ruins of Waterside's old hospital. They'll be there long after we've all gone.'

For Clara, in that moment, it felt as if that day couldn't come soon enough.

2

The wet lap of water burbled into Clara's skin, into the most private parts of her naked body. She lifted her leg to meet her hand holding the razor. The water turned a little red as she dipped the blade in and out. Three days ago she had stepped foot inside Waterside House and still the bathroom made her feel something awful, something she couldn't explain. It felt as though it was watching her, as though it had eyes. But of course there *was* someone watching her, at all times, even in the bathroom.

'I'm all finished here,' Clara said. The woman rose from her chair, her black skin glowing under the naked bulb fixed to the ceiling. She took the razor from Clara and told her she had five minutes left. Clara covered her privates with her hands and turned to the window, where she could see the raindrops crawling down. She wished that she was the raindrops. She wished that she was anywhere but here. She yanked the plug from the basin and the water started to disappear. She groped for the cold tiles for balance as she reached for the towel. The tiles had pictures on them. Pictures of birds. Clara wondered if they were crows from the nearby trees, screeching over the scattered leaves where patients walked the grounds. She had been told that it would be her turn soon, to see the outside world, even if it was just a walk around the old ruins. And most probably with a nurse at her side. She noticed then that the peephole in the door, much like a bull's-eye port hole on a ship, was covered over by a thin, sandy cloth. But still she rushed getting her knickers on, just in case someone was to lift it and amuse themselves. Clara left the bathroom as the November rain continued to tap against the window. It was now dark outside.

***

When James Hudspith, who was architect to the Cumbria asylums board, designed St Luke's – a lunatic asylum in the parish of Furness, he didn't anticipate that a hundred and seventy years later Sal Blackwell would take a piss on the cherry wood floor of the television room. Being among England's other high secure forensic psychiatric services – Broadmoor, Ashworth and Rampton – Waterside House (as it had been renamed some time ago) was still full of surprises, even after all this time.

'I had to go bad and the bathroom was fucking locked,' said Sal, pulling up her knickers.

'Get a mop and clean that up,' said Lindy. Her black braids hung over one shoulder, her face fleshy and her short legs desperately trying to avoid the mess on the floor as others gathered in the hall for their meds. Clara wanted to apologise but no words were forthcoming.

It was dark in the television room, and every chair was faded, grey and had teeth like a croc. Clara put the orange headband back over her chestnut hair and waited in line. In the hallway, where the others stood, there was the pungent smell of vinegar. She mused over the ward round from yesterday as she waited, listened through the slam of heavy doors, waited for her name to be called. She still wasn't really speaking much, not to Lindy Robson, not to Francis Bird, not even much to Kath Jennings – or The Kathometer – as she was nicknamed by other patients on account of her constant weather updates. Kath was nice, and she had a motherly tone in her voice. There was something rather wholesome about hearing her Yorkshire accent, especially when she was being supportive to the girls. Dr Bird had asked Clara how she was faring on the medication. She could only respond by telling them that she was thirsty. Kath poured some water from a jug and placed a cup on the table. In her green eyes there was a vast sea of sympathy. 'I was so tired this morning, I think I could probably have slept all day,' said Clara, after she gulped down her water.

'You will feel a little drowsier than usual. That is perfectly normal,' said Francis Bird. She wanted to laugh at that. How could anything be normal in this place? It seemed that she had flown very far from normal. She just sipped at her water again and smiled. 'So, is it working?' she asked.

'It will take time to figure that out,' the doctor responded. 'We have you on observations at the moment. I want a staff member outside the room at night. At least until you're climatised. It would simply be bad practice if we didn't.'

Kath leant out a hand and stopped just short of touching Clara, her dishwater blonde hair dragging across her narrow shoulders as she leant. 'It's just to monitor your condition throughout the night. Make sure that you don't harm yourself wandering around. You'll hardly notice,' she said, smiling beautifully. 'Best not look at those dark clouds up there,' she added, pointing through the sun roof. 'I think we better expect a hail down.'

'I don't think we will be giving you any grounds leave at this moment,' said Francis Bird. 'It is better that we can monitor your condition from inside the walls at this early stage. Let us not go complicating the issue by moving too fast.'

'I think the assessment is going well so far,' said Lindy Robson, her slender hands propped on her thighs, long black hair done up in braids like a bun.

'Have you got any questions for us?' Francis said.

'I just want to get better,' said Clara, breathy and weary.

'We will get you to see occupational therapy when we are satisfied the meds are doing their job. In the meantime, staff on Eastview will look after you,' said Francis Bird, wearing a paper cut of a smile. He slipped some notes into a black leather case. 'Have we made any friends on the ward yet?' Francis asked.

Clara thought it through for a moment, saw that there was indeed hail coming down towards them, at the sun roof. It sure was a 'hail down' as The Kathometer had called it.

'I like Marcie. . . and Garnet. She's so young. Has it all ahead of her,' Clara said. After she left them, through the blizzard of hail, she saw through the courtyard to a huge wire fence where the best view of the grounds was. Above the barbed wire and the nets, on a clear day, you could see for miles.

***

Clara heard her name being called from behind a large blue trolley full of pills. A woman reached out with a paper thimble in her hands, her orange hair lapping at her square shoulders like waves. She was a squat young woman with a set of huge, round green eyes.

'Dr Bird has given you 15mg of Olanzapine,' she said. Clara took it from her and chucked its contents into her mouth. 'Watch for any spasms,' she added. Clara bowed her head, a move she was becoming used to, and trudged in the direction of the lounge, already feeling sleepy. Her footsteps were lonely and the echo they made sounded like a marble running down a wooden staircase.

She spied on the girls for a minute, leaning against the doorframe. She began to read from a notice board pinned to the back wall of the games room just behind her. One of the posters was about the summer of 1919 when a national asylum workers union organised a mass strike. But Waterside House was named Coniston Asylum back then, she read. It said that the strike lasted for six days and volunteers were drafted in to aid the staff. They came from Ulverston Community Hospital, Westmorland General and Mary Hewetson in Keswick. She read the next poster, treatments in the 1930s: Metrazol convulsion therapy, which was discovered by Ladislaus Von Meduna in Budapest. Originally, he planned to treat morphine addicts, but when they awoke from an induced coma, they felt a change in their mental health. There was a picture on the poster of a man wearing a doctor's coat chasing a patient around a table. It humoured Clara into a smile. It said that a survey carried out by psychiatrist John Godbold found that patients experienced mind-bending terror before each session, resulting in the doctors having to catch them and strap them in. The next poster had a picture of a man's head sticking out of a steam cabinet, looking like a slice of salami in a bread roll. It was also right here, in a little offshoot of an annexe facing the cricket pitch on the west side. She skipped to the next poster which showed a woman lying on a table wearing a rubber heel in her mouth. Above it were the letters ECT. Clara yawned violently and almost stumbled onto Margot's lap.

Margot's story was just as every other woman's in here, all apart from Clara, that is, if her word is taken and not that of her husband's: the dangerous liaison with suicide.

***

It was Margot's father who had brought her in, one winter morning, almost two years ago. It was Margot's father who had stopped her from drinking a pint of bleach in the cellar. Hugo Mandeville, an airline pilot, was looking for his old pickle cans he had stored down there sometime during the last summer. It had been a hot one that year, as everyone he met while pruning his conifers said. His great hobby in life took no amount of risk or adrenaline, but instead a great deal of patience which was required in the art of making dill pickle. Margot thought it was silly. 'Who makes this stuff?' she often said, and then, 'oh, right, my square of a father.' It was disgusting, thought Margot. She thought he should be at the races, or even zorbing in one of those polyurethane balls - that would get the heart pounding. But he was out of all that a long time ago. When you have your children to provide for it kind of stunts the growth of any thrill seeking.

As Hugo's lug boots creaked down the stairs, he was alarmed to see the light already on.

'I thought it was just me who came down here,' he said, not knowing who he was saying it to. The silence that followed made him wary. He grabbed a cricket bat from under the shelf that stored tinned food, flower bulbs and paper towels. He accidentally clipped the water heater with the tip of the bat, and that was when he saw Margot.

She was sitting on the ground in her underwear, her faded matching bra and knickers, and at her bare feet was a pint glass filled with household bleach. Hugo could smell it as he walked the last step. 'I wasn't doing anything,' she said.

'That's not what it looks like,' Hugo responded.

He threw the bat to the floor and grabbed Margot by the naked arms, her flesh bony and thin. He threw her on his shoulders and carried her up the stairs, her shrieks growing louder and louder. But nobody else was home. Mother was at the spa and health club in Grange-over-Sands. As she was every second Thursday of the month. When they had reached the kitchen, Hugo threw her down to the chair, and it was then that she bit him on the side of the face, drawing a little blood. He screamed at her, slapped her across the cheek. Then he opened the refrigerator and took out a carton of milk. He grabbed Margot again, pried open her mouth, and poured the milk down her throat. 'I didn't drink any,' Margot screamed. The milk splashed down her neck and soaked into her cotton bra. She jumped up when he had let go of her and ran outside. It was then that she decided she was going to borrow her dad's drill. It would be more painful, she imagined, but it would all be over in a flash.

3

The lounge was brighter than the television room. It smelled worse than it, though; it reeked of stale vegetables and vinegar. Clara apologised for almost sitting on Margot, then stumbled to an empty chair under the window. She could feel the eyes on her, burning into her.

'Who the hell are you?' Margot asked.

'Clara.'

'Clara what?'

'O'Hara.'

Margot snorted with laughter then. 'Are you sure it's not Cuckoo Sue, or Insane Jane?'

The other woman in the room was Jeannie Newton – dark cropped hair, almost raven black, carrying a load of weight at the gut, and always looking older than her forty-four years. Everything was moving south - breasts, chin, sacks below the eyes. She was an artist, both outside in the real world and in here. She'd had the odd exhibition out there, but in here she painted the birds that plastered the bathroom tiles. 'It's a beautiful name. It means. . . clear and pure,' Jeannie said, as though she were reading off cue cards. Then she turned back to the open magazine resting on the arm of the chair, sipped from a stained mug held by her trembling, puce hands.

'Jeannie knows the meaning of names, boohoo,' said Margot.

'Margot's just unhappy that she has no meaning,' said Jeannie.

Margot turned to her and stuck out her tongue, lapped with it in the air, then burst into laughter.

'Who's your psychiatrist?' Margot asked Clara.

'Dr Francis Bird,' she said, then gazed out through the hailstorm to see a battered washing line in the courtyard, swaying as though it were being electrocuted.

'It comes from the Latin for Frenchman,' Jeannie said. 'St Francis of Assisi. It is in giving that we receive, it is in pardoning that we are pardoned, and it is in dying that we are born to eternal life.'

'That's beautiful,' said Clara.

Margot whipped her head to the edge of the chair and stuck out her tongue again. Casey Harper walked in the room, well dressed in a collar shirt. She was quiet, usually, and caused little trouble to staff, although to look at her you'd never have guessed that she had been a heroin addict since the age of nineteen. She had also attempted suicide on several occasions, the last being with shears. She had tried to decapitate herself but only succeeding in leaving a scarred neck that she covered over with a scarf or a tall collar. She saw Margot and told her that she was as buggy as a fruit cake.

'Have you got any leave yet?' Jeannie asked Clara.

'I can't go anywhere without them watching me,' she said, rather tired, as though it were a great effort to speak. 'What happens when you do go out?' Clara asked, watching the gathering of leaves in the courtyard, spinning round as a hurricane.

'They don't let us too near the water,' said Jeannie, deadness in her voice.

'What happened to Sharne?' Casey asked, then plonked herself down hard in the final chair by the corner. Now all corners were taken.

'Sharne is a gimp,' said Margot. She turned to Clara, pressed her fingers to the side of her head and mocked being electrocuted.

'Why is Sharne in here?' asked Clara.

'She killed her mother with a claw hammer,' said Jeannie.

'Why are you here?' Margot asked Clara.

She paused for a moment, seemingly thinking of a valid reason. *They don't let us too near the water,* Clara could hear ringing around her sleepy head. 'I'm trying to get better,' she finally concluded.

4

Clara's bedroom was the only one with a decent view of the grounds, apart from the men in The Old Forge. It had the gravel path which snaked around the dining room, and one of the oak trees. She could also see the thicket of wildflowers that started at the base of the shelter and ran around all the way to the small pond near the old ruins. The mist rolled off the sky as she closed the window, rubbed her arms to get warmer, then sat on the hard bed. There was a nurse sat outside her door. Every half hour the slip of privacy cloth lifted and Clara saw a pair of eyes looking at her, measuring her for all she was worth. She thought of the past in the moments after, specifically of the friends she had let go during the last few years. Shirl and Jenny and the others from John Ruskin. She wondered now why they had never kept in touch. She could do with a few friends right now, even if she felt that they would all laugh at her. Laugh at her for making such a mess out of her life. She tried to bat that feeling away, and the horrible images that were created in her mind. She felt the need to urinate. She bent over double, holding her stomach, feeling it cramp. She held it until the pain was unbearable. Then she staggard over to the door, lifted the handle and saw the darkness out in the hallway. It was like a big hungry mouth waiting to swallow her up. Marcie had her door open, wedged by a trash can. She was sitting with all the lights out, a flicker of the television sprayed around the walls sporadically. Marcie then began to rock forwards and backwards on the edge of the bed. She looked at Clara and her face darkened, as though there were bad thoughts swimming up inside of her. She had rings around her eyes, dark hellish rings and it scared Clara. It scared her because she could see herself in those eyes, in that harbouring face. Clara walked on down the corridor, holding her aching stomach and hoping her bladder did not cave. She stopped when she saw the nurse sitting on a hard and uncomfortable plastic chair. Her shoes were scattered on the floor and her foot was resting on her knee. The smell of overripe vegetables and acidic vinegar was replaced by the noxious scent of fresh sweat. Nurse rubbed at the dead flesh on the bottom of her foot, flakes of skin falling to the floor like a shower of wood chips. She glanced up at Clara and seemed cross with her, at least that is what she made Clara feel. As though she had done wrong by just being there. Clara searched for her voice, knew that it was in there somewhere, but where she couldn't quite tell.

'The bathroom is that way,' the nurse said, pointing a bony finger to the end of the hall. 'I suggest you move quickly,' she added.

Clara never spoke. It felt as if her tongue had been nailed to the bottom of her mouth. She went past the nurse and felt her stomach turn at the smell. The bathroom wasn't far now. She was going to make it, she felt sure of that. But the sickness that was riding up to her mouth wasn't going to wait forever.

She bent at the sink and threw her insides up all the way down into the gaping black hole. The food tasted like refried mush after you have dental surgery on the way down, but on the way back up it was much worse. She ran the water and flushed the vomit away. She stared at her reflection in the mirror. The brown eyes were sore underneath, baggy and swollen almost, like they had taken a fair amount of pain recently. A whole shed load of tears. But she couldn't remember crying. Perhaps she had, perhaps that is why she was here. She studied her long nose, the scar on its side once russet and itchy and now white and hypopigmented – character her mother had called it. As she felt at the scar, Clara thought back to when a young girl named Rosanne had carried the blade in her snotty fingers. A complete fuck-up now pissing away her late father's inheritance money on flights from the Philippines. It was her online boyfriend – Eric Ocampo – who needed the money, so he says. A man called King Sting on account of his fraudulent conquests across the dark web. Clara couldn't even remember her full name. It was Rosanne something. Rosanne Fuck-Up. She had made Clara bleed, for that she would always remain as that snotty little twat who couldn't be trusted. Clara had shapely lips, heavy on the lower, thin on the upper and smiley sides as pink as cotton candy. She flickered as she touched the mirror with her hand, thinking of when she was back at home applying lipstick in her own mirror. She thought again about the girls she had left behind, or rather the girls who were leaving her behind. She wondered where they were, and then she remembered her need to urinate.

She sat down on the seat, after closing the cubicle door. Then she emptied her aching bladder. Before she flushed, she heard the outer bathroom door click shut. She held her breath for a few seconds, expecting to hear footsteps on the tiles. But she heard nothing. She knelt down to the cold hard tiles and spied out from underneath the cubicle door. There were no feet. No sound. Just the repetitive whirr of her own breath falling from her sour mouth. She could still taste the vomit as she rose to her feet and flushed the toilet. She opened the cubicle door and walked bare foot to the sink. In her aching state she had forgotten to wear any shoes. The silence was crippling, making her loneliness an even greater force than it already was. It was hard enough being in here, the last thing anybody wanted was to feel alone in the middle of the night, questioning every single decision you had made in your life. But her heart missed a beat when she saw what was written on the mirror.

She turned round sharply, gasped at the closed door and suddenly felt wide awake. When she turned back around, she examined the words on the mirror.

It said, quite simply, quite unfathomably: GET OUT OR

5

When she walked out of that bathroom, she felt the same eeriness that had escorted her in the first time. She looked at the empty chair in the hallway, empty save for that wonderful smell of vinegar again and not the foot odour that made her sick. There was no sound of anyone around and Marcie's door was now shut tight. Clara shivered in the darkness. The light storm outside battered the branches against the long hallway window. She was heading for her bedroom when she had the urge to investigate a little more. If someone besides Marcie had come into the bathroom and written in the cloud of breath on the mirror then she would surely see them wandering the hall. Perhaps she would catch the tail of them leaving the scene. She couldn't help but wonder where the nurse had gone. What would make her leave her station? Perhaps she could shed some light on the mystery, Clara thought.

Clara started off in the direction of the dining room. As she passed another dark window, she saw – in the flood of light coming from the street lamp – a shower of rain, and the tree that was bending to its power. She was at the turn of her corridor, in the end nook with the built-in sofa which reminded her of all those caravan holidays they went on when she was too young to fly abroad. She turned left and headed toward the open dining room. She passed the metallic lift doors that went down to the basement. It was creepy in this dark, stormy night. Whatever lies beneath them seemed a long way down. Then she heard a jangle of keys coming from up ahead. The double doors that sectioned off the mid-way point in the hall started to open. When they had opened fully Clara was met with another cross look. The nurse asked her if she was alright. 'Did you see anyone?' Clara asked.

'Only someone who should be sleeping,' the nurse responded. 'I'll take you back to your room.'

'Where did you go?' asked Clara.

'That's none of your business.'

Clara had to quicken her step in order to keep up with the nurse. 'You're the only one awake, madam,' said the nurse, as she twisted the keys in her hand. Clara felt the need to apologise, but instead kept her mouth shut. It seemed the best thing she could do. *You're the only one awake* still ringing in her ears as she moved. They reached the empty plastic chair and kept on walking until they were at the door of Clara's bedroom. Room six.

'Well, what are you waiting for?' asked the nurse. Clara wasn't sure what she was waiting for, but sure enough that she wanted to say something about what she had seen in the bathroom. 'You really didn't see anyone out there?' Clara asked, a little desperately.

'Get a move on.'

'Goodnight,' said Clara.

'Goodnight.'

Clara locked the bedroom door. She sat on the edge of the bed, yawned and closed her eyes. She knew that her medication would soon start to kick in. She knew that soon she would dive into a deep sleep. This brought her more comfort than she could ever have imagined. At the same time, it also absolutely terrified her. The raindrops rolled down her window and she drifted off into a dreamless sleep.

CHAPTER 3

Six weeks ago

1

Bill waited out in the lobby most times, but today he said he needed to run a few errands in town. It wasn't unusual, he did bank here occasionally, and he loved to check out the bookshop where a copy of his novel *Sundays in Paradise* sat on the shelf next to the likes of George Orwell's 1984. They had driven the twenty miles south east from Coniston to Kendal in complete silence again, as they had the last few weeks. Clara was growing quieter all the time these days. It seemed to sap her energy – the constant battles with her anxiety, and the blackouts. But Dr Nicholls was sure he could help.

He checked his watch. He was tall, even sitting down you could tell that he was probably around six four. His brown suit was expensive but looked cheap. He wore brown rimmed spectacles which framed his small blue eyes, had a square forehead, pointed chin and was always clean shaven.

'Tell me something from your childhood,' he said.

Clara turned to the window and gazed into the grey clouds. She heard the river humming below. It always seemed to relax her to hear the music of the water. 'I saw a spider one time when I was a little girl. A bird eater. It was so big I thought it was a bat. I was so scared. I get so confused,' she then paused. 'I'm so afraid.'

'The spiders make you afraid?'

'Why do they look so frightening?'

'Maybe you're not supposed to be looking.'

Dr Nicholls pressed his fingers together as though he were about to pray. He wasn't the kind of therapist who believed that one size fits all. That would be too limiting. He offered a range of therapeutic approaches from dreamwork, hypnotherapy, relaxation, CBT, NLP, play therapy, attachment therapy, and inner child work. He also offered counselling on a range of issues such as depression, relationship difficulties, bereavement, abuse, anxiety, suicide, PTSD, and the list goes on. He covered everything from abortion to phobias to sex problems and charged fifty pounds per session.

'We are meant to enjoy life, but sometimes we get blocked by fear or trauma and this manifests as anger, anxiety and phobias,' he said. He straightened his tie a little. 'Tell me about your father.'

'My father was a bookshop owner. Rare and antique books was his speciality. First editions. Of course, he is retired now. Mum and dad moved to Cornwall five summers ago.'

'You love to read?'

'Well, I married a writer. When I was a little girl my father gave me the best present I ever received for my birthday. It was a rare first edition of Jack Pumpkinhead of Oz by L. Frank Baum, although the author of that particular book was a woman named Ruth Plumly Thompson. My father said he could never get my attention again after giving me that book. I think I must have read it about a hundred times. It seems a hundred years ago. But I still remember. It's raining in Philadelphia and that means no baseball. I really got that, the rain I mean. I suppose growing up in Cumbria you kind of get used to the rain being there all the time. Peter Brown wishes himself back in the yard of Jack Pumpkinhead. They head for the Emerald City but lose their way. Sniff the iffin makes them a threesome. I think I can relate to the griffin that's lost his gr.'

'Do you feel lost, Clara?'

Clara licked her dry lips. 'Oh, I don't know, Bill says I am like a little sailboat alone in the vast ocean. Just bobbing along without a care in the world. Except that I do care, about a lot of things.'

'Do you and your husband get on?'

'We're still married, aren't we?'

'A marriage doesn't mean you are entitled to a harmonious relationship was my point.'

'We are fine. Except that I forget things.'

'What do you forget?'

'When we got back from San Francisco everything had changed. I need to keep my mind healthy, as a runner would keep their body.'

'But you forget things.'

'There have been some incidents.'

'What kind of incidents?'

'I fed the cat on Xylitol. I blocked it out. It resulted in liver failure. We were in the States where Bill was promoting a new book. He was adamant that the beloved cat came with us. Then. . . like I said, I don't remember.'

'You tend to block things out.'

'I think it's a part of my anxiety. Sometimes I find it hard just to concentrate. But that's why I'm here. I want to get better.'

'What makes you feel anxious?'

'I know I have to be there for the children. I have got to be there for them growing up.'

'David and Rita,' Dr Nicholls said.

'Do you have any children, Dr Nicholls?'

'I have two daughters; they both go to QKS. Now back to you,' he said with a little smile parting his paper-thin lips.

'Some days my heart is beating so fast I am afraid it's going to burst out of my skin.'

'You need to breathe, Clara.'

'I feel like I'm going to die.'

Dr Nicholls picked up a small red ball and began to squeeze it in his hand. Clara listened to the river and then watched the leaves blowing around in a strong autumnal breeze. It might just rain today, but that would have been no great shock. It was in the forecast on the car radio coming here. Dr Nicholls placed the ball back down on the desk next to a photograph of his family.

'You need to drink plenty of water and make sleep a priority. How is your routine – do you get much sleep?'

'Bill says I get too much sleep.'

'And what do you think?'

'Oh, I don't know. Sometimes I dream about him and the children.'

'That sounds perfectly normal.'

'Except that they always end in violence.'

'Do you remember any of these dreams?'

Clara shook her head. But all she thought of was the lines to a song from a movie. One she couldn't sing aloud for fear she may be off key.

'Do you instigate the violence in your dreams?'

Clara shook her head again. 'I don't know, I can never remember. I just hold on to the feeling, those awful feelings.'

'Perhaps you should keep a journal. Then you could write down your dreams or indeed any thoughts that you might have that seem. . . troublesome, shall we say. It's a good way of tapping in to the unconscious. Freud believed that dreams concealed conscious thoughts.'

Clara stared at the little red ball and wondered what the fascination was all about. She tried to guess what power it gave its holder. She was feeling a little anxious as she saw the leaves of an elder tree fall to earth. The sky had darkened to the point where it may burst soon. It looked bloated and gravid as it hovered above them.

'I would never hurt my husband, Dr Nicholls.'

'Nobody is suggesting that you will.'

'Good. Because I wouldn't.'

'Going back to what makes you anxious, can you identify a trigger? We did this a couple of weeks ago; I want you to try and remember.'

Clara ironed out a crease in her skirt, laid her hands in her lap. 'I tend to get headaches.'

'Good. What else, Clara?'

'If a situation arises, I could get tense.'

'What kind of situation?'

'Meeting new people, or something that makes me worry. Then I would usually make my excuses and leave. Or avoid it at all costs.'

'That is something that I want us to work on. Have you had any thoughts on our sessions and what treatment I could give you?'

'Right now, I am just happy to be offloading some of this shit.' Clara took a sip of water. It had been standing still ever since she had poured it from the cooler.

'The universe has a habit of putting everything in its rightful place,' Dr Nicholls said with another smile. He then closed his book of notes and that marked the end of their session.

'Then I guess I am destined for someplace,' said Clara, watching the weather turn.

2

She gazed at her reflection in the wing mirror, and told Bill, after he had asked, that she was making real progress. She said that pretty soon she wouldn't need the help of that Brobdingnagian, which brought a sharp whistle from Bill's mouth. He knew he had written that word somewhere, but couldn't place it right then. He certainly knew Clara had not read any of Swift's giants and monsters, so it had to be one of his books.

'I'm impressed you've been reading my novels. I know how the fantasy genre gets up your nose a little.'

'It means sexy, right?'

Bill laughed, sped up and then drove the car close to the side of the road that was shrouded in shrubbery, just to get some of his own back. The motor boat place in the background gleamed in the late autumn sunlight. Its various assortment of boats sat upon the coruscating brilliance of the water.

'I take it back,' Clara screamed through her laughter.

'Well, you better, missy, because I am deadly serious about giving you a new dramatic haircut. I'm sure the ladies down at the salon will admire my handiwork.'

'You're a brute!'

'I'm a giant and you're stepping on my shoulders.'

Bill again drove into the shrubbery on the narrow roadside. Then they turned out onto the A593 and were soon under the imposing mountains. Minutes later they were home safe and sound, he reminded her.

'What *did* you mean back there?' Bill asked as he shut the door. The lightness had vanished from his voice.

'Nothing, I meant nothing.'

'You think that Dr Nicholls is sexy?'

'Come on, Bill, it's a joke. Leave it.'

'So, if I thought your hairdresser was a stone-cold fox, you'd be able to just leave it?'

Clara waited for his words to sink in. It knocked her off kilt a little. 'Do you think that?'

'I don't know, maybe I need to read a few more books first to find the right words.'

'Oh, come on, Bill, sleeping with the therapist is so cliché. I thought at the very least you'd think of me as having a bit more originality.'

'But no more class, it would seem.'

Clara dumped her bag onto the glass table. An easel haunted the corner of the kitchen while the breakfast bar remained empty, clinically clean, as everything always was – thanks to Bill's incessant nature and routine – but empty. Clara had painted since sixth form, abstract work which Dr Nicholls encouraged. *Let the right side of the brain have its little moment,* he had said once. The old timber stud walls were barely visible underneath the paintings Clara had finished.

'That's a cheap slur,' Clara said.

'Well, if the cap fits. . . isn't that what they say?'

Bill turned away and walked through the hall into the lounge. Clara followed him. Brickwork surrounded the cast iron open fireplace with a slate hearth. Bill stood at the window, holding his reading glasses. He'd had them three years now. He scanned the top shelf of the bookcase, where his latest novel *Sundays in Paradise* sat amongst his others, and the several poetry collections he had written since the age of twenty-three. The novel was about a photographer who catches people's dreams, and while the people always seemed nice enough, their dreams were horrific, filled with hatred. The photographer goes to extreme lengths to change the course of the future and prevent a series of murders. The lounge was furnished with leather sofas and shag carpet, but it didn't make use of all the space. In the corner there was a floor lamp, and a Dorchester armchair with a round marble coffee table sitting by its feet. The modest mid-terrace house sat in amongst a row on the fringe of Coniston village. Hardly a word passed between neighbours these days. It suited Bill just fine. The back was what really sold it to Clara, where she could picture herself sitting on the balcony just at the tip of a tiered garden where her flowers could grow tall. It was beautiful in the summer. Bill sometimes wrote there too, when he'd had enough of his hot, breathless study.

'If the cap fits. . . yes, I believe that's true,' said Clara. 'Don't they also say if you're going to be crazy you will have to get paid for it or else be locked up?'

'You're seriously telling me that *I* am crazy?' Bill said.

'No, you are a child flinging sand in a sandbox.'

'That's not exactly fair.'

'Why are we arguing?' Clara asked, throwing her arms into the air and then letting them fall limply by her side. It was a question she sometimes dare not ask. Why are we arguing when I know I can't win?

Bill caved. He sometimes liked to do this, to test her as it were. At least that is what it felt like. He took her in his arms and gently kissed her on the brow.

'I don't know, my love. Crazy is what makes the world go round. You're not crazy, Clara, not yet anyway.'

'Oh, thanks,' she said, 'I thought money made the world go round?' Clara punched him playfully in the chest. 'I'm going to see what we have for dinner.'

'As long as it is not snozzcumbers,' said Bill.

Clara's laughter chimed into the kitchen, sweet and euphonious, like the ringing of church bells. It made Bill smile.

3

The smell of beef cooking wafted in to the hallway, where Bill stood, still holding those reading glasses in his hand. He had knocked out a few hundred words in the study where it was quiet, but he wasn't satisfied when he had to look something up at the bookcase in the lounge. It would only be another hour before David and Rita came home from school. They both went to John Ruskin, Rita being in the class two years above David's. Then the noise would ramp up to levels far from conducive to writing, even when the door was shut, given the close proximity to the playroom. David would perform his wrestling moves with his large stuffed bear, and Rita, well Rita wouldn't actually make much noise, but she would always be asking questions, usually to her mother in the kitchen when she was making dinner. Rita was going to be a wonderful young woman. Bill could just tell she would make some lucky man very happy one day. Bill searched for the missing bits of knowledge in a dusty book at the end of the second shelf. But it was missing. There was a gap in the row of books that looked like a hole in an infant's mouth where a tooth should be present. He sighed and knew instantly where that book would be found. He walked through the hallway, stacks of photographs on the walls, white paint and large doors framed and panelled. A pair of blackout curtains let only a slither of afternoon light spread its wings across the carpet. He opened the door to the playroom, saw the sunlight creeping through the curtains and was hit by a wall of dust that made him slightly cross. There was a tepee open beside a small sofa, the children's toys endlessly spread on the carpet and an inflatable chair that looked half deflated. He bent to the open door of the tepee, hoping to find his missing book. It was a volume of encyclopaedias covering the late nineteenth century. It was vital to the story he was writing, and although he had rather a good memory for most things, it was dates that sometimes got lost. He was hoping to find the book, but instead he found his own reflection staring back at him in a shiny meat cleaver.

It shocked him so bad that he fell backwards, felt a sting in his wrists and found that he could only scurry on his hands and knees back over to the playroom door. His mouth was open, shaped into a terrified O. He had seen his bushy eyebrows in the blade, his quiet green eyes, his slim nose with a vicious spot on the right side and his dark brown hair greying slightly in those long sideburns. His cheeks had looked fleshy and flushed. He crawled over to the tepee again, picked up the meat cleaver, which looked nasty and well-endowed, and he held it in his hand. It was just like the tacks in the coat pocket. But that was six months ago. Bill had passed it off as an honest mistake, it was an accident which never led to any harm. Until now there had been no other mistakes.

He leant against the wall, holding the meat cleaver by his side, his breath coming on hard. As he passed the downstairs bathroom, he felt his heart murmur a little. Just a little gap in the ticks, that's all – he thought to himself.

He could not remember their argument word for word when they left the school that day, but he knew it had been bad. At least bad enough for them to get a therapist involved. He waited until his heart wasn't fluttering anymore. He gripped the handle of the knife so hard that his knuckles were turning white. He could hear the clank of pans coming from the kitchen, and water being run from the tap. He even heard the faint sounds of Clara's voice humming as she went about cooking. It angered him and so he hollered for her. The water shut off and the pan went down to the counter. 'Bill? Did you shout me?'

'In here!'

She appeared in the mouth of the doorway, under the arch that led from kitchen to hall. She was holding a tea towel in her hands. It took her a few seconds to spot the blade. Then it was her turn to be agape.

'What have you done?' Bill said.

'I haven't done anything.'

'First you put nails in our son's pockets, then you leave this fucker lying around our kids' playroom.'

'But I didn't put anything anywhere. It couldn't have been there. It couldn't have.'

'I can't trust you. It feels like I'm just waiting for a serious accident to happen. Will you be satisfied when you kill one of them?'

'How could you say that?'

'This says it all, Clara,' Bill said, holding the cleaver out for her to hopefully grasp what she had done. Clara's face turned a little sour. There were tears in her eyes, a look of confusion straddled her. 'You've blacked out before, but this is something else entirely. This is unforgivable.'

'I'm sorry,' she said through a breathless sob. 'I must have left it there this morning when I went to check the bags had been taken to school. Because last week, David forgot his books.' Clara started to cry. A stream fell down her cheeks and her next words were lost in the tears. Bill couldn't look at her, now feeling a little guilty about riding her so hard. But he was still angry. He walked past her into the kitchen and slid the meat cleaver back into the top draw.

'You've got to stop!' Bill shouted, his words bouncing off the recessed spotlights. 'What are we paying for if that son of a bitch can't help?'

He slammed the drawer shut. Clara was right behind him, dabbing her eyes with the tea towel.

'Please forgive me, Bill. I don't honestly remember leaving it.'

'It's always the same.'

'I need help.'

'We've tried all that and look where it's gotten us.'

'Just give me more time. I know I can get better. It really did go well today and Dr Nicholls has given me a great idea.'

'Fuck him! He's useless.'

The silence between them both felt thunderous.

'What are you saying?' Clara said, breaking the deadly quiet that was swallowing her up.

'I don't know, Clara. I really don't know.'

Clara touched him, gently, on his stubbled cheek. 'I love you,' she said. 'Don't you love me? Don't you love me?' she repeated.

'We need to get you sorted.'

She kissed him softly, tried to pull him into her bosom, tried to hold him tight against her body.

'I love you,' she whispered in his ear.

'I love you too,' said Bill. He cupped the back of her shoulder as she hugged him tight, still whispering.

'I need to write,' he said, then turned away from her.

Clara watched him leave and felt sick. She grabbed her hair in her hands and pulled as tight as she could, a strand becoming tangled in her fingers. She wondered exactly where along the line everything had become so fucked.

It was the first time she had ever thought about killing herself.

CHAPTER 4

1987

It was still hot even after tea, as hot as any day Tim Hindle could remember of the whole year. He left the men, who had been gardening, at the fence and called out to Sharon that he would catch up with her later. Sharon was cute – a blonde pixie cut and pretty blue eyes. Tim had fancied her for years, but never made a move. She had a boyfriend who worked as a chef out in Calgarth. One of those roadside takeout places that opens until late. Tim envied him, but never showed much of that envy to anyone, especially not Sharon. He sometimes had an after-work drink with Sharon and a few of the other nurses, usually Jim McEwen and Martin Talbot, sometimes Sara Hartigan and occasionally Paula Kunach. He was hoping for one tonight. He made his way out of the nature area - *growing well again* they called it, passed the unoccupied gym, and was almost at The Octagon when his pocket alarm screamed at him.

He knew he had a matter of seconds to make it onto Eastview. He quickly calculated that he was about a minute and a half away, but if he ran, he could make it in forty seconds. He began to sprint.

When an alarm sounded it meant that there was trouble. It meant that wherever you were, you had to get there quicker than was humanly possible. Somebody's life might just depend on it. It was a rare occurrence on Eastview but lately things had been a little hectic. Things had started to happen on that ward. Tim could only think of the last time he was called out. When he had to wrestle Terri Jones to the ground after she had stuck a fork in Lisa Matthews's eye. That was horrific, just seeing the blood sprayed down Lisa's shirt was enough to give him nightmares. He wondered what awaited him as he neared. By the time he was inserting the key to the door of Eastview ward, he had sticky sweat patches at his armpits and his forehead was wet.

'It's about fucking time,' said big Ben Wilson. He was called big Ben because he was the size of two men. Tim had wondered if he was working this ward today, but doubted it seeing as he could no doubt handle most situations single handed. He was a little taken aback when he saw Ben, but rushed over to the commotion in the centre of the hall, where two other nurses besides big Ben held a woman face down. The screams were violent, maddening screeches and the patients all looked horrified. There was yogurt splashed over the walls, and a little running down Peter Farmer's back. Peter was like a mother hen with his charge, always running after them, always making sure that everything was done right. Tim knew that he didn't deserve to look like a cornetto on a hot summer day.

'I came here as quick as I could,' said Tim, out of breath and wishing he had taken the week off like he had planned a month ago. He jumped in straight away and piled on to the woman, pressing his knee into her neck. 'What's happened here?' Tim asked big Ben.

'It kicked off in the dining room between one of the agency staff and this one,' he said, pointing to the woman. 'What's her name?' Tim asked.

'Brenda,' said big Ben.

'Alright, Brenda, I'm going to stand up now, and you're going to slowly get up to your feet, do you understand?'

She hollered out from beneath Tim's knee, a rasp in her voice. 'Do you understand, Brenda?'

'Yes,' she said.

Tim slowly rose up from her, straightened out and willed for her to do the same. She started to rise, keeping everybody on their toes. They were all ready to pounce should it be needed. Ben wrote something on a clipboard and then readied himself in case he needed to do something. Brenda was now upright and breathing hard. They all were.

'Why don't you start by telling us what happened? Tim asked her. She nervously looked at Ben. 'Don't matter about him,' Tim said.

Then Brenda turned around and raised a hand. Facing the end of the long hallway she pointed at something out of Tim's view. He stepped to one side, steered his gaze through the small gap in the group that had gathered and saw that Brenda was pointing to a woman in a wheelchair.

Tim looked back at Brenda and waited.

'It was that bitch,' said Brenda. 'She's fucking evil.'

'That's no language to use,' said Peter Farmer, still trying to dab the yogurt stains with a damp cloth.

'What did she do?' Tim asked.

But she never answered him with words.

Brenda began to scream, a shrill cry shocking the other patients into cupping their ears. She held up a tin can lid in her hands, moved it swiftly to her throat and began to slice open her own skin. Ben rushed in and took a hold of her. The others started to follow suit. Tim looked on in horror. He saw the scatter of blood just like he saw the yogurt, only he wished it was yogurt. Ben got the tin out of her hand and threw it to the floor. It was stained red at the edges, dripping off the side like a can of tomatoes. Peter Farmer picked it up urgently. Then he looked at Tim, who was still frozen to the spot. The glare in Peter's eyes was enough to move him from his trance. But as everyone else rushed in to the mess that was occurring on the wood floor, Tim couldn't take his eyes off the woman in the wheelchair sitting quietly at the end of the hallway. The light over her head flickered and Tim could have sworn he saw her smile. It was there for a second or two and then it seemed to vanish. He felt a prickle on the back of his neck, and suddenly it didn't feel as hot anymore.

CHAPTER 5

Present day

1

Clara spat the toothpaste out into the basin, and looked at the space on the mirror where she had seen the message late last night. She thought about the way Marcie had winked at her this morning on her way to the bathroom. A sort of conspiratorial gesture on her part. But it was hard not to get paranoid in a place like this. Perhaps Marcie was just being friendly. Clara was sure it was something else though. Maybe it was her who came in last night and wrote on the mirror. Whoever it was, it was a sick thing to do, she thought. She knew, just like every woman in here, that there was no easy way out. You had to do the hard yards and she was here for three months at the very least. Clara ran the tap and mopped the toothpaste away with a towel. As she opened the door she was almost knocked over by a sprinting Sal Blackwell, who skidded at the turn of the corridor in her white sport socks. Behind her were two male staff nurses, also running, in their lug boots. One of them they all called Whiteface, because he was an albino with a thin cloth of white hair, and the other they called Fatso on account of his bulging gut. But they were always together, like a bughouse version of Holmes and Watson. Sal was screaming now. She hollered about rape and Nazis whilst giving them the middle finger.

'If you keep acting up, Sal, you're going to go to Gatesgarth,' said the man with the paunch.

'They won't stand for any of this shit,' said the albino.

They had their arms outstretched as they crept up to her, as though they were going to catch a wild animal.

'Wait until Dr Bird hears about your behaviour,' Whiteface added.

'Dr-Fucking-Shit-Bird!' Sal shouted, and backed up to the end of the hall, still holding up the middle finger.

The two nurses pounced on her, pulled her to the floor by her hair, to which she screamed, even louder this time. Whiteface sat on her backside while Fatso took her arms in his grip. There was now a gathering at the mouth of the game room, where a group therapy session was taking place, one which Clara was late for. She thought Sal a suspect now in light of her rebellion, but nobody was *not* a suspect. The two nurses lifted Sal to her feet and, holding her arms, they marched her to the seclusion room, passing Dr Bird's office. Dr Bird was at the window, his hand lifting up the blinds. His steely eyes were watching the thing unfold. He knocked against the glass and said, 'I need a word with her first.' The men pushed Sal against the door, held her firmly, face pressed to the wood. The door opened and they shoved her inside and the ward went quiet again. Quiet until Lindy roared above her sore throat and tried to herd everyone back inside, but the excitement was overwhelming. She spotted Clara at the bathroom and scowled at her, waved for her to join the others.

Inside the game room there was a circle of plastic chairs next to the pool table, a huge window behind that where the autumn morning was posing in the mist and a stereo sat upon a bookcase in the corner. Along the walls there were posters, some of which Clara had read already, some of which she stared at for the first time now, wishing all the while that she was dead.

2

Lindy had been ward manager on Eastview for four years. She had seen a lot come and go in her time, and plenty return too. She hadn't made up her mind on Clara. But it looked touch and go for now whether she would make it through the system or become a lifer. Clara didn't speak much and that was a concern, but even greater was her unwillingness to mix with others. A solo bird wasn't a good fit inside these walls. The flock must learn to fly together. Clara ran her fingers along the poster showing the gymnasium from 1978, where the plaque hung. In the poster the reverend Martin Stokes was pictured alongside his own words: Let the light in and the darkness shall perish. We are all God's children. Amen.

He looked like a good guy, but they all did in the dog collar. There was a short biography about him underneath his photograph. It read:

Martin came to us as chaplain in 1963 and as counsellor he treated the spiritual needs of our patients. Together we prayed, sang, read scripture and listened to sacred music. Martin emphasised forgiveness. Nobody was lost. The time that he spent at Coniston Waterside Psychiatric Hospital has brought greater peace of mind and, in some cases, a much speedier recovery for the patients that he sat with.

Clara blew a bubble of spit out of her mouth. It hung from the corner of her lower lip and dropped to her chin. Lindy came to her side holding a tissue. 'It gets easier you know,' she said. Clara turned to her, mouth open, eyes glazed. 'Why don't you come and join us? We were just about to announce the patient of the week at sports club,' Lindy said.

Clara began to smile. But it was a smile that scared Lindy. It had rage. If it was touch and go before, now it was perhaps a little clearer: she was going to be here a while. But Lindy loved a challenge. She wasn't going to give up on her, no matter what. She held out her arm and Clara took it. They walked over to the circle and Clara took a seat next to Garnet Morecott.

'Don't listen to her,' Garnet said. 'She's full of shit. It gets worse and worse.'

Clara smiled again. But this time it wasn't filled with rage. It was full of madness. It was a smile out of place.

As Lindy whispered back and forth to a junior med staff called Sarah, Clara began to feel the after effects of her dosage this morning. It made her awfully sleepy and some of her joints ached. She stretched out her bare legs to the side and touched the back of Ann Piggins's ankle, causing her to turn around and cast an accusing look at her. 'What are you looking at?' Garnet said.

'I don't know, they don't label shit,' said Ann.

'What the fuck did you just say, bitch?' Garnet said.

A scuffle broke out between the two girls. Ann seemed to be losing, despite her height advantage. Lindy rang the alarm on her pocket before the albino burst in. Garnet was laughing hysterically as she was lifted up and towed away like a busted car. A little clarity came back into Clara's head like the mist had rolled away and left her with a ray of light. She crossed off Garnet's name mentally, thinking it would be unlikely to be her who had written on the mirror. It wasn't her style.

3

Outside the game room Sal Blackwell left Dr Bird's office in a worse mood than she had come in with. Francis had upped her meds again, even threatened her with a depot if she continued to act up. Everybody knew about the side effects. It wasn't nice, your whole system could be put out of whack. She was escorted away to seclusion by Whiteface. Then the phone rang. Francis picked it up. It took a few seconds for it to sink in.

'Bernie,' he said. 'What a pleasant surprise.'

On the other end of the line, tucked away in her cottage by the woods, Bernie Waller had to practically force out her words. Francis was the last person she wanted to call. In fact, he was going to be the last person she called. The other six had given her no encouragement whatsoever. She stared down at her list of names and numbers and saw six big crosses she had made with her pen. They were her so-called contacts for a new story. It was, however, proving to be a bunch of dead ends, each one more depressing than the last. Francis Bird's name was still visible. He was the last hope. They quickly got down to business, neither of them needing, nor wanting, any small talk.

'I just wondered whether you'd consider letting me in,' she said.

'Waterside House is no place for reporters,' he said.

'I know you want your patients to be safe, and they will be.'

'We have nobody who will be of interest to your paper. Why don't you try one of the less secure wards up in the north?'

She let out a deep plume of breath. 'Is there anybody who's just come in? Maybe if I'm extra tactful I could write something about the experience of being inside, or get the family's version of events? I could really help with the adjustment period.'

'Don't flatter yourself.'

'I'm sure we could come to some sort of agreement over this,' she said.

'You're dead wrong.'

He was about to hang up when she said, 'And what about the girl, Francis? Was she dead wrong too?'

She could have sworn she heard a gasp on the line, or maybe it was just crackle, or just the signal becoming lost. 'I don't have any idea what you're talking about,' he said. She knew he was lying. He must have thought about that night as much as she did.

'I was there, remember? It was pissing down, and you were in the room, and there was somebody else there too,' she said, leaving a breathless silence on the line. She thought back to the night in Vienna, and the dead air came flooding back to her again. That place where all bad things go, or come from. Whatever the way it worked, it caught her out every time, made her breathing seem like pulling teeth.

'Look, if it helps you out of a jam, I can have a word with one of our new arrivals, maybe she understands and wants to be a part of it, and maybe she hasn't got a scooby what's going on. But that's really all I can do for you.'

Bernie thanked him. Then they said goodbye. Maybe she would have a story to write after all. It wasn't supposed to be like this, she thought to herself. She wasn't supposed to be chasing after fish at her age. By now she should be writing for a major player. She should be covering important news events, not scrambling around for tiny morsels of food. She looked out of her window and saw the trees being shook by the savage wind that had ridden her garden all morning long. She heard the screams of the lambs up on the hill. She heard the screams of a young woman fourteen years ago in a hotel bedroom and then she closed her eyes and waited for the dead air to pass.

CHAPTER 6

Five weeks ago

1

Bill grabbed Clara by the arms and shook her awake. He was sat on top of her as the moonlight lit up a spot on the wall above them. Other than the drips of moonlight the room was dark. It seemed to ring out like a siren, the darkness, and it ate up everything in its sight. Bill took her head in his hands, partly to stop it from moving with rapid force side to side and partly to wrestle her from sleep. He told her to wake up. Slowly she began to open her eyes, seeing only dark shapes in front of her. Instinctively she clutched at her stomach, felt that sense of relief wash over her. It was still flat. At least it was still flat. But her next thought was that she was in real danger. She screamed into the hand that was pressed now against her mouth, damping the frenzied sounds. She bit down on the fingers and was surprised when she heard a familiar voice shouting her name. She was awake now, wide awake and confused. Bill switched on the bedside lamp and rolled off her, panting as he sucked at the pain in his hand. She had drawn blood. He leapt off the bed and stumbled into the bathroom. The light forced Clara to raise her hand to shield her eyes. There must be something wrong, she thought. Maybe one of the kids had done something, or had a nightmare and needed company. That was more likely. Perhaps David had had a nightmare and couldn't get back to sleep. She glanced at the clock through her stinging eyes. It was just after four. She could already hear birds outside the window. She watched Bill at the sink, dabbing his face with a cloth and running it under the tap. But he wasn't so bothered by his hand. That's what made Clara sit up, anxiously waiting for him to turn out the bathroom light and climb into bed.

'I'm sorry,' she said.

'You don't even know what you've done,' said Bill.

He left the light on and walked back toward her on the bed. She thought he wanted sex, maybe that was why he had been on top of her. Perhaps that is why he had held his hand on her mouth. But that thought quickly vanished when he turned his face to the left and she saw blood oozing from a nasty gash on his jaw.

'What's happened to your face?'

Bill dabbed himself with a towel, still unable to say the words, unable to tell his wife. Clara sat up on the bed, pulled the duvet over her knees, her mouth twisted with anguish.

'It doesn't matter,' he said. 'You were sleeping.'

She gasped, held a hand to her mouth and whispered, 'fuck.'

'It's not your fault,' Bill said.

Clara started to cry into the duvet.

'You were lashing out,' he said, 'and that's when I tried to calm you.'

'So I hit you hard enough to make you bleed?' Clara said, unbelieving but sure that it happened. All she had to do was look at his chin, which was still bleeding and had started to darken. Bill gathered up a blanket from the corner chair and a pillow from his side of the bed.

'I think it's best if I sleep downstairs tonight,' he said.

'No, you mustn't, you mustn't leave me, Bill.' Clara reached out a hand hoping he would take it and fall back into bed with her. Hoping he would take off her nightdress and place his hands on her, his mouth, his cock. She hoped she could make him forget.

'I can't trust you like this,' he said. 'I'll see you in the morning.'

Clara sank into the softness of the pillow and hugged it tight. She heard his footsteps on the stairs growing fainter and then she noticed on her knuckles a speck of wet blood. It was Bill's blood on her, staining her with guilt and fright. She no longer knew what she might be capable of doing and this terrified her. She thought that she was losing him. She howled into the pillow and it seemed hours before she fell back into a deep sleep.

2

A week after the meat cleaver episode and the morning after the blood on her knuckles, Clara sat on her balcony nursing a mug of tea. Mist hung over the land and the faint glow of autumn sunlight peered out through cloud like a torch through the bedsheets. From her vantage point she could see the stone steps that led down to the tiered garden stocked with small trees and shrubs. In the distance she could make out Coniston water and the hills that rode above it. She knew in these moments where her husband had derived inspiration for his poetry. She remembered one now:

The wind lashes against fronds of fern, scattering spores. Misty heavens tangle with skylarks. The pompoms gather in arching sprays, awaiting the whites of juneberry. A vertical dogwood basks in the mid-morning rain, missing the bold white bracts of summer. I miss the bold white bracts of summer, and the unsung beauty. I hear the rain in children's footsteps. The patter of their voices rings out over glistering waters. As far as the moon can show, it rings out to the loneliest light.

It was a poem from his third and final collection to date: Sketches for Drunk Lovers. It often came to her in the morning. It gave her a sense of place and perspective. It rooted her and she liked that feeling. She heard the sudden eruption of a child's laughter coming from behind her. It was David on too much sugar before school. It made her think of the tacks in the coat pocket again. Which in turn made her relive the meat cleaver. She could never truly forget any of it. But what was worse was how it made her feel about the future. Whether it was all done and dusted with. Or if she was going to keep on placing her family in danger. She gulped her tea, which was getting cold, and ran her fingers through her hair. She wriggled the loose strands from her palm into the morning wind. It was then that she remembered about her appointment at the salon. It was booked for an hour from now and she was still wearing her dressing gown and hadn't yet brushed her teeth. She entered the bedroom again, spread apart the curtains and picked David up in her arms. Her voice was strained as she told him how heavy he was getting. He made a noise, sounding like he was embarrassed at being cradled like a young child, and pulled his face as far away from Clara's mouth as he could. But still she managed to plant a kiss on his fleshy cheek. Bill appeared in the doorway, a dark bruise clearly showing on his chin. He was naked from the waist up and had a towel draped over his shoulder. The hairs on his chest were damp but his head was dry. He had used the shower cap Clara bought as a novelty Christmas present last year. She smiled at him and put David down. He ran to his father and held on to him by the knee. A gust of wind moved the curtains and touched the backs of Clara's naked legs.

'You'd better get ready for school, young man,' said Bill.

'Okay,' David replied.

'And go wake your sister.'

He ran out of the room and pounded the landing with his bare feet. 'I wish I had his energy this early in the day,' said Bill.

'You would if you ate the breakfast he eats,' Clara said. 'Are we okay?'

Bill didn't know how to answer that question. He mopped himself dry with the towel and pulled on a clean blue shirt. 'What time's your hair appointment?'

'I'll get a taxi,' Clara said.

'Nonsense. I'll drive you after I take the kids to school.'

'I love you.'

Bill smiled. But he couldn't reply. He still felt the pain in his jaw, in his heart. He turned away from her and knew that she was watching him walk away. At the bottom of the stairs Bill checked the inside pockets of the coats his children would be wearing that day. It's something he had started doing since the incident. He found only a soiled tissue and a wrinkly foil once used to wrap a tube of sweets. Both David and Rita ran down the stairs, causing him to shout at them to walk. It made Clara smile. Then the door was closed and she was alone in the house.

On the balcony she stood, holding an empty mug. She thought of her mother and her favourite topic: their marriage. Clara recited her mother's words in a voice that was whiny. 'Be thankful for the little things,' she said, thinking of her children. 'Take care of your appearance.' She drew an imaginary tick in the morning sky. 'Always remember humility, patience and honesty.' She parked the urge to call her mother on the phone. She wouldn't know where to begin. She walked back down to the lounge and began to fold the blankets Bill had used last night. The light was beginning to come round, like a punch-drunk boxer slowly getting to his feet. The room looked different now, almost a sad loneliness to it that made Clara feel guilty all over again. It knotted in her stomach and so she hastily left the lounge and was on her way back upstairs to dress when she noticed the door to Bill's study was open. It was an unusual sight. He always kept the door locked. Bill didn't want David running around in there, poking at his work, making paper aeroplanes out of it. She hovered by the door and, after a moment of indecision, she decided to go inside.

She ran her fingers over the spines of Bill's books, none of them collecting any dust – it was Bill's incessant cleaning at work again, she thought. The curtains in here were half drawn so that the only light that slid its way inside was shining on the first book Bill had ever written: Secrets of the Spider People. It was Clara's favourite. Bill not so much. He never parted from the joy that he felt about the book that broke him, but he moved on very quickly. He soon tired of speaking about a group of nomads with extra limbs from the Never World, and the imposter who gains entry. He never said, however, that he had based the imposter upon himself. He never said that he felt the same way his protagonist felt. Clara picked out a poetry book on the shelf, but not just any poetry book. This one was when they had first met at a bookstore in town. Bill was signing copies, and Clara was in the store by chance. She was just killing time until her mother showed up for their lunch date. It was to be the very day that she would tell Clara of her plans to move out of town for good. Until that day Clara's parents had only flirted with the idea of moving away, the ideal was somewhere a little roomier, a little warmer.

Cornwall had seemed a good fit. She was browsing the latest fiction titles when she turned a corner and saw a handsome man wearing an Edgar Allen Poe necktie. He was sitting down talking clumsily to an attractive woman, if a little old for him, Clara thought. She liked the fact that his hair kept getting in his eyes, and the way he brushed it behind his ear. She also liked his grungy cardigan, and his cargo trousers that bunched up at the crotch when he stood up. He introduced himself to her and when she waited a while to answer, he knew then in those silent, awkward moments, that he could see himself marrying her. Seven months later they were standing side by side in the Sacred Heart church, signing away their lives to each other. A ceremony which lasted, due to William being a devout Catholic, over an hour: three biblical readings, exchanging of the vows, the exchange of rings, the Prayer of the Faithful, the nuptial blessing and plenty of music.

Clara put the book back, felt a little sad at the memory and then was almost out of the door when she saw something interesting by the side of a stack of papers. There was a box on the table. She stooped to read the fancy font which adorned the top: Karl Lagerfeld. It was then that she remembered she had a birthday coming up. It was next week in fact. She had been so thrown by the events of the past few weeks that she had completely forgotten about it. A smile cut through her steely refrain and shivers fizzed up her spine. She carefully opened the box, feeling like a kid on Christmas morning. 'Bill, you old fool,' she whispered as she removed the gold chain bracelet with *real* Swarovski crystals. She smiled so hard that it ached at the side of her mouth. She placed it on her wrist and danced in the mirror out in the hallway. She had to laugh at herself and, still admiring the shimmer the bracelet created, she had a bout of embarrassment. She took it off and put it back in its box. Then she noticed a card at the bottom, and in another fancy font it read: *My darling, my love, my greatest fuck buddy x*

Laughing some more, she closed the box and strutted out of the room. 'Always be thankful for the little things,' she said aloud as she dressed in the bathroom, a pin held in her mouth. 'Take care of your appearance,' she said in that motherly, whiny voice. 'Foster relationships outside of marriage.' Clara grabbed her warm winter coat and made for the door. 'Agree to disagree.' Then she was gone.

3

Clara walked fast, buoyed by her little find in Bill's study. She was so consumed by her glee that she had forgotten about him driving her to the salon. But as it was dry out, she didn't give a second thought about going on foot, once she had realised that she had left the house far behind. She made it onto West Street and crossed the road onto the village square, mindful of the bus that almost sent her flying backwards. There were plenty of people milling around, looking through the windows of every café and pub in the vicinity. Probably tourists making up for lost time in the fine weather. And it was growing finer all the time, the sun starting to cast its warmth, finally. At every window she slowed a little to watch her figure in the reflection, until she made herself laugh aloud on the busy street. The salon was on the corner of Tilberthwaite Avenue, half a block away from the butchers they bought their meat from. It was almost empty save for an elderly woman sitting under a roll of aluminium foil, her leathery face pocked and sagging, and what was presumably her elderly husband sitting in the waiting area reading a copy of *The Herald*. There was a woman sweeping hair from the floor who refused to catch Clara's eyes. Clara took off her coat and then she was greeted by a slim brunette who rushed over to the reception desk from the narrow slip of stairs in the corner that led up to the second floor. She ushered Clara into one of the empty chairs. Offered her tea or coffee, which Clara declined, but she did ask for water. The brunette scurried away through an open arch and then the stylist arrived armed with a black cape.

After her hair had been washed, trimmed and blow dried, Clara could hear again, and what she heard was like a gunshot to her heart. It was a trigger for all that pain and anxiety when the elderly man reading the paper piped up and spoke to his wife. 'Did you hear about this girl in the paper?'

'What's that, Sam?' his wife said.

'This girl in the paper,' he said a little louder this time. The woman shook her head, held her mouth open in suspense. 'Not something you'd expect from a childminder and an ex-teacher,' he said. 'They found cigarette burns in the little girl's pyjamas, burns on her face. It's an evil thing to do - to keep your own daughter locked up in a cellar, away from the world.'

'Whose daughter?' the woman asked.

'It was a suicide pact. The father killed himself but the mother couldn't go through with it. Thankfully the girl is still alive. Although I'd hate to be the one who has to sort that mess out. There's a job for someone.'

'Whose daughter?' The woman repeated.

'The Rothmans' child,' he said. 'Used to go to John Ruskin before they left for Hawkshead.'

'Oh,' the woman said. 'Never heard of them.'

'The mother was suffering from anxiety, was seeing a psychiatrist,' he said, chuckling as he spoke. 'It says here that authorities believe they failed the family. Huh, she doesn't know what anxiety is. Try sleeping through an air raid night after night afraid if you close your eyes you'll lose everything you care about.'

The woman muttered something under her breath, all Clara caught of it were the words 'air raid' and 'silly sod.' But she was getting hotter as she felt the cut hairs crawling down her neck. She slipped a finger under the cape and itched a spot on her feverish skin. Her breath was becoming rapid. She started to sweat heavily. It burst through her clothes and wet her like a rain shower. When her heart started to double in beats, she rose from her chair and fell at the sink, knocking bottles of spray to the floor. She tried to speak but her tongue felt like a cotton ball, stuck to the insides of her mouth. The elderly woman asked her if she was alright, but Clara still couldn't answer. Her eyes were wide with terror. The terror that she thought she might die right here in the salon, away from Bill, away from her children, and the thought that she may never see any of them again made her scream until she saw only red in her eyes, and then complete and utter darkness.

CHAPTER 7

1

Dr Nicholls knew he had asked a stupid question, but his excuse was that it was habitual this time of the morning. He had barely sipped his coffee when the phone rang. Clara was hysterical on the phone, barely making sense. He told her to breathe, and said he could meet her in his Kendal office as soon as she could get there. It was all he could do, even though he felt that she might be better off in a psych ward. If just for a night or two. He thought about calling the hospital himself, and then the crisis team, but the money was too good to turn away. So when he asked her how she was, he pinched the skin on his hand to shut out the thoughts telling him that he was a fool.

'I know I sounded crazy back there,' Clara said.

'Your illness is real,' he said. 'There is no shame in having to reach out for help.'

'I feel so dumb.'

'You are not dumb, Clara.'

'In the salon there was a man talking about something in the paper. It involved a little girl who was tortured by her parents.'

'The Rothmans case.'

'I felt the breath come pounding out of me. I couldn't breathe.'

'Did you talk with Bill?'

Clara shook her head.

'Can you trust him?'

'With my children's lives.'

'Then why didn't you confide in him?'

Clara bit her lip, thought back to something that troubled her.

'I hear the birds singing,' she said, 'but sometimes it sounds like they're saying something. Something else.'

'What?'

'Something awful.'

'Awful?'

'It sounds like they're warning me, or asking me something, or telling me something.'

'What do they have to say, Clara?'

She stared out of the window where a flock of blackbirds perched in the elder tree. The mist had remained in the sky. It was ringing from those dark, stormy clouds.

'I know it's crazy, but it all seems so real sometimes. It just seems so real that I freeze. I can't move, I can't speak. It was like that until I blacked out. I need my family but I am scared I might yet lose them.'

'The support of loved ones cannot be underestimated. They are our lifelines.'

'Bill bought me something – an expensive gift for my birthday. I saw it today by accident.'

'And how does that make you feel?'

'Honestly? I feel guilty.'

'Why such a negative reaction? I mean, it was – as you said – a nice gift. Doesn't that mean he loves you and wants to show it? Should this make you feel something bad?'

'I suppose not to a sane person.'

'You are sane, Clara.'

'I left a knife in the children's playroom.'

Dr Nicholls definitely flinched. There was something in his eyes. It was like they just shivered.

'Another blackout?' he asked.

'I think so. It's not just that. Last night Bill slept downstairs.'

'I'm guessing he wasn't just drunk and passed out?'

'I hit him. I clocked him pretty good. So good there were blood stains on my hands. I can't trust myself to not put my family in danger, and what the hell am I supposed to do about that?'

'Psychogenetic blackouts are caused by an overload of stress or unusual levels of anxiety.'

'How can I stop them?'

'Just coming here can help enormously. Patients often find that talking can start to unravel some of the reasons behind why they are experiencing blackouts. Other things we can try are eliminating alcohol from your diet, increasing your activity levels, and by learning specific techniques we can hopefully control and reduce these attacks.'

'But I am talking. I'm talking to you and I talk to Bill all the time.'

'Clara, we are making excellent progress, believe me on that. I see many people with these sorts of issues and, without crossing any lines here, I think that you're doing so well. Keep talking and keep up with your diary. This will help, Clara. You need to stay positive and remember to live your life.'

'I just want to hear the birds singing again. Like they used to. I don't drink, Dr Nicholls, by the way. Never liked the taste.'

Dr Nicholls smiled. But his eyes betrayed that smile. Clara noticed it, stood to leave and then almost asked him what he really wanted to say.

2

The mist had miraculously all but disappeared by the time Bill had shut off the engine. Clara pocketed her notebook in the inside of her jacket. She thought about what she had just written, that she was living in a small part of hell at the bottom of a dark and lonely sea. It wasn't quite what her husband would have written, and a part of her envied him for that, but it felt honest. She turned to the window and drew with her finger on the glass, a little heart with an arrow shooting through. The arrow was the illness. The heart was everything she cared about, everything she had. The light was coming on stronger now, the parting of the clouds giving way to the early autumn sun. It was chilly out, but the sunlight felt wonderful on Clara's skin. Bill put his arm around her waist as they neared the house. She buried her nose in his chest. Bill pointed up to the sky. 'You see that up there?' he said.

'What?'

'That fat old thing. The one you shouldn't look at.'

'You mean the sun.'

'Is that what they call it? Well, yes, the sun.'

'I see it.'

'That is exactly what you are.'

'A fat old thing,' she said, and lightly punched him on the arm.

'No, love. You are the brightest, shiniest star that rises every day with the same hope that everything is going perfectly to plan.'

'I could do with some hope right now.'

'You will beat this. *We* will beat this. Keep shining, Clara.'

'All is going perfectly to plan,' she repeated as they closed the door behind them.

'Dr Nicholls tells me that you are doing really well. I'm so proud of you, Clara.'

'Apart from embarrassing myself to death at the salon, you mean.'

'They'll forget it all as soon as there is some other news to gossip about.'

'Speaking of news, I wanted to ask you if you read about the Rothmans in the paper today.'

'I may have seen something on my phone, remind me again.'

'The Rothmans,' Clara said, sounding annoyed that he hadn't known it off by heart. 'The parents who tortured their little girl, kept her prisoner, beat her, burnt her, did God knows what else to her.'

'Oh, yeah, I remember. It's terrible.'

'Is that all you got to say?'

'It's shocking news, I know, these monsters in our part of the world.'

'Yeah, but it hit me hard. I mean the mother was suffering from anxiety, and she was seeing a psychiatrist. It just made me think that I . . . well, that I . . .'

'Don't you dare compare yourself to that wicked woman,' he said. 'You're nothing like her.'

Bill wrapped his arms around her, the hallway where they stood letting in the light, bouncing off the mirror. 'There are certainly no monsters here,' he said.

'Sometimes monsters don't look like monsters,' Clara said. Bill released her from his grip. She stood at the mirror and saw that her face was drawn and tired. Her eyes were sleepy. She groped at her face and hiked back her flesh. Over her shoulder she could see Bill, looking worried. It saddened her. It felt like she was losing him as much as she was losing the best parts of herself.

'No monsters,' said Bill.

CHAPTER 8

1987

It was a cold December 18th and Tim Hindle was still thinking about his imminent transfer from Brantwood to Eastview. He watched the first falls of snow outside the window, pulled his polo neck up even further and nervously tapped the desk in front of him with his jittery, icy fingers. Stuart was late. Not a great start to his interview. Tim opened the window slightly, enough so that his cigarette smoke had a place to escape, but not enough so that his fingers might drop off his right hand. He lit the fag and blew out a perfect O into the troubled, grey sky. He wiped away at the fallen ash on the CV beside his cold left hand. Stuart Pillman was the name at the top. He was the last candidate for the job. At this stage it was going to go to the portly and arrogant, but very keen, Jim Craft. He hadn't impressed Tim that much but he had a great past. Had worked at Rampton before volunteering at the Riverside Home as a buddy/companion. Tim took another long drag on the cigarette. Below him, on the ground, a car pulled up to the vacant white lines and stopped. A red Ford Orion with a scuffed grille. It looked a little weathered. A man got out. Shoulder length blond hair, which he hurriedly hid under a baseball cap, and then he took a long stride towards the huge oaks. Tim watched him walk. He thought you could always tell a lot about the way someone walks. It gives off a sense of character. Stuart walked as if he was being chased by the devil himself. Perhaps he was, thought Tim. Maybe that's why he was so late, he was making a deal at the crossroads. Tim checked over the CV again. Stuart had worked in another hospital up in Carlisle. A secure unit called The Wellness. Tim wanted to know why he left three months ago. That would be the first question, he decided.

Stuart's face was bony and white. He looked like a Halloween prop, one that tells the kids it is a good place to start if they want any sweets. He sat down, placed his hands on his lap and smiled at Tim, hoping that he wouldn't want to delve into the reason he was so late. It would have been easy to lie, but he feared his eyes might tell the truth, or some other part of his body. He had watched a documentary some nights ago about body language and how it gives little signals to what the person really thinks. Anyway, he was relieved when Tim asked him about his time at The Wellness.

'I got a reference from Paul Varney. He'll tell you how devoted I am to making a difference in people's lives.'

Tim grunted and met Stuart's eyes. They were icy blue. As blue as the ocean. 'I also take care of my mother,' Stuart said. He hoped he hadn't given anything away. If Tim knew why he had been late, there was no chance of getting this job, and then things at home would get worse. Much worse.

'Tell me about your mother?' Tim asked.

'She started with mobility problems,' Stuart said. 'She needed assistance in getting up the stairs, up to bed, in and out of the bath, you know, things like that. Then about a year ago she got diagnosed with Dementia.'

'It must be hard on you.'

'It's worse on her,' he said, feeling a little triumphant at his caring nature being so visible in front of the man.

'So you take good care of her,' Tim said. He smiled at him, then felt a shiver crawling up his spine. It was still cold with the icy air inside the room and the entrails of smoke were present. Stuart knew he had got away with it again. Just like when the social came to visit and mother couldn't talk. She couldn't tell them what Stuart had done. She couldn't breathe a word about his temper and how it had burnt her in the most sensitive parts of her body. How he had humiliated her at breakfast by pouring milk on her head, how he had forced her to eat off the floor, or how this morning he had hosed her in the freezing snow, risking the onset of pneumonia. He had done it all holding a cigarette. A cigarette that he threatened her with every time. It was her hatred of the things that started this tirade. He was always told to put it out, before she stopped talking sense, that was. Put it out or I'll put you out, she used to say. Now he always looked like he wanted to put it out on her, in her, in her eyes. He said it with a dangerous grin. He made the movement towards her but he always stopped short of touching her. He knew one day, and she probably knew somewhere inside of her, somewhere where she still had something ticking, that he would stick in right in her. He probably wouldn't even care if they saw the burn marks. He always had a reason to explain himself. Maybe he would stick it in a part of the body where he himself came from thirty-six years ago next week.

Tim asked him some more questions about his time at The Wellness, then a few scenario questions - just to get him agitated enough to let his guard down. But that didn't happen. He was as cool as a cucumber, Tim thought to himself. Stuart had aced his interview. More than aced. He was the best man for this job and Tim was just happy the whole process was over. Tim stood and held out his hand. Stuart shook it. 'I'll expect you first thing Monday morning,' Tim said.

'Thank you, boss.'

'I think you're going to enjoy working here,' Tim said. 'We have a few patients that are probably about your mother's age. You'll get to know them all in time.'

'It's just what I've always dreamed,' Stuart said.

Tim watched him below on the icy gravel making his way back to his tatty red car. There was that walk again – as though he had hot coals in his shoes. It seemed like he was one of those people who always had a place to be, thought Tim. 'Lucky bastard,' he said to an empty room, and then blew the cigarette smoke out into the chalk dust that was falling from the sky. By Monday Tim would be on Eastview with the women. He had a list of names sticking out from under Stuart Pillman's CV, a list of patients from the ward. He was eager to make a good first impression on all of them. Even on Mary Dunn, the grey-haired woman in the wheelchair. He thought of her as he watched his cigarette fall to the distant ground. He thought of that smile of hers, of her beady eyes, but most of all he thought about her silent mouth (silent in the aftermath) and how it had the power to cause a shitstorm.

CHAPTER 9

Present day

1

Garnet couldn't help but be reminded of her much-documented suicide attempt. She had been sitting on the shed roof of their semi-detached house for an hour, hoping that the sixteen aspirin pills she had taken on that misty winter night would kick in and send her off to sleep forever. When she started to feel weary, she stood up and tried to climb back inside the house through the bedroom window. She just could not bring herself to go so violently like that, with all that blood-shed. It ran through her mind like a hurricane, before she decided to turn back and hope the pills would work. It used to be her little brother's room but, at some point in the last year, she had taken it because the neighbours on the side of her old room could hear her moving through the house. At least that is what she told the doctor. They were tracking her in case she told people about their mission to stop the farmers polluting the water supply. The room still had her brother's garish wallpaper of Pokémon characters but it was quieter in there, so it was a good trade off. The doctor had put her on some pills she couldn't pronounce properly, but they were ineffective, she would be told later. Even the thirty-milligram dosage would have been dud. She had spaghetti legs when she tried to move. The light had faded with the sun setting behind the huge fern at the bottom of the opposite house's garden. She turned to the sea of windows in front of her eyes, wobbled a little on the asphalt roof and planted her hands down on the gravel. It reminded her of the monkey races at school sports days, the one she used to win hands down, pardon the pun, every year since year three, every year since Fabian left to go back to France. She could hardly move an inch without the stones ripping apart her skin. Just when she had her balance back, she took one step too far to the right and came tumbling down with an enormous thud. A broken wrist and a badly bruised collar bone was not quite as painful as the hospital order they issued her with. Garnet was sectioned and taken to Waterside House, where just an hour ago she had watched her friend struggling for air.

It was the scariest thing she had seen in a long while. Even scarier than Sal Blackwell running at Whiteface with a coffee jar wrapped inside a hand towel. Clara's eyes had rolled back, revealing a sea of white. Her lips twitched and her whole body had begun to tremble. It was as if she was possessed. When she began chanting, that was when it got frightening. The words were jammed together, but Garnet recognised some of them: Water. Get out. Get out or.

The speed of her tongue was rapid, as was the flickering of her eyes. It seemed to last for ages, but in reality she had come round in less than two minutes after collapsing on the floor. It made Garnet think about what Jeannie always said, about the water, and specifically about how they couldn't get near it for the fence.

Now she watched Clara twisting the telephone cord around her fingers, looking tired and probably hoping for some comfort from home.

'Bill it's so good to hear your voice. How are the children?'

'It's good to hear you, Clara. The kids are fine. They are in school now.'

'I miss them so much. Did David's show and tell go alright?'

'It's not until next week, honey, you're getting confused again.'

'Oh right. Of course,' she said. But she couldn't stop herself from thinking about the note she had just slipped underneath Ann Piggins's door. *I know it's you, so back off now* Clara had written on the back of a take-out menu. It felt good when she pushed it under, but now she wasn't so sure. Perhaps she had made a mistake. Maybe the message on the mirror had nothing to do with Ann, maybe it was someone else. Perhaps it was foolish to jump to conclusions after she had seen Ann writing on the windows of the game room. The good, light, feathery feeling she had was now dissipating like a terrible realisation that everything she had lived was just a dream.

'Rita lost her tooth yesterday,' Bill said.

'My little girl is growing.'

'She now has more money to spend on sweets so more of the damn things can fall out. How is the treatment there?'

'The meds make me nauseous, and sleepy, very sleepy. I wish I didn't have to take them.'

'You wish for so much, Clara, the angels don't know where to start.'

'I'm still having the blackouts.'

'How do you feel about that?'

'You sound like Dr Nicholls.'

'Is that such a bad thing?'

'You're the one who always says he can't drive ducks to water. Please say you'll come and see me, Bill. I know you don't want the children in a place like this, but please say you'll come.'

'Hang in there. It's going to get you back to us.'

In the silence Clara heard a voice, a female voice. It came through the line from a distance away. 'Who was that?'

'It's just Connie,' Bill said. 'The neighbour from hell,' he whispered.

'What is she doing there?'

'She brought an extra-large portion of lasagne round in case we had all forgotten to eat.'

'It doesn't sound like any neighbour of ours,' said Clara.

'It's good that you've still got your humour.'

'Maybe it's the last thing to go.'

'Stay strong. Listen, I have to go. But it's good to hear you. I promise you I will come and visit as soon as the doctor says it is possible.'

'He's keeping you from seeing me?'

'Not for too much longer. I love you.'

'I love you too.'

2

Clara hung up feeling dreadful. It seemed like he couldn't wait to get her off the phone. Perhaps he just had that feeling that he gets when he knows he should be writing his book. Or maybe it was more sinister than that. Clara saw Ann Piggins taking her seat at the dinner table. She always sat near the door, always prowled the room with an apple in her hand, offering it to anybody in exchange for cigarettes. Clara felt her skin crawl as the day was growing into night. The Langdales were still snow-capped and the fine rain had ridden down the scree. The big freeze held its grip over the ward. Clara took her seat by the window with the image of a naked Connie Brooks sitting on her husband's lap firmly in her mind. The smell of vinegar reared its head again inside the dining room, which always reminded Clara of that night she saw a message on the bathroom mirror. It was something that she couldn't forget. Her investigation wasn't exactly going well, either. Suspect number one seemed oblivious, however. So maybe that was a blessing in disguise.

After dinner the meds began to take hold of her, just as they always did at this time of day. It was usually this time when she began to take herself to her bed and sleep away the evening. But on this occasion she tried to fight it. She met Garnet in the tv room. She was watching a soap opera Clara had never bothered with in all of her thirty-two years. It sounded like a bunch of histrionics. She never could understand the pleasure it brought to people. Even her own mother. But at least she was in her forties when she began watching. Garnet was a young buck at the age of twenty-two. She shouldn't be glued to its flabby guts, Clara thought.

It was hard keeping her head above the water of her meds, but she tried a little conversation and Garnet began by telling her a story of how the huge windows came to be locked.

'So whenever Fatso does his rounds in the afternoon, he checks the locks on the windows in here last. Just to make sure that nobody is sneaking any more Gin.'

'I can't believe Sal snuck in a bottle of booze, what a kook,' said Clara.

'Oh, Sal is always on the take for something, whether it be fags or booze, any type of contraband really. She even set up a wagon wheel business not long ago.'

Clara knew a version of herself would have laughed at that, a version she hadn't been in here. But the realisation that she was having blackouts in here, and the state of her thinking made her wary of such luxuries as laughter.

'Can I tell you something, Garnet?'

'Sure.'

'I think somebody is watching me.'

Garnet scoffed. 'No shit, Sherlock.'

'I mean somebody who isn't supposed to be watching. Do you ever feel that?'

'Clara, I am a paranoid schizophrenic, there is always a feeling that I'm being watched. But that usually is because I *am* being watched. Just like you are, just like we all are.'

'I think there's someone, or something, in Waterside House that wants me,' said Clara.

'Wants you to do what exactly?'

Clara stopped herself before she told her about the bathroom mirror. She didn't need those details. It would only bring fear and until she had a better idea of who it was, she wasn't going to spill the beans, not yet.

'I don't know. But I'm going to find out,' Clara said as the darkness around her eyes scared Garnet into a nervous laugh.

CHAPTER 10

Four weeks ago

1

The boat had been rented for the afternoon. Bill had handed the man a wad of cash and, wearing a boyish smile that lit up his face, turned to Clara with his hands thrust deep in his coat pockets, which made her forget about the icy air for a moment. Just as the sun began to skulk behind the mountains, Bill uncorked a bottle of champagne and filled two paper cups. He handed her a cup and she felt a little sick as the boat rocked. 'Are you trying to get me drunk?

'It's hardly a night on the tiles.'

'You know I don't usually drink,' she said.

'Yeah, but this is a very special occasion. It's not every day that my wife turns thirty-two.'

Bill lifted his phone to take a picture, but as he did, Clara hid behind her hand, smiled into the drowning sun and sank some of her champagne. 'You know I hate my picture,' she said.

'I just thought that maybe today would be a little different,' said Bill.

'I'm just a little anxious, more so today than any other. You know how I hate birthdays.'

Bill finished his champagne, hid his hand underneath his coat and, when it returned, it was holding a brown paper bag. Clara threw her drink into the water when he wasn't looking. Then she saw the bag and her head flooded with the memory of the little box in Bill's study. It was the crystals in the bag and she lit up for the first time since breakfast. It felt good, until it didn't, that was. It felt good until it felt like a waking nightmare.

Bill leant towards her and planted a warm kiss on her face. She felt shy all of a sudden. It was the same feeling she got when she was complimented by a stranger, or receiving a grand gesture, or in this case an expensive gift. She took the bag, couldn't help a breakout smile appearing and said, 'you shouldn't have gone to any expense.'

'It's something I know you will use,' said Bill. He poured another drink into the paper cup. He did the same for Clara. But she looked confused when she stared down into the bag. 'Come on, I know you don't hate birthday presents as much as you hate birthdays,' he said. 'Open it up.'

She opened the bag and took out a box. Only it wasn't the box that she had found in the study. It didn't read Karl Lagerfeld, and it didn't contain any crystals either, but instead, on it were the words: Winsor and Newton Cotman watercolours. 'It's so you can keep painting me those beautiful roses.'

'I don't understand. It's a joke, right?' Clara said.

'Don't be ungrateful, Clara.' He finished his second cup in one swift move. 'They're not cheap knockoffs.'

Clara dropped the box of paints to the floor of the boat. 'Hey, be careful with those,' Bill said. 'Where is the box?' Clara asked.

'What box?'

'I saw it in the study.'

'I know how much you like to paint,' said Bill. But she thought he was trying to change the subject. 'This will keep you active. They're supposed to be the very best.'

'I saw the damn box,' she said.

'There is no other box. Don't you like the paints?' Bill waited through the silence. 'If they're not right we can get them exchanged. It's just that the guy in the store said that these ones were the best half pans in the shop.' Bill took the box of paints and began to read the back, examining it like you would a paperback novel. Clara felt the icy air at the nape of her neck and pulled her collars up. She inched away from him as far as she could without leaving the boat. She inched until she was at the back of the boat. Its prow jutting gently at the lick of the water. The oars were resting listlessly between their feet. Clara pulled her knees up to her chest, teeth started to chatter, mumbled words that were lost in the wind. Bill was still holding the paints, his brow furrowed with concentration. 'How could you say that?' Clara whispered, staring at him, pouring her confusion and her anger and, at that moment, her hatred right at the man sitting in front of her. 'I saw a box.'

'Are you having one of your episodes?'

'Don't you say that. Don't you dare. This isn't fair.'

'Fair isn't a four-letter word – isn't that what your mother always said?' Bill poured the remains of the bottle out into his cup. 'When are you going back to see Dr Nicholls?'

Bill sank the rest of his champagne and gazed up into the hills where the sunlight was now starting to drown behind a sea of white cloud. Clara got to her knees, then she was up on her feet, and then like a ballerina she was up on her toes. She crept back towards the stern. The next words out of Bill's mouth were a blur. He may as well have been talking to a deaf woman. Clara spread out her arms like a bird. When Bill turned around, she was gone.

2

Bill knocked the oar portside. He scanned the water around him, saw a steam yacht gondola in the distance merrily skipping along, but only ripples on the surface beneath his feet. He shouted for help, knowing that nobody could possibly hear him. The gondola must have been about a hundred and fifty feet away. He waved his hands in the air in the hope that someone on board would see him and raise an alarm. He couldn't wait for them to arrive; lord knows how long it might take. He shouted his wife's name over and over but all he saw when he stared into the murk was a darkness that scared him into jumping headfirst into the cold water. It was so cold his chest heaved at the drop in temperature and he thought he might well suffer a heart attack. It was so cold but he thrust his arms forward and dived down into the water, going deeper and deeper thinking she might have sunk to the bottom. It would be about one hundred and eighty feet in total, but this he knew having written a poem about it only a year ago, a poem that featured in a Cumbrian magazine this February just gone. He couldn't see anything but the light above him. But that was the wrong direction. His lungs swelled and it felt like he was carrying iron. He had to retreat and so he swam upwards. He gasped for air when he got back to the surface and knew that time was not on his side. Back down he went, knowing that he had this one shot to find his wife, or else she may be lost forever. If he went back up for air again, he may never find her. With all his strength he plunged himself forward, down toward the bottom.

He opened his eyes under the water, saw only murky shapes in front of him. He could only just make out his own hands frantically swatting at the water. At the broken bits of debris listlessly floating around him. He thrashed and kicked and clawed until he was struggling to hold on to his breath. He couldn't see it but the gondola above him was nearing the empty boat now, a passenger enjoying the afternoon tea had informed the captain, telling him that he had seen an agitated man diving into the water, leaving behind the boat to rock aimlessly alone. The captain had called in via radio and the pier was awaiting further information. A crowd had now gathered at one end of the gondola, cameras and binoculars ready to spot any potential action. Mouths were agape, eyes were wide open. Bill thrashed and swatted water away from his eyes. He was sure that she was nearby, she had to be. He was risking his own life now but he had to bring her up this time. If he went up without her now, he may never see her face alive again. The thought of her lifeless shell of a body laying stiff on a slab inside a morgue made his heart beat just a little faster. It also gave him a thrust of energy, a burst that made him plunge the depths a little quicker. He could not see her, but above him there was action coming from the gondola.

He felt a hand grip him around the waist, tightly – so tight that he felt himself sink a few feet. He clasped his hand on the ones holding him and tried to unhook himself, but the grip was too strong and he was losing his breath. He managed to turn a little, felt the grip loosen but not enough so that he was free, and then he kicked out with his legs, using all of his strength – that which was still left in his body – and at last, the hands were off him, and he could turn fully, gasping now with his very last breath. Looking up at the light felt like his rebirth from the womb, plunging out into the open air, the fantastic sizzling sun. He could see it all and that's when he saw a figure splashing down into the water. He tried to scream but it was all muted. He felt the life drift away from him. He closed his eyes and sank.

3

Clara heard the graceful sounds of migrating red kites and drifting coots roaring through a darkening skyline. She sat at the rear of the boat with an overcoat wrapped around her shoulders – given to her by the man who had rescued her from a watery grave. She watched the shadows of the late afternoon, the hump of hill that was shading the sunlight, silently arcing over a glistering bed of water. She watched the nomadic clouds arriving over the boat like hungry pochards along a glassy river. A man was holding Bill, desperately trying to breathe life into his bones. She was still shivering at the cold that engulfed her as she looked on at the dreadful scene only a few feet away from her trembling toes. He gave one big plume of breath to him and pumped his chest with so much force that Clara thought he had broken his ribs. The man turned to her and his face was ashen, washed out by a mixture of grief and terror. It was then that the other man, the one who had brought Clara to the surface, stepped in and began giving mouth to mouth to Bill. Clara never blinked, not until she saw her husband splutter back into life, which he did after thirty or so anguish-filled seconds. Everybody on the boat breathed a sigh of relief. The two men hugged each other. The applause from the passengers on the gondola rippled out over the water and Clara turned to see the flash from a camera sparkle in the late afternoon light. Clara got to her knees and crawled over to Bill, who was lying on his side coughing tremendously. He looked into her eyes and she to his, both of them knowing that this was the moment that would define their marriage. Clara couldn't be sure why she had thrown herself into the water, or what she wanted to achieve by doing so, and Bill thought he knew everything. The look he gave her was one of contempt, fuelled by anger and hatred.

The man who had revived him came to help him to his feet, but Bill said he could do it. He thanked them both and ran a hand through his soaked hair. The feeling that coursed through him was humiliation. A humiliation that his wife had caused. He cared for her wellbeing but he could not brush aside the facts of the matter: Clara was deeply sick. So sick that she put her family in trouble. It was going to take everything he had to put this one behind him. The tacks in the pocket episode was easy, the meat cleaver was just as easy as the tacks, the blood she drew from his face was easy after a night on the sofa, but a suicide mission bringing himself to danger also was not going to be that way. 'Phone Dr Nicholls, phone the hospital, phone anybody,' Bill said before he collapsed back to the boat. Clara heard him, and felt it was like a siren for the cue to abandon everything and finally face the rumblings of war.

4

'Were you trying to kill yourself?' Dr Nicholls said. There was a curious look on his face, almost as if he was debating whether or not he could trust the answer.

'I don't think so. I don't think I really wanted to die in that moment. I can't say that I definitely wanted to live, either,' Clara said.

'Now that sounds like a humdinger of a contradiction to me.'

'I don't really know how I can explain that. I just felt like dropping to the ground. I was waiting to be buried, you know?'

'Then you were disinterred – dug up by your husband?'

'Actually, it was another man who saved me, but Bill did jump in to the water. Another man saved him too.'

'Tell me what your husband said, about this phantom bracelet of yours.'

'He said I imagined the whole thing.'

'And what do you think now?'

'I believe him. He wouldn't lie to me about something like that. There was no bracelet.'

'Good.'

'I'd had another episode the night before,' Clara said, 'only I know now that I didn't see it, did I? I didn't see the bracelet, Dr Nicholls. I didn't see it.'

'How is the journal coming along?'

'I'm not much of a writer, but I try to capture my moods.'

'How is your mood today?'

'Today is the kind of day where I feel like shit but I don't tell anybody about it. Or I don't give in, whichever makes most sense.'

'You're concerned about making sense – the opinion of others?'

'Just like anybody else, right? We all care what people think of us.'

'But if you knew that you wouldn't be able to walk down the street.'

'I guess it's like having an itch you can't scratch – wanting to know what other people think about you.'

Dr Nicholls leaned back in his easy chair, puffed his chest a little and exhaled while he crossed his arms.

'Bill phoned me last night, my wife actually answered the phone, but he told me how worried he was about you. He thinks that you could benefit from a little extra help.'

'He wants me to go someplace and heal, doesn't he? A place where I can be alone, be forgotten about, missed off Christmas cards and be the subject of every bit of gossip this side of Cumbria.'

'Don't you think you would benefit from a little extra professional help?'

'I come to you, don't I? Isn't that enough?'

'I can only do so much. I can help with your anxiety, give you practical help and advice in terms of exercises – but it will never be enough most likely.'

'I look forward to coming here, Dr Nicholls.'

'Pleasure is not always the start to recovery.'

'Haven't I already hit rock bottom?'

'Nobody denies you. Nobody is out to humiliate you. I think what your husband is saying makes sense right now.'

'So, you think I should go to the madhouse?'

Dr Nicholls never answered her. He picked up the red ball next to his keyboard and squeezed it firmly within his palm. Huge blocks of hail began hurtling towards the small window. It was becoming more unclear as the weather turned foul. Sheets of rain washed the glass, the noise a welcome break from the tension.

'While you are here I think we should work on some stress-reducing exercises.'

'What is the deal with that red ball of yours?'

'It helps,' he said, 'and what could help you is some mindfulness meditation, some biofeedback and repetitive prayer.'

'You think I should ask God for a full recovery?'

'Does that contradict something?'

'You didn't even ask me if I believed.'

'We all believe, Clara, sometimes we just don't know it until we see for ourselves.'

'See what?'

'What power really means.'

5

Clara shut her eyes tight and focused on the birds tapping at the roof gutter outside the window. She blocked out the sound of Bill's frantic breath - his shuddering, rhythmic, heaving body atop of her as he moved through her with all the force of a man eager to lose his frustrations, his anger, his torment. As he neared climax, Clara bit down hard on his cheek. It was the most pleasurable thing she had done to him in a long while, since they were first married in fact. It was the first thing that came to her mind when she thought of him, the first thing that would exorcise her fury. He let out a guttural moan, clawed at her naked flesh and quickened the pace until he did climax. Even at that point Clara was thinking about her first line in what would be the next argument. He rolled off her, tried to catch his breath, and the thought of lighting up a cigarette came to him again. It had been eight years since he last lit one – and that was bummed off a fan at a book signing. Clara threw her legs to the soft rug and began to dress. Bill touched her lightly on the arm, to which she shrugged off. 'Trust can go both ways, you know,' she said.

'Trust has nothing to do with—'

'It does, Bill. You calling my therapist says a lot about our marriage. Going behind my back like that, it is just downright shitty.'

'I called Dr Nicholls because I was worried about you. There is no betrayal here. This is our life, Clara, it is not a rehearsal.'

Bill leaned out over the bed and picked up his shirt from the rug. Both of them began to dress, almost as hurriedly as they had undressed. David burst into the room brandishing a replica handgun. 'Bang! Bang!' he shouted at his mother. Clara clasped at her chest, feigned injury and said in a whisper, 'and life is too short for secrets.'

David charged up onto the bed, shooting his way through the room. 'Go put that thing away and get washed up for dinner,' said Bill. Clara picked David up and carried him over to the balcony door, where she pulled the curtains apart. 'Don't you know not to shoot your father?' said Bill.

'Somebody ought to,' said Clara.

She set David down in the playroom next to Rita and kissed both of them on the head. David's hair wet with perspiration, matted to his scalp. Rita's smelling of Rosemary and honey. 'I got star of the week from Mrs Mitchell,' Rita said.

'That's great news! My little star,' said Clara. 'Go on the pair of you, get washed up before dinner. I thought you were star of the week last week?'

'No, that was Harriet Parker.'

'Who's she?'

'She's the one who got her little finger stuck in the door jamb.'

'Smart girl, eh?'

'She reads at year six level.'

'Shame she doesn't see as one too.'

Bill passed the children and ruffled their hair as he went into his study. He ignored the cold stare from his wife. It seemed that afternoon sex wasn't the remedy he had hoped it would be. But he could always manage a few hundred words before dinner. He did most of his writing in the late afternoon, feeling the muse very much with him as the light faded. Clara watched the door close and still felt the same. She could still hear that phone call in her head. Bill going behind her back and telling the therapist about how worried he was. If he was that worried he could have come to Clara first, he could have told her his fears. Was she that sick, really? She clenched her fists as she passed the door, thought about the techniques Dr Nicholls had taught her about anger and focused on her breath. Just one breath after another. It was nearly six when Bill emerged from his writing room.

'I hope we're not keeping you away from that computer,' Clara said.

'Not at all. Dinner smells good.'

'It's just what we had last Tuesday.'

'What do you know about Waterside House?'

'Just that it's a psych ward.'

'There are many types of wards actually. They help people get back on track.'

'Why are you telling me this, is it something you're writing about?'

'I was thinking that you might benefit from a little time away.'

Perhaps she knew this was coming, although it still stung. 'What I need is a little trust.'

'You have my trust, Clara. They have specialist doctors who know about this sort of thing that you're going through – what with the blackouts, the anxiety, the stunt you pulled on the boat. They know better than that crook, that smoothie, Dr Nicholls.'

'If he's such a lousy therapist then why did you call him to complain about me?'

Bill sighed. 'We need you on the right tracks,' he said, leaning over the breakfast bar. 'Just a few weeks at this hospital and you'll soon see the light again. I want to see the light in *you* again,' he said as he brushed a strand of chestnut hair from her eyes. 'You need some help before something goes dreadfully wrong.'

'Have you telephoned already?'

'No. I thought we should discuss it first.'

'How noble of you.'

Clara pushed passed him and almost knocked a picture from its nail in the narrow hallway. It was the back cover of Bill's second book. She took the stairs two at a time. Bill followed her up. He watched her from the open doorway.

Clara stood on the balcony as the rain hit the awning. It made a patter like pellets being fired from above. She counted them until she could no longer hold the beat in her head. The sky was inky over her and in the sallow lamplight beyond the dogwood she watched the rain coming down in sheets.

'Are you okay?' Bill asked.

'Do you even care?'

'I care. I care so much.'

Bill approached her, touched her skin, kissed her neck in the mouth of the doorway. The curtains blew in the night air. 'Is this what we are becoming?' Clara asked. 'One of those couples who fight at every turn?'

'It sounds like my parents,' said Bill.

Clara laughed, said, 'mine too.'

'I only want what's best for us,' he said.

'Maybe it isn't the worst idea in the world,' said Clara.

'Nothing needs to be decided tonight.'

'I don't know if I'll cope being away.'

'We can manage in the harshest of climates, when we really have to.'

Bill squeezed her arms then rubbed them warmer. 'Don't be too long out in the cold,' he said. She caught hold of his hand and planted a kiss before he turned and walked out of the room. Clara watched him disappear. The moonlight was cutting through some of the mist that hung close to the fells beyond the garden. A rattle of fence panels down below in the neighbour's yard was accompanied by a dog's bark. It started to sink in – the sounds of life that she would be leaving behind, and the safe world that she knew. It was dark and it was wet out there and it seemed that the rumblings of war had finally come crashing in on her, all hell and fury.

CHAPTER 11

Present day

1

Bernie Waller wore her long taupe trench coat with an ecru trim, a pair of fawn cone heels on her feet, and in her handbag, she had a Dictaphone, a notebook and a pen. Eastview ward looked like a film set with extras dotted around in the nooks and crannies of its cherry wood halls. Kath Jennings was on one side of her and Sal Blackwell was on the other, sporting a gaping black hole where her front tooth should have been. The excitement was not lost on Bernie, and it even gave her a little spring in her step. It made her think of those documentaries she watched on repeat, the ones where an outsider infiltrates a sacred space – where the public are usually shut out. She only hoped that this story was going to be good enough to get back in the good books of Michael Rainford. Even if she had no idea what the story was yet. Maybe it would be about this strange creature hanging off her arm, the one who kept skipping along as they moved through the lumber of the hallway. This strange creature who had spent the eternity of their time together thus far recanting the tale of how she lost her tooth in the first place.

'You should see the other guy,' she had said, and went on to explain further. 'This fucking drunk had me up against the trash cans outside a Dixy Chicken, so I socked him hard. He went down but then he didn't want to lose face so he clocked me back and here I am,' Sal said. 'I think Whiteface has it now.'

Kath Jennings seemed to be ignoring Sal and so Bernie felt safe enough to do the same, even though she hated doing that. Kath talked about the weather, prompting Sal to use her nickname – the Kathometer, which brought a smile to Bernie's poker face.

'I've got three words for you, hotshot,' Sal said. 'Take. Your. Medicine.' She held up three fingers, stained black at the tips through charcoal and dirt. The fine, stringy remains of nail were bitten down to about halfway from the tip. Bernie only knew that she was on her way to meet with Francis Bird. She had no idea who the patient was that had just come in and who would be her story for the paper. She silently prayed it wasn't Sal.

'I've got stories, you know,' Sal said.

Bernie couldn't stay quiet much longer. 'How interesting,' she said.

'I came third in a Miss Cumbria contest.'

'Yeah, as a baby,' said Sharne, who had joined the three of them.

Margot looked on, leaning against a noticeboard as though she was wating for a bus. Her wary eyes sunken and angry. Kath knocked on the door. All the blinds were drawn inside the office. Sal skipped ahead of them; her fingers raised above the back of her head giving the V sign. Kath's face lit up with a warm smile and then she turned to leave. Bernie wanted to say to her, 'don't go,' but she knew that it was silly to think of Francis as some monster. The way she thought of him when she was alone in the cottage by the woods. It was daft to think that her memory was perfect anyway. It was far from perfect and it played tricks from time to time. The door opened and Francis, despite his small frame, stood tall in the light like a devil.

2

The first time she'd had a flashback was when they had met on the street twelve summers ago under a fiery sun that made the earth arid and apt for flames. The talk had been kind of small between the two, nothing very memorable. Except the stains of blood, the awful screams tearing through her, threatening to suffocate her. These all came back to her in a moment and cut off her tongue. Now she looked at him on this cold wintery morning, the hair had greyed and the face had sagged a little but the eyes were as steely as they had ever been. 'It's been too long,' he said.

Bernie stepped inside. It didn't feel long to Bernie. It felt like he was there with her every time she closed her eyes. But she didn't let him know this, she couldn't or else she would break down and never be able to write her stories again. 'It's nice to see you,' she lied.

She took a seat facing the window, back to the door. Francis lifted the blinds and a shard of light swam in, lit up the desk where Bernie placed her hands – the cold, shivery hands that nervously tapped the wood in a scatty rhythm. 'She's quite a character, isn't she?' Francis said.

'You mean Sal?'

'She's got a vendetta against me,' he said.

'You sound as paranoid as they do,' Bernie said.

She crossed her legs and instinctively pulled down the lower part of her skirt which had ridden up. Francis saw it but kept on undrawing the blinds. At least everybody can see us, Bernie thought. She relaxed for the first time that morning and her thoughts turned to business. 'I'm eager to see who you have for me to interview,' she said. Francis took a seat behind his desk, in front of Bernie and her sheer tights catching the light. He pawed at a stack of papers, took two off the top of the pile and adjusted his spectacles. 'Ah, yes. A new fish in the pond. I think you'll get on well.'

Bernie dug out a notebook from her bag. 'What's her name?' she asked, pen in hand.

'Clara O'Hara.'

She wrote it down. 'That's some name,' she said.

'She's due to see Occupational Therapy at noon,' he said, 'but her schedule isn't overly busy. She hasn't talked much, not even to her case worker. Her husband is a writer – William O'Hara, known to us as Bill. He writes fiction. Not a bestseller yet but I'm guessing he does alright. He was the one who brought her in a few weeks ago.' Francis stopped, then mouthed the word 'suicide' slow and purposefully. His smile returned, the one that haunted Bernie and then he placed the confidential papers in a drawer out of sight.

'How stable is she right now?' Bernie asked.

'I think with a combination of the meds and some real therapy she'll come out of her shell a little.'

'But I asked how stable is she right now?'

'She is what she is. Do you still want to go ahead?'

'Yes.' She almost added, it's all I've got, but stopped herself. No intimate details – she had sworn to herself before leaving the cottage.

'When can I meet her?'

Francis instinctively checked his watch, then looked at another stack of papers. 'I can have you meet with her in five minutes, if that's what you want?'

'Of course, that's why I'm here – isn't it?'

'Of course. Why else?'

She felt that aching pang of guilt again. The one that sticks a knife through her body when she's about to turn out the light and sleep. Or when she's at the airport. Or singing to herself in the shower. 'Five minutes works for me,' she said.

'Great. Let me show you to the room we use for our ward round. You can get acquainted today and if you feel it's working then I can give you more time, providing that she's game.'

Bernie followed him to a small, square room off the west side of Eastview ward. The sole window was covered in ivory and a pair of checked curtains matched the garish carpet. It had two large seats facing each other, which took up most of the space, and there was a small wood table in between. Bernie sat down, took in the posters on the walls promoting healthy living – there was a picture of a young woman drinking from a bottle of oil and a bag of crisps next to it, and waited for a meeting with the quiet, mysterious Clara. She waited for Francis to leave. But he hesitated by the open doorway, smiling again. 'You know, I always stop to think how lucky we are,' he said.

Bernie's facial muscles tightened a little. 'Lucky?' she asked.

'You'll soon figure it out,' Francis said. He closed the door behind him and Bernie needed a large, stiff drink.

3

Clara thought that she looked like a slightly older version of Natalie Dormer. That's who she reminded her of, with that crooked smile – maybe just a darker complexion, but she was a dead ringer. She stirred her coffee with a wooden strip. It was the kind that comes in silver foil (glass was a banned substance) and tasted ghastly. It wasn't the good java she used to buy for herself in town, the fresh heavenly type that when brewing casts its own magic spell with the aroma. She thought about the question Bernie had asked her again. There were so many ways to answer it, probably too many to be able to pick one and articulate it to a stranger.

'I have these blackouts,' she said, ending the unbearable sound of the silence in the room. 'They're pretty awful.'

Bernie hoped that her exhale of relief hadn't been noticed by Clara. She checked to see if the Dictaphone was working, even though she was taking shorthand notes. It never hurt to have a backup. 'It must be so hard being away from your husband and children for such a while.'

'Bill said he'll be here soon.' Clara sipped at her scalding cup of instant coffee and shook her head when she felt the heat on the tip of her tongue.

'It must be a relief to know that you have all that support on the outside?' Bernie asked. Clara never answered that question, so she tried a different approach.

'Tell me about your children.'

'David is seven. Rita nine. They're in school and doing well,' Clara said it as though it were a distant memory, as if she were desperately trying to keep a lid on it before it escaped from her mind. 'I think me being here is going to be great for all of us in the long run.'

It sounded like doctor spiel, the kind of bullshit that they tell patients with severe mental trauma, thought Bernie. It sounded like Francis Bird.

'Tell me about your life before Waterside House. Before these nosy doctors got into your affairs.'

Clara sipped from her cup, licked her lips and then almost broke out into a smile. 'I had a therapist on the outside. Bill never liked him – said he couldn't lie straight in a bed. I kind of think he was right. He couldn't keep me out of this place for starters.'

'I've read your files, Clara. You've had it rough for a while.'

'You know about the nails and the knife?'

'I'm not here to judge you. I just want to understand what it's like being you. Being locked inside this hospital. Being a voluntary patient sectioned for three months who has a loving family waiting for them on the outside. I just want to know what it feels like to be a victim of your own head.'

'I tried to kill him,' Clara said. 'I jumped in the water to make him drown.'

'You don't believe that,' Bernie said.

There was a long silence before Clara looked her in the eyes and said, 'there is someone in here who knows.'

'Knows what?'

'I can't say any more than that,' she said, lifting a finger to her lips.

Bernie studied her face, a tired, russet brokenness to it that looked sad and terrified.

'I just want to remind you that what you say in this room is just between me and you. I mean I know I'm a journalist, but I know discretion. In fact, it's a huge part of the job.'

'It wants me out of here so I can see.'

'What wants you out of here?'

'It wants me to find out.'

'Find what out?'

Clara thought back to the writing on the mirror. Then she thought about what had happened a day ago. She remembered the trail of water leading from her bedroom to the turn of the corridor. The smell of fish that wouldn't leave her fingers, the tips of her chestnut hair, the hairs in her nostril. She remembered the sounds of whispers in the night. She remembered the clippings from a newspaper that had been shoved underneath her door. Letters that had been cut out of headlines. She had no idea what they meant. Or what they were trying to say. The letters simply spelled out

T H E P I L L M A N

She thought about it now in the cold light of the day and almost broke down with the ache behind her eyes.

'I just want the screaming to stop,' Clara said, before she bent to her lap and began sobbing.

Bernie leant out a hand in comfort and caught a lump in her own throat. Clara grabbed her hand tight and said, 'tell Bill. Tell him about pill man. He'll know what to do.'

The bell for the lunch trolley sounded out in the hallway and Clara wiped her eyes dry with the back of her hand. She stood and Bernie did the same. 'I have to go and eat, otherwise there will only be jam and crackers.'

'Please let me see you again,' Bernie said, a little desperation in her voice.

Clara smiled at her. At least her mouth was smiling, but the eyes. . . they were troubled. Then she was gone.

CHAPTER 12

1988

In the cold afternoon mizzle, Tim Hindle led the group of bird watchers back to the warmth of Eastview ward. They had only seen one other bird – apart from those deafening crows that sat at the tops of the thicket in the ruins. It was a corncrake. It reminded Tim of long walks through Walla Crag with his ex-wife. The picnic she made them overlooking Derwentwater, and then the heavy rain that showered them both into a mild panic. He remembered the run back to the car and then his mind stopped suddenly. Stuart Pillman appeared through the throng of patients, just as several papers had blown out of Katie Thorogood's hand – sketches of birds now at the mercy of the winter wind. Tim jogged over to the smoking post where the group had taken shelter from the light rain. Stuart was picking up the papers. 'I didn't expect you to be in so soon,' Tim said.

'It's better for me that I keep busy,' Stuart said.

'Yeah, but you need to process what has happened.'

'I'll be fine, Tim. Really. Just let me get on with my job, please.'

'Okay. But you talk to me if you need anything. *Anything.*'

'Will do, boss.'

'Some of us are going out for a drink tonight after work,' Tim said, 'if you feel like some company.'

'Oh, thanks, but I need to sort out mum's belongings. You know, there's about a million photographs, a suitcase full of jewellery and about a hundred phone calls I have to make.'

'Well, if you change your mind just call me.'

Stuart smiled and handed the pictures back to a lank haired young woman who stood at about five feet tall. 'I'll get them back inside,' said Stuart. 'You take a break.'

'If you're sure,' said Tim.

Stuart called the patients over by the fern bush where his car was parked. The back entrance to Eastview was just around the corner, through a small lane shrouded either side by bushes. They all walked in step, back up to the ward without uttering a single word. Stuart liked that. It gave him a good feeling.

Past the row of office windows they went, until they came upon one bedroom window that was slightly ajar. There was a light on and a figure was sitting at the sill. It caught Stuart's attention. Ever since he had been introduced to her he felt a strange kind of carnage in the pit of his stomach. He stopped and the rest of the women stopped walking too. He waved them all on. He whispered to himself. 'You think you're champagne in a tall glass.' He repeated it again and again.

He approached the open window, placed a hand on the white frame and gently closed it shut. He could see her clearer now. The grey hair bunched up on her head, the eyes that were pale and sunken, the mouth twisted and whiskered. She was his mother then. Screaming at him to put out his cigarette. Put it out! Put it out! He clenched his fists, unclenched, then clenched again. He had shouted at her, couldn't remember what he said exactly, but he definitely shouted back at her. They went on like this until he couldn't stand it anymore, until he did something about it. He could still see the look on her face as he placed the plastic bag over her head. He could see that terror in her eyes, and the bulging of the throat as she tried to breathe. He could smell the urine on her clothes and the grease in her stringy hair. He watched as the recognition came and went. One second she looked like she knew who he was, then the next, she had no idea again. He pulled the straps tighter, felt her neck against the plastic and held on for what seemed like an eternity. Soon enough she would be dead. Soon enough it would all be over.

'What do you see around here?' Stuart said to the old weathered face at the window. 'I bet you know everything. I bet you know everybody's dirty little secrets. What about Tim Hindle? Is he still pining for his ex-wife to come back and blow him? All those lonely nights with just his right hand for company. I bet you know, don't you? What's the matter, don't you talk? Not even to little old me?'

The rain started to hammer down and Stuart turned to see Tim running towards him, a cigarette in his hand. Stuart waved. 'Let's get them back inside,' said Tim. Stuart nodded and broke out into a jog. The patients were stood hooded and wet by the time they both joined them. Tim inserted his key in the lock. 'Was she speaking to you?' Tim asked.

'Who?'

'Mary. I saw you at the window. I just figured she was talking.'

'No, she wasn't talking. I can't get a word out of her. But I will.'

'That's the right attitude to have. It can get you through a lot of shit in a place like this.'

'I actually feel quite comfortable with her. She reminds me of my mother.'

Tim smiled handsomely, until he saw the ring mark on his finger again for the millionth time that day. Then his brightness disappeared. 'It gets rough sometimes, don't it? Stuart said. Tim didn't try to pretend that he had no idea what he was talking about. He was beyond all that now. They walked the group of patients back inside the great lumber of the halls, Stuart locked the door behind them and said he was going to try and speak to Mary one more time.

'You know, just to push her some more,' he said.

'I like your determination,' Tim said. 'You'll do fine here.' Then he gave him a thumbs up.

As Stuart walked on he heard the sounds of his mother, back when he was small enough to be carried in her arms. He heard the lash of a belt against his thighs. He heard the silence of his mother as his father walloped him again for dropping his dinner fork on the carpet. He heard his mother sobbing in the bedroom, alone and afraid but just as guilty as him. As culpable as his crazy daddy. The one who does things to him at night when he pretends he's asleep. But he is always awake. He always remembers it too. He always remembers his mother in the morning cooking eggs and bacon with a big fat stupid smile on her face. 'When is that old bitch going to leave me the fuck alone?' he whispered to himself. He wished then that he hadn't killed her. Instead, he wished he'd done it years ago when she was well enough to know who the fuck he was. When she would've felt it more. When she would have been sorry.

Mary sat in her wheelchair facing the hard rain hammering against the window. It was seeping in through the gap, sopping the edge of the check curtains and the fringe of the sill below. Stuart watched the back of her head for a moment. It could almost pass as his mother. It could almost have been her. Her neck was long and it had veins sunk deep into its weathered skin. Stuart stood at the open door and laughed quietly to himself. She had no idea he was there, and it almost gave him an erection. He could feel the blood pumping down his torso, into his stomach, then to his penis. His heart fluttered when she turned her head to the left, saw a shadow on the cream wall and opened her mouth so the breath would come flowing out. He hoped it would. He had heard stories about her, depraved stories that made her seem worse than mad. Being mad was a requirement inside this place, but hers was a strange madness that drove others wild. At least that is what he had heard. 'What's an old witch like you doing in a place like this?' Stuart asked. He stared at the back of her head, which was still unmoving. He held his breath. He could have sworn he heard a gasp, or more like a tired rasping breath that had escaped. It sounded like she was communicating to him, something along the lines of 'at last.'

CHAPTER 13

Present day

1

Clara couldn't believe her aching, tired eyes. If it wasn't for the medication they drilled into her body, she might well have thought she was going crazy. That is what it stopped you from doing, wasn't it? She stared at the window again, almost too afraid to maintain eye contact with it. She wondered if her sleep could be that deep that she wouldn't know who had just come into her room. But somebody had.

She ran a finger along the steamy pane of window, and let it fall to the wood sill that was also wet with the run of condensation. Another message. Another haunting for her to deal with alone. Written in a glass marker, same penmanship as before, this one said:

YOU'LL DIE IN HERE

So that made two messages now. The first she could remember clearly, just after her run to the bathroom to throw up that awful scent of foot odour from her stomach. That one had told her to get out or. . . now it made a little more sense. *Get out or you'll die in here* was the full message. But who the fuck was writing it, and why?

Clara jumped back into bed, almost fell with her feet tangled in the maze of her bedsheets and covered her face with the papery duvet. She heard the mechanical trap of the door opening outside in the hall. Then she heard footsteps. Those heavy lug boots that squished the floor like someone was slapping the face of a hammer against it. Somebody was coming for her. She looked at the clock and knew why. It was morning meds. She shut the curtains and waited for the knock at the door.

Clara eyed Jeannie Newton in the tv lounge feeling that the marker had to have come from her. She stared at her own fingers, stained with the ink she'd removed hastily and felt a wave of anxiety creeping in to her bones. Those fine white bones that looked more brittle as fine white China every day she spent inside this brick house. She told herself to breathe. Just like Bill had always done. She heard his voice too, although it wasn't like the others in here. She heard her own impression of him, that was all.

Clara sat at the window, through which she saw the courtyard and its empty washing line – apart from a robin that swayed unevenly along its spiny wire. She tried to focus on the morning magazine tv show, but it was brain-sapping at best. The nurse arrived with a handful of pills and a thimble of water in her hands. Clara took it from her and knocked it back. The nurse smiled and left. Jeanie, sitting in the opposite corner, dug her finger in her ear and asked, 'what is up with you? You've been rubbernecking me like I'm a car wreck all morning.'

She sniffed the tip of her index finger and rubbed it along the seam of her trousers.

'Nothing. I'm not looking at anything,' Clara said, then her voice dropped a decibel or two, it was barely a whisper. 'But if you wanted to tell me something, then you know you can, right?'

'Tell you. . . what exactly?'

'I don't know. You have all kinds of paints and markers, don't you?'

'I have some decent art supplies, bought them from the Craft Store a town over. You need something?'

'No. I don't need anything. It's just that. . .' Clara couldn't finish her sentence. Just the thought of it made her stomach turn and her legs buckle. Her breath just wouldn't let her get the words out. 'Can I ask you a question?' Clara said.

Jeannie just looked at her, open mouthed, and a pair of eyes that were dark but very impatient. 'Do you sleepwalk?'

Jeannie laughed. 'No, I don't think so. Well, nobody's ever told me that I have. Why do you ask?'

'No reason.'

As Margot walked in stomping her boots, Clara shrank back into her corner chair and gave up her pitiful investigations. Who was she kidding? She was never going to find out what was behind those messages herself. But that is when she thought about the woman who comes to see her. That's when her hopes began to rise again.

2

Bernie fed Hemingway a can of tuna and a saucer of milk. He lapped it up like there was no more coming for another month or so. He was getting a little chubby in the underside of his gut too. A bulging neck that barely had room for a collar to be fitted. But Bernie didn't mind a fat cat. It was better to look at than Mrs Welsh's scrawny excuse for a kitty a few cottages down the road. She stroked the tip of Hemingway's scalp, felt him brush against her and cry out with glee. He always cried out when she treated him with milk. She grabbed her trench coat and picked up her car keys from the quaint old fruit bowl that had seen less and less of actual fruit over the years. It was made from teak and when she had first bought it she had kept grapes and oranges in it, but now it was lucky if it held a bag of mentos. She stepped out into the cold harsh wind and pulled up her collars. She hoped her car would start at the first attempt, but it did not. In fact, it was the third. Not bad for a tank of junk on a winter morning, she thought to herself. Then she was cruising down the road, thinking about Clara O'Hara and her writer husband. She reminded herself to visit the bookshop in town. At least she could read what he had to say before she interviewed him, get an insight perhaps. Maybe help her build a rapport. She was good at her job, even Rainford would agree on that – and she hadn't had a drink now (even though Francis Bird made her think of it all the time) for seven straight days – but even the best need a little helping hand, she thought as she opened a bottle of Alprazolam and chucked back a couple of pills. It was given on a private prescription, her anxiety meds, but she insisted that she'd never been any more sober than she was right now.

She pulled up to the hospital feeling the cold breath of winter rattle its way through her bones. It was mid-November but it felt like January. It might even snow soon, they said on the radio. But even if that was always promised, it rarely delivered. Still, the skies looked dark and moody above. Bernie pressed the buzzer and waited to be let inside. It couldn't have happened soon enough.

The warm smack of the central heating hit her in the face and made her ears sting. She asked Kath Jennings, who was eager to share her weather predictions – once she had arrived at the central hub of Eastview – where she might find Clara at this time of day and then she followed her into an unlit and fusty room where the atmosphere was dense. Bernie could feel it trickling down the paintwork, seeping in through the window and in every creak of the unoiled door as it opened.

Clara was quiet at first. Bernie only knew her starter for ten, as it were. She only knew that she had no idea what yesterday was all about. She didn't know who or what *pill man* was, and she didn't yet know what role Clara's husband was going to be playing in this little story that was about to be written. About to be contrived out of a load of shit that made little sense at this point, thought Bernie. But she was intrigued. She had to talk to her again, and Francis had given her the green light. 'Do you remember what you told me yesterday?' Bernie began.

'You seemed pretty shook up about something.'

'They've been in my room again while I was sleeping,' Clara said.

'It's just nurses, Clara, they're looking after you. I was wondering if you could just tell me about your time in here and whether you think that it's doing some good.' When she didn't respond Bernie tried a different tack. 'I'm going to speak with your husband later today. We spoke on the phone last night. He's really supportive of you, isn't he?' When that didn't loosen Clara's tongue, she tried to humour her. 'A writer of fantasy who's just been given his latest story no doubt.' Bernie tried a laugh but it had no real punch. Perhaps it was just in poor taste. So she conceded. 'Okay, Clara. Tell me. Tell me about pill man.'

3

Newspaper clippings, give me a break, thought Bernie. She didn't know who or what it was or why it had been in her head in the first place. The pill man was a figment of her imagination. It was as real as a fifteen-pound note. Bernie felt less and less sure of her 'brilliant angle on an old story.' She didn't feel that Michael Rainford was going to go for it in this state. She had a woman on the edge of reality babbling about a ghost it would seem. It wasn't supposed to be like this. Her story was going to be heart-warming, but it was also going to be a first-hand account of life behind the walls of one of the top psychiatric units in the country. People loved that kind of thing, but maybe as a guilty pleasure or something like that. It was always the same with buildings like this, whether it be prisoners at her majesty's pleasure, or the mentally unwell, people just went gaga for it. If she could only find a way to humanize her subject – Clara, that is – then maybe she could pull on all those heartstrings and give a genuine insight into what is thought of as a scary institution. A place where you don't want to be, but you read about it biting your nails, or you watch it on the telly hiding behind the sofa.

No, Clara had not said who or what pill man was. But she had said that there was someone writing on her mirror, or her window, or both it had sounded like to Bernie. Big deal. So someone with a magic marker was scribbling down messages, it hardly equates to espionage. She mentioned the torn-out letters of a newspaper spelling out the words 'pill man.' It sounded a little bizarre to Bernie. But she humoured Clara and told her she would ask her husband all about the pill man.

When she arrived at their modest mid-terrace house, she took one last look at the notes she had made since reading through Bill's latest novel, *Sundays in Paradise*. It was a fantastic hook, she thought. Quite original. Not your average murder book. She picked up the book and flipped it over to study the black and white photograph. He was handsome, if a little stuffy. But his eyes were frightfully full of intelligence. She knocked on the door and waited. Bill offered tea or coffee, then pulled out a stool at the breakfast bar for her to take.

'Herbal will do just fine,' she said. It was awfully clean inside. He obviously didn't miss that womanly touch either. The place was pretty as well as sterile. She noticed a vase of flowers on the table, and a single rose on the window sill where the afternoon gloom had begun to settle. Soon it might just snow. Maybe the weather reports were right about that. The kettle clicked off and Bill poured them both a cup of steaming green tea. Bernie wished it was wine, then she pinched the skin on her chapped hand to tell herself off for the thought. It had just been banished to the dead air, where all her bad thoughts go. Ever since that afternoon in the breathless attic. Bill saw her notice the paintings leaning against the kitchen wall. 'The artwork is my wife's,' he said. 'I was just in the process of moving it upstairs.'

'She never said she was so talented.'

'Why would she?'

Bill sat down at the opposite end of the breakfast bar.

'I suppose she has other things on her mind right now,' Bernie said.

'How did she seem to you?' Bill asked. 'I spoke to her on the phone, she seemed in good spirits, but I just wonder.'

Bernie waited for him to go on. 'I just wonder whether we're doing the best we can for her. Being in that place, it can't be easy for anyone. I still don't know if I can fully trust Dr Bird, either.'

Bernie perked up a little at the mention of Francis. 'Trust him?' Bernie said. 'I don't know about that.' Suddenly the tea wasn't so hot that she could gulp it down her throat without really feeling it burn. She had left a nail bomb hanging in the air, so she spoke quickly. 'But I do know that Clara is in the best place right now.' She felt a stab of heartburn and another excruciating pang of guilt.

'It was the only thing I could think of doing, you know. If there had been a different way to go then I'm convinced it would have found me,' Bill said. 'We tried a therapist in Kendal for a long time. He gave her all the exercises, all the knowledge, all the techniques, but in the end it was all for nothing.'

'I'm going to recommend that Clara keep a journal of her journey through the hospital. I think it may help.'

'No, you're just trying to write a better story with none of the juicy details omitted. Come on, cut the shit, what do you really want with us?'

Bernie was thrown back, mouth open, steaming tea rising like hail fog up to her nostrils, her pretty brown eyes. 'I'm just here to do good. I mean, yes, I am going to write a story about Clara, about Waterside House and its function in this town that we both love. But I am also here to offer my full support for the both of you. We can take it as slowly as you like, Clara too. Please don't be mad at me.'

'Maybe I just have some trust issues. I'm sorry I didn't mean to take it out on you, it's not your fault we're in this mess.'

'Mr O'Hara, I completely understand. It can't be easy on either of you right now.'

'It's no excuse.'

Bernie smiled, wide and beautiful. 'Mr O'Hara, can I ask you about something?'

'Sure.'

Bernie paused, took some tea, then said, 'Has Clara ever mentioned the words pill man before?'

'Pill man?' Bill looked puzzled, his brow arched and deep thick wrinkles burrowed into his forehead.

'It's probably just something she's heard on the ward. I think she's been getting messages from someone inside Waterside House.'

'From who?

'I don't know that yet, and I presume that's what's on your wife's mind right now too.'

'And you think pill man is one of those messages?'

Bernie nodded her head. 'I think so. But I wouldn't worry about it, Mr O'Hara.'

'I've never heard of any pill man before. Did she say anything about its context?'

'The last thing I want to do is add to your worry. It's just I think some other patient is sending Clara these messages. I'll speak to someone on Eastview, maybe they can warn them off.'

'Thank you.'

'Now you do something for me, Mr O'Hara,' she said, smiling again.
'Tell me about Clara before Waterside House.'

'I think it's alright now if you call me Bill.'

'Okay, Bill. Tell me everything.'

4

So he told her everything he could remember. The awkward teenage years that she had confessed to him about, including her silly crush on Dicky Clarkson. The first boyfriend that made her cry for days when they had broken up. The attempts at singing for a career, until she realised, she could barely hold a tune – by which point she had already made her reputation: Coniston was a small place, he said.

As Bernie drove back home to her quiet cottage, she played the recording on her Dictaphone, resting on the passenger seat. She laughed at the part where he said Clara had once walked past a member of the pop group Take That in town, stopped only to tell him that the guy looked like one of Bill's characters in Secrets of the Spider People. Bill spoke about her love of books, her love for her father and mother, but her father especially as he was the one who nurtured her interest in literature. Bill said she had worked at the bookshop her father owned during her last years in school. He also said that he thought it was probably her happiest years. Although he said she seemed full of vigour and resolve when the two of them had gotten hitched. He told her about her part time job at Julia's – an upmarket dress shop selling everything from formal work clothes to party outfits – until Bill said she could quit if she wanted seeing as they didn't need the money. Clara, he said, was relieved to give it up. It meant she could spend more time with the kids at the weekend. Plus, she didn't exactly pine for the stuffy clientele who came in expecting five-star attention, coffee and their ego massaged. Clara was a spark of electricity. A shining light. She was funny and beautiful and kind and he almost broke down when he said that she had saved every memento of their courtship: a cinema stub, a teddy bear won at the funfair, a receipt from their first dinner, a shell singing with the muscle of waves from their first walk along west shore beach. Then he said something Bernie hadn't heard right when she was there the first time, sitting in his kitchen and sipping the green tea. He said something that made Bernie rewind the audio a couple of times, just to make sure she had heard it correctly. 'Marlie would agree, Clara isn't the type to act on jealous emotions. It's what I love about her.' Bernie rewound it again. 'Marlie would agree,' and again: 'Marlie.'

The snow started to fall. The weather reports were right, who would have known? Bernie switched on her wipers and turned off the tape. She was a half a mile away from her cottage on the outskirts of town, neatly pocketed in the valley, adjacent to a wild thicket of spindly wood trees and roaming hills. She drove home in silence. But that name kept gnawing away at her. It was all she could think of, even though she was trying really hard to focus on what Michael Rainford would have done. She drove up to the winding spit of a path that led to her cottage. The snowfall was getting heavier and it was settling on the tops of the fern at the edge of her small garden.

The kitchen seemed a messier one than when she had left it this morning. Bill O'Hara probably had something to do with that. His kitchen was that of a showroom. He was also responsible for the whirring brain that was about to give her one hell of a headache. She picked up a bottle of wine, then placed it back in the door of the fridge and closed it shut. She threw her coat, which had been dusted with a layer of snow, onto the arm of an accent chair underneath the window and fished out her notebook and pen. Looking again at the photograph of Bill on the back cover of his latest novel, Bernie could feel herself being drawn into a murky place, it reeked of murk – a kind of murk she was becoming used to now, ever since she picked up the phone to call Francis Bird. She was back in that attic, and back in that hotel room on a rain-soaked night in Vienna. She shook the dead air from her head, unclipped the pen and began to write.

On the blank page she wrote: Number 1: who is pill man? Number 2: why is Clara being sent messages? Number 3: who is sending them? And Number 4: who the fuck is Marlie?

The last one she underlined, twice.

CHAPTER 14

Present day

1

Bernie tossed and turned all night. It was one of those nights where she wasn't sure if she had been asleep at all. But she concluded that she must have been, as her brain was giving her that kind of signal when she unravelled her body from the web of her duvet and made hastily for the bathroom. At least she was sure she had not touched the wine. The thought of her sobriety made her face contort into a half-smile in the morning gloom. The snow had all but gone now thanks to a little light rain in the early hours. The hills that loomed above the cottage were still steeped in it though, a blanket of pure white snow that reminded Bernie of the festive season, a long time ago. It had been a while since she'd had a happy Christmas, thanks largely to her fractious parents – now divorced – whenever they got together, and her younger brother Frank who still wound her up, even though he never knew it sometimes. Secretly she envied him with his wife and young daughter in tow, flaunting it around as though he knew that Bernie would most likely never have what he has. Frank knew she was having troubles with her alcohol addiction. It seemed like it started a long time ago, when she was flying through her reporting career with *The Herald*, which included trips abroad, such as Vienna in the spring. It seemed to start then, and lord knows how it was going to end. Barely a phone call passed between them now, although they followed one another on Facebook.

Bernie slipped on her jeans and noticed there was a little more room in the waist. Another half-smile crossed her lips. She grabbed a clean shirt from her wardrobe and picked up her heels from underneath the bed. She sniffed her armpits, not bad, she thought. Her trench coat was still on the arm of the accent chair. She grabbed it and her keys from the fruit bowl. The icy air of the unforgiving morning smacked her nose and stung her ears. There was a trail of slush on the garden path as she walked to the car. It was still dark out. But it was one of those days that seems like the sun will never rise. She started the car, waited for the windscreen to warm up and thought of how she was going to tell Francis Bird about the pill man.

She took two Alprazolam before she shut off the engine in the gravel drive of the hospital. The huge oak trees sent down a litter of leaves as she walked beneath their lumbering hovel. She needn't have worried about explaining herself to Francis, he already knew about pill man. More than that, he was able to shed a little light on the subject. He actually knew who pill man was.

'His name is Stuart Pillman. He got called the pill man because he used to divvy out the meds to the girls on Eastview. Christ, I haven't thought about that guy in years. Where did his name crop up?'

'Oh, it was just some research I did into the history of Waterside House. Only I never knew his role exactly. So, he worked right here on Clara's ward?' Bernie did her utmost to keep her voice light and engaging, even though inside she was a ball of fire.

'Yes, he worked on Eastview the whole time he was employed here. He left under a bit of a cloud, I might add,' Francis said.

'How so?' The air in her voice was almost nauseating for Bernie, but Francis didn't show it.

'It was more of an admin failure on our part. He wasn't vetted correctly, or thoroughly, I should say. It relates to his previous employment with The Wellness, up in Carlisle. I blame our manager. A guy called Tim Hindle. Couldn't lie straight in a bed. I arrived in this hospital in 1991 and when I did, Stuart was going in the other direction.'

'Was he sacked?'

'We found something out. It was back in The Wellness. What he failed to disclose was that when he left The Wellness he was under investigation.'

'Crikey, what was it?'

'He was being accused of assault on one of the patients. But the investigation was dropped when said patient died a few weeks later. Unconnected apparently. Old age. She had no family, no one at all and she just perished like a fart in the night. Pillman was let go from Waterside on account of his lies. It's a serious thing to not disclose something like that. We had no choice.'

'Is there anybody working here that might remember him?'

'We have some staff that have been here as long as I have, but I doubt they'll recollect a man like him.'

'A man like him?'

'A greasy haired chancer who you'd cross the road to avoid if you saw him in the street. He was one of those people you just don't notice until it's too late. Thankfully we found out in time. Who knows what could have happened?'

'Did he have any problems with staff here?'

'He kept himself to himself if I can recall. Like I said, I doubt there's anybody who would remember a little fucker like that.'

'But he was here three years.'

'You can speak to Tim Hindle about him. But I doubt he'll be in any sort of mood to talk. Not when it comes to the Pill man. It's a touchy subject. Besides, I believe he's sunning it up in Portugal these days. Lucky get-out I say.'

'What about this Wellness place?'

'They may have better memories. Or worse.'

Bernie filed the information away in her sober mind, and almost half-smiled again. But then she changed the subject, which almost certainly would have wiped off the smile if she had one. 'Is Clara okay for a visit today?' She asked.

'You two are getting close, eh?'

Bernie fake laughed. 'I'm just doing my job.'

'You can see her after lunch.'

'That works fine for me. I have some admin to do of my own.'

Francis laughed, none of it was faked. Then he stood and pulled up the blinds. There was a moment of awkwardness as they slipped past each other, almost brushing the other with their chests. Bernie ran a hand through her hair and looked to her shoes. But she saw a different person wearing those heels. What she saw was a young Austrian woman with a pair of ripped tights begging for her life. Then it was gone.

2

The Arc 4000 electric fly killer, with its UV tubes, zapped another one, killing the beast instantly. Its dead body dropped into the catchment tray as Clara watched in fascination. The kitchen she was standing in was a complete mess with stained worktops and cold tea bags strewn along the brown wood. She reached for the milk but gasped when she smelled the smoke on the rim of the carton. Sal had been drinking from it again. She had been warned about that. If she carried on, the kitchen would be off limits to patients. They would need to ask a member of staff to open it and they would watch everything like a hawk. Lunch had been alright. It seemed like she was becoming tolerant to the food in Waterside House. Refried dental surgery mush it certainly wasn't anymore. She even let out a hearty burp now, tasting the hamburger and mustard in her mouth again. It tasted nice. She left the kitchen and scurried down the hallway, hoping she hadn't been seen by Lindy or anyone else. The last thing she wanted was to spend the afternoon washing dishes and scrubbing worktops that she hadn't even been responsible for. The mess was someone else's. Let them clear it up. Besides, she had work to do. Investigative work.

Ann Piggins was selling wagon wheels to Sharne and Casey, the three of them were huddled in secrecy beside the heaters. Money was wafted around and then hidden in the baggy pockets of Ann's cargo trousers. She kicked the empty box that had once contained the wagon wheels to the side of the hall, beneath a long window dusted with white snow. Clara heard Sharne saying something about why she was so tired, and then the three of them turned to stare at her, all of them quiet and disturbingly still. Clara quick-marched down the corridor. She never looked back. She sat in her room at the chair beneath the mirror and was reminded of the messages again. She shut her eyes tight so that everything faded from her mind. But one thought kept intruding on her: where was Bill?

3

Bernie wasn't lying about needing to do a bit of admin. She slipped out of her car and turned up the collars on her winter coat. She had a simple plan, and if it went the way that she thought it would then she was going to be turning super sleuth. Maybe it was catching in this place. Or maybe there was something here that needed uncovering. Maybe this hospital had some dark secrets. Then it all sounded a little silly to Bernie. But she reminded herself of the facts and thought it odd that nobody seemed to know about it. This pill man character was here, that she knew. But why has he come back in the form of newspaper headlines? And what has it to do with Clara? Bernie checked again that she had brought the sheet of paper with her notes on them, felt it inside her pocket. Then she rang the buzzer and waited.

In the same room as before she placed the sheet of paper on the little wood table between each of their feet. It was blank side up. 'So, Clara, as you know I am here for the duration of your stay. I am going to follow and document your journey in Waterside House. I'll be writing about the basic things, such as your routine, your daily progress and the practices of the hospital and its staff. In the end I am going to focus on how this place has helped you to reunite with your family. In other words, I want to write about how it has done you some good. I'll be interviewing your husband of course, and I hope to reach out to anyone else who you deem important in your life, and for your well-being. For instance, how about your mother and father? Or close friends and neighbours, a work colleague? It could be anyone really. So how about we start by writing down all of the people in your life who might want to know of your situation. Anyone who might be able to help you in your hour of need. How about it, Clara? How about we name everybody who is important?'

Bernie handed her a pen. She took it hesitantly. Then she leant on the table and started writing on the blank page. After a couple of minutes where it seemed Clara was visibly thinking hard, she handed the pen back and turned the paper around so that it faced Bernie. Bernie felt relieved. Perhaps this would get the story going, finally, and it might just shed some light on something else too. She read it aloud. 'Bill, David, Rita, Louise (mother), Colin (father), Connie (neighbour), Dr Nicholls, Dr Bird, Marcie, Garnet.' Bernie reached the end of the list. 'Is that everyone? You're absolutely sure about that?'

Clara nodded. 'It's everyone from the last year that I haven't already lost contact with.'

Bernie looked at the list again. There was one name that was missing, but she did not disclose that information. Where was Marlie?

She flipped the paper around and glanced at her brainstorming session in the car. *How much does Francis know?* screamed at her. But maybe she had another reason to doubt him. Whatever her reasons she didn't want to go there again, not today. Another line from her notes stuck out, hit her in the eyes: *is Bill squeaky clean?*

Then she began to wonder what the real story was here. Was it the impact of hospital life and the long journey to be reunited with loved ones? Or was there something between the lines? Something darker, something more dangerous? Something neither of them had envisaged when they woke up this morning. Bernie smiled and thanked Clara for her input. 'If you want, I could telephone your mother and father? I know it's a difficult call for you to make, so I am here if you need me. Just give me a shout.'

'They can't know. Not yet. They would only worry themselves sick. Perhaps when I am closer to getting out. When these blackouts stop. Maybe when I'm better.'

'It's your call.'

'Besides, I've got Bill. He's enough for me.'

'I'll chase up that visit, see if we can get him to come and see you soon.'

'Did you ask him about the pill man?'

'Yes. And no, it's not something he knows.' Bernie kept her tongue from saying anything else. Francis knew, she was almost about to say. But she kept quiet. She just flashed that crooked smile of hers and said, 'sorry.' Maybe it would come out eventually but right now she kept it to herself. She was going to do a little investigation first. Better to keep Clara in the dark, for her own good, at least until she'd had a chance to visit Carlisle.

Outside the wind was picking up. She checked the forecast on her phone and it was looking worse for the snow than it had early this morning. Carlisle was going to take about ninety minutes and, if she got going about now, she could make it before lunch. She pecked at a banana and sipped at a flask of coffee. She turned on the radio and started her tank of junk. She wondered what John looked like – the man who she had spoken to on the phone from The Wellness. She figured he was tall and bone white, like the flakes of snow trapped in the ridges of her wipers. She set off thinking that he was her ray of sunshine.

CHAPTER 15

1988

Stuart rewound the tape, even though he was due to set off for work in about fifteen minutes if he wanted to avoid Tim Hindle's warning. He certainly didn't want to be disciplined today for being late. That would really spoil his good mood. The film had been okay. But it was really just a big-titted bimbo of a film. Even so, he watched the part where the mother falls down the stairs and breaks her neck again, smiling to himself. Then he rewound it and watched it again, this time a little laughter broke out. He brushed off the popcorn from the buttons of his shirt and tied his laces tight. 'See you later, mum,' he said, looking at her empty chair, the cushion still dented with the imprint of her spine.

There was a scattering of petals on the ground. The blossom had rained down as though it were a cheering parade of confetti for someone's wedding photograph. Stuart crunched over them with his lug boots and rang the buzzer for Eastview's entrance. The sun was just peeking out through a cirrus roof, its strength growing all the time now. Spring had begun and there was no better time to be alive, thought Stuart. Then he thought about his mother lying in the cemetery under all those black trees. She was always in the shade now. Always in the dark. Just like she had pretended to be all those years.

Tim waved him inside. He was smiling that same smile he always had – a smile that looked like it burnt his mouth, as though it really hurt him. It was in the eyes aswell, the hurt and the desperation. Stuart felt relieved he didn't have to perform like that. Not for some skank like Sharon from growing well, anyway. He didn't even know her last name. No, it was not for him. He preferred to look at photographs. That's how he took care of himself. Photographs of women, not little girls, no, he wasn't one of those. He found the women around here too fat anyway. Too fat and spoiled.

He removed the baseball cap to reveal a shower of blonde hair, now getting a little long. So long that he had to blow it from his eyes when a gust of wind howled through the courtyard. 'I hope you've got a good stomach on you today?' Tim asked, still wearing that pretend smile. Stuart looked at him blankly. 'You've drawn the short straw. It's your job to clean up Mary Dunn,' he said, handing him a pair of slippery gloves.

'I thought it was Paula who did that usually?'

'She's had to phone in sick.'

Stuart followed him through the doors. 'It's alright, isn't it?' asked Tim. Stuart nodded, pushed his fingers through the gloves and smiled. There was no hurt or pain in it, and for that he felt superior. 'It's as fine as candy,' he said, fondly remembering his mother's voice saying that exact phrase. 'It'll put hairs on your chest,' Tim said, jokingly. Then he gave a titter of a laugh which Stuart felt was also hiding something ugly.

Stuart stood in the light of the sun that was gleaming through the window. Mary had her back to him, and again he was struck by the similarity to his dead mother. The neck in particular, and the way the hair was bunched up on the top of her head. Streaked grey and wiry to the touch. 'Okay miss fussy pants,' he said, 'how about we get all that dirt off you.'

She did not move her head, perhaps her eyes had twitched, but she remained stationary, still in the wheelchair that faced the sunlight. 'Paula,' she said, in a whisper.

'Paula's sick. You've got the pleasure of me this morning. Now let's get you washed so you can smell like a new born.'

He took her ankle in his hand and with a sponge soaked in hot water and soap, he brushed her skin, gently at first, then firmer once she had got used to the temperature. He was soft on her, never gripping too hard or going too fast. He was being thorough, and kind. The toes were yellow and the thick nails that pricked his hand were chipped at the ends. He moved up to her legs, brushing along with the sponge, always soft. 'I'll give you a minute to get off your underwear, then you can take the sponge yourself.'

He waited outside her room, peeking through the crack in the door. He watched her getting undressed, taking his eyes away at the last second before he saw her pubic hair. He had seen his mother's before, plenty of times in fact. He had bathed her in the tub and washed her hair, and her anus and her old, wrinkled vagina. But he never got an erection. Not once. He was so proud of that. Just the thought alone sickened him. He never got the whole incest thing, perhaps it was just the revulsion of his own flesh and blood that put him off. Mother was a sickening thing to behold. He heard the splash of water from the bedroom, then heavy sighs as she scrubbed down there. He snuck a peek in when she had turned around to face the drawn curtains. He saw her bony arse, and her shoulder blades that looked skeletal and frail. Her legs were long and russet, knees knobbly and thighs thin. Stuart came in with a bath sheet in his hands. 'Stay facing the curtains,' he said. He wrapped her body in the towel, rubbed at her back and helped her back into the wheelchair.

'That hair of yours needs washing.'

He started to run his fingers through the thick grey strands, felt its grease under his nails, curled her locks around the edge of a finger.

It wasn't Mary anymore. It was his mother.

He pulled hard on a wiry strand and he heard a gasp, a choking sound that could have come from a child. 'You're hurting me,' she said.

'Stop your whining, you're always whinging about something. It's too cold, it's too hot, it's too fucking late. Well, guess what, mum? It is too late. You're right about that one! It's too late for you.' He continued to pull at her hair, saw strands coming out in the ridges of his slender fingers. They were tangled with grey – long, thin, tired old grey hairs. He pulled until she turned swiftly and bared her ruin of a mouth full of teeth that were yellow and bruised from years of neglect. Stuart saw mother. He saw her walking away from his bed, turning out the light and climbing into her own. He saw his devilish father come into the room, undoing the clasp on his leather belt. He felt the feel of his soft pillow in the spaces between his teeth. He felt the scream swell up inside of him, the yearn for mother to come in to the room, stop him, stop him for good.

Mary dug her long, sharp nails into his raddled cheeks. It was only then that he was back in the room, feeling the warm trickle of blood swarming down his face. He let go of her, swiped at the blood with his sleeve and watched her fall back into the chair, hair sprayed like a rain shower pulled by a gusty wind. He watched the breath falling out of her mouth, looked at her eyes that were narrowed and then he smiled. He liked the feeling he had in his stomach. It was warm and fuzzy. His heart was beating fast, almost jumped right out of his chest, almost slipped out of his mouth and slapped her in the face. He took off his belt and then had to hike up his trousers to stop them falling below his backside. 'You're going to wish you hadn't done that, mum,' he said, walking toward her. But he never really thought that it was mother, he only said that for effect. To see, or let her see, how mad he was, how irate he had become, how very pissed off he was at her. If she felt it, she never showed it to him. Her eyes remained locked on his, her mouth left slightly open letting the heavy sighs come tumbling out of her lungs. Then she smiled, wide and creepy, showed her missing teeth in the front of her mouth, and the whiskers hanging from her chin caught the light from beneath the window. Stuart Pillman held the belt in his right hand, let the buckle hang below his hips and sway back and forth inches from the ground. He bared his teeth, lips peeled back, nostrils flared as each breath came fast and heavy. He took another step toward her chair. She never moved but her smile vanished and the teeth, and the black spaces where there should have been teeth, were gone. She pursed her lips into a kiss and made a smooching sound. It angered him more, so much more that he almost charged at her, and wanted so much to push her off that damn chair, hear the smack as her head hit the hard wood floor. He wrapped the belt around his clenched fist. 'Any last words, mum?' He expected her to start screaming, holler for help, but she disappointed him. 'You're a bully,' she said barely above a whisper. 'Bullies always get what's coming to them.'

As he neared her, he felt a stirring in his pants. It excited him. It enraged him. He felt his penis bulge out against his fly. He instinctively felt it with his free hand, stroked it over his pants. He hasn't been with a woman since he was in his early twenties. He remembers it well, though. He remembers the smell of her on his fingers. The smell of the bed even. He remembers but he doesn't like to remember. It makes him feel sick. He would much rather think of all the photographs he has in his bedside drawer. The ones he took of women when they didn't know they were being watched. But they were all women, all of them, not children, no, he is not one of those. He despised those kinds.

He heard a sound coming from out in the hallway. He turned to see. The belt went limp again. It was Tim Hindle. Shit. Stuart turned back to face Mary. She had a finger pressed to her mouth, covering some of the fine grey whiskers protruding from her wrinkled skin. Her eyes were laughing. Stuart was angrier now. He could barely hold it together, then he wondered if he could still go through with it. He wondered how much time he had left before Tim spoiled it all. The next thing he knew Tim Hindle was patting him on the behind and telling him what a great guy he is to a woman in a wheelchair who is barely awake.

CHAPTER 16

Present day

1

Marlene crossed the bedroom floor, still in her fancy underwear: the floral lace panties that Bill liked. The heat was turned up inside the room so that it felt like August. It was the first time that she had been in his house. In the house where Clara went mad. They haven't spoken about her yet. Not today anyway. But she will come up soon. She always does. Bill leant up on a pillow and rested his head against his hand, watching her walk over to him. She swayed a little on her feet, part sexy, part drunk. It was mid-afternoon but she has started early today. She often does these days. It is one of her days off. Sometimes she even sneaks in a hip flask to work, the children don't know, they're too young to notice these things. But if the headteacher ever found out then she would be sacked, and this she knows, this is part of the thrill of doing it. The risk of getting caught is high, but as long as she chooses her time carefully, then. . .

Nobody knows she is here. They have been discreet about it and it is after all only the first time. She could have been a cleaner, or a friend just come to pass on her sympathies, there have been a few of them these last few weeks. She climbed back on the bed and playfully hit Bill, straddled him, laughed and brushed the hair away from her eyes. It is longer than Clara's and blonder too. It is wavy and full. Bill asked her where she parked the car. She told him and then bounced off the edge of the bed to show him through the window exactly where she parked the car. 'See,' she said, holding up the blinds. She pointed to a rusty saloon sitting on the drive, its bumper sticker just about visible through the slip of a small window facing the front. It reads: when in history did the climate NOT change?

She allowed the blinds to fall back and then she passed a picture of

Bill and Clara hugging each other, the mountains hiding behind them underneath a glorious filament of sunlight mashed into the crevice. She picked it up and immediately noticed Bill's manner shift. He has gone from relaxed and carefree to stiff in seconds. 'Please put it down,' he said.

'I don't see what the problem is,' she said. 'We've been at it for months. Don't go getting all soft on me.' As she said that, she ran a hand up his naked leg and cupped his crotch. There was that smile again, and Bill loosened up. He leant back on the pillow and she clambered up his body, dropped the picture to the rug and began kissing his lips with a softness that excites him to the point of another erection.

'The kids need picking up from school,' he said with a mouthful of her flesh. He wanted her to continue, but his words left her cold. Perhaps it is the mention of the brats. She has never felt like she wants to hear about them. But it is important to Bill. So she must endure it, for now. 'Don't I get you all to myself today?' She asked.

She leaned away from him, her lips parted and it felt to Bill like she was teasing him, wanting him to lust after her some more. He did for a second, then the children came into his mind again. 'I really should get some clothes on and drive over to Ruskin.' She seemed pissed off. She tapped him on his nose and edged off the bed, picked up her skirt and blouse and wrapped herself in them, hiding her beautiful body until the next time they meet. And there will be a next time, she is sure of this. Then she asked about her again. She wondered if that mad woman of a wife of his is still out of the picture. He reassured her that she is, for now. 'I'd hate to see us drift apart,' she says.

'Never going to happen, we've been through too much,' said Bill. Then he kissed her on the stomach that's showing through the open shirt. She knows that he is already falling for her. It is the way he looks at her after they've made love. A sort of animal vibe – one sick pup that has been rescued and is more than happy to show its affection while lying in the owner's lap, goo eyed. She waved goodbye and strutted out of the bedroom, looking back only to see that same expression on his face. A man of good taste, she thought to herself.

2

Dr Bird let his hands do the kind of gesturing that Clara had become accustomed to now. He wafted them about in the air, as though he were helping pilots land their aircraft. She watched him carefully. She heard every word and thought how great it was that she will get to see her husband, finally. He doesn't mention the children, but perhaps Bill will when he arrives. She can hardly wait. Tomorrow, tomorrow, tomorrow. She drew in a huge gust of air and expelled it from her pink lips, blowing the corner of a document in a neat stack of papers upwards. When Francis speaks it seems like a ceasefire. Before he has been deadly and acicular, now it is different. Now he is telling her she can see Bill at long last.

'You've earned this,' he said. Clara doesn't know what she has done. She will not know either. She will also not know about Bernie's investigation, her questions. Clara didn't know that Bernie was on her way to Carlisle. On her way to speak with John 'the stick man' at The Wellness. Francis smiled at her and it feels like she has just picked up a rose and been punctured by the thorn attached to its stem. But she didn't know why. Perhaps it was a test, and she may be right. Is Francis testing her with a visit, see how she behaves?

Marcie stopped mid-walk. She turned to face Clara and her eyes were wide with glee. It was the first time Clara had really noticed Marcie's beautiful brown eyes. They were like huge shiny buttons set back in a deep socket with her pencil thin eyebrows framing that cute round face. She bounced on her toes. 'Tell me what it feels like,' she said.

'I'm still in shock,' Clara replied.

I'm still also thinking about the notes someone pushed under my door, about the ink on the window pane, about the damn mirror, she didn't say, but she couldn't erase those doubts from her mind. But never mind, tomorrow everything will feel different. Everything.

Clara nervously tucked a strand of hair behind her left ear, saw the wrath of cold wind blow the oak beside the smoking shelter and sat on the hard bed. Marcie waved a goodbye before shutting her door. In the silence of the room Clara laid back on her hard bed, her head touching the soft pillow and she closed her eyes. She saw herself, and Bill was there too. So were the children, not at first but then they appear, happy, smiling, giddy almost. Clara let a smile stretch her mouth. But then she saw that boat again, and the water that filled up her lungs. She flinched at the vision. She saw the gondola gliding above her head, then she felt the mouth of a stranger on hers. He gives her life again. Then all the visions vanished as the dinner bell rang in the lofty reaches of the hollow corridor outside her room. She whispered to herself as she moved from the bed. She told herself it is just one more sleep, like a kid at Christmas, until she can see him, smell him, tell him everything. Just one more sleep.

3

Bernie shut off the tired engine of her beat up BMW, which had made the journey to a freezing Carlisle despite all the odds. She gazed up at the long building ahead of her, its huge grey concrete walls screaming institution. It looked like a film set, some portrayal of a psych ward that some devious mind might create. She saw the cages on the windows and noticed a figure in the top one. It was the head of a man looking down at her. Her body shivered. Not from the cold bite of wind outside but from a nervous kind of fear. It was fear that she felt and she didn't quite know why. She grabbed her bag, which hid her notebook and trusted Dictaphone, and exited the car. She had to pull up her collars to keep the cold off her neck. There were more traces of snow on the ground. But it was fading like it was back home. At first glance there is one discernible difference between this place and Waterside House. There are no godforsaken crows.

'It's Bernie Waller come to see Mr John Lynch.' The woman behind the buzzer made a series of noises before the click sounds and Bernie stepped through the bolted door. It was cold and sterile inside. It was like a prison. She moved through a ring of cages where she passed the mail room and the staff doors that looked like Fort Knox. The woman who let her in had to present a card that was attached to her neck to a reader machine in order to keep progressing through this maze of locks and passage ways. It was dark until they walked beneath a spot light which came on when their feet tap along the right step. The lights made a hum when they came on too, and Bernie felt like her moggy Hemingway might feel when he enters gardens carrying motion detector lights. 'Security's tight here, eh?' Bernie said.

'It has to be,' the woman replied. 'We house some of the worst in here. You wouldn't want them getting out.'

It didn't reassure Bernie. Instead, she clutched her coat and bag a little harder. She smelled the faint scent of lemon floor cleaner as she climbed the stairs. The footsteps chattered against the bare brick walls either side of the stone steps. She had to take two at a time to keep up with the woman leading her in to the den of sick patients. They must have climbed three flights before they came to a stop in front of a cobwebbed black door.

'No turning back now,' Bernie said as they entered. The woman barely broke her deadpan face. Then she saw a man thin as a rake standing by the caged window with a clipboard in his hands. The room was bright, pure white walls and high ceilings. Spread out along the roof was a row of oblong strips of lights turned on even though the natural light was already spreading in through the windows. 'Aren't you coming in?' Bernie asked the woman. She shook her head, pointed to the rake of a man and left through the same back door.

'You must be John lynch,' Bernie said, heels clacking loudly on the tiled floor as she made her way, arm outstretched, over to him. She noticed a couple of patients swiping a glance at her. They were milling around the dispensary, shuffling feet along in a lazy walk. She has seen a pair of eyes similar on the ward at Waterside House. The dark rings, the sunken expression, the bags. It feels more in here. It feels more desperate, as if getting out is possibly the hardest thing in the world.

Then she thought of Clara and felt more positive for her sake. At least she is in a place where the end of the road was visible. It is long, but it is in sight.

'You must be the curious woman I've been speaking to?' the rake of a man said, as if they have shared countless phone calls. It is only the one, Bernie has to remind herself. Then they shook hands. His grip was strong, purposeful and authoritative. He wiped his hand against his trouser leg, as if she has cooties. It must be a habit, she has to tell herself.

'Is there somewhere we could go to talk?' asked Bernie. She noticed, as she asked, a man looking at them with a face full of enthusiasm, as if he was hanging on their every word. Bernie shrugged it off, no big deal. He may just be crazy. John signed his spidery signature on the clipboard and folded his arms across his slender waist. Bernie looked beyond him at the back of the patient's head who she was sure was looking down at her when she got out of her car a few minutes ago. She senses he is sad, a kind of sadness that tears at your soul, mind and body. It is nothing she has experienced, but she is sure of its power nonetheless.

'Is he okay?' She said, gesturing to the head at the caged window. John turned the clipboard around so she could see. At the top of the paper there was one line that chilled her to the bone: Danny is trying to accept the fact that he raped his mother while holding a knife to her throat.

Bernie felt lightheaded, almost as if she'd been spun in a tumble dryer. She didn't look at the back of his head any more. Instead, she was captured by the other man, who is now munching his way through a shiny red apple. He doesn't take his eyes of them both and suddenly she was wary, very wary of what was around her. 'Let's go to the rec room,' John said. The man watched them all the way to the door and then the phone rang. Bernie just had enough time to see him pick it up, still his eyes were fixed on her, before John rattled his keys in the lock and the door clicked shut with an almighty wham.

'He was a nice chap for a long while,' John began after Bernie had sat. 'Good with the patients, especially the older ones. Always there to listen and never seemed to judge anyone. I think he had a rough childhood or something like that.'

'So what went wrong?'

'He became colder. Harder. Less patient. It seemed like a switch had been flicked. But it didn't happen overnight. These things never do. I blame myself for not spotting the signs earlier.'

'Signs?'

'He had a cruel streak that I had not noticed when he first came here.'

'When did Stuart Pillman come here?'

'I checked the records after our phone call. He started on this ward in March, 1983. I remember that year very well as it happens. It was just after a big freeze we had up here, cold snow had blown in from the east. Covered all of Cumbria in a thick white blanket. It was a chap called Philip Quear who hired him. He's recently deceased so don't bother going after that fish if that's what you're thinking of doing.'

Bernie stopped writing.

'I'm told there was an investigation.'

'Indeed. You were told correct. Pillman was accused of assault while serving here, an elderly lady who was very frail, unfortunately.'

'Meaning?'

'She had taken to falling quite a bit that year. That meant that she could have suffered the bruising after one of her little mishaps.'

'Is that what happened?'

'It's what Pillman says happened.'

'What do you think?'

'I think he's a little runt who can't be trusted anywhere near vulnerable patients. I think he gets off on it to be honest.'

'What happened to the woman?'

'She died before any investigation could even get off the runway. Old age they said.' He laughed at that.

'I'm guessing you don't agree with that conclusion.'

'Let me tell you something about men like Pillman. They're cowards and they don't like it when you get the better of them. But that's what I did. I got the better of the little bastard when I sacked him.'

'I thought he left under the investigation. Isn't that how he came to be at Waterside House? Or how else could he have got that job?'

'He's a liar and a schemer. Okay, so I didn't sack him but I would have had it gone on a little longer. I used to see those beady little eyes of his narrow and darken to the size of apple pits. He was the devil himself when he wanted to be, you know.' John shivered at some memory. Bernie guessed it was still a sore point. Maybe he dreamed these days of doing what he wanted to do at the time but never could: sack the little bastard or hit the little bastard.

'Did anybody ever say that they were sent messages in The Wellness? Maybe something concerning Stuart Pillman?'

John frowned and shook his head. 'Nobody ever came to me if they did.' Bernie guessed it must be the only answer she was getting on this. She didn't want to go into detail. She feared if she did she might be sectioned here along with the mother-rapist. Better to leave it alone. She asked more questions but after a while she felt it was going stale. She thanked John and shook his hand again. He only seemed to be repeating himself anyway. It was all he could do to dismiss Pillman as a scoundrel, a bastard who needed his teeth knocking halfway down his throat.

She was about to leave the ward when a hand tugged at her trench coat. She turned to see that face again, the one that was munching an apple moments ago, staring straight at her with a look of absolute fascination. She readied herself for one of those moments you get in a place like this. She was getting used to it by now. But what came out of that mouth was something that took her breath away.

CHAPTER 17

Present day

1

Clara held the scent of fresh air in her lungs. The wet bracken and the gunmetal mist hung around at the split ends of her chestnut hair. Beside her was the student called Helen, but she had forgotten her name on several occasions and now was afraid to ask it again. Things were becoming lost. They were fluttering by without introducing themselves properly. Things like names and places she had been and things that she used to know. It was like bloodletting, until she was raw from needles and their frightful sting. She felt drained but she could still think, at least she still had her mind. It works a little differently now, though. Now it tells her things she never used to know. Things like what might be down in the basement waiting for her. And it is waiting, she can feel it more than ever. It is like a vibration through her bones, a humming in her joints. It is leading her to the water too. But she knows that in Waterside House they never let you too near the water.

Helen stopped on the footbridge beside the large pond. They were standing on the west side of the ruins of the old hospital. The crows were screaming high up above in the listless branches of the overbearing oaks. She said something to Clara, but it was muddled with the cawing of the crows. Clara stopped on the bridge. She turned to the pond where a spawn was laying atop the glabrous surface. She watched a frog march down the pond's brick sides and a leaf that was lost to the water's guts. 'There's something downstairs,' Clara said. 'Something awful. I just know there is.' Clara turned to face Helen now. Clara's face was pudgier these days, and at the same time a shadow of what a face should be. It was sad. Helen couldn't hide her concern, it showed in the eyes, in the smile she pasted to her lips. For someone so young she had a knack for reading the situation, and she did it perfectly this time. She even knew what to say. 'Are you excited about Bill coming later?'

Clara shook the mist from her eyes. 'Is he bringing the children?'

'I don't think so. I could ask Dr Bird when it is likely. I'm sure it won't be much longer, if you play ball, if you do what they ask and don't give them a reason to lock you down, or up your meds.'

Clara looked beyond Helen, into the crack of sunlight that was breaking through the ghostly sky. 'So he's not bringing the children,' she said with a deadly flatness.

'Come on, let's get you back to Eastview,' Helen said.

They passed several men approaching the footbridge from the opposite end. Their bellies huge and round and stuck out like gravid women. One nodded at Clara, who pasted a smile to her candy lips. They all passed in silence.

Back on the warm ward now Clara was free of cobwebs, but there was a haunting in her eyes and her colour ashen. The weight had gotten to her, too. There was a slight bulge in her face, a broadening at the hips, a protrusion in the flabby midsection where her tummy burst through her size ten blouse.

She kept her body perfectly still on the turn of the corridor. Her feet were pasted to the cherry wood, stuck out at an angle that looked and felt (although she still doesn't know it yet) rather a painful position. Above her head there was something that made her stiff. It used to be fright that she felt (especially the one that she thought might have been a bat when she was a little girl in the bathroom), but now it was suspicion. A deep and terrible suspicion.

She thought it was a test. Some design to see how she reacts. She thought Francis Bird had placed this mechanical spider, with its hidden camera, here on the wall to see just how she behaves now that Bill is finally coming. She turned on her heels like an overstuffed ballet dancer. She kept her pose, caught in the dull light skipping through the sun roof overhead. The spider moved too. One darting leg tickled the plaster of the wall, moved up an inch then stopped dead again. Clara could feel her breath coming out. It was heavy and loud. She wondered if there was a microphone in the spider, and tried to suck in the noise, causing her heart to quicken, and she felt as if she might suffer one of those awful panic attacks. Then, right on cue, she did.

It was like a kick to the solar plexus. She dropped to her knees with a sickening thud as her bones met the hard floor. A sea of sweat broke out across her forehead, carpeting her flushed, raddled skin. Her heart felt wickedly quick, as though it may burst out of her chest, burn so hard that it catches fire. She had been here before and she could hear Bill's voice telling her to breathe. Just breathe. Then she heard the echo of her own voice the day Bill brought her here to Waterside House. *I'll be all alone, Bill, all alone.*

She saw a bloody cloud of red before her, a collection of dots that swam around manically. She was on her haunches now like a knackered horse, finished from the races for good. Her crest and withers stock-still, fearing death, her barrel down. A thought came to her, almost like a vision; a terrifying image of Bill holding a shotgun to her temple. Just like a knackered old horse run its last race. Before he pulled the trigger there was respite. A flesh-coloured blur swept across her eyes. A voice that cast a spell. It was Marcie. It was the deep, contralto voice of Marcie Claybrook that she could hear. Now Clara was on her side as she looked out beyond the red mist that bled through her eyes. She saw the strands of brown hair skipping along Marcie's sweet shoulders, the eyes wearing black rings below and around those bright pupils. The mouth was moving but the sound dipped in and out. Suddenly the sounds grew into audible makeshifts.

'Clara, can you hear me?'

Marcie rubbed Clara's shoulder. She leaned in close, so close that they could kiss. She handed her a mug of water, told her to drink it all up. 'But for God's sake do it slowly or else you'll be fit for the morgue down in the basement.' Clara pricked up. Marcie just mentioned that place, the place that had trapped Clara in her dreams lately, and even in her waking state as she stalked the corridors in broad daylight. It was there, waiting and watching like a doll watches its child through the night. Waiting. She laid her head on the cool wood of the floor, reached out and stroked the shoelaces belonging to Marcie's size five feet. She couldn't hear all of what Marcie was saying, it dipped in and out. She pulled on one long strand of lace, undoing the tie that Marcie made this morning while Clara was out on her very first grounds leave with the student Helen. 'Take me down there,' Clara whispered to those size fives.

2

'Don't stop it. Please don't stop Clara's husband from visiting today. It wouldn't be right,' Marcie said. Dr Bird was shaking his head. The bristles of his new grey beard shone under the glow of artificial light that weighed down on them both. His office was warm enough for a bead of sweat to trickle down the nape of Marcie's neck. She pleaded again. 'Can't you see what's good for her?'

Francis considered this a moment. He thought he knew what was good for her, what was good for them all, including Marcie. Marcie with her horse's tail hanging down her left shoulder, and her eyes like big bright buttons glowing at him. He smiled. 'I think you are what's good for Clara,' he says. Marcie puffed out a breath of air. She had been ready for a fight. Now she feels lighter. A whole lot lighter.

'You'll allow Clara's husband to visit?' The words came out a little girlish, weaker than before, and her legs have started a little wobble as she shifts uneasy on the balls of her feet. Francis could sense her sudden stutter in the way she has presented, and he knew he had the power. He had been here before, one night in Vienna, one night that Bernie Waller remembers a little too well. Perhaps she remembers it a little differently than Francis, though, in the cold light of day. 'Of course she is allowed her visit,' he said, looking her up and down, taking in every inch of her. Yes, he liked having the power. Marcie nodded her head, turned on her jelly feet and started for the door. She was keen to leave now, aware that he was watching, aware that he was ticking something over in his mind. Then he took it, the power, the control. 'But it's on your head,' he said, 'if anything should happen.' She stopped mid-walk, the deathly sound of nothing clambering up the woodwork. She left the pounding silence to swell inside the office.

Marcie walked out, didn't look back over her shoulder, for if she did, she knew his face will be in her dreams tonight. And that new beard is just plain fucking goofy, she thought to herself.

She saw Clara sitting in a large tub chair, the back of her head still looking attractive, even if the front was starting to swell. Clara reached a hand over the arm of the chair and dropped a chocolate wrapper to the floor. She had been eating them since she was handed that mug of water by Marcie half an hour ago. Marcie picked up the garbage. 'Litter bug,' she said. Then she saw the extent of her littering. Around the chair beside Clara's feet there were twenty or so empty wrappers. She had gorged nearly a whole box of chocolates. 'It makes me weak,' Clara said. 'After a panic attack I get so hungry to the point of nausea.' She unwrapped another and stuck it on her tongue. 'You might want to slow down,' Marcie said. 'Dinner at four, remember?'

'Fuck dinner. I need chocolate.'

Marcie tried to hide her eyes from the protrusion escaping above the sash belt – Clara's stomach, which rippled with every thrust forward – as more chocolate went inside her mouth. There was a smear across the lips up to the cheekbones which were becoming fleshy. Marcie asked her if she was still excited about the imminent arrival of her husband to this strange place. Clara didn't answer at first, instead she was still gorging on the choccy that was stuck in one of her molars. She forked a finger inside her mouth to remove the debris. As she sucked the tips of her smudged finger, she made a little sigh like she has just been given an early Christmas present. It was the sound of pleasure which made Marcie feel a little uncomfortable. Then she answered. 'Do you think he'll bring me any treats?'

'I think you've got enough of those,' Marcie said with a short laugh. It was a nervous sound, too. It did nothing to hide the anxiety, the angst, the terror that Marice felt right now. The words *it's on your head* still reverberating around her mind, echoing in to the dusty regions that were kept quiet most days, but there are some days when it wasn't. Those were *the shits*, as Marcie calls them. The shit days where she was her own worst enemy. But at least she knew it is her and only her in battle. At least now she has what Francis Bird calls that little bit of good insight. It will serve her well is what he has said in the past. But here I am, she thinks, still socking it to the world behind the wire fence, behind the barbs, beyond the water. Here we all are.

'Do you think he'll bring the children?' Clara asked with a sudden bounciness, an urgency that erupts through the spaces between them. Marcie knew the answer already. It was always like this with new fish. They all want it all, and now. She didn't crush Clara with her wisdom, not this time. 'I'm sure it won't be long,' Marcie recited, thinking of all the times she had to hear this from the nurses and the doctors and the therapists. Clara will be hearing this too, she knew. As hard as it is, she almost understands that this is the way. This is their way, but shit, it's all you have.

3

Bernie clicked the record button on her trusted Dictaphone. The man who had touched her a moment ago, said his name was Ray, had already begun, but nothing too pivotal had been said. In fact, in the time it took Bernie to root it back out of her bag, he had only spoken about Danny. His voice was pleasant, low and barely above a whisper. They sat in a corner of the large white brick room, Ray with his hand on a card table propping up his head. Bernie was sitting in the hard chair opposite, not at all aware of her bare legs showing. Not like she was with Francis just days ago when she saw him for the first time in a long while.

'It's an awful business,' Ray said. 'A crazy child who has designs on own mother. Can you imagine what you would do if you were his father?'

'If my son had raped my wife while holding a knife to her throat?'

'He killed himself. Shotgun wound to the stomach. But he had drugs in his system. It all came out in the post mortem. Barbiturates. He was dead already. He was dead a long time before he picked up the gun. Or the pills for that matter. So where do you want to start?'

'Let's start with you telling me again what you said before, for the benefit of the tape,' Bernie said.

'You want to know about Stuart Pillman again?'

Bernie nodded. She held her breath until she realised what she was doing and then she let it out in a slow huff. Told herself to calm down, reminded herself where she was, who she thought Ray was – a patient, a sick man. But then she silently berated herself for even thinking that, even if just for a moment. For thinking that he's crazy and that his word doesn't mean shit.

'Like I said before, he made a woman disappear. I don't know how, I don't know why, but Pillman – as patients called him – made Mary Dunn vanish like a fart in the night.'

'Were you in Waterside House when he worked there?'

'Yes, I was. But it's not quite how you might think. I was staff nurse back then. I worked Eastview ward after a stint on Newfield – that was one of the men's wards. Everybody finds that quite fascinating at first, then they speak to me and realise I'm as crazy as a bughouse rat.' He smiled when he said this, showed his smoke-weathered teeth like headstones with the engravings wearing thin. Bernie was surprised, but she kept it from showing on her face. 'Did you speak much?'

'Only from time to time, but by the end of 1991 we were hardly crossing paths anymore. Then he left a little abruptly, after the lady vanished.'

'Tell me about her.'

'She was old. So old she had to get around in a wheelchair. But she was quiet, too. Some folk ignored her but they were stupid to, I mean I got this vibe off her that she knew a lot more than some think. Pillman was fixated. Couldn't leave her alone whenever he was working. He was always taking her for a spin around the grounds. He was always watching. At first I thought she had been transferred to another ward, then another hospital. But I got this feeling that she was still around, still watching us. I asked people about her but all I got was this shrug of nonchalance, everybody did it, drove me crazy.'

'Did any patients ever say they were receiving messages on the ward? Maybe newspaper clippings like you would find in a ransom note kind of thing?'

Ray looked at her in a way that spells he hadn't got a clue. He shook his head. 'Only messages were from the devil and occasionally Jesus H Christ with a northern accent.' He laughs. 'Voices, my darling,' he said, then touches the side of his head with his long, nicotine-stained finger. Bernie felt he had said more than he wanted. 'What do you think happened to her?'

He shrugged nonchalantly, wore a big smile and almost erupts in ironic laughter. 'Beats me,' he said. 'One day she's wheeling around the old ruins and then the next she never existed. If I were you I would talk to a doctor down there, find her old records, they can't delete them.'

Bernie knew a doctor alright, a dangerous one goes by the name Bird. 'I'll try to speak with someone,' she said.

'If you find out what happened to her could you let me know?'

'Sure.'

'I'm sorry I can't say much about Stuart Pillman.'

'It's OK, I have some new information thanks to you, Ray.'

'Her name is Mary Dunn,' said Ray. 'Please let me know if you find her records. Let me know what really happened to her.'

Bernie said she would. She stood up and extended a hand. Ray shook it. 'It's Ray Spivey, the ex-nurse turned bughouse rat,' he said. Bernie handed the man a card with her phone number, he took it and kept his slightly sad smile, just something in the eyes that knocked a little bit of breath out of her. Bernie waved for the orderly who was stood behind a wire mesh. He unlocked the door and escorted Bernie out to the echoey stairwell. 'How did he end up here?' Bernie asked.

'Nobody's perfect,' the man answered.

Bernie liked that. Nobody is perfect.

4

Bill took another step forwards towards the back of his wife's head. She still had the orange headband in place. He sniffed the faint scent of Marlene Bonner on the collar of his shirt. He should have showered and changed his clothes. But it was too late to worry about that now. He thanked Francis Bird at the door then it was closed and Clara still hadn't turned to see him. He spoke to her softly, called her name but she didn't hear. He was almost afraid to walk any further, to walk into her eyeline, but he had to, he had to see her or else he'll be guilty again and he can't have that, not on top of everything else. As he neared the edge of the lounge chair, he saw that Clara was eating something out of a box. It was chocolate. He even smelled the sticky aroma as he approached. He heard the whispers from his wife's mouth as each chocolate went in. 'He loves me, he loves me not. He loves me, he loves me not.' Suddenly he was in front of her and she stopped eating. She put down the chocolate. She smiled.

'How are you?' Bill said.

She raced up from her chair and fell into his arms, against his chest. She kissed him, the smell of chocolate was stronger and he could see the smears starting at the corner of her pink lips and travelling up her mouth. She broke away from him so that she could study him closer. She looked at him as though she hadn't seen him in years. Bill started to get worried. He could see a change in her that frightened him. If she could alter this much in a few weeks then what would happen in a matter of months?

'You're finally here,' Clara said. She hugged him tight. He sniffed her hair. Just a habit that he has never forgotten. It was still sweet, except there was a different aroma lingering amongst the hair wash. It was sour. It was like sweat, but it was mixed with the scent of vinegar. 'Where are the children?' Clara asked him, a spread of distress plastered her face.

She looked behind him, to the wall, to the door, then back at his eyes. She needed an answer.

'They're in school. Maybe at a later date they can come and see you. I'm sorry.'

'Don't be sorry. Look at you all dressed up,' she said as she eyed him, rubbed his arms with a jovial hardness that made him worry a little more. Worry and ponder his guilt at the same time. He had left Marlene in the car outside the hospital. He thought about her now. He thought about her departing words to him just a few minutes ago. 'Stick to the plan,' she had said. He does.

'The doctor told me you were outside today, that's a positive step forward, don't you think?'

Clara didn't answer at first, hardly heard the question through her busy mind, he thought. 'They don't let us too near the water,' she said. Bill furrowed his brow in confusion. It was the sort of non sequitur that they used to joke about when Clara would sit down with a pot of coffee and read through Bill's manuscript. In the good old days. The days before hospitals and affairs. But it was these days that Bill was concerned with now. The plan.

He tried to take the box of chocolates off her knee now she had sat down again. She gripped the side of the box and a tug of war ensues. It would have made Bill laugh if it wasn't so painful to watch. He gave up and let her carry on eating the chocolates. She stuffed the chocolates into her brown-smeared mouth. Not at all concerned with the busting gut or the flabby chin that had started to show in recent days. She stopped suddenly and eyed him in a rather suspicious manner. He felt a pang of concern. She couldn't possibly have known about Marlene, could she? Maybe she saw her waiting in the car. But that would have been impossible. They were parked on the opposite side of the building, away from all patient confines, all windows, all unlocked doors. He loosened up at this thought and continued to play it cool. She doesn't eat and it nearly killed Bill into saying a stupid remark about the weather. Like she would care if it was cold out, or dry, or sunny, or pissing wet. 'You don't love me anymore,' she said.

Maybe she *has* seen the other woman in the car, he thought. He stiffened a little, just a straightening of the spine, the neck, and he felt a little hotter under his fragrant shirt collar. The scent of Marlene, maybe that is what she had smelled on him, knows something is going down. Bill tightened his lips. Prepared himself for a flat-out denial, but they had never spoken about that in the car, and he now curses that silently as he waited for his wife to shatter everything with that cocoa-coloured tongue of hers. He waited until he could bear it no more, but before he had a chance to say the words 'why do you think that?' he was cut off. She threw a chocolate at him, hit him on the chest, made a smudge on his nice sweet-smelling shirt at the breast pocket. 'You don't love me anymore!' she screamed at him. 'Just go if you're going,' she added. Then she curled up on the chair, her legs tucked up behind her backside like she used to do out on the balcony on those rainy days when the awning would shelter her, the rap, tap and peck of the drops soothing her as she held on to a warm mug of green tea. Sometimes he would join her, but mostly he liked watching, observing, taking it all in. The days before affairs and hospitals, the days when he could not think of a reason why his marriage might fall apart. Before blackouts, before the master plan.

Before he had a chance to respond a second time, Francis Bird opened the heavy door with a tired creak. He stuck his face around the gap and his gaze was fixed on Clara, then he turned to Bill, who was standing beside the window, wiping a smear of chocolate off his chest. He had seen it all over the years, this was no different to when Margot Mandeville threw the contents of a cleaning bucket over Harmony finch, or when the notorious Sal Blackwell poured a bottle of ketchup into Ann Piggins's socks. 'I think this visit is over now, don't you, Clara?' Dr Bird calmly said. A burly staff nurse appeared behind him, shadows fell across the doorway, only the light from the window shedding any clarity on the scene inside the room. A scene which is comical and at the same time terribly sad. Francis felt this even if Bill didn't. But he doesn't know that yet. He doesn't know anything that Bill might feel. Clara began to sob, gently at first, then she bent her head down over her breasts and a muffled cry emerged from her mouth, into the fabric of her denim jeans. Bill gave the doctor a look that told him he had no idea what had just happened. Francis nodded his head and moved closer to Clara, gently, his arms outstretched before him just in case, like he has seen it all before. A look was all that was needed and Bill said goodbye, and then he told her that he loves her, which was not true. How could it be? Clara looked up at him, red eyes and bags. The words were left hanging in the air around them. So long that it made them seem like a drunkard's last attempt at an awful apology. Maybe it was.

5

Bill opened the car door and settled back into the driver's seat. The heater had been on and it was a warm twenty-five degrees Celsius. He looked across to his passenger. He began to smile. It was temperate at first, a little shy, but then it bloomed into a wide grin, a silly grin that made him feel giddy, like a schoolboy who has just asked out the hottest girl in the class and managed to get her phone number. Marlene placed a hand on his knee and she gave it a playful squeeze. She knew now that he had done well. He had kept up appearances, and made Clara feel like she was still wanted. But now she was well and truly out of the way. She is certified, and she is going to be there a little while. And that's all she needs.

'So the plan went without a hitch?' she said. Bill was still wearing that stupid grin. But he had something on his shirt, which Marlene presumed was Clara's way of telling her that she is indeed crazy. This made her smile. She didn't even need to hear it from Bill, she knew. 'Soon it will be over,' Bill said, a glint in his quiet green eyes. He placed a hand on her knee and now they were in perfect symmetry. 'We need to proceed with the next stage,' Marlene said, as though she were telling him casually to pick up the right kind of potatoes from the supermarket. She flicked her long blonde hair back and put on her seatbelt. Bill started up the engine. 'You need to get the papers printed out, sign them and then go ahead with the rest of the plan,' she said.

The car turned out of the wide gravel drive, onto the quiet road out towards the motorway and steamed onwards at a fair rate. Morning was nearly over, and the afternoon looked good. He will have a nice lunch of salad and couscous, Marlene's favourite, and then he will set about getting the office of public guardian to register his claim. He felt great now that he thought about it in the silence that had overcome them. They were both dreaming. Both dreaming about the large sum of inheritance that will soon be theirs.

***

Marlene never liked being called a thief. She had struck the last person who called her that when she was living on university campus down in Staffordshire. A wiry, pathetic little bitch called Natalie Barber who accused her of filching her bottle of wine. Marlene never took it. She knew the cleaners had taken it instead. But she didn't persist with telling the truth, not after she was labelled a common thief. No, instead she slept with Jordan, Natalie's boyfriend of the time. Not once or twice but for the rest of the semester, Michaelmas if she remembered right. She remembered the falling leaves and the soft ground wetted by the hard rain that autumn. She remembered the look on Natalie's face when she walked in on the pair of them rubbing their bodies in aromatic oils, Marlene sitting on Jordan, a wide, dangerous looking smile on her face. She remembered because she was called a thief. She didn't like that word. But this wasn't stealing. This was business. Good business. It had been her major. She had always been shrewd and this was as shrewd as she got. 'Are you sure she'll be a nice little doner?' Marlene said. 'And the doctor will go along?'

'Just leave it to me, it's all in hand. Soon I'll be Clara's lasting power of attorney, and then the money is ours.'

'And Clara will be out of the picture?'

'The way she's going it looks like she may be there for life, or certainly a damn good chunk of it. They'll be none the wiser. The doctors, Clara, anybody and everybody. They'll assume that we aren't together because of her condition. It's too hard on me and the kids. When we move to Portugal it will just seem like I need a fresh start. Then they'll never see me again. And we'll be rich. And alone. And sitting pretty.'

'I think I love you,' Marlene said. She kissed him on the cheek as the car sped down the road, past a wagon carrying horses, the smell of them creeping through the open crack in the window. 'We'll need to apply for the health and welfare part of lasting power of attorney as well, just to avoid suspicion,' she said. Bill nodded at her, kept his eyes on the road ahead and smiled one more time. He thought of the way it had worked out. Even the dumb Doctor Nicholls played a big part, and he wasn't sure if he would be up to the job. But he came through. None the wiser, he thought. Then he turned into the empty street, except for a white worker van parked up against the rear of a blue Ford, and parked in the usual spot. The house was empty. The street was deserted. No one saw Marlene and Bill enter the house. He got to work as soon as he sat in his office chair. Printed out the forms, grabbed a pen and began the next stages of warfare. Only right now, he and his lover were the only ones playing. None the wiser, he said to himself.

CHAPTER 18

1988

The wind had picked up in the last hour, spoiling some of summer's last hurrah as the season was about to go out of fashion, and autumn was on the starting line, waiting for the pistol to snap and then it would be on its way. It was late August and the pond had dried up, the frogs were marching away as the late afternoon was coming to an end, and so was Mary Dunn's grounds leave. Tim Hindle had the back of the chair in his grip, pushing her through the old ruins, where the savage sounds of crows hurtled through the sky above them both. Tim set her chair at the path leading up to the cricket pitch. He noticed how nice it was, how peaceful with no noise pollution, except for the birds of course. He stretched out his arms and clasped them behind his head. 'It's beautiful, isn't it?' he asked. 'Come on, even an old battle-ax like you can appreciate a little quiet in the late sunshine.' Mary stared into the orange above the hills, the mashed fruit sun that was pouring down like honey. Her face was creased with the strain, the eyes were watery and she remembered something that Stuart Pillman had said to her several weeks ago. She recalled how he looked when he said it, like he wanted it to happen so much he started hopping around the room, his eyes glowing, his lips twitching into a smile. He had said that he hoped she would scream loud enough for his mother to hear her. Then he had apologised, and said that he was out of turn. He actually hoped that she would not be able to scream at all.

Mary set her frail arms with the arthritic fingers on the side of her chair, kept looking at the scalp of those hills and told Tim to move onward. She said she needed to take a piss. Although she phrased it as 'go number one.'

'Piss it is, then,' said Tim, and quickstepped down the gravel where the shade felt quite cool against his bare arms. After a few paces treading through the crisp blossom trails he heard the crunch of feet against hard ground, and slowed down at the turn of the path. Waited for whoever it was. Then he saw who it was making him wait. It was only Ray Spivey with two more patients from Eastview, two quiet ones never in any bother. Two who could slip in with the rest of society and not be noticed. The old adage – too crazy for the street, too street for the crazy. Nevertheless, they were here and they might as well get used to it, Tim thought in the split second before Ray pulled one of his best yeeha cowboy! impressions as they neared. It made Tim smile again, if a little forced this time. 'Hello, Ray, or should I say howdy partner?' he said, nodded at the patients. He knew their names but they were honestly quite forgettable. Ray slapped his side with his hand and acted as if he was rocking on a horse. He galloped onward sharing his best cowboy smile. Tim played along with a sporting laugh. Mary reminded him that she needed the toilet and then they were on their way again, a hundred yards from the entrance door and the loo that was inside, just a hop to the right once through the buzzer.

At the mouth of the blue door Tim heard the terrifying scream of his alarm vibrating like hell against his right hip. He snapped his hand away from the back of the wheelchair and groped the alarm with a frenzied swipe. The trouble was coming out of Newfield ward, a couple of buildings down on the west side of the hospital, next door to the gym and opposite the library, about a minute's walk. But Tim couldn't walk, he needed to run and run fast. He saw Mary knocking her knees together, her mouth pinched and her cheeks sucked inwards. He only had seconds to spare. The sounds that came from her pursed, puckered lips were almost feral, whining moans that rang on in the late sunlight shining through a breast of cloud. He considered leaving now, considered leaving her on her own, considered the option of letting her piss her pants. But he couldn't bring himself to do that, even though he was still considering it as an option. He was still considering it when his saviour arrived to poke his head around the other side of the entrance door.

'Stuart, you are a life saver!' Tim gleefully shouted. The alarm was still sounding from his hip pocket as he rapped Stuart's slender frame with his hand. He almost sent him falling backwards he did it with so much force. Stuart almost dropped the papers out of his grip, the documents relating to new medication instructions for poor Katie Thorogood. The new regime will now include a depot once a week. Stuart was about to explain that he was on his way to the library to photocopy the papers for the file, given that the one on Eastview had given up the ghost, but Tim had no time for that. 'She needs to go to the toilet,' he exclaimed as he backed off towards the trouble on Newfield ward. 'Thanks Stu, you really are a life saver.' He broke into a jog then went full pelt at it until he became a little tiny dot in the eyes of Stuart Pillman.

'Well, isn't this a turn up for the old book-er-roo?' Stuart said. 'Mary, Mary quite contrary.' He took hold of the wheelchair and spun her around so she faced the oaks and the tall wire fence. Beyond that there was the water, gently humming along under the warming summer sun. It was low and at the grass bank there was a trail of dried muck where it looked like shoes had trodden its surface. Stuart gasped at the sight, and whispered in her ear, 'Who's been down to the water?' Mary began to groan; her bladder was about to burst and it was the last person she wanted at the helm of her chair. The last person she wanted to see the dribbles of urine escaping down her trousers. 'You know you're not allowed down at the water's edge, don't you?' he said in her ear, still whispering as though there were plenty of folk around to hear him if he were to talk a little louder. There was no one within earshot, there was hardly anyone else on the grounds, except for the guy who runs the blue food bins to the kitchen and he may as well have been on the moon for he wouldn't hear Stuart if he had a megaphone. Mary closed her eyes, let out a guttural moan and almost let her bladder cave. 'Come on, let's get you to a water closet before that chair becomes a water slide.' Stuart charged through the door, pushing her in the chair until they were both through and then he smiled for the receptionist who looked a trifle confused at the sight. He opened the toilet door and pushed her inside, then he locked the door with the hand holding the papers. They were both locked in now. He turned and his smile widened into a sick grin. His teeth yellowing and crooked, his lips dry and blistered at one corner. There was a smear of sweat pasted to his forehead, and the pits of his shirt were wet. Mary leant out a hand groping for the rail. He watched her. She knew he would stay and watch her take a piss. She knew she couldn't do anything about it. She thought of telling Tim Hindle when he came back but her stories have not been believed before. She doubted whether they will now. She also knew that he and Stuart were practically bosom buddies in here. They have each other's back. Besides, what could she say, other than he made sure I was okay? In the end all people deal with are the facts. The facts and the facts alone.

She had her knickers down at her ankles, her shoes were poking out from underneath the white cotton and she kept her eyes at the floor while the trickles of urine crawled down the porcelain throne. Stuart folded his arms and stared down at her, shook his head and bared his teeth one more time. 'You almost had me in trouble,' he said, 'when you told that little tale about me.' He made a tut with his mouth, licked his teeth as though he were sucking off a layer of peanut butter and crouched down on his haunches. 'Let's see if you can cause any trouble down in the basement, mother.'

She didn't know if he was crazy or just playing crazy, but the dread she felt was real all the same. She tried to speak but her tongue wouldn't budge from the dry spot at the roof of her mouth. She finished urinating and waited. He knew she had finished because he could no longer hear the splash of water against water. 'He is so stupid, just like you,' he said. 'I mean, it was so obvious at the funeral, it was there for anybody to see, especially a close friend like Tim is, don't you think?' Mary sat and waited and wished she could not hear this next part. 'Yes, you both have a lot in common, and I think you'll both regret the day you met The Pill Man,' he said as he neared her, stood over her head, pulled the chain before she could gasp in fright. 'He never even asked if we were close, mother and me. He just assumed. I'm tired of people assuming, thinking they know what's best. Mother didn't know so how the hell is he supposed to know? But she did know, didn't she? She knew all along what that fucker did to me. Well, now she's in the same place as him.' He spat on the floor, landed right at Mary's feet, beside her cotton knickers. She clenched her hands together and locked them as if in prayer. She closed her eyes. 'Good riddance to the pair of them,' he said. 'You know, when I choked her, it felt like I was floating on air.'

'Oh dear God,' Mary said in one gasp of breath.

'When I saw those lights finally go out it was better than sex, better than any orgasm you've read about in those nuddy magazines. When I put my hands on her throat and squeezed the life out of her, I felt reborn, as if it were a gift from heaven.' His face lit up with a strange kind of smile, as if he was reliving the part right here. His eyes wandered to the ceiling, then to the window at the right of him, which was open just a crack letting in the late summer breeze. He pushed it until it creaked against the wood frame, then it snapped shut. Stuart took hold of the empty wheelchair and positioned it in front of Mary. He tapped her on the knee and told her to pull up her knickers. He didn't want to see *it* any more, he said. He'd never liked seeing *it*, only in those nuddy magazines his mother was always deploring, and even then, he felt sick afterwards. Ashamed. He wondered now if he'd get an erection. He wondered if he'd think about it later, tonight perhaps. 'Get on it,' he said, pointing to the chair. 'And don't scream,' he said, taking out a pen knife and holding it up to her eyes. 'Or I'll take out your fucking eye. Do it now.'

Mary gingerly lifted herself off the toilet seat, her body feeling heavier now, as though she were carrying the stone bathroom with her legs. She got back on the wheelchair and found it felt different than it did before. As though it had been gutted of its memory, of her memory.

'We're going for a little walk,' he said.

'Where?' Mary whispered. It's all she could do was to whisper.

'The basement,' Stuart said. 'Where you'll never be heard screaming again.'

The afternoon hadn't aged well. In the tail end of August 1988, the sun was losing its strength, the sky had turned a smoky grey and it was now bloated with rain. Mary Dunn took a look at that sky as she was wheeled through reception and she hoped that she would see it again tomorrow. She wouldn't even complain about the weather if she could just see it one more time. She could feel the sharp prick of the pen knife at the nape of her neck as they waited at the desk. They were buzzed through the second door leading to the small courtyard of Eastview, where there was nobody in sight. No one even out smoking a cigarette, how rare? she thought. Stuart pushed her through the jagged cobbles, then over the gravel and then finally past the washing line which was empty. At the door he walked around to the front, still holding the knife out. He bent to her, which to anybody looking would seem as natural as sharing a laugh on grounds leave, as natural as hearing the wretched crows in the clouds above, and he said, 'any last words? I didn't give mother that chance and I kind of regret it now.' She didn't answer for the fear. 'Nope? Okey doke.'

He pushed her around the door and headed off to a corner of the courtyard she had never been down before. It had another door, this one looked like a fire escape, a heavier door with a bar across its chest. Stuart pushed the bar and the door unlocked. Nobody saw them go off inside. The lights flickered on when they passed underneath them. It was a narrow corridor, long and winding, which barely had room for the wheelchair. It smelled of paint as though a new coat had been recently added. Then they approached a second door, which also had a bar on its front. He opened it and the scene was familiar. They were on Eastview's west wing and suddenly Mary was delighted to see the notice board at the end of the hallway with its warnings and dos and don'ts sprawled across in colourful font. But her relief only lasted a few seconds. They turned into a corner, a dark corner where no light infiltrates, a corner where there was only one way and that was down. They stopped at the metallic doors of the lift.

The lift opened and Stuart began to whistle a tune as he pushed her inside. It was familiar to Mary because it was one she has sung herself many years ago. She was taken back to a time before Waterside House. It was a time when people actually looked at her in the eyes, not at the feet or over the top of her head when they talked to her. It was a time that had been forgotten until now. The song came to her and she realised it was that one that tells you to not worry and be happy. Stuart went on whistling as the lift descended to the bottom. There was a slight delay before the doors opened again. When they did, the dreadful darkness that floated around in the stale air squeezed every bit of hope out of her. Stuart saw her deflate and had to stop the laughter from escaping. He didn't want her to get the wrong impression. He meant business. But nonetheless he found the situation rather funny. Here he was wheeling a patient down to the basement to face her future and no one was any the wiser. Nobody had seen them since the toilet and he remembered the look on that ditzy receptionist, the one with all the jangly jewellery hanging off her wrist. She saw them but he doubts if she would remember either of them if she was asked. Nobody ever remembered him. But somebody would. Mary would remember him. At this he canned the urge to laugh and stopped whistling. In the dank of the underground, he pushed the chair forwards, past the door that said MEDICAL SUPPLIES, and through the mechanical areas and then rested at the door that said MORGUE. The chemical lights flickered and hummed against the sliver threads of cobwebs hanging in the dusty regions of the ceiling. It had a strange, sterile smell down here. It reminded Mary of the hospital you went to when you bashed your skull, not the one where they stuck needles inside you, watched you scream and wrote it all down on a fucking clipboard as you wailed for your mammy to come take you out. She tried to plea, made a whimper of a sound but it only made him angrier. He took the keys hanging from his hip and unlocked the door. He hoped that she would make a fuss, a song and dance about it as his mother used to say. It almost gave him an erection.

He remained silent as he wheeled her through a row of empty beds. He was deep in thought but he had planned it some time ago, so there was no need to get flustered now. He knew how to take care of this, with the doctor and with that pudden-head Tim Hindle. Another one of his mother's favourite sayings. Pudden-head. The milkman was a pudden-head, and the bailiff was a pudden-head, and even the damn cat was a pudden-head. On his ninth birthday, Stuart Pillman was a pudden-head too, when he spilled the litre bottle of coke on the spanking new table cloth.

He stopped at the end of the row of beds. There was only the dreary chemical dim above them for light. No windows, not down here, only artificial yellow light. She was frail and scared and when she opened her mouth to scream, even though no one would hear her – and she knew it, she was struck dumb. It's as though she was stricken when he took off his belt. It's as though she was in a bad dream when he dumped her on the hard bed, legs splayed like a knackered umbrella, face down on the pillow chewing into the cotton just as he had done a long time ago. 'I know you're not asleep, you dirty brat. I know a lot of things. I know you've been looking at those nuddy magazines,' Stuart said. Mary whipped back on to her side, then to her back so she saw him straight in the eyes. The look was scary, as though he were someplace else, as though he didn't even see her anymore. There was a glaze in the pupil, a blackness in the iris, a narrowing down of the white space in his eyes like fruit pits. It made her shiver, then panic again as she tried to get off the bed. 'Don't fucking move!' he screamed at her. Took his belt back and hammered it down on her legs. She yelled out in pain, a searing pain that made her see ribbons of red in her grey eyes. He spun her back on her front in one sweep. She was momentarily surprised at his strength, then she heard a crack in her spine, then she felt a warm sensation crawling up her body, up to the nape of her neck. 'Little brats get their due sometimes,' he said in a dead voice. 'And that due cometh now.' They were the last words she heard before everything went dark.

CHAPTER 19

Present day

1

Bernie looked out at the blinking yellow lights of the neighbouring cottage, the one that sat on the last hill of the town looking like a ghost story. She tossed the book she bought to the floor and rubbed her tired eyes. She stared down again at the name on the front cover. William O'Hara. Then back to the slip of a window where the night had come to rest. Since she returned from Carlisle, she hadn't been able to rid herself of the conversations she has had with John Lynch and with Ray Spivey, especially with Ray. His words were pasted along her memory now: *let me know what really happened to her.* Ray had said a lady had vanished, this played over and over until Bernie could bare it no longer. She rushed to her feet and yanked the blind down so that cottage, and its haunting light, vanished from view. She marched into the kitchen and opened the fridge door. Inside there was a bottle of wine. She reached for it, stopped, pulled away, reached back and held the screw top in her hands. She shut her eyes and the only image she could see was Francis Bird. Or as she called him that fateful night, the devil himself. She gritted her teeth and pushed back the urge to remove the bottle. She slammed the door shut and returned to her accent chair. She felt the clouds of dead air ringing in her head, the dead air that came for her when she needed to get control. The dead air where bad things are stored. Then the phone rang. At this hour it can only be bad news, she thought. Someone has died, or someone is in the hospital. She almost didn't answer it for fear that if she did it would be made real. But she does answer, hesitantly and afraid. 'Hello,' she said, then waited for the world to come crashing down on her. But it didn't happen. The voice was familiar, but strained, as though it were carrying too much weight and must unload.

'Miss Waller, it's Ray Spivey from The Wellness. I hope I haven't woken you up?'

Bernie breathed a welcome sigh of relief. 'Hello, Ray, what's happening?' she said, hoping it was not bad news.

'Oh, it's nothing really. It's just that I remember something that might make you think again about Stuart.'

'Go on,' she said, barely able to hide the anticipation that had crawled up her throat. She clenched her jaw together in an effort to conceal her hope in case it was dashed and wondered what was coming next.

'One thing I forgot to tell you about Stuart – about a year ago I wrote to a buddy of mine, Phil McQueen, a therapist working on Waterside at the time Stuart was there. He says to me in a letter that there was something wrong.'

'Wrong? With Stuart?'

'Phil was working with the staff on their mental health. I know, how ironic, the staff getting treated along with the patients, and they don't know shit about it, for good reasons I suppose. Anyway, he tells me that something just wasn't quite right with him. I thought it must be something huge because Phil wouldn't break the confidentiality rule for anybody, let alone me – a psych patient. But we are good friends. What he told me shocked me. But then now that I think about it, I'm not at all surprised really. I believe him. Maybe back then I didn't think nothing of it, but now I see it all so much clearer. I think the meds have helped.'

He was rambling. Bernie pushed him. 'Can you tell me what your friend said, Ray?'

Ray apologised, then went on.

'He had many sessions with Stuart. He didn't go into detail on all of them, barely any of them as it happens, but he did say some things which I've never repeated to anyone until now.'

'What things, Ray?'

'Phil was worried about Stuart, said he had a lot of emotional baggage, some trauma that concerned his mother. It sounded disturbing.'

'Please go on.'

Bernie couldn't see it, but Ray took a look around him, and only saw crazy Danny sitting in his chair by the window with its frightful cages. He was reassured. He went on. 'Phil told me that he had recommended Stuart take some time off work to process his father's death. Only he didn't take that advice. He told me that Stuart had suffered an immeasurable amount of torment at the hands of his father for years. I'm talking about sexual abuse here.'

Bernie drew a large breath and pushed back her will to scream into the receiver. She thought of Francis Bird again. That's twice in the last half hour, not exactly a record, but it did piss her off all the same. It was the sound of Ray's voice that helped keep the feeling at bay. The feeling that makes her reach for that bottle in the fridge. It's been there since she walked out of Michael Rainford's office half cut, pleading for her job. Ray continued.

'It seems that Stuart was a victim of his father's sexual deviancy. And his mother knew all about it. It was all about control and discipline according to Stuart. Nothing but a way to keep him obedient in the house. If you ask me it sounds a lot more like some sicko getting his incestuous ways out of his system. His father was a paedophile, Miss Waller. A nasty piece of work.'

'Christ, I don't know what to say.'

'Phil also told me that he thought a period of absence from work might help him with feelings of antipathy.'

'Towards the patients?'

'Yes indeed.'

'Holy shit.'

'Now you know why I called you so late.'

'I suppose you think that Mary Dunn's so-called disappearance might have something to do with Stuart Pillman?'

'I don't know. But I remember what Phil said in his last letter, "in the end we are born to serve our own demons, whether we like to or not. It's this that takes us to some pretty awful places". He believed that Stuart was capable of badness. I don't see any reason to disagree with him.'

'Do you know where Stuart is living now?'

'No, and I wouldn't go poking the hornet's nest either, Miss Waller. I mean that sincerely. Pillman is dangerous.'

'Thanks for the heads up, but I may have to find him if I am supposed to find Mary.'

'Do what you got to, Miss Waller, but take my warning, he's nasty. Goodnight.'

Before she had a chance to say goodnight the line had gone dead. A chill rose up her spine as she looked out the hallway window to the darkness riding her cottage. She jotted down some thoughts on a notepad. She wrote Pillman's name and then she asked herself why Clara is receiving messages with his name on them. Then she wrote Mary Dunn's name and another question popped into her head. Where the fuck is she? Before she could even think about William O'Hara and this woman called Marlie, she sat down on her accent chair, grimaced at the creak that had recently come into the legs and switched on the radio for company. Perhaps some jazz will ease her mind. Within six minutes of the saxophone blaring at her she was asleep and dreaming about one rainy night she still hadn't forgotten, and probably never would.

2

When Clara woke up she forgot to feel at the prominent pouch of her stomach, where a roundness had developed since she first laid down on that rain-lashed night in October. She heard the rattle of something tinny outside her door. Then there was a great commotion, not usually heard, that made her skip out of her bed and slip into her jeans and sweatshirt from the day before. She forgot to look at the mirror, and didn't see her tangle of hair swept over one side of her scalp leaving the other side looking threadbare. She forgot the headband too, and began to blow away the falling strands from her eyes. The rattle outside became a crash of cymbals, or something like that, like a tambourine shaking to some winter beat. It got louder as she opened the door. When she did, she saw Lindy hopping down the hall carrying the hospital's only Christmas tree in her hands. She was singing a song that Clara knew sounded familiar, but what it was she had forgotten. Margot stood at the open doorway connecting the bedrooms to the main corridor which led to the dining room and further ahead the kitchen and tv rooms. She was holding a long strand of tinsel and looked pissed off at the same time. She wore a frown like most people wear a nondescript resting face. Clara followed the singing into the lounge where the tree was being positioned in the corner by the small window.

'Don't block the telly,' said Sharne, who was still complaining about feeling so very tired, to which Casey mocked: 'You're literally the laziest one in here, you don't move from that chair, you little tv whore.'

'Fuck you, needle face.'

'That's enough, ladies,' said Lindy, who was unwrapping a tangle of lights.

'How do they get so muddled?' she asked no one in particular. 'Next year we are chucking this thing out and getting a tree with lights already on,' she said. 'Margot, how is that tinsel coming along?' Margot dropped the tinsel to the floor and walked out of the lounge, maintaining eye contact with Lindy as she moved, looking as sullen as she ever has. She pushed past Clara who was still mesmerised by the sounds of the festive season. She didn't even realise it was December. But she kept this to herself. That and the fact that she has noticed a patch of strange white liquid smeared across her sweatshirt at the chest.

She tugged at it with a clawed fist, scrunched the sweatshirt up and pulled its coldness away from her breasts. It snapped back again and wetted her naked skin. A door slammed behind her and she turned to see Harmony Finch wearing her Dead Kennedys tee shirt with the slogan *bedtime for democracy*. Her hair was sticky with gel and she pulled on an earring as she cast a mocking look over the half-dressed tree in the corner of the room. She dumped herself down on the chair facing the window and took a look at Clara, unsettling her in the process. She snickered, then told her to eat her breakfast properly next time, eyeing the wet splash across her sweatshirt. Clara didn't remember eating anything this morning. She was sure that she only just got out of bed, didn't go to the dining room, didn't go anywhere until she heard the frivolous sounds of Christmas out in the hall. She ignored Harmony. She was always casting scorn somewhere about something. Clara leant against the brick, watched the tree coming along with the hanging of baubles, angels and the coloured tinsel Margot threw to the floor. She wondered what it could be as she felt its cold wetness writhe against her body, hardening her nipples, soaking her sweatshirt. She stood like this for a few minutes, watching the room turn into a grotto you would find in a little offbeat town's shopping centre, replete with a fat man in a red suit ringing his little bells for the kids and the even bigger kids accompanying them. There was a plastic Santa that went on the sill, a wreath that went against the door, and a small wiry tree that got dumped on the tea-stained coffee table where Harmony's legs were resting listlessly. Jeannie Newton barged in to the scene holding a mug of tea, her fingernails stained black from ink, and she was barefoot. The soles of her feet were thick with grime. She rested a hand on Clara's shoulder and gave her a warm smile as she manoeuvred her way to the only empty chair in the lounge. She brushed off the crumbs from the seat, mainly Doritos – the real cheesy kind, and plonked down with a thick thud that made Lindy smile. She switched on the lights to a round of applause from Jeannie, and another snicker from Harmony. Clara stared on with a vacancy in her eyes, a wisp of fog in her brain and a trickle of milk running down her front in torrents.

It was Jeannie Newton who saw it first. Then Casey appeared when she heard Clara screaming, followed by Margot who returned with a look of disgust, not at the milk inexplicably pouring out of Clara's breasts, but at the annoyance of having to take out her headphones when Bad Brains were playing. 'Ho-lee-shit!' said Casey. Then she offered a bemused laugh, which started out that way but then ended in dread. Margot stared on, only a flicker of emotion behind her brooding eyes, the music still rattling through those headphones. Jeannie had grabbed Lindy by the arm and turned her to face Clara. She was still whistling a carol as she went about readjusting the positions of some of the lights on the plastic tree. Clara had looked down to see what they were agape at, and found some howl beneath the blanket of fuzz in her mind, a howl that brought the whole ward to a standstill.

After an hour of tears Clara laid on her bed with her breasts bandaged in a cloth. The lactating had ceased when Lindy called for backup from Whiteface. He had arrived in time to catch Clara as she fell backwards to the hard ground. She had fainted, not a blackout as the doctor had said, but one of those 'blood rush' episodes. It happened from time to time, he had said. And what about the milk coming out of her? Lindy was intrigued to know. He had looked at her as if to say well, you're the woman, and she to him in response, well, you're the doctor. Neither of them could really tell what had happened, only that some meds can have very strange side effects. Very strange indeed.

The sweatshirt was currently spinning round in the washing machine. Clara could hear the faint Dickensian sounds coming from Marcie's bedroom. It was some version of A Christmas Carol on the telly. Clara's door was to remain open tonight, and the nurse was still watching and listening from her chair out in the hall. It was three in the afternoon and the gloom had already set in and was making itself at home. The curtains were open allowing it to spread its darkness into her bedroom. She watched shadows of light as cars pulled in to the car park, and then she watched some of them leaving. It was shift change in Eastview and Clara was trying to guess whether it would be Fatso and the tall Nigerian fellow or Pauline – one of the only few names she knew – the squat young woman who talked the hind legs of donkeys. She concluded that it shouldn't really matter, she was going to go down to the basement at the very first opportunity she could find, and nobody was going to stop her. It was the hum that did it, the hum from down below, where the dead go to sleep. Where the bodies pile up in their saddened, lifeless forms.

3
Bernie woke up in a cold sweat. The accent chair creaked as she

moved to go piss. Her neck ached where she had slept awkwardly. She flushed and checked the ticking of the living room clock. It was already nine. She showered slowly, let the water rinse her skin. It felt good to stand under the ring of the hot water and she stayed there a few minutes. She knew she would have to phone Rainford at some point but she reckoned she could postpone that particular job until tomorrow. He would understand, eventually. Right now she needed to clear some space in her head and what better way than to hit the keys. She started up the computer and stared blankly for a few minutes. Then she got hungry and raided the kitchen for food. She didn't have much, say for a box of pop tarts past their date and a pack of celery in the fridge that was turning brown. She slipped into her rain slicker, grabbed her purse and went out of the door. When she returned, she had a breakfast of an almond croissant, a TREK bar and a fresh cup of coffee. She downed it as if she hadn't eaten in a while, who knows maybe she hasn't. She can't remember eating yesterday but the dirty plate in the sink says she did. It worries her to think she may be losing her shit over this, over the missing woman and her friend Clara. And what the connected them both. But she can't afford to stop just when she might be making a breakthrough, and the story that she needs might just have begun now – largely thanks to Ray. In the next few hours she considers everything that she knows about the story so far. She has an idea, but she doesn't want to play that way. Not yet. Not until she has had chance to think of another one.

She tapped her fingers along the keyboard of her laptop, not actually writing anything, but making the sounds as if she is. There was nobody that would hear it, but she senses something there. Something perhaps watching over her as she sipped her green tea. She was actually getting used to the taste now, it was not quite so bitter and hard, more mellow and, more importantly, alcohol free. She shivered in the afternoon light, not that there was much, but what is present she is glad of. The cottage over the hill had smoke bellowing out of its small chimney. She took her empty cup to the sink and slipped in another bag as she waited for the kettle to boil again. She tried to think about it now, in the fading daylight, even though she had dreamt about it all last night. She tried hard to think of the situation. She still couldn't figure out what Stuart Pillman's name was doing in Clara's messages, or what might have happened to Mary Dunn. People don't just vanish in a hospital. There are procedures, rules, organised chaos, every chance that nobody can ever be left behind. But somehow a patient just went missing and nobody even knew, or so Ray Spivey claims. The kettle switched off and steam was ejected from its spout. She thought of the article she was supposed to write for Michael at *The Herald*, and wondered if she might be better phoning him to get all of this off her chest. But then she thought he may find it too dangerous to be working on, who knows what the truth of the matter is, and who knows who or what is involved? So far all she knows is that there is a missing woman from around the late eighties, a man who has been fired for lying about his past, and the fact that Clara is now caught in the middle means what exactly? Then she thinks about Clara, and her husband, and the name Marlie and pours herself a large mug of green tea. 'Hmm, delicious,' she said sardonically to nobody but that ominous feeling.

As she sat back down at her desk, she shook off the sudden panic that had come over her. She reached for the bottle of Alprazolam and knocked a couple back. She needed it. She does if she is going to open up that old can of worms. The one that comes for her at nighttime, usually when she slips out of her casuals and into her soft bed. She does if she is going to email him. If she is going to write Francis Bird, that is.

She opened her email and began, tentatively at first, as though every letter is cutting her skin, flesh unravelling as the words form on screen. She feels like she is writing Krampus – the child snatcher who comes for bad children in the night, or some other bogeyman from folklore. As she wrote she could hear the hum of the dead air again and still wondered what it was. It felt like a blanket of darkness where her bad thoughts are stored. It felt like she was wading through the sea and she could just about keep her mouth and nose above the drink. As she felt this, she also felt the urge to take that bottle out of the fridge. Christ, how many times was that now? But she was adamant about keeping it there, just like a smoker might wrap a pack of cigarettes in tin foil and let it howl to them. Part temptation, part reward, and the reward bit is good. So good it just makes sense. Bernie wondered if her email is making any sense, so far she has:

Hello Francis,

I've been doing a little digging. I've spoken to some folks up in Carlisle, like you suggested, and I've come across a chap named Ray Spivey – I think you'll know who he is, and he has given me some info on Stuart Pillman. It is somewhat overwhelming, I have to say, given the specifics of his termination at the hospital. From what Ray knows there appears to be some missing information on a woman's discharge from Waterside House around 1988. Her name is Mary Dunn and we don't know what happened to her or where she is now. For the life of me I cannot work out what Ray is insinuating, however there does appear to be some discrepancies in paperwork. In that there appears to be no record of the woman leaving. My request is simple: can you fill in some of the blanks for me and Ray – he is very keen to know more, I think it may put his mind at ease. Mine too.

Regards

Bernie Waller

Then she shut off the screen and closed her eyes. The cold afternoon was turning into a black wintery evening. It was the kind of night that brought terror to trees and rooftops, loose slates and rickety old fences. The kind of night that might make somebody bash in someone else's brains. It was one of those nights and she was unaware right now. She didn't know it yet, but she was already sleeping the dark sleep of someone who visits the land of the dead air.

CHAPTER 20

2005

Vienna was washed with a hard rainfall. It hit the roof like a round of pellets smashing against a tin hovel. The downtown Pentahotel had a warmth that felt homely, yet it had some dangerous charm that made Bernie feel alive as it bucketed down outside. Its walls were painted dusky orange and in the bathroom a rain shower made the room feel quite chic. The danger came with its loose guests who paraded the hallway in scanty clothes, the gables that seemed garish and frail. It was the way that it loomed over the town like a tall, rickety church spire caught in the hard winds like some storm chaser. It was the first time Bernie had been abroad since taking part in a sailing holiday with six close friends from university four years ago. It was early March (the spring was rearing up with the bloom of hardy English bluebells) and it was only nineteen days before her twenty-fourth birthday. She had taken the mid-afternoon Eurostar from London to Brussels, then the Nightjet sleeper from Brussels to Vienna and slept most of the way in preparation of the night ahead. She checked her pass again, flopped out on the springy bed and swiped a nip of bourbon from the mini bar. She dug out her worn copy of the BJPsych journal from her bag and it fell open at the page she wanted. The page she had thumbed and doodled. She had underlined Dr Naraghi's name. He would be leading the discussion on the subject of women increasingly occupying the spaces of mental health wards. He had worked in hospitals across the globe, from Calcutta to Berlin, and his expertise was in schizophrenia and bipolar disorders. She read some of his bio again and noted that none of the women featured had won any of the awards he had. Perhaps it was just that he was ahead in terms of life experience. But the RCPsych Awards 2003 were littered with male names. It angered her. It scared her a little. How far could she get up the ladder with her breasts and her womb and her childbearing hips? *The brightest teams and individuals in their field*, it had said. Naraghi had won Patient Contributor of the Year. She scoffed at that and thought about Michael Rainford. Could he ever see the potential in her? He had paid for her to be here in the first place, so perhaps she could ascend just like her male counterparts. Or maybe that was just wishful thinking. Had she hit a glass ceiling already?

Naraghi was a bughouse expert according to the dog-eared journal. 'He's a bughouse bitch,' said Bernie, holding the small bottle in her teeth. She rocked back on the bed and sank it in one breath. She unzipped her suitcase and took out her clothes. She would be wearing her black dress with stockings, not the white one without, given that the weather had turned rather inclement just a few hours ago. It did not look like relenting one bit, either. She heard the commotion of garbage men in their trucks down on the street. She went to the window to see them in their orange uniforms, clambering up the sides of the truck, lifting the bins onto their pulley. She came away from the window and let the sash fall back to its resting position. She opened the mini bar again and decided on the Gin. She flicked through the journal, even though she knew most of it by heart, and picked up her pen. She decided on one of her games: which ones would she marry, screw and avoid of all the doctors who had their photographs printed. She drew a pair of breasts for sex, a ring for marriage and a huge penis for the one she would avoid. Tonight's conference would be all about the subjects that she thought always newsworthy: sexual abuse, substance misuse, child abuse, treatment for schizophrenia, women on the mental health ward, the relationship between cancer and mental health, and how to rehabilitate those affected. Michael knew the score, too. It would be good for *The Herald* to be seen mixing in these circles with some of the brightest minds in the field of psychiatry. It was something he shared with Bernie, but something that he could *not* share was his own mother's experiences with her mental health problems. Since the age of twelve he has had to deal with psychotic episodes. Sometimes they come and last a couple of days and sometimes months on end. The places he has been to, the things he has heard his mother say – they always stick. Once heard and once seen then never forgotten was his way of thinking. And it happened to be quite true.

Bernie stumbled a little in her heels. It made her laugh. She saw herself in the mirror and began to brush her hair. Then she applied a little lipstick to that crooked smile of hers. She opened a fresh carton of cigarettes – camels, and pried open the window. She lit it and blew out an arrow of fresh smoke into the Austrian night. The moon hung like lace over the blackened sea of concrete below her room. It was busy down there. People with a place to be, people who they needed to see. It was rush hour and it was happening. She took out her perfume – Chanel, and used it to mask the smoke in the room. She closed the window and had to rub her arms warmer. The noise tailored off. She placed the journal inside her bag and repeated a mantra in the mirror: 'I'm the cook to dig up the muck.'

She dumped the hotel key into her bag and heard it whump against the journal. She let the door crack shut behind her and clacked her way down to the lift. She waited half a minute for the doors to open, when they did there was a young woman and a child going down to the lobby with her. They spoke German. Holidaymakers, Bernie surmised. The kid looked at Bernie and then back to his mother, he said something that made his mother shush him. She then smiled at Bernie and said in her own Germanic lilt, 'English?'

Bernie nodded.

'Holiday?' Bernie said.

'Ja,' the woman said, grinning wide.

The doors opened and the woman and child went first. Bernie followed them out into a luscious reception area.

There was a dazzling water feature (it was a cherub angel pissing into a basin) adjacent to a long winding staircase which eventually led up into the eaves. Among the crowd there were several women, which gave Bernie a nice reassurance that she wasn't going to be the only one wearing heels. It looked formal. She momentarily had a slight panic at the thought of going over and introducing herself. Then she batted it away. It would only be later, much later, when she would see her family doctor and get herself a prescription for Alprazolam. After a battle with the booze too for that matter. The battle which started to get serious after this very night.

She watched a man with a grey quiff talking animatedly to a middle-aged woman who occasionally spat little bits of her cava out in front of her. She watched three men all around the same age, say fifty, fixing each other's ties, and then they borrowed a pocket mirror from an attractive woman who was clearly done with her conversation over by the set of double doors which would open out into a large opulent dining room. She placed her glass down on the third step and reached into a burgundy handbag and produced the mirror for them to see. She held it under the light, moved it side to side to avoid any glare and smiled generously at them. When they had finished, she returned to her drink and left them staring awkwardly at her backside as she bent over. One of them tried to make small talk. A short, sinewy man with a long neck and a receding hairline. The woman talked with her hands a lot. He started doing the same. Arms were spraying everywhere. At one point he almost slapped one of the other two in the face. Then Bernie saw someone that she would never forget again. She saw a man with a beak of a nose stuffed inside his wine glass.

His eyes were grey behind his spectacles, a washed-out grey that looked like another one of those drab winter mornings that she would come to hate. He had a nice suit and there was a fleck of grey also in his mousy hair. He tapped the side of his glass with a ringless finger at regular intervals, almost like he was beating along to the rhythm of music only he could hear. He stared at the group as Bernie stared at him. Then he turned to face her. Instinct told her to look away. But she held on. She expected him to smile, but he didn't.

She walked over to the man in the black suit, him tapping the rim of his glass as he looked at the crowd of people in turn. His face never wavered from sharp and studious. Bernie felt hot. She dug out her journal and began to fan her face. He looked at her again. Up and down.

'Are they always like this?' Bernie asked.

He turned to face her fully. His nametag read: Dr Francis Bird.

'Are what always like what?' He said.

'Well, take those people over there, they wouldn't give me the time of day, would they?' Bernie said.

'You see that woman over there?' he said, half turning his body toward the edge of the staircase. 'The one with the ruffle trim dress and the huge fake tits,' he said.

Bernie snatched a look at her. She was laughing into her wine as two young men encouraged her along. 'I see her,' Bernie said, covering up her mouth with the tip of the glass, knocked it back and swallowed hard.

'She comes to every one of these events. From Berlin to Paris to Milan. And she does the same thing every single time.'

'And what is that?'

'Fucking blanks me.'

He burst out laughing. Bernie chirped along mainly out of politeness.

'So it's not just me then?' she said.

He shook his head. He held out a hand, she took it, they gave names.

'So what happens now then?' she asked, placing her empty glass down on the table. For the first time she noticed the bowls of crisps and crackers and caviar.

'Anything you want to happen,' he said.

There was a moment of quiet. It felt seductive. Bernie knew she didn't fancy him – for there was something hidden in his eyes. Something that kept her libido in check. But the longer he kept the silence between them the more she felt compelled to try and find him attractive. She was about to blurt something rather trivial out of her mouth when she was cut off by a hefty woman in a blue house dress. She ushered everyone through the mysterious double doors and into a room.

The room looked like a lecture theatre, with chairs that had little side tables attached to them, and a stage down front with a huge black curtain at its helm. The lights came on above them and shot the room in fluorescent yellow. Bernie took her seat at the end of the second row, placed her journal on the table and dug out a notebook from her bag. As the man on the stage spoke, she wrote: women on the ward and how we might rehabilitate.

Then underneath that, she wrote: grey eyes needs me! he wants to fuck me so hard my pussy won't stop meowing.

She scribbled down fast as the man talked, showed slides on a projection and made everybody apart from Bernie laugh heartily at a joke about side effects of the anti-psych meds. She got bored rather quickly and decided to play her favourite game that did not involve shots. Who she would marry, screw and avoid. She hadn't decided on Dr Francis Bird yet. But after this night, she would very much like to avoid him at all costs.

The conference was over for one night. They would return tomorrow afternoon for the speech by Dr Liam Hart on preventing relapses in the community. Bernie was gathering her belongings when Francis Bird tapped her on the shoulder. She spun around with a look on her face that he read as interested, but it was far from that. It was a look of disbelief. She hadn't thought she would see him ever again in her life. But that would have been too good to be true. He had his jacket folded over one arm and his hair looked wetter than before, like it had been swept back with the aid of the tap in the bathroom.

'Come up to the room later, we are having a small get together,' he said.

Her first thought was that he definitely wanted to get her knickers off. She almost politely excused herself and said that she needed an early night after all the travelling, but she didn't say that. If she had maybe she never would have ended up in Doctor Thompson's square little office, taking a prescription for her crippling anxiety. He was the man who gave her mother the premature HRT, her father the anti-depressants and the blood thinners, her brother the statins and her grandmother the Busulfan before her bone marrow transplant. He had seen it all had Doctor Thompson. The Wallers were preferred customers.

She hesitated a little. Then she stammered. Eventually she agreed to go up to Bird's room when she saw two other women approach him from behind and nip his arm with huge beaming smiles. They all seemed friendly enough and that was alright by Bernie.

'I'll just grab a drink and meet you up, shall I?' she said.

'I have a bottle of champagne upstairs,' Francis said. 'But if you want a short or something, we'll listen out for your knock.'

She hadn't heard a man say 'short' since her father when she was a little nipper. She was reminded of him, and of the way he left her and her mother one rainy night in Coniston nearly fourteen years ago. She could almost smell the alcohol fumes that she remembered as a little girl when mother and father came home from a party. It lingered on them like perfume.

'I'll be up in a few minutes,' she said, looking over his square shoulders at the open bar in the distance between the conference room and the foyer. He smiled a thin, paper cut of a smile at her and then the two women (one of Austrian descent, and one English – she being the older one by at least a decade) held on to him, linked arms and laughed their way through the reception and up past the desk towards the lift doors. He turned at the end of the hall and stared back at Bernie. 'Room 208,' he shouted back at her.

Bernie asked the barkeep for a vodka martini and said to skip the olive. She sat on a high stool and placed her jacket over her stockings. She looked around her and saw a young couple almost neck deep in each other, and a group of men she vaguely recognised from earlier.

She sipped her martini and thought about the man she had just met. There was a charm to him that she would not have thought was there at first sight. He also had something about him. Something she failed to put into words at first. As she sipped it became a little clearer. He did have something about him. He had a poker face and he had ice in his veins.

She opened up her notebook again and saw her scrawls from earlier. In this light they looked different. They looked a little churlish. A little uninformed and incomplete. She began writing again. She wrote: ask Dr Francis Bird for a little inside info. What is it like to treat the mentally unwell?

She finished her martini and hopped down from the stool. The rain had started to become ragged and heavy. Bernie thought she heard the rumble of thunder, or maybe that was just her beating heart. She told herself she would be careful. She told herself she would leave if it became just the two of them. She was not going to take any chances.

CHAPTER 21

Present day

1

Marcie crept into Clara's bedroom like a thief. In her hands she had what Clara had craved since she first heard the humming from down below. It had started when she had seen the second message on her window, telling her she might just die in here. Then she had got the newspaper clippings and the hum had grown deeper. Every time she passed those cold metallic doors, she felt it in her bones like a magnet. It pulled her inside. Marcie dropped what was in her hands onto Clara's pillow, next to a tuft of chestnut hair stranded on the feathers like a sea creature waiting for the tide.

Marcie kissed Clara on the forehead, swept away some of those tufts of hair, which were growing long and frayed at the ends, and whispered in her ear, 'go get your truth, Clara.' Then she left the room.

Clara woke up. Her head felt heavy when she moved on to her stomach. Lying flat against the pillow she saw something catching the pallid moonlight sneaking in through the crack of curtain. She fished with her hands, but they were tingling and numb. She shook them and moaned with the sensation. She managed to roll on to her side again and the feeling dissipated. Then she was able to claw at the foreign object lying next to her in bed. She picked it up and flipped it so its tag could be read under the moon glow: BASEMENT KEY.

She thought hard but came up with nothing. Perhaps the nurse had come in the night and had dropped it onto her bed, fished for it but could not see in the darkness and then left until morning had broken to come back for it. It sounded quite plausible.

Clara slipped on her jeans and checked the bandage around her chest. It was still tight and it was dry. She opened her wardrobe and fished out the first thing on the hanger. It was a plain tee shirt stained black with ink, from one of the art therapy sessions on the ward. It hugged her as she moved her body through its cotton. She snuck her feet into a pair of white trainers and crept to the door. It was open, which meant less noise unlocking the damn thing in the dead of night. That was good, maybe the nurse had left it that way to avoid any noise when she came back for the key card.

Out in the hall there was an eerie silence. It was black until she stepped out from the mouth of the door. Then the lights came on accompanied by an earthly drone. She crept around the corner of the corridor, past Marcie's room which was shut tight, and into the end of the passage where an empty seat was placed against the white brick wall. The nurse, like a night watchman who had given up, was nowhere to be seen. Clara walked slowly with her hand up and outstretched grazing along the wall. She made it to the first set of double doors, which were open. She could see down into the kitchen and the dining room that were next door to each other, and then she could see the outer door of the staff office, and next to that the first tv room which had shards of light escaping. The television was still on. She told herself to go quietly, there is bound to be a nurse sitting in that room watching a movie or some late-night show. She peered around the set of doors and eyed the cold steel of the lift. It was then that she heard, or more like felt, the strange humming again. She batted it away. It was just her anxiety talking to her, that's all it was, she was sure. She reached the door. A crack of light swam up to her, then a rumble that sounded deep and resounding. It was just the damn television. That's all it was. She reached out a hand and felt the cold skin of the lift. It was almost vibrating against her flesh. But she put that out of her mind too. It was only her anxiety. That's all it was. She held the key card over the reader and after a few lights flashed she gasped as the lift doors opened up to a river of darkness.

2

Bill slept until three in the morning. Then he was wide awake with the anticipation that today could be the day his wife signs the forms that would make him a little richer. He placed his phone back into its position on the nightstand next to the alarm clock that was red and pulsing with each passing second. He heard the rain smashing against everything outside – the fence panels, the awning, the window. He could see through a slip of curtain a hollow and bloodless moon. Marlene was lying next to him on Clara's side of the bed. The children were fast asleep next door. The house was silent. Marlene slept soundlessly too. He watched the rising and falling of her chest in slow rhythmic cycles. He pictured her seven months ago, sitting on a pew in the Sacred Heart church. The smell of her gloved hand in leather, earthly and sweet as he took it in his. It was the first time they had met, but as Marlene said at the time, it was not the first time they had laid eyes on each other. When she spoke to him it was soft, and he could feel her already under his skin. She said she'd been recently widowed, which explained all the black, including a veil which she kept on as she told him about her late husband. It was late May and the blossom was crashing down from its branches, the sun had grown warm and the silk of blue sky could be seen again after a dismal winter that seemed to last an age. They walked along the deserted street on Sunday morning, only passing other church folk in their Sunday best. The smell of roast chicken was in the air. They talked at length about Father Brogan and his service. His habit of exhaling a puff of air like a horse might before the Liturgy of the Eucharist commences and a basket is handed round. His knack for telling the re-enactment of the sacrifice of Christ (washing his hands) as some might do to teach children of the dangers of deadly airborne viruses.

She told him that the next time they meet she would not be wearing her black clothes anymore. He had asked, politely, cautiously, how her husband had succumbed to an early death. She has told him it was a quick, earth-shattering heart attack. He said no more other than that he was sorry, for what else was there to say?

She rose on her toes to peck him on the side of the face, and then she had to dash. She smelled good. It stuck in his nose afterwards when he returned to his wife and young children. He could not wait until Sunday morning to see her again, but she failed to show. A couple of weeks passed and she still had not returned to Sacred Heart. Bill even dared to ask Father Brogan if he had seen her or heard anything from her, but he had not. He left that day feeling wistful, melancholic. He was quiet for a couple of days. Spent most of his time working on his new book. Then after three weeks since he first met her, and she had stolen his heart, he saw her again, propping up a bar downtown. He had only come in for a quick loosener before his writing had to be done for the day. It was a regular haunt of his – the bar called The Rum Dairy in the alley just off Main Street. There she was, looking hot out of her mourner's clothes, her breasts stacked and her legs tanned and shapely. She saw him when he first walked in but she blanked him. It stung. She was talking fast to a guy on the stool next to her, his ring finger blank with the white space of divorce. She laughed hard at something he had said and then turned to see Bill in the doorway, the misty overhead light casting him in lovesickness. It wasn't long before the other man had taken a cue to leave, and then Bill and Marlene were alone at the bar at three in the afternoon when the mothers were rushing about town collecting children from crowded school playgrounds, including his wife of ten years.

He said he'd been thinking about her a lot, all the time actually. He confessed that he'd wished he had been single when they met. But his wife wasn't well. She was struggling with some anxiety. She had also had some blackouts recently where she seemed unable to remember what she had said to him. Pieces were missing. It had taken its toll on the marriage and only the children were keeping them together. He divulged something else to her in that bar on that pleasant Spring afternoon. He told her, after several beers and a shot of tequila, that he was up to his eyeballs in debt. He had a gambling problem – horses, slots, dogs, and football. He was telling her he was on the edge of sanity himself and thought there was no way out but to declare bankruptcy, which would all but kill his family and his own reputation.

Of course, his wife had money – a hefty inheritance from her grandfather passed down through generations, but he could not ask her for it, she was not to know about the debt. He made that perfectly clear. When Marlene asked about the amount, Bill drew breath and said it was two hundred and thirty thousand.

Marlene slinked into a lazy posture, her head resting upon her arm and told him that she had graduated from University of Kent with a bachelor's degree in Criminal Justice. She told him that she had a job working in fraud investigations in the southwest of the country. It was before she got married, at the age of thirty-one. He said she'd lived a busy life, but he had no idea where the conversation was heading. She said she had picked up a habit or two in the art of making money, and knew a few tricks of the trade. It was the anxiety and the missing bits of life in blackouts that made her think of it. Poor wifey, she thought, with a dangerous kind of smile. She said there was a way through it, a way past all of the bureaucracies of the system. A system designed to fuck you, she had said. Then she said, 'how about I show you a way you can fuck the system, and then fuck me?'

It was dangerous at first, and that is what turned Bill on. But the more she went through it the better it sounded, the saner it began to feel to him. It was simple, really:

Make Clara think that she is going crazy, she already suffers anxiety attacks so it shouldn't be too hard. The blackouts could really clinch the deal, so to speak. Get her to agree to see a therapist, again it shouldn't be too much trouble. Then comes the harder part: have her voluntarily sectioned in the hospital. Marlene stressed that it should be far away, but Bill, still caring in his own way argued that it would have to be Coniston's very own psychiatric hospital: Waterside House. Once she was inside, then they could legally declare her insane and obtain lasting power of attorney over her finances. She said they could also decide on where Clara would live, what treatment she could receive and so on. Bill told her he would have to think it through. He spent two days torturing himself, and when he kept getting phone calls about his sobering debt, he decided on that day, the twenty-sixth of May, that he would go through with it, that he would all but end his marriage and send his wife to her fate. The following morning he booked a flight to San Francisco and said his private goodbyes to the beloved cat, Macdonald, who he had been feeding on a large amount of Xylitol.

3

Clara stepped forward and inhaled the breathless, coppery air. It was must and sulphur – the scent which hung in the darkness like cloud hovers over the Old Man. It was dank and seemed to stretch out for miles as Clara's eyes slowly adjusted to the dark. Her trainers slapped against the cold hard ground and when she had moved a few feet a strip above her head ignited and there was a shard of white light. She moved along, hearing the humming that grew louder with each step forwards. She passed a grave looking trolley with a slimline bed sitting on top of it. One for the dead bodies, she presumed. I'm hardly Sherlock, she thought to herself. Then she thought of Bill, and him telling her never lose your humour. Then she thought of her kids, and what might become of them now their mother is in the loony bin. She hoped they still were at that age where they didn't know fully what was going on with their parents. Just how young children can seem oblivious, and resilient for that matter. But they all cotton on eventually, she reminded herself. Still, she hoped they might understand in time, even if she didn't understand it all. She walked along the basement floor, touching the wall for balance with her outstretched arms. It felt cold and coarse to her soft hands. She faced a corner of darkness, a silver thread of cobwebs in the reaches of the bricks, enough for her to draw her hand away, and then another strip of light above her head shone down.

Around the corner she moved, walking slowly and always hearing that hum which had started to become rather loud. It was a throbbing, earthly drone, a drumbeat that sounded as if it were calling her name. She stopped. The door in front of her said MEDICAL SUPPLIES with a layer of thick dust smouldering over its font. She tried the door but it was locked. The humming went on. She bent to see through the keyhole but all she saw was blackness. By the size of the room she guessed it was only a few feet short of a cupboard, a little cubbyhole with a few stacked shelves and trolleys full of meds. She turned in the half light, sweating slightly at her pits. It was from a mixture of dread and anxiety. She hoped to God that she didn't have a full-on attack down here on her own with only ghosts for company. She would be in serious trouble if she was caught. Anyway, there were no ghosts, she told herself. She wasn't a child anymore. The thing underneath the bed had probably died of old age, even if it was a ghost. The man in the corner of the room was just a pile of old clothes from the days before. There was no 'thing' behind the curtain, either. It was all a fantasy. She groped for the wall again in the pitch black and the hum was louder than ever before.

Then came the mechanical areas: heating, lighting, an electrical room replete with meters and panels, cooling, steam, vacuum, water and ventilation. She passed them still holding the wall upright as if it might fall if her hand was taken away. As she passed a row of spare beds (and thought how in the hell would they get them up there? Maybe there was a bigger access point through one of those heavy-duty doors that led somewhere else) she not only heard the humming but she felt it vibrating through her small white bones. Finally, she came to a door and the hum was at breaking point. Whatever lay beyond that door might just have some answers. Clara, feeling wretchedly anxious, placed a trembling hand on the surface. She wiped away the layer of dust and read: MORGUE. She put her ear to the door, heard the hum which now sounded just like a drum being pounded by a beastly hand. It seemed to have a rhythm of its own.

She tried the handle, slowly. She closed her eyes and hoped there would not be the face of the bogeyman on the other side. The door opened and its blackness showered Clara. But most of all the thing she remembered about that moment was that the awful humming had suddenly stopped dead.

CHAPTER 22

2005

Bernie Waller made sure her bag was still in the grip of her left hand. She wasn't pissed yet, but she was starting to feel the martini bursting through her bladder like a water shoot. She slipped inside the bathroom located adjacent to the reception desk in the hotel. It was nice in there. It matched the outside with its rich, earthy tones. It smelled great too, and they had little fluffy towels with a gold rim around the edge for that extra opulent effect. She washed her hands with some expensive-smelling gluey soap and hung them under the dryer. She told herself that she would come back one day for a little break when she didn't have to work. But that all changed in the next hour.

She straightened out her dress and patted down on her thighs where she thought a rip had torn the stockings. It was just her imagination. It was always just her imagination, is what she told herself when she couldn't get off to sleep. She told herself the same thing as she did when she was a little girl and the monster was hiding under the bed, or in the wardrobe. She told herself it was just her imagination, then, and later. She knocked on the door, waited a little while and then knocked again. It opened and the noise inside fluttered out into the lobby.

Francis Bird was holding a bottle of champagne, true to his word, and he stood aside for her to walk in where she was greeted by a few head nods by the two women who she had seen earlier pinching Bird's arm. One of them, the Austrian, was lying on the double bed, head against the propped-up pillow. The older one, who was English, was standing by the floor lamp lazily holding a half-filled glass of wine in her hands. The window was ajar and Bernie could smell the entrails of a tobacco pipe winding its way outside. Then she saw a man sitting in the corner, a man with a large black nest of a beard and furrowed brows, waiting for her to say something, waiting for her to allow them all inside her head like eager tenants. She felt nervous, but pleased at the same time that there were others here, others perhaps just like her, women who needed the presence of other women in order to feel safer in a place like this. It could have been worse, she thought, it could have been just the two of them, Francis and her.

The rain had turned to a sheet of hail and it was sopping upon the sill. The man in the corner did not move. Instead, it was the English woman who turned and shut the window closed.

'This is Bernie Waller everyone,' Francis said, closing the door. 'She's a journalist back home.'

Bernie waved, smiled shyly and put her bag down on a dresser next to the hotel telephone.

'And where might home be?' asked the man in the corner. He tapped some tobacco into the chamber of his pipe. Then he sucked on the lip for good measure. It wasn't lit yet, to the delight of the woman who had just closed the window for the hail raining through.

'I'm based in Coniston,' Bernie said.

Francis walked over and placed a full glass down on the dresser for her, then ushered her to sit down on a vanity stool he had pulled away from the large mahogany mirror that reflected her temperate, diffident face.

'Up in your neck of the woods, then,' said the man, pointing his pipe straight at Francis. He played about with a Zippo lighter in his hands, toying with the idea of lighting up, never giving the English woman a chance to relax, even when she began to rub her arms theatrically, staving off the already cool temperature in the room.

'I'm based in Preston for a short time,' said Francis, 'at the hospital.'

He took a seat on the corner of the double bed, his glass resting on the carpet at his feet. The Austrian woman sat up and crossed her legs, showing faint scratches along her thigh underneath her tights. Her feet were bare, toes painted red and now went sliding from view underneath her bottom. She played with a strand of her long auburn hair and looked a little bored to Bernie. She tried to guess her age and figured around twenty-two, or twenty-three, give or take a couple of years.

Francis leaned his shoulders forwards, picked up his glass and said, 'we were just having a little giggle at some stories we've heard over the years.'

'The bad effects of anti-psychotic meds!' The man burbled out.

'Tell her about the Vegas man, Tom,' said Francis.

The Austrian woman rolled her eyes, perhaps Tom had already told this story to the room, perhaps she was just sick of them already. Bernie feigned an interest, sucked at the champagne, felt it slide down her throat in scads. It made her lightheaded, but she concentrated on Tom's voice. A voice that was forceful, priggish. To Bernie at least.

'I had a patient one time, a while ago now, but he had the strangest story to tell,' Tom said. The English woman holding the glass by the light of the floor lamp sat upon the lip of the sill, her backside resting on the very edge, a slight crumple of her mouth as she did so. The Austrian went back to playing with her hair. Bernie began to wonder what connected them all inside room 208. But Tom went on, egged on by Francis Bird. Bird laughed in anticipation of the story and refilled his glass. It was full about two minutes ago, Bernie couldn't help but notice. But who was she to be counting other people's drinks? This, she already knew, was not some great revelation on this cold, wet Austrian night, here in the sallow lamplight of room 208: Dr Francis's hotel bedroom.

'He was taking a moderate amount of a drug called Aripiprazole.' Tom paused for good measure, tapped his pipe on the wood table beside him and then a grin appeared above the chin hair. 'Do you know what he did?' Tom asked Bernie, who had to admit she had no fucking idea. She simply shook her head for politeness. 'He jetted off to Las Vegas without a spur of a thought, neglected to tell his loved ones I might add, and spent twelve thousand dollars on a damn slot machine.' Tom's grin grew wider and then sadder, thought Bernie, as though he were reliving it right now, the moment when he received the news. It placated Bernie, relieved some of the anxiety she felt toward him, the anxiety and the dislike, the connection, as she was becoming to feel. Perhaps there were more connections to be made in this room, she began to think.

'When I asked him for "God's sake why" he just looked at me mournfully, but remained perfectly natural, like he'd just been out to the pub all day, and do you know what he said?' Bernie was growing tired of the questions that nobody could obviously answer. She sank some more champagne, felt it ride all the way down her gullet. '"It must be a side effect of the meds, Dr Bower",' said Tom. 'Well I laughed and laughed. Then I spoke to another chap – Dr Griffen, do you know him, Francis?'

'Can't say that I do,' said Francis Bird, then he leant over the bed and refilled the Austrian's glass. It was then that Bernie noticed the ice bucket standing upon the mahogany dresser, and inside it was another bottle of champagne, cooling away for afters.

'Dr Griffen said that this particular drug can cause the patient to develop an inclination towards gambling,' said Tom Bower. He lit the pipe. The English woman turned and opened the window where the hail had now come to an abrupt end, and there was only a smattering of light drizzle coming down in the pallid light of the bustling street. The pipe smoke smelled oaky, earthy and crisp, like a patchouli joss stick Bernie sometimes lit.

'So what do you make of that?' Tom asked, again.

'That's quite a side effect,' Bernie said, 'are there any drugs you can give that make you write better stories?'

'Loads, but they're all illegal,' Tom said, with another one of those silly grins stretching the skin that was still visible above the thick tufts of facial hair.

'So you are a journalist, Francis says?'

'Yep.'

'A good man once said to me that journalists are like rats scurrying to lick up spills of bird seed given out by well-meaning folk.'

He gasped at the end of his sentence, making a face that said he wasn't sure if that was a correct assumption or not, in other words he left himself free from judgement. He didn't know what journalist were, only that he had been told this from somebody else, a good man apparently, which Bernie took as he really did know what he thought about them, about her.

'I like journalists,' the Austrian woman said, with her native lilt, taking Bernie and most of the others by surprise. 'They write importance of the day,' she said, not looking at anyone but at the ragged ends of her long auburn hair.

'Exactly,' said Francis Bird, then he swilled back the half full glass and turned to the ice bucket, gripped the neck of a second bottle of champagne and poured another one.

'And where might we find your work?' asked Tom Bower, exhaling a shoot of smoke out of the corner of his bearded mouth. The English woman coughed and muttered something under her breath. Bernie felt the tension in the room, she spoke quickly.

'I write for *The Herald* newspaper,' she said.

'A fine publication!' Tom said, then he laughed one of those condescending laughs, one which made Bernie hot again. Suddenly she was glad for the breeze blowing in through the open window.

'I know it well,' said Francis Bird. 'Don't mind Tom over there,' he said, pointing to him with the end of his glass. 'He struggles with real emotions anyway. Sometimes I wonder who is treating who.'

Tom laughed once more, a heartier one which once again placated Bernie. It was becoming something of a roller coaster in room 208, Tom Bower the one in control of the speed and the dips in the tracks. Bernie could sense the growing boredom coming from over by the window where the English woman stood. Then almost right on cue she leapt off the edge of the sill and bent to pick up an expensive mac and a handbag from the floor. She said she was sorry to have to leave, but she didn't exactly look sorry, thought Bernie. She hadn't even known what her name was. 'Sure you won't stay for another? Perhaps the rain might stop in a little while,' said Francis Bird.

'No, I really think an early night might be good, what with the second part of the conference starting so early tomorrow,' she said.

Then she waved a small goodbye which could have been for Bernie or Tom, or both and she walked out of the room looking relieved. As if she had just left the dingiest bar she had ever set foot inside and was on her way to a much more pleasant one, one with nicer people and nicer drinks. Still, there was more champagne for those that were left, thought Bernie. She finished her drink and waited for Francis to top her up, which he did almost immediately. Now she was starting to feel it. The bubbles had fizzed their way through her body and were settling nicely in her bladder. She was feeling a little drunk.

'Couldn't stand the woman anyway,' said Tom Bower, and another one of those laughs followed. Francis laughed too but Bernie could only force a polite smile, even though she wanted to say something to Tom, something like: why don't you stick your stinky pipe up your snotty arse.

But she didn't say that. If she had done then she may not have had to sit in Dr Thompson's waiting room with all the other mad ones. All wondering where their lives were heading and wishing they could all turn back the clock. Not to take that drug, drink all that booze, mix with that crowd, stay in that hotel room on that piss-soaked night in Vienna. If she had said that then she wouldn't have so much on her conscience now. But she didn't.

'She should take a leaf out of your book, Johanna,' said Tom. The woman on the bed smiled, a lovely, wonderful smile that showed her brilliant white teeth. Then it clicked. The Austrian woman who had kept rather quiet was Johanna. But what did he mean by taking a leaf out of her book, presuming he was talking about the woman who had just and so left the room to what was now a drunken threesome and Tom? Bernie asked him straight, feeling a little braver now the alcohol was swimming inside her body.

Tom blew his smoke in Bernie's direction, away from the open window. 'I was referring to a conversation we had before you arrived, dear,' he said. 'For fear of repeating myself, which is a greater fear the older you get, I shall say only this: the woman who abandoned ship earlier wants to travel more, see the world as she put it. Johanna here is a seasoned traveller, you see. She saves up money by working in hotels such as this fine one and then goes off. My point is that working as a doctor can have its drawbacks on the travel bug. No bloody time off!'

'Except for things like conferences,' Bernie said.

Tom laughed again. Bernie wasn't sure why. She also wasn't sure at this point how to feel about it either. Tom looked tired and he had stopped smoking his pipe. He rested his head on his hand and placed the pipe down on the table. 'What did you think of Naraghi's speech?' asked Tom.

'I thought it was enlightening,' said Bernie without hesitation.

Tom made a face, a searching face that made his eyes wander up to their highest point without becoming lost under skin. 'I can see why you might think that, being a woman yourself in such a demanding role,' said Tom. Francis Bird had creased his mouth into a knowing smile. A smile that said he knew Tom was getting at something, again, probably for the fiftieth time that evening. Or maybe that was an exaggeration, but Francis told himself that it was a great many times tonight when he had poked the hornets' nest. He had already got one of them to leave, Francis did not want any more departing before he'd had his fun. What fun there was he wasn't entirely sure but he had hoped for something, just to take the edge of this weekend trip. A single man like him needed something.

He'd been engaged only four years ago to a woman who painted. He'd even posed for her to draw him, but the relationship had ended abruptly. He never said why. Those closest to him, and it was only a smart couple from Ambleside who ran a hotel and his elderly mother living in Cockermouth, were told that his woman wanted to run away from Cumbria for good. They had talked about it for a few years, but Francis had no intention of actually upping sticks. To him it was a childish fantasy. He had no desire to leave and had no intention of marrying someone who wanted out. This was his home. It was only a short stint in Lancashire, he would return at the end of the year to Coniston's Waterside House, and there, some years later, he would regret ever letting her go.

Tom Bower smiled wearily at Bernie. 'I'm getting old, dear,' he said.

'Nonsense,' said Francis Bird. 'Have a drink, Tom, it will loosen those knots.'

'Can't touch the stuff nowadays,' said Tom.

Tom Bower and Francis Bird began talking. It was a conversation about the increasing of prescriptions for antidepressants against the decline of antibiotics. Tom mentioned a CDC report on suicide rates, and Francis started on about something to do with The American Association of Suicidology and the conversation deepened until Bernie had to stand up and then fall back down again with a mighty crash.

One moment she was in the room, the next she had seen red blotches where the room should have been. Her body hit the ground with a hard smack and she remembers now only the face of Francis Bird staring down into her blurred eyes.

'Stood up too quickly,' said Tom, who had not moved from the chair. The Austrian woman, Johanna, was lying face down now on the bed, her head hanging of the edge staring down at Bernie with a troubled look spread across her angled cheekbones. Francis reached across Bernie's forehead, held his hand there a moment before declaring that she had no fever.

'I think Tom is right,' he said. 'Just a rush of blood to the head.'

He helped her up to a sitting position, rinsed out her glass, which Bernie thought a tad aggressive (even though a few seconds ago she was out of it, and in a room full of doctors there was only one way through and that was to lose the booze) and then went to the sink to fill it up with tap water. Bernie drank and then insisted that she was fine. Francis helped her to her feet, watched on by Tom Bower who had put his wretched pipe away, and Johanna who was now back to a cross legged sitting position on the double bed, champagne in her hands.

'No more drinking for you,' said Johanna.

'I think I need to use the bathroom,' said Bernie.

'Maybe there is a story for *The Herald* here,' said Tom Bower, and another one of those laughs followed.

'Yeah, maybe you're right,' said Bernie, no longer bothered about the man's imperious remarks. Or his laughter that had grated on her many times this evening. It was over as far as she was concerned. It was all done with. She closed the bathroom door behind her, drowning out the sound of Tom's voice, and that laugh that sounded like a murder of crows. She ran the tap and wet her face, looked at herself in the mirror and thought of home. She thought of how many people would be missing her right now and stopped counting after her mother. She sat upon the toilet seat and let her head fall backwards, closed her eyes and promised herself that she wouldn't drink again. Then she amended that promise and said that she wouldn't drink again this evening. She felt tired and almost fell asleep right there on the toilet. The tap was still running, still drowning out the sounds of the bedroom. After a minute or so she turned the tap clockwise until no more water came shooting out.

As soon as she had she heard raised voices from the next room. A female voice that belonged to Johanna and a male voice that was Francis Bird's. It sounded like an argument. Great, thought Bernie, another fucking episode to have to endure, or referee, depending on how it was going out there. Then she made her mind up to leave the evening where it was and retreat up to her bedroom two floors up. As she pushed the bathroom door open she felt uneasy, almost like she could feel a drastic change in the air. As if a balloon had just been pricked by a knife. The life had been sucked out. She rounded the corner and could see that Tom Bower's chair was empty. The window was back in its closed position. And on the bed Johanna was screaming.

Bernie quick-stepped around to the edge of the bed where she looked on in shock. Johanna was lashing out at Francis with her bare feet, striking him several times in the stomach. That's when he struck her the first time. A slap across the face which left a red mark instantly. Johanna's eyes flared. She screamed again, called him something in Austrian and tried to get him off her body. Again she kicked and again he hit her. Bernie felt paralysed. But she had to do something and so she yelled at him to stop, grabbed him by the ankles and tried to pull him off Johanna. But he was too strong. She yelled some more and took him by the arm, the same arm that had hit Johanna twice to her knowledge already. That was when he stopped.

'She was being hysterical,' said Francis Bird.

'So you assault her?' asked Bernie.

'It's not what it looks like.'

'It looks pretty cut and dry to me.'

Johanna was now sobbing. Her hair was a mess of tangled auburn, sweat was matted to her face. Both were breathing heavy. Francis took off his spectacles and checked for any damage. Johanna said something in Austrian, which Bernie guessed was something like *bastard,* or *I'll kill you.* Perhaps it was, or maybe she was saying how she had a brother or a boyfriend who would gladly beat the shit out of him, if only they were here.

'Are you okay?' Bernie asked Johanna. Johanna checked her mouth for blood, and gave Francis an evil stare. Then she screamed at him. She charged off the bed and ran at Francis with intent. Her eyes mad with rage. That was when Francis knocked her unconscious with an almighty slap across the face with the half empty bottle of champagne. Glass smashed into tiny little pieces and flew about the room with the shrill cry of tiny bellbirds. Johanna collapsed to the bed, blood sprayed like a water jet, a cut above the eye dribbling down her left side. Francis asked Bernie to help him with the fallen body, put it on the bed the way she was before she ran at him. Bernie froze. Her mouth was agape, shocked. She could only stammer out something that she never can remember all the years after that night. She guessed it was something like *what have you done?*

'Help me with her,' said Francis.

He pulled her body up the side of the double bed, brought out a hankey for the blood on her face and started to wipe away some of the claret. He laid her body out so that it looked like she was fast asleep. Asleep while the room was in chaos. Glass from the champagne bottle crunched under his weight as he moved. Bernie inched backwards until she hit the edge of the dresser with the small of her back. She still did not believe that it was real. Just a few minutes ago the place was dying a slow death with the winding down of a drab conversation. What had happened while she was in the bathroom?

When she looked back on this night, as she couldn't help but try, more often than she wanted, she wondered if she could have done anything different. If there was anything she could have done to not be tormented by the harrowing way Johanna fell silent.

It all seemed to happen so quickly. Francis started sweeping up the glass with a dustpan and brush. He opened the window for the air, which was blowing in with the lash of rain. It had started again, that's what Bernie remembers looking back. The damn rain was back. Then he kept asking Bernie if she was alright. Bernie could only stare in horror at Johanna. She wasn't sure if she was still breathing. The next thing she can recall of that night is picking up her handbag and walking out of the door, and Francis's departing words to her: 'She'll be ok. Trust me, I'm a doctor.'

Bernie walked to the lift, slow and unsteady. To any passer-by, and she doesn't recall seeing anybody, it would have looked like any old drunk woman staggering back to her room after one too many in the hotel bar. She thought about going back to room 208, even after she had undressed for bed and was starting to drift off. It was this thought that went all the way with her until an unrestful sleep came in the early hours of a bright and sunny March morning on her last day in Vienna.

CHAPTER 23

Present day

1

The sheets and top pillow were damp when Bernie woke up at a little after six in the cool morning. The sweat smelled sour as she lifted her legs from the bed and gazed at a ghostly moon slithering in through the gap in her hefty curtains. She moved lazily, nudging a sleeping Hemingway from the foot of her bed, heard him purr and then she yawned, just as he did. His eyes were a wonderful shade of green as he looked at her in a way that suggested he was rather content with his lot in life. She wished for the same feeling when she suddenly remembered the last thing she did before she fell asleep. She would need to check her messages, and the feeling that she might have to do that from behind a cushion almost crushed her right then in the half dawn.

The bathroom light stung her tired eyes, and the birdsong flittering through sounded dangerous. Perhaps her dream had not ended when she awoke, maybe she was still dreaming now. Dreaming of a land she had once visited, a foreign land where somebody was screaming into the torrents of rain until (here was the disturbing part) she was screaming no more, until everything went silent. She lowered her face to the warmth of the running water and blinked away a few droplets from her lashes. At that time, she had a flutter of a memory. A memory of her life fourteen years ago when being in a stranger's hotel room was something of an exciting adventure. A carefree version of Bernie Waller who drank, ate and fucked anything she pleased. Then the screaming started and she was back in her rather isolated, and at times, lonely cottage with the hot water gushing down her face.

She patted a towel to her wet nose and chin and stared back through the door at Hemingway, who was now licking parts of himself that she would rather not see this early in the day. He had never gone out at night like some cats prefer. He had always been a house cat, lazy that way, she supposed. He liked his comforts, as did Bernie these days. A warm bed and a nice wet plate of Felix was all he wanted. The cottage grounds had plenty to offer during the day, birds for one thing, where the thicket of trees crowded the space, but after dark he was always scratching at the door to come back in and rest up for the night with his feeder human beside him. Bernie dressed in her slacks, the comfy sort that stretch out as you do, and slipped on a collared shirt. She scratched Hemingway under the chin and he jumped down off the bed and began to rub himself against her leg. When he started to whine then she knew he needed his breakfast. She could do without for now. She never liked to eat first thing, just the thought alone brought her to retching point. She waded into the kitchen and brought out a saucer and a pack of Felix. Hemingway got excited and rubbed some more, whining all the time with a great honking of his own horn.

She stood at the table in the open plan kitchen, hands pressed together at her mouth as if in prayer. The dawn was growing lighter all the time, spreading through the small lounge window with an inquisitive charm. It was as if the air around her was waiting for what comes next. But she had to know what Francis knew about Mary, about the pill man, about anything from that awful night in Vienna. But that was too hard to ask him about. For if it wasn't, she would have done it already.

She entered her emails. There was the usual smattering of stuff: remortgage calculator, a hotel booking site advertising great last-minute getaways in Canada and tours of Australia, an offer for solar panels with no upfront cost, the digest of film monthly with an article on films that were so bad they destroyed the actor's career, and then there was an email which sent a shiver up Bernie's spine and stopped her breathing for a split second or two. It was from Francis Bird. She hovered over the inbox with her mouse, felt the cold morning on the back of her neck and swallowed hard. Suddenly the dream came back to her mind. The blood gushing from a young woman's nose, the screech in her throat as she screamed, the battering rain at the open window. Bernie closed her eyes. She felt the dead air. Before she opened the message, she guessed she needed a little help from her refrigerator, her percolator and her radio. It just seemed to make sense.

2

It was silent down there. Silent and black. Only it had been loud before Clara had opened the door to the hospital morgue. She stood in the dank of the room, her hands trembling, but still holding the metal bar attached to the front of the heavy-duty door. The silence was what scared her. Maybe it should have been the humming before she came in through here, but it was actually the silence, as if all she had known was that strange hypnotic beat that seemed to crawl its way inside her mind and planted itself there forever. She tentatively put one foot in front of the other, just like she had forced herself to do over the last few months. Whenever she had a panic attack, she told herself, with enough practice, to simply try putting one foot in front of the other and take it from there. One foot. One breath. One day. One at a goddamn time.

As she moved gingerly over the cold hard ground, taking her first steps, a light flickered over her head. She stepped back immediately, hoping not to find something stranger than whatever had been in her head a moment ago. All she saw when she dared to look was a row of sharply dressed beds, fitted with crisp white sheets that snapped across them. She let go of her breath and gasped at the sound it made coming out of her mouth. Almost as if she was unaware she had been holding on to it for more than she knew. She moved again into the crowd of darkness ahead of her, slowly and with trembling hands that were now growing wet with sweat. Another shot of bright light blinked on up over her head. She began to smell the room, and found it sickly, like the wards she knew from a girl when she came into those sterile, bleached confines. Again, she let out a deep plume of breath, and felt her heart miss a beat in the process. It wasn't exactly the best activity when you had an anxiety problem and suffered from chronic panic attacks. It wasn't wise at all, and she knew this, but she moved on ahead despite knowing this. She moved ahead because that strange humming had stopped. She moved on because she felt obliged to move. Almost as if she had been summoned down here. That's what she felt, as if she had been called to some great service. She felt it inside, somewhere amidst all the chaos and trauma she had felt these past six months. It all felt like she belonged down here in the dark, in the strange quiet of the basement.

Another few feet and another light came on above her. Another few feet and another bed sitting in the room like a relic from long ago. She moved again, this time with a little more confidence in her stride. Another light. Another bed. The room couldn't stretch on for much more now. It would have been physically impossible for there to be many more beds. Although the basement had been surprisingly big, it couldn't be that big, surely.

Another light. Another bed.

Then.

As the overhead whiteness barked out of its oblong slip of a casing and showered Clara with the glow, she gasped and rubbed her knee where she had just banged it against the metal sides of an empty wheelchair rolling off a few feet to the side.

It came to a standstill in the centre of the room. Its wheels squeaking as they moved. It was fully out, not folded up for storage. Clara managed to catch her breath again, stopped an attack at the source and stood upright facing the strange chair and its shadow looming over the ground. She crept over and reached out a hand towards the seat. At first, she couldn't quite believe it. Thought it may just be a patch of wear and tear, or a shadow even. But as she neared, she leant out a hand, trembling, and felt at the leather seat. It was wet. It was icy cold. She lifted her hand to her nose, to that scarred nose where, as a little girl, she had learnt to be wary of other girls carrying scissors, and then she sniffed her fingers. She gagged, dropped her hand to her thighs and wiped them against her denim jeans. She had just smelled the remains of a human. She had just touched and sniffed human urine.

3

The day had grown into a murky pool of window condensation, and outside a mist crept up to the pane like a thief. Bill had now been awake for several hours, ever since he shot open his eyes at around three in the morning. He had made coffee and the smell was wondering all around the house. Soon the children would be awake and would want their breakfast cereal the way they usually had it when Clara was here. Clara would always pour the milk in first, just like they did on the advertisements, then rain down the cornflakes into the bowl and all the while singing one of those jingles they had on the television. It always made Rita laugh. Bill stood at the breakfast bar and drank his coffee. Outside he could tell the sun wasn't going to be making any appearances today. It was just too dank and grey. He thought about getting some writing done, which he rarely would at this time of day. But his energy was high, nervous energy at that. He usually worked in the late afternoon, when his brain had a chance to put things in order, things that were necessary and proper. What was necessary and proper this morning was making sure the papers were ready to be signed off by his wife and the trusted doctor, Francis Bird. Marlene said it would be like taking candy from a baby. He didn't like her talking about his wife that way, but kind of felt the same. He just didn't want to admit it, perhaps for the sake of his kids. He put the empty cup into the sink and ran the water over the remains of his breakfast which had been one slice of burnt toast and orange marmalade. He went to the study where the air felt warmer, less hostile too. In this room he was king. No matter what went on in the rest of the house. But that was when his wife was around. Now it was different. Now Marlene was here. The house was becoming *un-wifed*. A term he had recently coined and written in his new novel. He ran a finger along the sheet of the paper form where

Clara's signature would be placed. He told himself to think of the life he could have. The money problems would all be solved. No more headaches. No more gloom. A new wife perhaps? Yes, he even thought of the advantages Marlene could bring in that department. A new life with his sexy new friend, which she would be in the eyes of his neighbours and acquaintances – a new start. And while people mourned the loss of Clara, her being incapable of normal life, he would still be the thoughtful and loving husband he had always been, but they would understand his needs and wish him every bit of new found happiness. This brought an early morning smile to his lips and he slipped the forms into his leather manuscript bag. He went to the bathroom to shave.

As he cut across yesterday's growth with a week-old razor, he saw himself from a few months ago in the mirror. He saw himself looking back over the bed where Clara lay frightened and confused. He saw himself just moments before she had woken up to see him riding her like a wayward bull, cupping her mouth with his hands. His hands that had purposely struck his own damn chin in the bathroom while she slept, and managed to draw blood. He saw himself wrapping his face in a towel and he saw as he turned away from his wife and started down the stairs to go sleep on the sofa. He saw it all in the mirror. It had been Marlene's idea, make her think her blackouts had become intolerable, make her feel guilt, make her believe that she is dangerous. Bill told himself to think of the money. As if it was a job to keep hold of in order to pay the bills. His job had been marriage, and his bills were spiralling out of control. It was necessary, Marlene had said to him in one of their bar chats downtown. And then again, in the reception of the Sacred Heart, while father Brogan was well out of earshot. Make her think.

Bill rinsed the razor and wet his face. He looked back at the bed where Marlene lay, sleeping still as the light began to rise. For a brief moment, and one that sent him stumbling backwards into the basin, he saw that it was Clara in bed, wearing that orange headband she was so fond of to keep the hair away from her eyes while she slept. But then she was Marlene again as she rolled over to face him, big brown eyes staring up at him, a gaping yawn and then a warm smile that set him right.

'You're up early,' she said, rolling over to pick a carton of cigarettes from the nightstand. Bill strode toward the window, pulled the curtains apart and let the cool air blow in.

'I couldn't sleep too well,' he said. The garden, he noticed, was wet from rain, and the wind rocketed through the dogwood at the bottom, rattled the fence and shook the ripples of water from the furniture on the balcony.

'It's going to be a stormy day,' he said, looking back at the curls of smoke as they rose upwards from Marelene's mouth. After a couple of drags she stubbed the cigarette in an ashtray, looked at him questioningly and figured he was just wound a little tight by the impending signing day.

'Come back to bed, it's too early to worry about things,' she said. 'My mother used to say you can't earn your corn by betting against yourself.' She pulled back the bed covers and tapped the empty space beside her invitingly. Bill stooped to pick up a stray leaf that had blown its way onto the stone.

'I guess that's why she never let your father play the hero after he'd done the dirty, or something like that,' said Bill.

'My father was a lost cause and mum just knew how to handle things better, with me and my sister.'

'Was it rough?'

'At first. But you kind of get used to it, and besides, kids are resilient, even more so these days. There is no such thing as a happy family, only moments where we forget who we really are.'

Bill thought about David and Rita. Would they simply get over it? Would they want to visit their mother in a mental hospital? And would they accept Marlene in time? These questions started to burn him, and then he said, 'I've got to do something.' He walked out of the bedroom leaving Marlene watching him and wondering if he was going to do something very proactive or something dangerously stupid. She thought it might just be the latter and promptly dressed in her white robe and proceeded to follow him down the stairs.

4

Bernie stared at the screen, unmoving for a full minute before she snapped out of it and, with one thrust of a finger, she clicked the email open and read it, mouth agape, heart racing, conscience hammering at her, telling her to stop it now and turn back before . . . but it was too late. She had already begun and there was no turning back now. Francis had messaged and it felt like the first time he had done since that March night in Vienna. She read it again, this time while she was breathing, in and out, in and out just like Doctor Thompson had said as he handed her the prescription for her Alprazolam. 'And don't be silly,' he had said, 'there is nothing so bad out there that we need to keep ourselves hidden from.' So much for doctor Thompson, Bernie thought.

She poured another mug of steaming coffee and thought about what Francis could have to tell her that he couldn't over the email. *I need you to come in for a chat* he had written. It left Bernie feeling both cold and hot at the same time. So she did what only she could do and began counting the sheep upon the hill whilst she undressed from her morning robe, stood at the window naked, sure that nobody was watching her, but feeling all the while like there most certainly was. She had from time to time been so free like this, only this time she couldn't do it without wondering just where along the line she had come to care for another human as much as she cared right now about the fate of a woman named Clara. Maybe it was the Austrian girl still haunting her, still screaming in her dreams that made Bernie care so much.

She dressed in a hurry as time was now slipping away and she needed to speak with both Francis and Clara before the dreaded dinner call, which was at a staggeringly early eleven-thirty in the morning. She had put on her winter boots when the telephone rang. She answered, and to her surprise the voice was comforting and familiar.

'Hi, Michael,' she said, and breathed a small sigh of relief that it was Michael Rainford and not bad news about Clara.

'Just asking you to check in,' he said, 'so how is it going at the hospital?'

'I was actually just leaving to speak with one of the doctors there. I think he may have some useful info on a story that is developing.'

'What is it? This O'Hara girl still?'

'I'm just following up on a few leads which relate to the O'Hara woman.'

'Leads?'

'Yeah, you know just to tie things together.'

'I thought you were writing an article on the necessity of our psych wards, you know, and how it benefits the patients?'

'Well, I am. But I've discovered something about the hospital. I can't say much at this point, you'll just have to trust my investigative skills for once.'

'Is it dangerous?'

Bernie hadn't prepared for the question on the telephone, but she knew if she let Rainford in on what was going down that he would ask her that. She thought about it for too long.

'Bernadine?' he asked, in a tone of voice that made her regret saying anything.

'It's not dangerous, Michael. But I really need to push on through. I promise I won't go poking any hornet's nest.'

'I want you to call me every day from now on. Give me a rundown on what it is you're investigating. I mean it, Bernadine.'

'Okay, okay, I'll call you.'

'Who are you meeting today?'

'Dr Francis Bird, then Clara O'Hara, hopefully.'

Bernie could almost hear the ink hitting Rainford's notebook, marking both names with his fountain pen. 'And you won't tell me what it is you're working on? How are we supposed to develop our trust in each other if you don't let me in, Bernadine?'

'I'll call you tonight, I promise. Then I will fill you in on everything I've gathered so far, okay?'

'Okay.'

'Can I go and do my job now?'

'On you go, kiddo.'

'Thanks.'

'And, Bernie?'

'Yes.'

'Be safe.'

Bernie hung up and grabbed her keys from the fruit bowl that contained no fruit. Then she stepped out over a family of snails that had set up camp on her doorstep, and was inside her cranky BMW, heating up the windscreen as the morning was just breaking. She turned on the radio and sped away down her path, passing the closed blinds that belonged to Mrs Welsh, and tutting at her lazy ways. The day of reckoning had begun.

5

Clara ripped at her bandages that had wrapped her breasts, feeling the itch worsen as she opened her eyes fully to a chorus from those manic crows perched in the old oak trees outside her bedroom window. She could still smell the scent of urine on her fingers, even though she had washed them several times in scalding water, so hot that it left her knuckles red and sore. She almost couldn't believe (if not for the smell on her fingers, then she might not have) that she had witnessed the wheelchair at all, dripping in urine, just standing down in the morgue, all alone, all inexplicably present when nothing else was (nothing apart from an item that scared Clara enough to run when she saw it, and clamber into bed before throwing the item underneath it). Now there was something to tell Bernie, and maybe others too, but not yet, she thought. She drank a cup of water and dressed in her denim once again, carefully removing the bandages that had encased her when she had been mysteriously lactating the night before. She was told that there would be a discussion about that with the doctor. Maybe even today at afternoon ward round. It wasn't meant to be Clara's day, but it had been brought forward in light of recent events. Then Clara reached from under her bed and pulled the item she found from the morgue, the pair of black shoes that she had taken. A woman's pair of black shoes, size four, and a little scuffed at the heel, almost as if the wearer had been scraping their small feet along a hard surface. She examined them a little closer in the morning light and thought it silly that she had been so frightened by its appearance last night down in the basement morgue. But it did unsettle her. Whose shoes they were Clara could not tell. How old they were she did not know. Why they had been left in the morgue she had no idea. She put them down on the floor and kicked them back under the bed. Then she heard the footsteps coming nearer. The privacy cloth was pulled upwards, and then she knew it was time for morning medication. She swallowed the pills down in one hard gulp. Stuck out her tongue to show that it had all gone and went back to the mirror and sink and began washing her hands again. For She could still smell the acrid stench of urine.

Marcie burst in with a face that looked drawn and harried. She held out her hand and made a *give it to me* motion. 'Where is it?' she asked.

'Where is what?'

'The key to the basement, where is it? I need it back. If you get caught with it it'll be both our heads on the chopping block.'

'It was you?'

'Of course it was, who do you think it was the tooth fairy?'

'Why did you steal it for me?'

'I thought it would make you happy. And shut you up at the same time. Now give it to me before Whiteface comes patrolling the rooms.'

Clara dug behind her pillow and came back with the key in her hands.

'Oh, behind the pillow, that's a great hiding place,' Marcie said sarcastically.

She gave her the key and held her wrist as she did. She was about to break the rule she had just made moments ago and divulge what she had found to Marcie, then she stopped herself, for it would only make things worse. What if Marcie went ahead and stole something else for her, perhaps a key to the staff office? It would spiral out of control and Clara couldn't bear that to happen. She suddenly remembered what the student nurse had said when they were on the bridge. *Don't give them a reason to up your meds or lock you down.*

Clara let go of Marcie and said thanks for the key. And no, it didn't amount to anything. It was just a rickety old basement with too many spiders for her liking. Marcie left with the key tucked inside her bra. Clara looked back at the shadow protruding from under her bed, the shadow of a small pair of black shoes that belonged to somebody. Or perhaps nobody. Perhaps nobody she knew. At least that is what she thought.

6

Bill picked up the telephone for the third time, and he was yet to try dialling a button upon the vintage landline that plugged into the wall under the two-tier side table, which also housed an antique lamp and a trusty notebook. He was having second thoughts about dialling because he knew it wasn't in the plan. The plan that Marlene (together with Bill) had approved all those months ago. He reopened the address book, with the number written in Clara's handwriting, and began to punch in the first digit. Followed by the second, then the third and then he thought he was too far to turn back now. He felt like doing the decent thing, and so here he was telephoning Mister and Missus Fernsby, from Cornwall. Also known to Bill as his in-laws.

The phone rang. Bill had no idea what his first words were going to be, it was either *your daughter is in the nuthouse and it's all my fault,* or *I've done something terrible and I'm afraid I'm going to do a lot more if you don't come back to Coniston right away.* Either way, it was going to put an end to all of this, and Bill for one felt a little relieved. But Marlene was not so for it. As she heard Bill stutter out his words, she marched into the living room, morning robe flapping about her elegant thighs, and grabbed the receiver from his sweaty hand. She slammed it down before he could do any damage, he had only said hello and asked how Louise Fernsby was before he was cut short. He didn't even get to hear her voice – the voice he was secretly very fond of after all these years of knowing the woman – before Marlene put a stop to it. 'What the fuck do you think you're doing? You want to ruin everything before we've even got started?'

'I don't know what I'm doing, I don't even know if I can go through with this, it's unfair to ask me to do something this horrible to my wife.'

'Cut it out. We've come too far to turn back now. Your wife is ill and she's not going to get any better.'

'But we've done that to her.'

'So you'd rather lose everything you've worked for and become a gutless coward.'

'I just don't know if I can take her money while she rots in that place.'

'You can, and you know what? You damn well will, William O'Hara. It's my neck on the line too. Just stick to what we discussed. Get her to sign the forms today and let's leave it to the authorities for the rest. And soon we will be sitting pretty far away from here,' she said as she sat upon his lap. She began to kiss his cheek with a softness that turned him on. He grabbed her by the waist and kissed her hard. 'No more talking to Clara's parents, okay?' she said. 'No more talking,' he replied. 'I'll get the signatures we need today.' Marlene couldn't help a laugh that just burst out of her. It was amusing to her to see him cave so quickly, so open and helpless. 'I'm going to have to watch you, aren't I? she said, running a finger upward along his cheekbone. 'Clara's gone, baby. It's just me and you.'

'And the kids,' he said.

'And the kids,' she said, looking like her cogs were turning rapidly, musing over something that Bill could see, but what it was he had no idea. It was the way she said it, *and the kids,* that made him a little uneasy. 'Let's take a shower,' she said.

'You can trust me not to make another phone call,' Bill said. 'I just panicked when you we were talking earlier, you know, about relationships, mothers and children and whatnot.'

'I know. You just need to be calm. Think of the money. This is a way out for both of us. Come on, I've got something to show you,' said Marlene as she led him by the hand to the foot of the stairs.

'I'm sure I've seen it all before,' said Bill with a wide grin.

'Baby, you've seen nothing yet.'

So they showered together, but Bill couldn't get that image out of his mind. The image of Marlene's face as she said *and the kids,* it was just something that bugged the hell out of him.

CHAPTER 24

1988

Stuart Pillman stared at the sheet of paper so hard he was getting a headache. One of those 'bastards' he gets when he thinks about his mother these days. It was all so hard to be reminded of that woman, and even harder when he had to be reminded of his father. That was not going to happen now, though. His hand was perfectly still as he held the pen above the dotted line. He had practised again and again all last night as he ate his mac and cheese, all washed down with cheap supermarket brand lemonade, the kind of drink that fizzes all the way down the throat and sits in the stomach like a gas pottage. He had torn pages and pages out of his diary, not that he used it anyway, but the fact that he even had one was something of a surprise to him. Why he'd bought it he couldn't quite remember, but it might have had something to do with getting the new job at Waterside House. Yes, that was probably it. On the torn pages he'd scrawled out the signature, making it look perfect, almost as if he were the man whose signature it belonged to. He even imagined himself as the man, the doctor who couldn't remember shit these days as the booze problem was so bad. If it had been a couple of years ago, he might have dressed in one of his father's suits and pretended he was the man in front of the mirror. But those cheap funeral suits had been slung out now, along with the photograph album mother kept in her bedside drawer. He shook his hand once, just to get the yips out, if there was going to be any. It was better to be safe now than sorry later. Another one of his late mother's sayings. He was startled when a branch from the elder tree outside crashed into the sill of the office window, instigated by a vicious autumn wind that had picked up several notches in the last hour. He removed the baseball cap and tugged at his blonde hair which had started to keep the sweat matted to the head, then placed it back on his scalp and pulled it down tight. He set himself again, holding the pen above the dotted line where he was going to forge the signature of doctor John Hill.

He had seen it many times on the forms for releasing a patient into the community and today the good doctor was going to be releasing Mary Dunn from Waterside House. He just didn't know it yet.

The ink touched down on the line. Then he moved it quickly just as he had practised last night, quick and purposeful making sure that the last letter was extended and whipped like a reverse tick. He blew on the page, laughed a little to himself and told his mother that he was cooking on gas, to which the dead woman made no sound and that suited Stuart down to the ground. He had signed the release form for Mary Dunn, or rather, John Hill had signed the release form, he just forgot about that, the damn booze again.

Stuart bounced out of the office, the paper now sitting on Dr Hill's desk along with the minutes of the last ward round with Katie Thorogood. She had not been participating in any group activities, Stuart had read while he waited for the ink to dry. She had also been given an increase in her meds – the dreaded Clozapine, usually a last resort – which had side effects such as severe constipation and neutropenia. In the notes it stated that Katie has grown delusional and lacks any insight into how she became unwell, almost three years ago now. When was the light going to flick on? Stuart asked himself. As if he cared, he thought, which then made him laugh.

He walked past the lift doors on Eastview ward, thought about the last time he had seen Mary in that goddamn wheelchair which stank of piss and shit. It made him angry. He clenched his fists into balls, and squeezed his own flesh until it began to throb. He muttered something to himself that Tim Hindle couldn't quite hear as they passed. Tim nodded at Stuart, who nodded back, but there was something in his smile that seemed strange, a little off to Tim. Who knows? Maybe he is still processing his mother's sudden death. Dementia can be cruel, thought Tim. And he left it at that. But when Tim knocked on the door to Dr Hill's stuffy office and read the release form for one of his patients, he demanded to know what the hell was going on around here. Those were his exact words, but the strength with which they came out was something more like *please tell me why I'm always the last to know anything?* The doctor stood by his decision, which was strange because up until two hours ago he had no idea that he had. But it was all there in black and white. He had read Mary's file all morning and noted that she was not even up for unescorted leave around town. It was very odd, but things had been odd recently. There had been an unusual spike in alarm calls, most of them from Eastview, there was the lockdown last month because a knife had gone missing, and a reporter by the name of Gail Sommers who worked for the BBC was hanging around the corridors making a documentary which was to air in the new year. Tim stood there as the doctor stuttered and slurred his words. Mary was fine, he had said. She had been released because she was no longer sick. Tim walked out feeling more helpless than he ever had, perhaps he needed a break, he thought. Spain sounded good, or Portugal. Somewhere far away where he didn't have to fight at every turn. He walked on by the lift doors which led to the basement, and then the morgue, which only housed ghosts anyway, he thought.

CHAPTER 25
Present day

1

Francis Bird had to grab his own hand to stop it from rapping the desk with so much rapidity. It was a habit he had when things were conspiring against him. His fingers would beat out a drum tune, and his face would swell with the tension in his body. In other words, he was a nervous wreck this morning. A little pissed off, too. As he stared blanky for a few minutes the page in front of him began to blur into a mishmash of symbols and lines. He removed his glasses and rubbed his eyes. When he returned to the page, he read it again but this time he managed to crush that little piece of self-confidence that he had woken up with before the words on the page did it for him. 'Dr Slinger, you piece of shit,' he said to the empty office. He heard the crows then and felt it stab at him like an insult. He opened the drawer of his desk and pawed at a bottle of Bourbon, thought better of it seeing as he had summoned Bernie Waller to his office today, and he picked out his leather-bound diary instead. He flipped to January fifth of next year and held the blue nib of his pen ready to write the details of when Dr Stephen Slinger had just arranged by common letter to pay Waterside House a visit.

Stephen Slinger was one of those doctors that always liked to stick a thorn in someone's side, whether they needed it or not. Over the course of the past three years, he had given countless second opinions on patients at various stages of treatment, and at various hospitals around Cumbria. Coming from The Oakfield Unit in the upper west of the county, a small branch of a larger tree, so to speak, Slinger was well rehearsed in the minor details. He was able to spot the signs of any misdiagnoses as easy as it was to dish them out like candied sweets, he often thought, of the many doctors who sat on their high throne cracking their invisible whip. He had a reputation as an unyielding, tough man with a fascination for making people look foolish. This was because he read between the lines, he thought outside the box and any other cliché that anyone could throw up about such a ferocious and formidable man. He was a good doctor above all and there was no patient, ex or otherwise, who had a bad word to say about him. He was, all in all, fair and who could want anything else to be said? If that was what was going on Slinger's headstone then he could sleep easy at night.

Francis wrote hurriedly, afraid that if he slowed down to a normal person's pace, he would feel the full force of whatever it was that was making him so anxious. Right now, it was manageable. January fifth was still a few weeks away. He had plenty of time to assess his patient. Reassess if needed. No, there was no way that Clara O'Hara was going to slip through his fingers. He had given her all his attention that there was to give and had found her to be suffering. The blackouts were being managed by the medication, and so was the anxiety. Apart from little histrionics the night before she was coping well with the routine of ward life, and had settled down, even made a few friends along the way. The suicide attempt, he reminded himself (and he would remind Stephen Slinger too), was the reason she was here, and it was good reason. She was a little different, he'll give her that, but she actually had a lot in common with the girls of Eastview.

Francis closed his diary with a hard snap. The last thing he had read as he flipped back through the pages was from December 25 which was a reminder for the dinner with his sister, and niece, who lived in Maryport. He wasn't so much looking forward to it before, but now it seemed a rather pleasant one, in light of recent news. He just hoped that he would be able to put Slinger's impending arrival to the back of his mind while he ate his turkey and sprouts. If not for himself then for his mother's memory. She would not have liked him being so gloomy over the festive period. It had been four years since her passing and he thought about it now, in the early light that was crawling up the wall. 'I thought you'd be around forever,' he whispered into the empty room. Then he felt a little silly for doing so, and placed the diary back in the drawer. That was enough of that, he thought to himself. He breathed slow and steady as the ward started to come alive. In and out, hard and deep.

Sal Blackwell knocked on the door, puncturing that thought about his mother. He sighed before he opened it and met her with a steely glare, one that he fought hard to place in his saddened grey eyes. It might be a brick wall that he put up but it was better than letting people see that vulnerability in him, he thought. Not even any of his fancy women, as his mother used to call them, would see that side of him. 'What can I do for you, Sal?' he asked wearily.

'I'm sick.'

'What's new?'

'I mean, I'm sick of the depot.'

He sighed again. 'Any problems with medication can be discussed at ward round, you know that, Sal, you've been here a long time.'

'I don't even know when it is. Lindy isn't here.'

'She'll be back later this afternoon. She has some personal stuff to sort out, it's nothing that concerns you. Anyway, I think it is your ward round tomorrow, if I'm not mistaken.'

'But I'm due to get the needle today.'

'Yes, Sal, you are.'

'I want a second opinion.'

Francis almost screamed at her. Not another one, he thought. Slinger would love to hear that, wouldn't he? Another chance to get involved in his business, make him look the fool again. Poke about in his affairs, all the while wearing that awful pinstripe that he probably bought at Age UK. No, Slinger was not going to get the chance with Sal. 'I'll note your request,' he said, wearing a fake smile. He checked his wristwatch and said, 'if there's nothing else, I'll see you tomorrow.'

He closed the door as Sal chewed on her bangs, which were growing long enough to match Lindy in the braid department. He sighed one more time as he checked his watch and this time made a mental note of the time, unlike a moment ago. No, that was a gesture for effect. He had thirty minutes before Bernie Waller showed up for their little chat. He wondered again why she was concerning herself with a former patient as far back as the late eighties. He made another mental note: ask her about the article for *The Herald*. He was intrigued, make no bones about it. Intrigued to the point of asking her to come in face to face. Just so he could attempt to read her reaction when he told her that Mary Dunn was released by Dr John Hill in late Autumn 1988. Then he would ask the important question: for God's sake why did it matter to Bernie Waller?

2

Bernie parked up next to a rusty saloon. Its driver – and possibly its other passengers – had vacated the car. She looked again at the bumper, where a sign read: when in history did the climate NOT change? It made Bernie sick. If that was what was out there, then we are all fucked, she thought. She wondered who it belonged to, and why they were so backward. She took out her bag from the back seat, unzipped it and checked her notebook and Dictaphone were packed. The saloon seemed out of place here in the hospital grounds. It just gave Bernie that feeling. She closed the door with a slam that was born out of a mixture of nerves (the impending meet with Francis Bird, made a little worse by last night's memory crawl through the soaked streets of Vienna) and anger (how could anyone drive around with *that* sticker on their bumper?).

There was a skin of ice on the tarmac, and she tread carefully until she was standing at the entrance pressing the buzzer to be let inside the foyer. She recognized the woman behind the huge pale wood desk and wondered if she was as familiar to her. As it happens, she gave her a reassuring head nod and a beautiful smile which Bernie felt privileged to receive. She met Kath Jennings (The Kathometer) on the other side of the door – the concourse – where the wind rippled through the large oaks and howled like the ferine mouth of a ravenous wolf. Bernie hoped she didn't show any of that anxiety to Kath. She had already taken her morning dose of Alprazolam and she wondered now if she needed to return to Dr Thomspon's practice for a bump up. It never hurt to be safe. Kath lit up, the way she did for her girls, as she called them when they acted straight (Kath's words). 'Francis sent me to greet you, it must be love,' she said with a dry cackle. If it touched a nerve in Bernie (and how could it not have with the sounds of screaming still haunting her?), she hid it well. 'Do you two go back a bit?' Kath asked. As they walked on through the grounds, snaked past the path that led to The Octagon – looking like a ghost house in the hazy winter light – Bernie stumbled over her answer. 'It doesn't matter, ignore me I'm just being nosy,' said Kath.

'It's a bit early for family trees,' said Bernie. 'You can ignore me too, I'm just caffeine deprived.'

Kath unlocked the door in the courtyard of Eastview. She let Bernie go on ahead. 'He knows you're here,' said Kath. 'He saw your car park up.' Bernie thanked her and turned to the din of the ward, where Margot was in fractious mood and poor Sharne was on the wrong end. Margot had a hold of Sharne's tee shirt; her face was mad with rage. Before any blows happened (if they were coming at all, and they would have been in Sharne's round, pudgy face if they were), Whiteface (is all Bernie knew of him, gathered from conversations with Sal on her way to see Clara) came skidding around the bend, almost fell into Margot as he tore the pair apart, ripping the tail end of Sharne's oversized plain white tee. Sharne hollered at the two of them, threw a wild swing in their direction and realised how close she came to a stint in seclusion. But she couldn't hold back the tears. 'Oh, baby Sharne gonna cry now,' said Margot, a full, luscious smile smearing her lips. It was said more of a statement than a question and Sharne turned away, wiped at her tired eyes and said something that was lost to the wild cacophony of Eastview on a winter's morning just before Christmas.

Bernie knocked on the door and then entered, noticing the dark inside Francis's office, where he sat head bowed to a stack of notepaper in front of him. He had his glasses in his hands when he looked up to the figure in the doorway. He didn't need to put them on, he knew it was Bernie alright. He could tell from the way she felt at her hair, a trick, or more of a habit, when she was nervous. She didn't know she was doing it; it was just instinct the way she didn't know she was blinking. 'Sit down, please,' said Francis.

'Your email didn't give much away,' said Bernie.

'I wanted to tell you in person.'

'It sounds ominous.'

'There's a record for you patient, Mary Dunn.'

'That's good news, surely?'

'Well, it's not the only thing I found. It appears that she was released in September 1988, her whereabouts are unknown, however.'

'Where did she go? You have records of where patients go don't you?'

'Normally, yes. But in her case, I can only presume she was placed in another hospital, or even a halfway house somewhere nearby, but probably untraceable now, it has been a while.'

'I'm aware of how long it's been.'

'The doctor who signed off was John Hill. Now deceased, I'm afraid. Liver problems for years, poor guy. I remember his funeral. Left a wife and three daughters behind. Nice woman, his wife. But when the body shuts down it's all over, goodnight nurse, as my dear old mum used to say. I'm sorry it's not what you wanted to hear. By the way, what do you need this information for, if I might ask?'

'It was just an angle. I'll have to try another way. Is that why you called me in? to try and unravel my article.'

Francis laughed. 'Same old Bernie, the whole world is an enemy.'

'Same old Francis, the whole world is his own.'

She got up to leave. 'Wait, there's something else you should know. It's about Clara.'

Bernie sat back down. The urgency in his voice had piqued her interest again. He sighed, a rather heavy one and then uttered the words that brought Bernie more comfort than she had thought possible from such a statement, especially one from Dr Francis Bird. 'There's going to be a second opinion on Clara O'Hara.'

'I didn't even know that was a thing.'

'Oh, usually it isn't. But in her case, there will be. Doctor Slinger will be the one to perform it.'

'And how do these things usually go?'

'Well, the doctor will go over the information that I've provided, the behaviour problems, the treatment, the reactions to meds, all of these things that Waterside house has provided for her, and then he will make a decision after a conversation with Clara himself. It usually takes a couple of weeks, then we'll have a formal decision on further treatment we can provide here in the hospital.'

'So there's no chance she could be released?'

'Well, technically yes, there's a chance she could be released if the doctor thinks it is right, but we have the right to reply, should there be a need of course.'

Bernie tried to hide her glee, but that was useless in the face of her tormentor for so many years, whether he knew that or not. She smiled. One that Francis saw clearly, but could not draw attention to, for if he did, he might break that steely refrain. 'Well, I've told you everything you need to know, do you have anything to say?'

'When can I see Clara?'

He checked his watch again, this time he managed to remember what the dial read. 'In the next ten minutes, before the dinner call, if that's alright?'

'That suits me just fine,' she said, not managing to conceal her good mood at all.

'Just out of interest, what is your article going to be about?'

'You'll just have to buy a copy of *The Herald* to find out.'

Bernie got up to leave and felt for the first time in fourteen years a sense of pride overcome her as she smiled one more time in the face of Francis Bird. Then she closed the door and felt a sense of closure. But she knew that the dead air was somewhere inside of her still. Somewhere that remained untouched. Like it was an itch she knew was coming but no matter how she prepared herself, she couldn't prevent it from happening. It was inevitable.

If she had known that there was something else Francis could have told her then she would have stayed and battled it out, but Francis wasn't really in a giving mood. If he was then she would have jumped up the wall at what he would have said. Like the itch, it was a bastard of a bind. Francis kept his mouth shut.

3

Bill placed his arm around Marlene now that they were alone on the bridge. They listened to the coots overhead, at least that is what Bill thought they sounded like, just like the ones he heard on the boat he had rented on that fateful day when Clara plunged into the depths of the water. He thought about that day now, for he couldn't help it, it was something that came to him time and time again. He had pushed her to the limit and he knew that, that was where the guilt sprang from. It wasn't exactly planned, for how could one plan for such an outcome. The gift he had left on his study desk was an accident, believe it or not. Clara was never supposed to find it, but when she did, it made the afternoon a prevalent one. The way she reacted was perfect. But he did not want her dead. And that is why he jumped in after her. Marlene squeezed his arm and planted a soft kiss upon his rosy cheek. They gazed into the misty sky and held each other like new lovers in a daydream. Bill watched a family of geese trotting through the gravel beside the pond. He watched as the mother led the way, couldn't help but think of his children and then that question raised its ugly head again. The question of what would they think of him, what would they think of their mother? He still kept them sheltered from the truth. Not the whole truth, not the truth that would make him the devil, but the sad truth that would make Clara a different person. A person who would change irrevocably in an instant.

It was when the crows started to caw that Marlene felt inside his coat pocket and happened to grip a piece of paper that spawned another argument. The only argument that seemed to be eternal. It should have been the one he had with his wife, but he had kept a part of himself hidden from her, that part of himself that he hated so much. The smile disappeared from Marlene's lips when she pulled the paper out and read it carefully. 'A betting slip? Are you fucking kidding me? Don't you understand why we're doing all of this.'

He told her to hush.

'Don't you fucking tell me to be quiet, you lousy deadbeat.'

Bill anxiously peered around the row of wild thickets that encased them on the footbridge, spying only those geese who were now across the other side of the pond beneath their feet. She read it aloud, in a voice that made him feel childish. 'Tottenham and Chelsea, both teams to score, match to end in a draw. You absolute idiot.'

She threw the slip to the ground; it caught a breeze and fell through the crack in the footbridge and ended up sailing down the pond amongst fallen leaves. Bill dropped to the ground, knees hard against the bridge, and tried to save the slip. But it was too late. He realised what he had done and then he realised next that she was laughing. A cruel kind of laugh that irked him a little. He got up as she kicked him lightly on the backside. Then she laughed some more. 'Come on, Billy Walters, let's shake a tail,' said Marlene.

Bill wanted to snap, he wanted to hit her, but he was helpless. He had come too far along the path, the metaphorical path, to turn back now. He couldn't help but be reminded of his plight by the woman he now shared a bed with. She had him, hook, line and sinker. And he knew it, he knew it bad. And he also knew that Billy Walters would have won the bet.

They made it to the office of Dr Francis Bird at a little after ten. He welcomed them in with a slight twitch of his mouth, rather than a smile. Bill could smell someone's perfume in the room. He had a good nose for that, women's perfume. It was warm and inviting, perhaps just the opposite of Francis Bird. They both took a seat and this time they all had a twitch. Marlene took out a folder from Bill's leather manuscript bag and placed some files on the desk in front of her. Francis picked out a pen from a tin can that he kept beside his computer. Then he checked himself and waited for her to speak. Or him. But it was obviously going to be her, he just knew it.

'Where is she?' asked Marlene.

'Clara is currently engaged,' said Francis.

'Engaged?' asked Bill.

'She is with a reporter, I believe you've met her, Bernie Waller from *The Herald*. A very good journalist.' Maybe too good, he thought. The article would probably be finished soon, and Lord knows what she is writing about, but he had the feeling that he was going to feature in it somehow, just how he didn't like to think. It could be any which way. Bernie had a knack for stringing you up, and he was in no mood to be strung. Not now, not ever.

'You didn't tell us about any journalist, Bird,' said Marlene.

'It's fine,' said Bill.

'And you met her?' Why didn't you say anything?' Marlene said, trying to keep her voice light, away from that dark place she sometimes went. Especially with Bill. Ever since the brats started to infiltrate their time together. One day they were just there, a huge part of his life, and she was forgotten for moments that she didn't like. It was only moments, but it was painful. 'She came round to the house once, we had a chat about Clara's condition,' said Bill.

'Oh, okay,' Marlene said, shrinking back into her chair, her ego a little more bruised.

'Can I just ask what the set-up is with you two?' asked Francis.

'I'm here as a friend for Bill, and Clara, he needs my support as much as she does.'

'It's funny she has never mentioned you,' said Francis.

'Well, she is in a mental hospital,' said Marlene.

The three of them sat in silence for a moment. Marlene kept her smile wide, her eyes fixed on Francis. 'Of course,' said Francis.

'Shall we get down to business,' said Bill.

'Right. May I see the forms,' said Francis.

Marlene slid them over the desk. Francis wiped his spectacles with the tail of his shirt and began to read, his mouth making the words as he went. Marlene swiped a sideways glance at Bill, who was sat with his arms crossed looking like he was going into battle. Marlene kicked him under the desk and scowled, forcing him to relax, like that was going to make a difference, he thought. It was only a matter of time before the whole plan goes tits up. But it didn't. Francis finished the form and smiled at them both. Then he checked his watch for what must have been the fourth time in the last thirty minutes.

'Clara will be finished any minute now. Then we'll bring her in,' he said. Marlene played the game. She placed her hand on Bill's shoulder and had the face of a deep sympathiser. Just look at how much I care about my friends, the look seemed to say. It satisfied Francis. Even though he knew that he should have informed Bernie of the situation. She was, after all, invested in the care of Bill's wife. Maybe too invested, he thought. And then that blasted article reared its head again. Like a thorn sinking into his skin.

4

Bernie was still hung up on that rusty saloon out front this morning. The one with that infuriating bumper sticker. The impact of global warming was no joke. It stung her like a thorn in the side. They were probably just people visiting a patient on one of the wards, God forbid it should be a doctor or a nurse, that would be too much to handle, a supposedly educated professional in this kind of a place with that sort of an attitude. The planet would have no chance if that were the case. She was still hung up on it, but she had some news for Clara which overrode the badness. Clara seemed better this morning, her eyes were sparkling, her clothes were clean and her smile was beautiful, if a little sad. 'Your hands look sore,' Bernie said. They were red at the knuckles, as if she had been burned by a scalding tap.

'Oh, I just had to wash some dishes in really hot water and I couldn't find any gloves,' said Clara. Bernie bought it. Well, it's not as if she was going to come to the conclusion that Clara had gotten some piss on her hands and couldn't get the smell out. 'How are you feeling?' Bernie asked, not sure if it would puncture her thoughts on Clara, or reaffirm them. Either way she needed to know before she gave her the news about the second opinion. She had learned to be tactful in these circumstances. Tread carefully, was the mantra.

The first thing that made Bernie twitch was the silence that followed her question, the second was Clara's answer, which crawled rather weakly out of her candy-pink lips.

'I've been down to the bottom,' she said. 'All the way down.'

Bernie liked metaphors but this one was a tad creepy. It was one way of putting it, another would have been that Clara was at rock bottom, but perhaps with some help she was on her way up, on her way back. If only, Bernie thought.

'I went down there last night,' Clara said. Bernie was about to speak, something along the lines of *You're doing great, Clara, just keep taking the meds*, when Clara said, 'I went down to the basement and there's someone down there. I think they need my help.'

Bernie was lost for words. If she wasn't then perhaps the words that would have come out of her mouth would have been something along the lines of *what the heck are you telling me, and why?* But instead of shouting at her, she stayed silent, long enough for Clara to expand on what she had said. 'I saw something that I'll never forget, Bernie. It was horrible. But I think that whoever is writing those messages on my mirrors is the same person that is hiding out down there. Down in the godawful basement.'

'I don't know what you've been up to, Clara, but you must try to stop, you must stop it now.'

It was all Bernie could think of saying. It was all she could do in the heat of the moment, well aware that her good news about the second opinion might well now fall on deaf ears. Clara could be like a dog with a new bone, she had gathered thus far in their relationship. Clara sat back and wore an expression that hurt Bernie. Have they come to the natural end? Was this the moment the entire article was put in jeopardy. Suddenly she could only think of Michael Rainford and that awkward (and it would be awkward) phone call she would have to make tonight. She told herself to breathe. In and out. Just like doctor Thompson had said. When she did so, she began to relax and then said, 'you're serious, aren't you? You're telling me you believe you found something in the basement?' Now she was listening, thought Clara. Now she was interested in some truth. What this place was hiding could be much bigger than her flimsy news story, something that could shake the foundations of this building and others that were just like it.

'I found the remains of whoever is hiding down there. It was a black, old-style wheelchair. And there was something on the seat.' (Now she was getting into it, now she was opening up.) 'Bernie, can I trust you?'

'Of course.'

Clara inched towards the end of her seat. Bernie naturally imitated her. Create a rapport, they always told her at school. Let them under your skin, Rainford had professed.

'It was urine. Human urine on the seat of the wheelchair.'

'My God.'

Clara's eyes flickered to the right, just for a moment, where Kath Jennings was leaning up against the window, her back to them, head nodding away at someone just out of sight. Bernie looked too, then lifted a finger to her mouth, she was telling Clara to keep it quiet. For everyone's sake.

'That's not all. I found a pair of shoes near the wheelchair. They were small, black, like a woman's shoes.'

'Holy shit.'

'Yeah, I know.'

It was instinct to tell Clara that she must tell someone. But then that same instinct also said to Bernie that it was better for now to keep it just between the two of them. Just like the deal with their mystery patient, Mary Dunn, and as for the messages Clara had received, well they were just fine kept secret, for now. Until she could find the right time, the right angle (there was her precious article again), it would be foolish to spill the beans now, before they had a chance to investigate fully. But Bernie was unsure if she was even able at this point. It was beginning to take its toll on her. And that dead air that came for her. . . well, it was like a noose.

'Do you think it could be our Mary?' said Bernie.

'I don't know, but it has to be someone.'

'It does indeed.'

'Do you think it could be her?'

'I was told something in Carlilse, something that doesn't sit right with me. It was about Mary and her sudden "disappearance."' Bernie held up her bunny rabbit fingers. 'It smacks of conspiracy if you ask me. If you ask Ray Spivey, for that matter.'

'Ray Spivey?'

'He was the man I spoke to. He used to work here in Waterside House, before he became a patient up in Carlisle.'

Clara raised her eyebrows.

'Well, if he says there is a reason to doubt the records then maybe there is one.'

'Perhaps that is true. But could she really be down in the basement after all this time?'

'It could be possible. Maybe she has had some help from whoever knows the truth.'

'Like The Pillman you mean?'

Clara shuddered when she heard the name. Then she looked Bernie in the eyes and said, 'We need to find him.'

'It could be too dangerous. If what we believe to be true actually is true, then we are dealing with one heck of a mad man.'

'Keeping a woman down in the morgue for years. How would he even get in and out?'

'I don't know. Everyone I have spoken to is adamant that I should stay clear of finding him.'

'Then that's the exact reason why we need to find out what's going on.'

'Maybe.'

'Absolutely.'

'Listen, there is something I need to tell you. There is going to be a second opinion on your diagnosis and treatment. I can say that it's got Francis Bird all riled up.'

Clara smiled. A wide, beautiful smile that made Bernie feel good. 'Then we go on,' said Clara. Find this Pill man and find out what's really down in the basement.'

'Okay. But we need to be careful.'

Clara zipped her lips with a finger and made a locking gesture. Whatever may come out was not going to come from her. Bernie could have bet her house on it.

Kath Jennings opened the door and said, 'I need to take you to see the doctor.'

'What for?' Asked Bernie, which shook Kath for a moment.

'I don't know, but he wants to see Clara. I think your husband is here.'

That was all it took for Clara to snap out of it. Now she was back as that scared, lonely, suicidal housewife. And Bill was on the other side, waiting.

5

Clara followed Kath down the hall, past the riotous Margot who was still in some mood over something. They walked quickly, well Kath did, and Clara just tried to keep up behind her. Bernie was following too, despite the fact that Kath had said she should leave them to it – the words of Francis, no doubt, thought Bernie. Kath turned at the end of the corridor, her smile was gone and had been replaced with quite a serious face, one that warned Bernie if she didn't do what was obviously asked by Bird, then perhaps the heavies would be introduced to her. Just then Bernie spotted who the girls called Fatso stretching out his arms behind Kath. Bernie stopped walking and hung her bag over her shoulder. Kath waved goodbye to her and then Fatso neared them all. Clara asked what was going on. Bernie backed her up but could tell that if she got out of line here then she was going out on her rear. Bernie told Clara it would be fine and she would see her tomorrow. Clara asked her to phone the ward when she could and ask for her. No doubt Marcie would answer but that was okay. She'd come get her if she needed to. Bernie took her own way out, before she was shoved. Clara waited for Kath to open the door. When she did, and she saw the room inside and its occupants, Clara was speechless.

'There is our girl,' said Marlene.

'Who the hell is she?' said Clara

'Don't you remember? said Marlene. 'I'm Marlie, your friend.'

'I've never seen this woman before in my life.'

Francis Bird twitched again. He looked at Bill for some help. 'Clara, it's us,' said Bill.

'I think she must be having one of her blackouts,' said Marlene. 'Are you ok, Clara?'

Clara turned to leave but she was blocked by the huge bulk of Fatso, who cast a gloomy shadow over her. He wrapped his giant arms around Clara and held her as she fought against his body. Francis held up a finger, and ushered the man to bring her towards the empty chair beside Marlene and Bill. He did so and plonked Clara down on the seat. Marlene turned away, seemingly unable to watch her friend in so much of a plight. Bill placed a friendly hand on her shoulder, then he leant towards Clara and reassured her that it was going to be alright. He did it with a series of head nods and smiles. Any words would probably have been lost anyway, he thought. And even if he was capable of speaking to her right now, he wouldn't have the first idea of what to say. This was where Marlene came into her own. In these difficult moments. He watched as she caressed Clara's shoulder. Clara's first thought was to back away. Then she realised that if she did so, she would look crazy. These were her friends, right? Friends don't mean any harm.

'Your husband is here to look after you,' said Francis Bird. Fatso backed off and retreated to the doorway. His work was done for now. Francis slid a sheet of paper over the desk. Then he placed a thick, fancy kind of pen next to the paper. It was bulky and black and had a gold trim like an expensive coat.

'These forms here are for your benefit,' said Francis. 'They are so we can make your life a little less complicated.'

'Complicated?' said Clara.

Francis tapped the sheet of paper with a ringless finger, hitting the dotted line with a thud, the dotted line where he wished Clara would just get on with it and pick up the fancy pen, sign her name and put an end to this, whatever this was. But Francis knew what it was, it was the natural way to go for her husband. And as for this Marlene woman, well, he wasn't so sure about her, but he understood a man's needs better than anyone. If she was giving Bill something that he craved, then who was he to start judging? *One of your fancy women, is it?* He could hear at the back of his mind, his dear old mum. Clara bent toward the paper, squinted at the fine print. Marlene shifted uncomfortably in her chair. Bill didn't know whether to put an arm around her or comfort his wife instead. In the end he did neither.

'What exactly is this?' asked Clara.

'It is a form to give your husband lasting power of attorney,' said Francis. 'He'll make sure that you are treated well, and he will have sole power of your finances, as you are currently in a state where you may not be able to make such decisions on your own.'

'I need Bernie,' said Clara.

She was half out of her seat, when Marlene attempted to hold her back, a light hand on the shoulder, then a firm pull as she came back down and hit the chair with a thump. Fatso began to walk over, but was ushered away by Francis Bird.

'I won't sign it,' Clara said.

'Love, it is for the best that we get this done today,' said Bill. 'Think of the children. This way they can be looked after.'

Clara weighed up the situation ahead of her. A strange woman was now holding her husband's hand, under the table where she wasn't meant to see. And the doctor? Was he in on this scam too? It was her money on the table, quite literally. And they wanted it for themselves? How could this happen? Now she really did want Bernie in the room, but she was long gone by now. She would be hitting the hard roads in her battered old BMW now. Oblivious.

Fatso grabbed Clara by the wrist and forcefully pushed the pen in her hand. He took her by then shoulder when she tried to release herself from his grip. Marlene looked away, showed her distress, while Bill gritted his teeth and watched as they made Clara sign the forms. As she finished the whip of her final letter, her tears fell uncontrollably down her face. She wiped them with the back of her hand. It was no good arguing. It was inevitable.

'Now it's my turn,' said Francis. He signed his name under the witness section. Bill signed his name on the dotted line, under the attorney section. The three of them smiled. Clara shivered in the morning light, the light that showered in around the considerable frame of Fatso. Francis pointed a finger at him and he duly left the room. Marlene brushed Clara's arm with a hand, a wicked hand, thought Clara. She had to speak to Bernie, the only person in the world who she truly trusted. It was time to let her write her article.

CHAPTER 26

Present day

1

Michael Rainford picked up the ringing phone, hoping that the woman on the other end was sober. He was just about to leave his office when it chirruped on the desk. He waved goodbye to Kristen and watched her leave through the automatic doors as he answered. It was a call that he never thought would happen, not that he had trust issues with his dear Bernadine, but he just figured that she'd have something else to occupy her tonight. Perhaps a date, perhaps something else concerning getting to the bottom of a wine bottle. But here she was, ahead of time, and telling him the strangest things from her quaint little cottage out by the woods. She told him what she knew about Clara, about Waterside House and its endless mysteries.

'Are these messages threatening the poor woman?' Rainford asked, gobsmacked at what he was hearing.

'They appear to be more of a warning *for* her, rather than against her.'

'I can't believe someone in there is trying to scare Clara. What do we know about the sender, or the writer of these cryptic crosswords?'

'Nothing yet. The first one told her she should get out of there, the second that she would die in there if she didn't get out, and the third, well, that's where it gets a little more cryptic. The third message was a set of letters cut out of a newspaper. It spelled a name: The Pillman.'

'The what?'

'I traced him. He was a member of staff at Waterside back in the day.'

'Are you talking back in my day or a really long way back?'

'Your day *is* a really long way back, Michael. Anyway, he worked there in the late eighties, and left around ninety-one. But the strange part is the disappearance of a patient. A woman named Mary Dunn. She seemingly vanished, according to our friend Ray Spivey. He worked the same hospital that Stuart Pillman did. He said one day she was there and the next she wasn't.'

'And he's the guy who is now sectioned up in Carlisle?'

'Yes. But don't discredit his words because of that.'

'I wouldn't dream of it. But you do realise that his word may be slightly compromised because of his situation.'

'All I know is that he was right.'

'She really did vanish?'

'I think so. But I can't prove it, yet. Francis Bird searched the records and found that she was discharged in eighty-nine.'

'Well, there you go, then. Clear as crystal.'

'No.'

'No?'

'I thought it may be a dead end too. Until I spoke with Clara this morning. She told me something. She told me that she went down to the basement. She went down to the morgue. And what she found truly shocked me. Michal there was a wheelchair. . . with urine on its seat.'

Rainford nearly choked. 'What?'

'Don't you see, if it was urine then that means someone is down there. She also found a pair of small black shoes, a woman's pair of shoes.'

'You think that the vanishing lady is still down there?'

'I don't want to say. Either someone is playing with Clara's mind, or there really is someone in danger. What if this Pillman character is keeping her prisoner? I mean I don't know how but I think I'm on to something here.'

'It sounds pretty dangerous. I told you I don't want you putting yourself in harm's way. Why don't you let the authorities deal with this?'

'Because they'll never believe me, or they won't do anything but take the doctor's word. They'll think I'm crazy, Michael.'

'So, what is the next logical step. I'm assuming you are still thinking logically about all this.'

'I have to find Pillman. Or go down to the basement and check it out for myself.'

'It's too risky. It's all too risky, Bernadine.'

'It's the only way to find out the truth.'

'I'll try some digging myself on this Pillman guy. But promise me you won't go down to that basement.'

'I can't do that.'

'Bernadine.'

'Okay I promise I won't go down there.'

'Good. Now tell me you'll warn Clara off too.'

Bernie thought about it. There was no way she could promise that. Clara was going to do what she thought was right. And Bernie kind of agreed. 'I'll speak to her.'

'It's going to be one heck of an article.'

'If it's true, it'll blow the socks of the millwright curse.'

Michael laughed. 'It sure will.'

'I'll call you tomorrow.'

'Goodbye, Bernadine. And stay safe.'

Bernie hung up the landline. She looked out at the grey blanket of cloud riding her lonely little cottage. Hemingway was lapping water from a bowl in the kitchen. Bernie felt a little lighter, like the load of what she had been carrying was lifted and she could breathe again, smell the cool winter air again. Then she called Eastview ward, spoke briefly to Marcie, and it all disappeared like a thief in the pitch-black night.

2

Clara shuffled along the cherry wood floor wearing the pink fluffy sheep slippers Sharne had left at the foot of a sofa in the tv room. She gave Marcie a hard smile. The kind of smile that convicts wear for their visitors in Her Majesty's Prison. Marcie handed her the landline attached to the wall and winked at her, a conspiratorial kind of wink. But Marcie had no idea of the levels of pain Clara was dealing in right now. She soon would. But not for now. It was hard enough getting her own head around it, and although she firmly believed in problems shared rather than kept, it was still too raw, still too painful, still too deep a wound to divulge to your nearest and dearest. But Bernie was different. Bernie was outside. Bernie was the shit hot reporter for a newspaper, and if anyone could help, and that's what she badly wanted, help not sympathy, then it was going to be Bernie Waller.

'Bernie, don't talk, just listen. Listen before they give me those darn pills and my brain fogs up. My husband is having an affair. Some woman called Marlie, apparently.' (Bernie had a moment, just a flicker of recognition that came to her then, and crept inside her brain like a leech.) 'And no, she isn't a younger version of me, and no she isn't any other cliché that some hack might have conjured up to hurt me. She is a shrewd and calculating monster. This I truly know. Together my husband and Marlie have conspired to take my inheritance money, and they think they've succeeded. This is paramount, Bernie. They have to believe that it's worked. That the plan has worked. So don't go calling anybody, especially not that bastard Bird. I mean that. No calls.'

'I don't know what to say. How?'

'They got me to sign a form to give him lasting power of attorney. I had to sign it, Bernie, I really had to, you know?'

Bernie thought she could hear the starting of tears, a break in the voice that up until now had been strong and captivating. It went weak for a moment, but she recovered. Bernie had to give her kudos for that, it couldn't have been easy. But while she talked, she sounded as if she really did have a plan.

'They forced me to sign, and if I had done what I wanted to do – bite that bastard's hand off – they would have just kept me in here longer, and Bernie, I'm coming out of here. It may take a little time but

I'm done with this sick girl thing. I haven't had a blackout for weeks, so they say, and my anxiety can go fuck off. I'm done.'

'I'm sorry about your husband.' Bernie didn't know what to say, how could she have found the right words for this? This just didn't happen, did it? Maybe in the movies, not here in little sleepy Coniston. Then she grasped what it was that had eluded her a moment earlier. It was the name Marlie. She had heard it before. Bill himself had said it on her tape recorder. What was it he had said? *Marlie would agree, Clara isn't the type to act on jealous emotions.* Bernie thought about the way Clara was reacting now and she had to give it to Bill, he really does know his wife. It was not jealousy or bitterness or even rage that was pouring out of Clara, it was pragmatism, it was self-worth, it was cunning. It was the first moments of sanity that Bernie had heard since she first sat down to talk with her.

'What's the plan?' Bernie asked.

'Well, you said there is going to be a second opinion on my treatment, right?'

'Yes, but it's not for weeks.'

'That's all the time I need.'

'I can get in touch with doctor Slinger, see if he'll move it forward. I'm sure in light of what is happening he'll be more than happy to rearrange.'

'January is fine. I need the time anyway.'

'Time for what?'

'To get those damn pills out of my system.'

Bernie only had a second of hesitation. But she knew it was right. The pills are making her unwell. She weighed it up and decided that any of those awful pills would make her unwell. Whatever she took it was going to—

Bernie gasped.

'What? What is it, Bernie?'

She was thinking hard, but then that thinking turned into thinking aloud. 'Oh my God. They planned it, Clara. They planned it. They've been playing you all along.'

Clara was silent. Until she thought about it some more. Then she said (as she was running through the dead cat in San Francisco – poor Macdonald – the tacks in the coat pocket, the meat cleaver in the playroom, the whack on Bill's chin, all the time she spent in therapy, the tears she had shed, the boat trip, the blackouts – every damn one of them), 'My children,' with a rasping breath that was both desperate and mad with fright.

3

Marlene held her fork tight, so tight she was turning colour at the knuckles. David had dropped his again, making an almighty crash on the oak wood table where the four of them were sitting, eating dinner together, as though it had always been this way. Rita opened her mouth to speak, but then closed it again with a burst of laughter the way young children seem to do for no other reason than they just had to do it. The two of them, David and Rita, exchanged looks and the laughter broke out again, this time it was coming from both of them.

'There's a good boarding school out in Fulneck, you know,' Marlene said. Bill stopped chewing his pork chop, looked up at her, swallowed and said, 'We think state schools are fine.' He went on back to chewing.

'It is only nine grand a term,' said Marlene. 'Just get that book finished.' She smiled at him, warm and pretty. She had always been pretty but now she seemed to be a glowing kind of pretty. The kind of pretty that makes a man want to learn how to sew a button to the sheet, Marlene's mother would have said. To Rita she was an imposter. A woman who looked like a two-penny coin, her skin was that bronze. She was here and her mother wasn't. That was cold hard fact. But what it meant was less solid. Her mother was only at a camp, a mummy camp and when she returned, she would be able to see her again. But she had to get better first. Her mother was sick, they had said, so until she was better, she was to look upon Marlie as a substitute, but she was not to make her cross.

'It sounds like an unnecessary expense to me,' said Bill.

'It could be the making of her. Don't you want the best for your only daughter?' she said between mouthfuls of pork chop.

'State schools never did us any harm.'

'Come on, Bill, you're being soft on them. She won't thank you when she's turning twenty-one and hasn't got the discipline to hold down a regular job, a relationship, an entire life.'

Marlene smiled again, wide and pretty and she took Bill's hand under the table. If she could get the brats down to just one for now, then maybe she could make this work. Just maybe it could be like she imagined it all those long months ago. If she could only keep her anger in check for just a little while longer. She placed the fork down on the plate, swallowed her pork chop and then said, 'who wants ice cream?'

'Finish your greens first,' said Bill. That was good, make him out to be the bad guy, she thought.

Both kids lit up and rushed their dinner down. 'We can talk about Fulneck tonight,' Marlene said to Bill as the children ran out into the kitchen, opened the freezer and took out a large tub of Ben & Jerry's. 'Save some for me,' Marlene hollered back into the kitchen.

'I suppose she would get the best education there is,' Bill said, frowning in deep thought. Suddenly the pork chop didn't taste that good. He was thinking and when he was in that thinking mood, food took a back seat. 'Well, there is no rush. But I looked online and found the next term syllabus. She would be reading Ursula K. Le Guin.'

'I thought all that had gone up the shoot years ago.'

Marlene gave him a queer smile, a playful grin that melted his steel a little. 'She could turn into a real little budding author,' Marlene added. 'Obviously her dad would be an influence,' she said as she rubbed his arm. There was a clatter in the kitchen behind them, breaking the moment yet again. But she held control over that side of her, the bad side that Bill never truly saw. The side of her that broke the nose of her previous boyfriend, the one from Pudsey who had only seen the good side until he kissed another woman. Perhaps it had been karma, a result of her actions, say when she slept with Natalie Barber's boyfriend, Jordan, for the entire semester. But for Marlene it was an act of betrayal and that wasn't on. Karma wasn't her thing.

'What are you guys doing in there?' Bill asked the kids. Inaudible sounds came echoing back through the hallway. 'So you'll think about it?' Marlene asked.

'Sure. In fact, if they keep making all that racket, I'm going to be sending both of them out to Fulneck.'

Marlene laughed for him. Her most beautiful laugh that lit up her face. She kissed him and said, 'I love you.'

'It won't be long until we have the means to touch the money,' said Bill.

'I know.'

'We should maybe think about finding a place for Clara. You know, somewhere she can relax with great views around her. I told you she likes to paint, didn't I?'

'Yes. You told me. But don't you think she already has that? I mean, Coniston water is right on the doorstep and all those mountains around her, it can be truly breath-taking, for a painter.'

'Yeah, I know. But we should keep an eye out for a good place anyway.'

'If it's what you want, darling.'

'I think it is.'

Marlene considered then that perhaps Bill had done what she had wanted him to do all along, and that was believe that Clara is sick. If he believed that, then there would be less guilt, perhaps in time no guilt at all. If she was sick then she was in the right place. If she was sick then Marlene herself was in the right place. And that hadn't happened in her whole life.

'I love you,' said Bill. The children came into the lounge holding spoons covered in chocolate ice cream. 'David has more ice cream on his face than he does in his belly, I'd like to guess,' said Marlene. That was good, make that bond stronger, play a little, be mumsy. He likes that, she thought.

The four of them laughed. David smiled shyly. Then put his chocolate hands on Marlene's white jeans. She gasped at first. Saw the smear of brown on her lap, the sticky, icy cold smear of brown chocolate. She nearly drew her hand back. But she caught it just in time. It was only a thought, an instinct, a reaction. But it was nearly fatal.

'David!' Bill shouted. 'Look at the mess you're making. Go wash your hands now.'

He apologised for his son. Marlene waited for an apology from David, but it was lost in his throat. Had he sensed that she was going to strike him? He looked up at her, stared into those piercing eyes and croaked out a whimper of a sorry. She said it was alright, they were old jeans and that it would only take a special tablet to get the chocolate out in the wash. Bill ushered him to the kitchen sink. Marlene watched them move, feeling sick at the sight of all that ice cream on her sexiest pair of pants. But at least it was looking like the brats were soon to be down to just the one. If she could only engineer something for the little boy. If only.

4

Clara lay on her bed, staring up at the curtain rail and spotting the flash of headlights that crooned in now and again through her window. It was dark out and it was cold in her room. Winter had set in with its frosted tooth and was biting everything with a viciousness that turned Clara icy. She cupped her mouth, and felt the cold breath coming in jet streams. She waited until the footsteps had disappeared around the bend in her corridor. Then she spat out the two pills she was keeping under her tongue, the two pills she had just been given a minute ago by the nurse with orange hair – Gemma was her name, Gemma the nurse who smiled at Clara with her laughter lines carved around her large mouth. Gemma who had no idea what Clara was up to. And why would she? thought Clara, she wasn't going to suspect the only woman in here who didn't have a full section three on her head of doing something untoward. Of sneakily not taking her meds. She felt them in her hand. They were warm and already turning to a pile of mush between her fingers. She wrapped them in a piece of toilet tissue and stuck them in the back pocket of her denim jeans. As she laid back on the bed she started to drift off. The flash of headlights was still casting its ghostly glow on the ceiling. Then the humming came back. At first it started low and soft, like an electric fan being switched on. Then it grew and grew into a drone that bit at her ears. Only it didn't feel like sound anymore, it felt like weight. Like a weight that was pulling Clara downwards. Under something. The humming went on and Clara was now awake and her body trembling, feeling the drone in the pit of her stomach.

She rolled off the side of the bed and planted her bare feet at the recently mopped floor. She couldn't deny what it was anymore. She knew where she had to go. She was hearing, or feeling, the noise from down below. It was happening again. She was going to have to go back down to the basement. It just felt that way. She stuck on her sneakers and made it to the bathroom where she flushed the pills in the tissue away. She felt good doing it, like she was taking back control. She checked her body in the mirror and saw that she had grown a few inches at the waist. She cupped her stomach which felt full of oil and animal skin and swore to herself that not only was she getting out of this place, but she was going to lose the gut too. Her hair was longer now, it was fraying at the ends, which had also grown lighter, and she combed with her fingers. She put the headband on and turned away from the mirror with all of its pain and lies. It was just how that felt too. Like the mirror was not the truth anymore. She wasn't ill, even Bernie had said as much. She wasn't some sick delinquent who needed to be locked away. She was Clara O'Hara, and she said as much to the mirror before she closed the door and started the short walk down the hall for Marcie's bedroom.

5

Bernie looked into the abyss. The wine bottle she had already opened. But the glass still remained empty. It was the closest she had come since the day she walked out of Michael Rainford's office, since the day she met Clara, to falling off the wagon. She sniffed the aroma of her favourite bottle – the Argentinian Malbec from Uco Valley. She passed off the notion a long time ago that they all tasted the same. This particular vintage was fruity and laden with alcohol. It smelled fantastic. But she didn't give in to her temptation. She put the cap back on and picked it up at the neck. She walked to the kitchen and placed it back underneath the sink. She opened the fridge and stared into the abyss again. But she didn't take that bottle of white out. She didn't need to, for she could smell it in her mind. Instead, she made herself a sandwich, remembering why she hadn't had anything to eat for dinner. She couldn't face eating at the moment. Everything she had learned so far, about Bill and Clara, about Waterside House, about her own memories, she had to rearrange. It was all a lie. She spread the butter over her wholemeal bread and slapped some salami and ham over it, picked up the mayonnaise and dolloped a generous amount on to the bread. Her stomach rumbled. She ate in silence, just as she had sat in silence since she came off the phone. Television would not have been the friend that it had been in those lost years after Vienna. Radio could have been more of a friend, but on this occasion, she simply sat in silence and ate her sandwich.

As she swallowed the final bite, she thought about Rainford. She ought to call him back and tell him what she knew. Or what she thought she knew. But she couldn't doubt herself, not now. She checked the clock: four past nine. It was alright to phone now. It wasn't too late, was it? No, you get special dispensation for news that could change everything. And besides, he had asked her to keep him informed, especially if there was a hint of trouble. And by God, if there wasn't before, there certainly was now.

He picked up on the third ring.

'Michael, there is a real story here. One that you're not going to believe at first.'

Before he could reply she had already begun.

She told him about Bill and Marlie, about the awful plan to have Clara sectioned, about the lasting power of attorney and about the way her phone call had ended just a couple of hours ago.

'Do you think that's wise? Her ending treatment without proper authorization?'

'Haven't you been listening to what I'm saying?'

'Okay, okay, calm down. I know how it sounded. But I'm just, well, I guess I'm just…'

'We're all in shock, Michael. But I believe that when Slinger arrives, then she'll be released.'

'I wish I had the same confidence as you.'

'But what?'

'These things might take some time. I believe you, Bernadine, and I believe Clara. I just don't want you to get your hopes up, is all.'

'We have to have faith in the second opinion. Until then I am going to see William O'Hara again.'

'Are you sure that's wise?'

'It's all I can do right now. Clara is locked away – her children are helpless and I feel that way too. If this is one thing I can do, then I'm going to do it, whether I have your blessing or not.'

'What about the article?'

She realised that she hadn't even thought about her article for *The Herald*, as much as she had thought this evening about a way to help her friend. The article was absent from her mind. Her mood lifted at the mere thought.

'I will write the truth, Michael. Whatever that turns out to be.'

Rainford thought about saying something along the lines of that is kind of the point of what we do in this industry, but decided to cut her some slack. It had been a long day for everyone concerned.

'Just go do your job, kiddo,' he said instead.

Bernie slept well that night. But she woke up hungry and raided the fridge, giving a haughty wink at the unopened bottle of wine as she slid out the salami.

CHAPTER 27

Present day

1

Marcie looked pissed off. It was almost Christmas (it was two days before Christmas Eve) and she hadn't yet had her visit which she was promised by Dr Bird at the beginning of December. She had whined all morning, then complained all afternoon before rounding off the early evening hours by arguing with Casey over who had the remote first. There was a showing of A Christmas Carol (another version of the popular movie – the third time this week) on the television and nobody was really watching it. They were all staring at the screen, but not one of them was focused on anything coming out of the little black box that stood on a wooden shelf adjacent to an antique and very dusty bookshelf. They were all thinking of something else. When Clara walked in, she found that she too was thinking of things that were a million miles away from Scrooge's ghost problem. Clara hung at the back of the room, brooding in her blue denim and white blouse, her hair beginning to clap against her shoulders it was that much longer now. 'Marcie,' Clara called. 'Marcie,' she called again, a little louder, a little firmer. She wasn't taking no for an answer. Marcie snapped out of it and turned in her chair toward the door, her face a picture of angst. Clara gave a little wave, her face stony and deadly serious.

Together they made their way back up through the hall and eventually came to a stop at Marcie's dark and moody bedroom. The curtains were half drawn and the moon was shining in with a sallow glow. The bed was unmade, something that Lindy would have addressed if she wasn't snowed under with other problems. The two of them had walked in silence to Marcie's room as though both women knew that what was coming was going to be taxing for the soul. Marcie had given up trying to guess so she just came out with it. 'What is it you want, Clara? If it's chocolate I don't mean to be rude but I think you've had enough for one lifetime.'

Clara hushed her with a finger. 'Let's go inside first,' she said.

'Now you're scaring me,' said Marcie.

'The humming is back,' said Clara. 'That's why I need something from you.'

'What are you talking about, you schizo?'

Clara smiled at that, the name that she thought at one point may just stick to her like glue. She took Marcie by the arms, gently, and stared into her troubled green eyes, a hard stare that almost set her alight. A shiver ran down Marcie's spine. 'I need you to get the key to the basement for me one more time.'

'Forget it, it's too risky,' said Marcie. She turned to leave but Clara grabbed her by the arm.

'I wouldn't ask if it wasn't important.'

'What's so important about a dingy old basement?'

'I can't tell you everything, and it's probably better that way, believe me.'

'Fine, then go ask somebody else to do your dirty work.' Marcie turned to leave again, and again Clara grabbed a hold of her, the grip firmer this time. 'Okay, since you won't have it any other way, I suppose there is something I need to tell you. I think you better sit down.' Marcie dutifully sat, tucked her legs underneath her backside and waited while Clara shut the bedroom door. Clara turned to face an intrigued, suspicious and excited Marcie Claybrook. All she knew was that this was going to be the strangest but also the hardest conversation she had had inside this mountain red brick house.

'When I first came in to Waterside House, I saw a message that was only meant for me. It didn't make any sense, not at first anyway. But how could it? It was incomplete.'

Marcie didn't interrupt.

'I got the rest of that message some time later, in my room, in ink. You wanna know what it said?' Marcie nodded her head.

'Get out or you'll die in here. Yeah, I was pretty disturbed by it too.'

Marcie buzzed with questions, but she allowed Clara to tell her story. Things were getting creepier with every word.

'Sometime later, I forget when, all the days blur into one around here, don't you think?' The question was rhetorical. 'I got some newspaper clippings shoved underneath the door. They spelled out a name: T H E P I L L M A N.

Marcie furrowed her brows, but kept silent, still.

'It turns out that this Pillman was a staff nurse in Waterside House during the late eighties. By all accounts he was quite disturbed. And he took a fancy to a patient called Mary Dunn, who vanished one day in 1988, and she hasn't been seen since . . . until now.'

Marcie's eyes almost burst out of their sockets. The room sounded different, as though someone had crept inside and flipped a switch that seemed to suck all the hospital banality out of it and replaced it with this unnerving simmer.

'Who is the Pill Man?' asked Marcie.

'His name is Stuart Pillman – The Pill Man is a nickname he got from patients, I guess you can see why?'

Marcie nodded again, solemnly. 'And this Mary Dunn woman – is she the reason you want to go back down to the basement?'

'Yes.'

'Why?'

'Because I think she never left. I think she is down in that basement right now.'

'After all this time can she really be down there?'

'I think so.'

'Fuck.'

Marcie hugged herself tight, sensing the shivers before they had even arrived.

'That night you gave me the key, I went down there, not knowing why. I mean, I just felt it, like there was something asking me to come. It was like this strange feeling. A humming I could hear, but feel at the same time. I don't know how I can explain it. But when I went into the morgue, I saw her wheelchair just standing there in the dark. When I went to touch it, I was grossed out by the puddle of urine still on the seat. There was something else too. I saw a pair of small ladies' shoes. I hid them underneath my bed that night. Marcie, I am telling you, there is somebody down there and I need to uncover the truth. I don't know how this woman vanished and I don't know why, but I need to find out who it is living down in the basement.'

'How is it even possible?' asked Marcie. 'After all this time – decades even.'

'I know how it might not make sense, but I have to find out, Marcie. Will you help me?'

'I don't know. This is way too heavy to go digging around in shit that don't make sense.'

'I know it's scary, but you're my only hope. Can you get me the key?'

Marcie looked Clara in the eyes, those beautiful sad eyes that looked more alive now than they had ever been in all the time she had known her.

'Yes, I'll get you the key. But you're not going down there alone, okay?'

'Thanks. But I think we'll need something else, too.'

'What?'

'I think we need to film it. Can you get a mobile phone from the office?'

'Sure I can. I'm Marcie Claybrook.'

Clara smiled. 'Oh, I should probably tell you something else, too. I'm not taking my meds.'

'Figures.'

2

Bernie ate like a horse in the early dawn, shovelling down strips of salami and seeded loaf with her steaming hot tea. She ate because of two things. The first was that she was nervous, a little understandably given the scale of the story that was blossoming before her very eyes. The second was that she was happy. It had kind of been a little while. She swallowed her breakfast and gazed out at the rise of the misty hills through her little lounge window. The darkness was abating to the promise of some much-needed light, finally. Hemingway jumped off the bed upstairs, a thud so loud she could hear it on the bottom floor. She could hear the patter of feet coming down the stairs in rapid time. Then she dumped her plate in the sink and opened a fresh pack of Felix. She could feel the nerves now more than ever as she pondered her drive up to the hospital. But that could wait for now. She showered and then dressed in a pair of black trousers and black shirt to match. She brushed her hair and wondered what it must be like for Clara. What it must be like to know you are not where you are supposed to be. Locked up for no good reason, other than greed and selfishness and a heinous and cowardly act from the one person you're supposed to trust the most. She dropped the brush to the table and threw her duvet back for air. Something her mother often did when she was a little girl. Before that afternoon in the attic. Before the land of dead air.

The road was quiet which added to the eerie feeling she had getting in to her car. It had also started on the first attempt, which was even more strange. It felt like someone had checked it over in the night, but that was fantasy – nobody gave that much of a shit for Bernie and she knew it. She'd tried to get the car back in to some mode of working order but finances and people skills were not great at the moment. So she did what most people tend to do and that was along the lines of it will be whatever it be.

She pulled up to an empty parking space and checked her mirror. There was a softness in her eyes that reminded her of the past. It reminded her of that night she walked out of Francis Bird's hotel room. It sent a shiver up her spine. She shook herself free of those memories only to find others in their wake. She thought of her mother again. The arguments and the crying and the bastard father who left his little girl to grow up with an emptiness in her heart. An empty hole that she would fill with booze and one-night stands. She didn't want to be her mother, stuck in an endless row until he decided that he'd had enough. She didn't want to be lonely either. She just wanted the screaming to stop.

3

Marcie threw her stump of a cigarette to the ground. She mashed it under the weight of her shoe and spat on it for good measure. It was early. The sun was just about over the arc of hill above the hospital roof and the mist was now clearing. The crows had gathered in the branches of the oak tree and their noise was hellish. It wasn't so simple as just hearing a caw in the morning, it was more than that. It was the sound of isolation. It was the sound of madness. She checked in her coat pocket one more time. She still had the mobile phone in there, clanking against her lighter every time the wind blew her coat outwards toward the smoking shelter. She took the phone out and checked her coordinates. She was facing east. That was where the wind was coming from. It was silent on the grounds. Apart from the howl from the elements. But other than the gusts and the godforsaken crows, there was nothing. A desolate nothingness that wrapped Marcie in its wings. Now the plan had to form. A way to get the mobile phone to Clara without it being noticed missing from the office drawer. She tucked her phone back inside her coat pocket and waved at the window where she could see a sullen Margot sitting in the tub chair giving Marcie the middle finger. A cold wind ruffled her clothes and swept her long hair over the shoulder. If she took it now, she would be caught by Whiteface on the way back inside. He wouldn't forget to ask for the phone and the lighter. It would only be one of the agency staff that might be complacent, as it had happened before in Waterside House. She thought back to that afternoon in August last year when Sal Blackwell placed a plastic bag over Sharne's head and tried to choke her out. The plastic bag that she had gotten through the door, and that had contained a jar of Reece's peanut butter spread, which she threw at Ann Piggins for good measure. Sal had been bad that day, almost killed someone. It wasn't the first time either. Marcie shivered in the cold misty morning, just the thought of Sal and that maddening grin. It had to be one of the agency staff. It just had to be. She knew that she had to check the rota, which was pinned in the office above the checkout times of patients on leave. She had seen it many times and many times she had used it to her advantage. Now she needed it more than ever. Then she thought that there just might be a way. A way to get Clara that mobile phone. She smiled to herself as the oak trees rumbled with the call of the wind. Then she returned the middle finger to Margot, who scowled like a woman devoid of all fondness. The plan was forming.

4

Bernie marched into Francis Bird's office with her Dictaphone already recording. He was sitting at his desk and he was on the telephone. If he was wondering how she managed to get in here, then he could only have blamed himself. For he had given her carte blanche, as it were, a key to the hospital, freedom of the city. She could come and go wherever and whenever she pleased, thanks to his authority. All she had to do was flash her badge which would allow her to gain entrance to the entire building.

'What in the hell do you think you're doing to Clara!?' she shouted so the whole ward could hear.

'I'll have to call you back,' Francis said into the receiver. He put down the phone.

'Why are you letting this happen?'

'I don't know what you think is going on but you have the wrong idea, Bernie.'

'She telephoned me late last night. I know the whole sorry sordid affair.'

'Are you recording this? You know you can't do that without my consent.'

'Bullshit. It's all a load of bullshit.'

'Just calm down for a minute. I presume you're referring to William O'Hara and his lasting power of attorney. Well, let me tell you something. It's for her own good. That man is going through hell as much as his wife. But in the long term it will be the best thing he could have done.'

'And what about Clara? Doesn't she get a say in her own damn life? How could you be so stupid, so gullible, so obtuse?'

'Be careful what you say, Bernie. I can have you out of here for good.'

Bernie could feel herself getting madder and hotter. But it was the first time she had stood up to him. The first time since that damn night in Vienna that she felt she had power, an urge to scream, finally. It had always been there in the back of her throat, but right now it was erupting like a volcano sick to its stomach. Maybe it was long overdue. She slammed her fists down on the desk. Tom Bower came to her mind, of his sarcasm and his vitriol. The Austrian woman who she never saw again after that night was in there somewhere, screaming bloody murder. Bernie felt them all and she ran with it.

'He is cheating on her you damn fool!' she shouted.

Francis leant back on his chair. He looked like he had just been struck on the chin by a heavyweight boxer.

'It's Marlie. She is the one pulling the strings.'

'Marlie?'

'Marlie the girlfriend.'

'No, you've got it backward, Bernie. Marlene and William are good friends, friends with Clara. I've seen them together.'

'You absolute fool. Marlene is the mistress. The one he wants to get Clara out of the picture for. And as for doing this for her own good – ha! let me inform you about Clara's precious inheritance passed down from her grandfather. That is what they want, her bloody money.'

'No, it can't be,' Francis said, putting his hands over his mouth, feeling the prickle of his new beard which was now becoming long and even more grey.

'Don't you see? It's all a con. It must be Marlene who has instigated this. But he is not blameless either. He may be going along with it but he knows his own mind. It's sickening to know, isn't it?'

Francis looked far off into the imposing hills, through the misty fogged up window of his small office. His eyes glazed and his mouth began to open and close without so much as a sigh coming out. He knew then that he had made the biggest mistake of his career. It should have ended with that night in Vienna, and if Bernie had been true to herself, then perhaps it would have ended there. But now he looked as if he were witnessing the last moments of a cherished time inside Waterside House. Then he thought of that fighting spirit which had almost blighted him before. The spirit that rallied something inside of him. The one that came to the fore fourteen years ago inside a hotel room. He was damned if this was going to be his last bow. Damned.

'I need to stop it, Bernie. I need to stop the lasting power of attorney coming into force. Before it's too late.'

'Damn right you do.' Bernie handed him the telephone and closed her eyes. The only thing she saw was Clara, smiling beautifully.

5

The next morning Clara wept as Francis told her the news. The news she already knew – that was not what brought her to tears. It was the sympathy that she saw in his quite often steely grey eyes. 'We need to obtain a deed of revocation, so as to put a stop to this barbaric charade,' said Francis Bird. 'I'm not having one of my patients played like a fool, nor me for that matter.'

Clara picked a tissue from the box that was placed in front of her. She wiped her tears way and sniffled into the tissue, blowing lightly.

'I'm sorry for having put you in this position, I really am.'

Clara could find no words. For this was a moment she hadn't prepared for, and now it seemed unreal itself, as though it were a dream. And in that dream, she had only thought of one thing and that was of her beloved children, David and Rita. She looked at the sign, the sign that had loomed over her very first visit to this office, the sign that read: IT'S BEEN A LONG TIME COMING. It certainly felt like it had been a long time, a very long time.

'We'll do everything to support you whilst you remain in Waterside House.'

'Remain?'

'You are still a patient under an imposed section. This means we can't just release you because your husband is having an affair.'

'I'm not sick, can't you see that you idiot?'

Francis Bird leant back in his chair, looked quizzically at Clara, and cupped that beard again in his weathered hands. 'If you continue with your treatment we can have a review in a couple of weeks' time, and then we'll discuss our options moving forwards. I think this is a big positive step in the right direction.'

Clara thought about telling him of her ordeal at her husband's hands, of the lies and the poison with which he had made her drink, metaphorically. She thought about it, but then she thought of something else. She thought of Mary Dunn all alone in a dark and dusty basement. She thought of Stuart Pillman and his poison and lies. She thought of the pills swimming down the toilet every morning and night. She thought of her friend Marcie, and her confidant Bernie. It would soon be over. This she knew. For Dr Slinger was about to read her file before he sat down for the festive period and did what he always did. Thought about his late wife and that endless mystery called love.

'Fine. Have it your way, doctor. I'll see you when the forms are ready to be signed.'

Clara rose abruptly, tucked a tissue into her denim pocket and turned away from Francis. She took one last look at that sign along the wall, and thought that it could wait a little longer. She was practically bouncing as she marched into the hallway and left a perplexed Francis Bird staring at that very sign.

CHAPTER 28
Present day

1

Marlene sat on the tangled mess of duvet and bedsheets, the light drifting to a sorrowful, mournful shade inside the room. She sucked her cigarette and blew out a plume of smoke in the direction of the open balcony doors. The flowers hung on to a shower of rain that had dipped them in water. She rested her feet upon the leather suitcase, a bulging case full of clothing and makeup and something else too. Something for Bill. She couldn't wait to show him her little surprise. She felt now that he was ready. She waited for him to come back to bed. She checked her watch and noted that he had now been gone for forty minutes. She sighed, then decided to holler at the top of the stairs. He decided to ignore her first call. He was in the middle of a sentence after all. Marlene stopped short of going downstairs to fetch her man, or of going back to bed, and instead did a comical u turn at the top of the stairs – her nightdress flapping about her shorn legs – and shouted again for her man. Bill heard her and regretfully finished up with his manuscript revisions. Marlene, now a little more satisfied, marched back into the bedroom, threw her cigarette upon the stone of the sodden balcony floor, and waited for him on the bed.

'What is it?' Bill asked, swiping his nose with a tissue.

'I just wanted to see you,' she said. 'And smell you, and kiss you.'

She planted a firm kiss on his mouth, and dragged him down to the tangle of sheets. They embraced in arms, tangled their mouths together, but she left him panting on the bed, left him to go open up her suitcase, left him to wonder what this woman was going to give him next. She had given him so much already. She smiled at him, wide and wondrous, and held his starry gaze as she unzipped the case.

'There were people – a long time ago now,' she said, 'who were called The Children of God. Some say they were a cult, a bunch of madmen who should be strung up by their you-know-what. But they were not like anything you have seen before. They were special people only God could have created.'

Bill watched her moving her hands deep under the valance.

'They had a saying and it goes like this: God is love and love is sex. There are no limits to this, you have to understand.'

She removed an object from the case. To Bill it looked like a long, wooden, and slightly misshapen coat hanger. It had a dip in the middle and screws either side. It looked rather like a paddle you might use to snap or strike somebody with, something that might be best placed in a knocking shop, he thought. Marlene looked to the doorway and shouted, 'you can come in now, David.' In he came, his hands covering his eyes just like she had told him. 'You can take those hands away,' she said.

'If there are no limits then you see that the young are not excused from this at all,' Marlene went on. 'Some of the. . . *children* started at the age of two or three. Some of them were whipped. Others just simply and quite beautifully had sex with their elders. It really was beautiful, you know. Kind of like a coming-of-age story, don't you just love to see those?' Bill tightened his muscles. His son just stood in the mournful light, as the wind knocked the curtains out of shape and the rain began to fall again, showering the flowers down below.

'It wasn't just in the crazy United States where they existed. Oh no, it was right here under your nose. They existed in Scotland also, in Renfrewshire, to be exact.' Bill was struck dumb. Why was his son in the room? He wanted to scream at her. He wanted to show his son that he loved him, that he cared for him. But all he could do was to whisper short exasperated breaths that made no mark on the woman who was now unscrewing parts of this weird assemblage. She held it up to her eyes and smiled such a wicked smile. 'They lived a communal lifestyle, a simple but wholly wondrous lifestyle. You really have to believe me on that. There was no music, no television, nothing such that would destroy the inner circles.' Marlene now had unscrewed parts of the device and it was in two different sections in her hands. Bill shivered as the wind ripped through the bedroom.

'The outside world became known as systemites. They were useless and quite boring and obviously so very, very wrong about the world and its creator. The children were taught this by house shepherds. Because things must be kept secret.'

David stuck his thumb inside his mouth. Bill wanted to break her spell, pick up his son and rush them both out of this room. The room that had once been enchanted by a woman's laughter. But he was stuck too, as though in the same trance as his infant son. Perhaps it was the strangeness of it all, or the power that she had, but it was almost impossible to move.

'The teachers were powerful people, all very powerful and straight up, you know. Not like these Catholic bastards with their guilt trips and paranoia. Their teachings were important to the children, as they knew what goes on stays on.' Marlene crept upwards to the edge of the bed where Bill was sitting. She had the thing in her hands. The thing which had him spellbound. The thing which she held aloft like a sacred offering.

She approached him like a lion sizing up its prey. 'It is called a Humbler,' she said. 'We use it to make everything that little bit more pleasurable.'

'What exactly is it?' Bill asked.

'It's a physical restraint. It has a testicle cuff which clamps around the base of the scrotum and a central bar here passed around the thighs at the base of the buttocks.'

'And why is he here?' Bill asked in a shrill whisper, throwing his worried eyes over to the little boy in the corner sucking his thumb. Marlene laughed, asked him had he been listening at all, then said it was typical of him.

'It won't hurt if you remain on all fours.'

She unzipped his trousers and patted him on the backside. 'For

God's sake take him out of here,' he asked. She smiled at him, patted him again on the backside and said, 'kneel down on the bed and keep your legs folded forwards.' Marlene crouched behind him and took his testicles in her hands. The humiliation made him erect. She had unscrewed the wing nuts on either side and it was now in two sections.

'Now you're going to thank me for trimming your pubic hair earlier, aren't you?'

Bill grunted as she pulled him toward her. She placed her other hand on the section of the Humbler which was against the back of his thighs – the notch facing upwards, and pulled his testicles through the notch so that only the scrotal skin was inside. His testicles remained on the outside. 'This will keep you humble, Mr Writer,' she said. She held his testicles and the Humbler section with one hand and slid the other section in place with the other. 'You'll have to crawl around on your hands and knees, you'll have to beg,' she said. His scrotal skin was now resting in the central gap. The two sections were now complete. She screwed the wing nuts back on. 'I'm going to be nice and leave the screws untightened,' she said. 'Seeing as you're new.' He could only gasp. 'I'll put you on ice after this,' she said. 'It'll ache for a while but then those endorphins will kick in and pretty soon you'll feel like you're on morphine.'

Bill gasped. 'I love you,' he said.

'Your orgasm will be so intense – your balls won't be able to push up so the climax will last longer.' Then he was inside the Humbler, and all he could think of was how much he loved this woman. He started to cry when he moved his legs, as the attempt to straighten up pulled hard on the scrotum and he felt agony. But it was a good kind of agony, the type that a man could get used to on the quiet. She stroked his naked backside and he groaned with pleasure. All of a sudden, he had forgotten about David. He wasn't thinking about Clara, either, but then again, he hadn't had one pure thought about his wife in a long time. Marlene disappeared from view again momentarily as she dipped behind the bed once more. When she rose, she had hold of another strange item. But one he had seen before, one that had set him alight. She let it fly backwards and then with a dreadful force she let it slash against his bare back. He started to bleed. His cries became louder and louder. She was whipping him again and he loved it so much he completely lost himself in the room. He may as well have been crouching in a muffled and dusty basement where no one could see or hear him. She whipped again and again, the skin breaking, bleeding and bruising with the lash.

2

Clara was so sure she need not be asked a second time. Marcie was the one holding the shaver in her hands. In the mirror she saw a young woman who was hell bent on taking back some control in her life. So, she started the blades and combed through Clara's long chestnut hair. 'It's too late to change your mind now you know,' said Marcie, as the tufts of hair fell to the ground. Clara smiled. She saw the scalp for the first time, the scalp that looked fresh. It was the moment then that she had a vision of herself. She saw that she was with her darling young children and she was smiling. She saw that she was on a hill eating strawberries and then she was looking right back at herself. The sun showered them in light. It was a good feeling. It was wholesome. Just her and the children. Just the way it ought to be. But that was just a glimpse of the future. A possible future. And to make it so, she needed to do something first. And then hope that her fate is kind.

'It needs to come off,' Clara said. And it did. It needed to come off because she was being reborn. The hell that she had come through was abating little by little. She was still in Waterside House but she was awake. Almost as if she had been in a coma for all this time, for months and months while her husband (the one person she was supposed to be able to trust, to rely on) had plans to ruin her. And he almost did. But the hope was that she could stop him before it goes too far, if it hadn't already.

Marcie cut through the hair with her steady hand, watched the ribbons of brown dance their way to earth, felt the same feeling that Clara had – as if they were both being reborn through this act.

'I'm going to the gym this afternoon,' said Clara. 'Why don't you come with me?'

'Something tells me you'll be okay on your own. Besides, I have a date,' said Marcie, holding up her wrists for Clara to see. Her wrists that were scarred and red from the cuts she had given herself. 'Therapy,' she said, and carried on trimming. 'But I do have a little surprise for you,' said Marcie. Then she pointed to her trouser pocket through the mirror's reflection. Clara turned to see Marcie open up her pocket and carefully take out a mobile phone just enough so that Clara could see what it was. She looked at Marcie and they both smiled. Then the two of them giggled like naughty schoolgirls. 'Tonight?' said Clara.

'Aren't you going to ask me how I did it?'

'I just presumed that you'd tell me if I waited long enough.'

'Well, waiting is not your style now. I hope you know that I love you and I'm here for you.'

'I love you too, you psycho. Now tell me how you managed to sneak a mobile phone past staff.'

'It was easy. I went into town carrying my original phone, the cool one. Then I bought a cheap pay as you go mobile from some market stall. Did you know they have speciality cheese on offer? Anyway, I switched the phones and gave the dumpy agency staff member the new phone, I mean like she would check. So now I have my old phone with a camera ready to roll.'

'Gosh that is easy.'

The two of them laughed again, a sweet ringing that chimed in the moody dining room, still smelling of fish and vegetables and vinegar. The sound brought Sharne inside, who took one look at Clara's new hair style and sharply whistled.

'Do you like it?' Clara asked through the mirror, showed her the sides and the front. Sharne yawned for the umpteenth time today and then said, 'it's cool.'

'Praise indeed,' said Marcie.

Marcie grabbed the broom and handed it to Clara. 'I do the cutting, you do the sweeping,' she said.

'So tonight we go?' Clara asked again.

Marcie nodded. 'Midnight,' she said.

'I'll come for you,' said Clara.

'Remember the special knock,' said Marcie.

'Three times, then pause, then twice,' said Clara.

'See you later alligator.'

Clara swept up the hair and plunged the remains into a black garbage bag. She examined herself in the mirror, but it was brief. This was not about fashion. It was about removing the old girl she had kept so well fed these past months. It was about freedom. It was about control. It was about being reborn.

3

Bernie hung up the phone. Michael Rainford wanted her to come in now as it seemed the whole story was even bigger than he first thought possible. It was gathering moss. And the latest developments were concerning, to put it mildly, he had said on the phone just minutes ago. In truth, Bernie felt relieved. For even she thought the gig was becoming bigger by the day. She wondered if it was too big for her, but then she batted that thought away and felt that strength come to the fore. She thought of her screaming at Francis Bird and felt wonderful with the memory. The only thing she hadn't divulged was that Clara was not taking her medication. She felt that would have been a huge betrayal.

It was Christmas Eve and Bernie had a dinner with her mother and brother and his family in just twenty-four hours' time. The big day had never before seemed so small. In light of her friend's situation Bernie hardly thought about the festivities. She couldn't escape the songs or the movies, for every time she turned on the radio or the television, she was hit with it again and again. She used to roll her eyes, or fake yawn whenever the big event got up her nose, but today she couldn't help but be swept up in its gleeful tunes and its merriment. For today was the day she felt she had some control again, after all this time.

She dressed in khaki and saw her slim waist in the mirror. During this time she realised that her diet was rather sporadic. She knew she was losing weight, but just how much she never gave a second thought, until now. She rubbed at her flesh, her stomach which was shrinking, and her hips that were becoming girl like. She vowed to indulge tomorrow. She would eat everything that her mother prepared, even the cauliflower cheese that she hated so much. She would not do it to please her mother, although she realised that she would do so, but she would eat too much and be thankful for it. She grabbed her bag and her Dictaphone and set out in the misty afternoon light, started the car and sped away past Mrs Welsh who was waving at her whilst holding her skinny little cat. Bernie wondered where Hemingway was. It was unusual for him not to be purring around her heels, or dragging some defenceless bird around the kitchen. As she drove on through the fog, she came to the conclusion that he was having too much fun somewhere. It was the only thought that she would allow herself.

Michael Rainford pushed back the seat and took his position on the edge of the desk, folded his arms and stared down at Bernie with concerned eyes. It was fatherly, and Bernie liked that. She had grown up without a father. She often mused on the things that she felt she had missed out on. No father meant no man to learn from. Her mother did date occasionally, and brought home some rather bemusing characters from time to time. But Bernie never felt that they were going to be in it for the long haul. That was sad. That was just the way it was. Just her mother and brother, no man, not until young Frank turned into an age where he could be considered an adult. Frank who was six years her junior. Frank who had it all, it would seem.

Michael Rainford asked her if she was okay. Bernie didn't know where to start. For once she actually thought that things may just be okay, but then they were awful at the same time. It confused the hell out of her so how would it seem to her boss?

'Tell me about the family?' Michael asked.

'I thought he cared. I thought he was kind of a decent guy.'

Michael raised his brows. 'William O'Hara?' he said. He knew Bernie never thought anybody was decent, especially not a guy. 'As for that rat Francis Bird, I could shoot him down right now and not feel a thing.'

'It seems like they have done a number on our girl.'

'The only thing that's kept Clara going these past months is her children and the bastard wouldn't even bring them in to see her. Something about not wanting them to see their mother in a place like Waterside House.'

'But we really know that he didn't want the guilt building up?'

'I think so. But more than that. He didn't want her to seem normal, or sane or whatever it is you want to call it.'

'So he kept them at arm's length.'

'It worries me what they are telling those poor kids.'

'Or what state they are now in.'

'I've been trying to think of anything else but the welfare of the children. But I can't focus now. I think we need to involve the authorities.'

'The only problem with that is that Clara is mentally unwell, and the husband isn't.'

'But she isn't, Michael.'

'I know that, Bernadine. But that is unfortunately the way that they'll see it'

'I need to write this story, don't I?'

Michael looked down at Bernie and smiled. 'What do I always say?'

'It's being passed to Kristen?'

Michael laughed hard, a sound that brought a little light into the darkness that engulfed them both. 'Just go do your job, Kiddo.'

'If I can just pay them a visit, I would love to give them both a piece of my mind.'

'It's dangerous. We don't know a thing about either of them. What is the woman like?'

'Marlene? She's trouble.'

'There you go then.'

'Anyone who drives around with a bumper sticker questioning climate change is deranged if you ask me.'

'Anyone who could persuade a once loving husband to do the dirty on his innocent wife must be deranged, who knows what else she is cooking up.'

'I have to do something, Michael. I can't just type up a story for the paper and be done with it. I need to go there; I just don't know what to do when I get there.'

'What about this doctor? Can we trust him now?'

'Bird? He's left a telephone message with Bill. I had to force his hand a little, in fact it was me who handed him the telephone.'

'So we all know who knows what, if that makes sense.'

'Bill now knows that we all know about the devious plan and it won't work so there's that at the very least. But we can't get Clara out of there. Bird is keeping to his damn word.'

'In time, Bernadine. In time. In time we will have our girl back with her children, you'll see. Now how about doing some writing?'

Bernie still wanted to go there, to the O'Hara house and confront the evil that lived there. But she knew it was a bad idea. At least it would sound like a bad idea to her boss. So she kept her mouth shut.

'I think I need to go home and rest. Maybe the writing will come when I've had a little time to process things.'

'That sounds very wise.'

She said goodbye and left the office. The square was bustling with last minute Christmas shoppers. She hurried to the car and had to rub her arms warm once she got inside. She started the engine and drove out of the pressure cooker that was Coniston Village.

4

Bill saw the little flashing light on the answering machine. It was concerning. Nobody called these days. Not his mother, not his wife, not anybody he could think of right now. He walked over to the machine, hands in pockets at first, then back out and by his side. Marlene was running a bath upstairs, a bath for the two of them. He could hear the gushing of water and the splash when she ran her hand through the filling tub. He could hear her voice humming as she waited, as she undressed. It was a tune that he was familiar with. It was the one his mother used to sing. The one that tells you not to worry and to just be happy. It had no effect this time. As his mother sang him to sleep, he would picture his life. A wife, a house, children. All the usual things that he thought he wanted, that everyone wanted, or thought they did anyway. He never asked his mother if he would end up like she had, a marriage that lasts, a house that pays in the end. But he assumed that he would. He just kept listening. The sound of her voice a comfort that he knew his children now had with Clara. And that is what conflicted his mind. Clara had been a good mother. All the hurt had come from him. Could he live with that? He was beginning to believe so. But things were getting serious and as Marlie told him often enough, he just had to man up and deliver for the both of them.

But now he was standing in the darkened hallway, his young son upstairs still sucking on his thumb. Still staring wide-eyed into the macabre. What little David had seen this afternoon shook him. It was horrible. It was what he thought badness may look like. He had run from the bedroom right about the time that his father was dripping blood from his naked backside and he never looked back.

Bill leaned over the machine. He pressed play and listened to a man who was at the end of his rope. It was Francis Bird. Clara's doctor.

'Marlene!' Bill shouted above the water. 'Marlie, we have got a major problem.'

The water stopped and she stood at the head of the staircase, naked as the moon, face twisted and her hand coming up above her head, as though she were about to slap somebody to hell and back. 'What problem?' she said, turning her head to the side, her hair wild and her eyes even wilder.

'It's Bird. He knows everything.'

Marlene opened her mouth but nothing came out. Bill was glad for that, the last thing he needed was a screaming woman in the house. He briefly thought of his son, still lying on his unmade bed, probably shivering from the cold, or something else. But that thought vanished when Marlene took to the stairs in thunderous fashion. Her face was contorted, her lips were moving but no sound came out. She was muttering under breath, Bill could see, as she approached the last two steps. 'How bad is it?' she said, rather calmly, Bill thought.

'Take a listen for yourself.'

'I thought you said we could trust in him to deliver.'

'Somebody must have gotten to him. Clara must have figured it out.'

Marlene pressed play on the answering machine. She listened as though they were the words from a sermon, facing the hallway window that looked out at the neighbour's garden, and the shrubbery that Clara had planted a year ago, now flourishing in the patch of soil she loved to water in the cool evenings of summer.

The tape finished. Marlene kept her back to Bill, but he could see how angry she was, it was in the shoulders as they tightened and raised up. He started to speak but she hushed him. A few seconds went by until she finally broke silence. 'It's over,' she said.

'He only said that he's going to speak to the authorities. What if he's—'

'For fuck's sake, Bill. It's over! he's going to get a revocation on the power of attorney. We're finished.'

It was Bill's turn to be open mouthed, silent. She turned to face him but walked past him, started for the stairs and broke out into a run. Bill followed her to the bedroom where she was flinging her clothes into a suitcase. The bathtub was still full of water and steam was pouring out the door. Bil tried to grab her by the wrist but she shook him off. 'Just listen to me, will you,' he said. 'We can convince him that it's the right thing to do, you can convince him.'

'It was never going to work, I can see that now,' said Marlene. She carried on throwing her clothes into the case, then snapped it shut and hauled it to the carpet.

'Where are you going?' he asked.

He tried to take hold of the suitcase, but again she shrugged him off. He took her by the hair, and that is when she hit him as hard as she could. She knocked him back onto the bed. 'If you try to find me, I'll make you pay,' she said as she stormed out of the bedroom and clambered downstairs with the suitcase in her hands. Bill heard the front door slam shut, and he moved to the window where he could see her parked saloon quickly motor onto the road out. He heard the murmurings of a little child coming from the next room, closed his bedroom door shut, left the balcony door open where a strong winter wind rattled through an empty room and closed his eyes.

CHAPTER 29

Present day

1

Clara's heart was beating fast. The last time it had done rhythms like this she was in the midst of a full-blown panic attack. She gripped the bars of the treadmill and slowed down to a gentle jog. She was still getting used to the short hair on her head. A habit of hers was to tuck the loose strands behind her ears and she found that she was still doing it even now. She was the only one in the gym. It was cool in here, and a lot less festive. She stopped moving altogether and draped a towel over her shoulders. 'Good work,' said the squat woman in the corner. She was the gym supervisor. She handed Clara a bottle of water. 'You seem keen,' she said.

'I've got my reasons,' said Clara.

The woman laughed. 'If I had a pound for every time I heard that I'd be sitting on my own yacht right now.'

Clara feigned a laugh and it felt quite good. She had forgotten the last time she was able to even if it was faked. 'As long as you've got reasons then you've got what I call the jumping mojo – a snake up your legs to make you run fast. That's what you looked like darling, like you were trying to shake off a rattlesnake.'

'There is definitely a snake involved,' Clara said. 'If I can outrun it then I'll be on my own yacht sometime in the New Year.'

The woman laughed again, said her name was Caroline. She said it was nice to see a young woman with so much oomph, as she put it. Clara felt the admiration, she also felt the burning inside of her, almost as if she were about to catch fire she had so much heat in the belly. It felt like she had swallowed stars straight out of the sky.

'Keep it up and I might make you patient of the month in our sport club.'

'I'll be here,' Clara said. 'As long as that snake is still breathing.' Caroline simply nodded her head, little realising the potent message of Clara's words, but still she was convinced of her appetite for fitness if nothing else.

Clara walked back to Eastview with an ache in her thighs and sweat patches covering her chest.

When she returned to the ward she headed straight for the shower. The image of the free bird murals on the walls took her back to that first night when she encountered the first of the strange messages. As she hung her head under the water she thought about Mary Dunn and what must be the nightmare that is her life. Down in that awful basement morgue with nobody to help her but the man who put her there – The Pill man. She shut the water off and shivered in the coolness, stood there for a few minutes feeling the winter breath on her skin. It felt good. It seemed like everything was feeling good again. Just as it had before she was manipulated into coming here. Just like it had with the family she had once known. But there in the freezing bathroom she vowed that she would again, maybe minus the cheating fucker who put her in this state. The man who she hated more than all the doctor Birds in the universe. The man who she now thought of as the devil incarnate. Him and the bitch he was screwing.

There was a knock at the door. A special kind of knock that could only have come from one person. It was Marcie.

Clara draped herself in a bath sheet and opened up the door a crack. Marcie was standing there with a silly grin on her face. She held up her hand without saying a word and showed Clara the mobile phone. She shook it and the grin got wider, sillier. 'Midnight,' Marcie said.

'Midnight,' Clara said. Then she shut the door and dried her hair in a frenzy. It was nearly time to go down to the basement. After dinner and after the other patients had gone to bed, it was time to finally free Mary Dunn. And it would be on record, thanks to the mobile phone Marcie had nabbed from the clutches of their keepers. It was time.

2

There was no stocking on the wall. There was no tree in the lounge. There was no sign of presents, just the awful silence that rang through the house like a siren. And the feeling that it was only going to get worse. David O'Hara walked through the dark hallway, still with his small thumb lodged in his dry mouth. He was carrying Mr Cuddles, his trusted teddy companion. He walked in to the playroom which hadn't felt the same since his mother left. It used to be a joyous, exciting place where his toys felt like an escape to another world. But now, in light of recent days and the festering feeling that it was never going to end, it felt for the world like a room without a soul. The door crept open with a creak, and the darkness felt solid, like a big mass of nothing. Only there was something there, something inside the room which did feel like a something. It was the strange sensation that it was now a room with a nightmare hiding inside. He switched on the light and it sprang to life. The tepee was still standing in the centre of the floor, its door slightly ajar, where nothing but a slither of shadow crept out. There was something else in the room too, which felt kind of odd. It was a suitcase with a tag hanging from the handle. David walked slowly up to it, still sucking his thumb. He bent down still holding Mr Cuddles and took the slip in his hands. He read it aloud. It said Rita O'Hara. Now he remembered something. Something he had heard at dinner the day before. It was when that woman who made daddy hurt was making burgers. He remembered the smell, and he could even taste it now. She had said Rita was going somewhere. It sounded like Full head, or Full something. He handled the tag in his hand and tried to remember. Felt it slip through his fingers as he let it fall. It came back to him just like the taste of the pickles in his burger. Rita was going to Fulneck.

A hand leant on his shoulder and he spun around, stricken with fright. Mr Cuddles dropped to the floor. He saw the woman in front of him. Her angry eyes, her snarl where there should have been a smile. She reached out to him and took hold of his little bones. She shook him. She shook him as though he were sleeping a deep sleep. He heard her voice shouting his name over and over, and then the voice started to change, became mellower, softer, lighter. 'David, it's Rita, wake up!' the voice said.

Then he saw the woman vanish. In her place was his older sister, standing a foot taller than him in her pig tails and check dress. 'I thought you were gone,' he said, a well of tears lodged in his throat. Then he hugged her tight. 'She's the one that's gone,' said Rita.

'Where's mum?' he asked.

'I don't know. But I don't think anyone is telling the truth.'

'Don't leave me here,' he said.

'I'm not going anywhere.' She shushed him as he sobbed in her arms. Then she picked up Mr Cuddles and wrapped her arms around her brother tighter than she could ever remember doing so before. 'We'll get mum home soon, I promise.'

'Where is dad?'

'I think he's in the study.'

'Is he mad at me?'

'What for?'

'I don't know. It's just that I saw them earlier. That's all. Do you know it's Christmas Eve?'

'Yeah, I know. Nobody is going to hurt you; I won't let them. Mum won't let them.'

'I'm going to paint mum a picture.'

'That's a great idea. What are you going to paint?'

'I'm going to draw mum.'

'She'll love it. When she gets back home.'

'When?'

'I told you. Soon.'

Rita closed the door behind them and sat on the floor, David followed her, Mr Cuddles too. She handed him a piece of large paper and some crayons. Then she sat in the mouth of the tepee and stared hard at the playroom door, hoping that it wouldn't open. Hoping that her father wouldn't come inside. Wishing that her mother would. She sat until the light started to fade.

Bill was down the hall, in the study where Rita knew he had been.

He poured another whisky into his tumbler and stared hard at the screen, where his new novel was looking more and more like a man's tortured soul laid bare. He tried the mobile again but there was no answer, just like the last five attempts at getting in touch with Marlie. She had gone. He had blown it. It felt worse because of the time of the year. It was midwinter and to be alone felt like a sin. He could still smell her on his fingers as he hit the keys on his computer. He typed her name, just to see how it felt. It was painful. It was pitiful. He knew if she could see him, she would mock. She would belittle him, but that had always felt kind of good in a way. It had made him feel wanted. He shuddered in the cool air. He drank his whisky. He typed her name. He repeated this action a few more times. He threw his writing slippers at the wall. Clara had bought them nearly a year ago. He thought about her now as the slap of leather rebounded against the plaster. He thought of the alternatives that were before him. He could come clean to her and also tell her about the debts. Perhaps she would forgive him. Or maybe it was just very wishful thinking. Or he could try phoning Dr Bird, maybe there was a way of getting him back on side. Maybe if he explained his plan differently, showed that he could cut his wife some slack and maybe go alone this time. . . maybe if he tried his hardest to appease him, or maybe he was just getting drunker and drunker. Maybe he should try Marlie one more time. Before the sun goes down. The phone rang and rang. He clicked it off. He stared back at the screen. He finished his drink. His head hit the desk and he started to snore.

3

Marcie looked over her plate at Clara. Ann Piggins was prowling the dining room as usual. An apple in her hands, which she offered to Margot, and only got a scowl in return. Jeannie Newton was rubbing the dye off her hands, and onto her cargo trousers. The blue food trolley smelled like fried cabbage. But on this evening everything smelled better to Clara. She ate her food in silence. Only snatching a glare from her friend who was sat to the left of her. Garnet knew that something was up, but what it was she would never be able to guess and Clara knew it, and she kind of liked it. It felt good to have a couple of secrets, Lord knows that Waterside House had its fair share of them. Clara smiled at Garnet then instantly regretted it when she made conversation along the lines of when she would be able to see her children, and why hasn't Bird let her home for Christmas? Clara brushed her off with an automated kind of response and then felt a little guilty. But that was alright. A little guilt never did anyone much harm in the end. So long as you were doing a good deed. And Clara certainly felt like she was doing good by going back down to that basement. She couldn't manage all of her dinner. Her hunger had evaporated with the thoughts of what was happening tonight at midnight. She looked over at Marcie who was playing with her food the way a child might when all they can think about is playing out afterwards. Either that or they were hankering after some dessert. In fact, Marcie could smell her dessert. Just sitting on the edge of the table. It was an apple crumble steaming away in the orange light of the dining room. The windows were solid black with the night, and the humming was starting to work Clara up into a frenzy. She waited for eye contact from Marcie and the two of them put down their (almost) unused forks on the table and waited for Ann Piggins to leave as she always did before anyone else. It was important to make everything look as normal (if that word could be used inside Waterside House) as it ever did. Don't be the first ones to get up, don't arouse any suspicion. And most important of all: for God's sake don't get caught.

They left one after the other. Clara had gone first, Marcie followed a minute later, chucking her half-eaten crumble into the trash. They both took their place in the queue for their medication. They never spoke to each other or anyone else. They simply stood against the wall where the notices hung unread and watched the people coming and going on a rather sombre Eastview ward.

Clara took her thimble of white pills, and kept them underneath her tongue, feeling them turn into mush in the warmth of her mouth. She knew she had to get to the bathroom quickly, and do so in a way that didn't alert the staff to her defiance. She would not swallow them. She simply would not. That would have been playing victim, and she was done with all that. She spat the mush into the toilet and rinsed her mouth, removing the bitter and salty taste that it left. She joined Marcie in the television room and actually liked the sound of the evening carols. It brought a moment of peace.

Harmony Finch was the first one to leave. She took her headphones off as she skulked out and wearily made her way down the hall to her bedroom. Sal Blackwell could be heard over the noise of the tv arguing with Fatso down the hall. It sounded like it was fairly tame this time, in good spirits and all. Then Casey Harper stood and stretched her aching legs, a symptom of the side effects of her meds, and quietly left the room at about seven pm. The night was black with anticipation. So that left four. Margot was sitting in the tub chair outside the game room, playing with her curls and sulking at something nobody could ever have guessed. They rarely could. She would get up to leave soon, probably at the same time that Jeannie Newton did. She liked to piss her off the most and, when she was no longer around, it just didn't feel the same. The fun was then over. Jeannie left at a quarter to eight. Margot got up at ten to eight and then there was just Marcie, Clara, and Garnet left to brood in that awful silence that engulfed their torrid existence. Christmas or no Christmas, the ward always had that knack of pulling a patient in, of tying them up in knots, and of keeping them on the edge of misery.

Garnet hummed in the corner, sang along to the hymn coming out of the tv set. She carried on even though nobody joined in. Both Clara and Marcie were racked with something, it was etched on their faces, but Garnet just couldn't figure it out. She had no idea that as this evening turned into tomorrow morning there was going to be a big shock on the ward. In the entire hospital. And things would never be the same again. It was nearly nine when Kath Jennings announced that there was going to be a special gift for each of her girls, as she called them, in the early hours. When everybody had had their breakfast, she was going to bring them something from outside. Garnet looked pleased. Clara tried to look pleased, and when she caught Marcie's eyes, she noted that Marcie just looked completely drained. She worried for her friend. She knocked her knee gently against hers and made her eyes wide in an effort to cajole her into a brighter face. But Marcie just turned away from her and watched the tv, where a Christmas concert was breaking into a chat show with celebrities neither of them were even aware existed until now. Kath sat down. Clara rolled her eyes. Then hoped it hadn't been seen. Kath asked Marcie why she was being so quiet. It was unusual, she said. Then Kath laughed at something the chat show host said and it was quickly forgotten about. Then Sal Blackwell, who both Clara and Marcie had forgotten was still up, came bounding in with a bunch of Wagon Wheels in her hands. Kath asked if she was going to share them out, and Sal laughed hard. Then Sal asked if she could smoke a cigarette outside, seeing as it was Christmas Eve. It was not customary to give additional smoke breaks to patients. They had their times, five breaks a day, and then whenever they wanted while on leave, including grounds. Kath didn't debate it long. She said no and it was a firm no. Then Sal asked Kath if she could shave her legs. Kath jokingly asked Sal if she had a hot date, Sal said she just wanted to feel festive, but Kath decided to give in to her demand. It was Christmas Eve after all. So then there was three again. Garnet closed the curtains on the night, said she was feeling tired but remained where she was. It was usually time for Marcie to go to her room and watch her movies, usually the one with Jack Nicholson and Helen Hunt. The cranky novelist and the waiter with the sick son. She had seen it probably around sixty or seventy times and it never got old. It was a classic and she enjoyed watching it over and over, even reciting the lines to herself when she wasn't plonked on the bed watching it. Garnet left at ten. She said goodnight and wondered briefly why Clara and Marcie were being so strange. Kath reappeared and asked the two of them if they were heading to their rooms anytime soon. Not that she wanted to get rid of them, she said. Marcie looked at Clara and Clara hoped that she had not changed her mind. She could feel one of her anxiety attacks in the far regions of her mind. She was breathing hard again until Marcie winked at her as she left the television room. It was nearly time.

4

Bernie blew out her candles and kissed Hemingway on the nose. Midnight Mass was in full flow. The night had a peaceful ring to it in the glistening dark. She eyed a spider web on the outside of the cottage window and when she opened her curtains a crack, she could see the lights from Mrs Welsh's Sedan shining on her unkempt lawn. She let the curtains fall together and for once she couldn't say a bad thing about her neighbour. Maybe as Christmas Eve turned slowly into Christmas morning, she had a heart that was going to sing for the good in people. And if the last few days had anything to teach her, then it was that there must be some good out there. Even if she had to force the issue just as she had by handing Francis Bird the telephone. She still hadn't touched a drop of alcohol since the morning she walked out of Michael Rainford's office half cut. She told herself that she didn't need it and that she would stick to being teetotal as long as she had something to live for. Right now, it was her friend Clara who she had to rescue from despair. Okay, so she was being manipulated by that beast of a husband and it was over as far as she was concerned, but she needed Bernie more than ever now given that she was still trapped in that hole of a hospital. She listened to the carols. O holy night was in full force and the carollers looked wonderful. Thoughts then turned to tomorrow, and the first time she would be getting together with her mother and her brother Frank since. . . well, since she couldn't even remember. How long had it really been? Months upon months, she figured. The phone started to ring, snapping her out of that place. No, not quite that place of dead air she so often felt, its musk and terror and all the unknown that came with it. No, not that place. But she was in a state of daydream when the shrill ring of the phone pierced through.

It was the Christmas morning tradition. It happened every year since she left home, even at university it would occur. Bernie picked up the phone and said, 'merry Christmas, mum.' When her mum asked her what she was doing, she told her the truth for once and it seemed to come out easier than it ever had done before. 'I was listening to the carols, mum. And thinking about a friend. And work.'

'Oh, you must rest your soul at times like these, darling. There will be plenty of time to right all those wrongs.'

'Thanks. I needed to hear that tonight.' She asked Bernie if she was looking forward to tomorrow and Bernie kind of half lied to her mother. 'Absolutely. Just the five of us, right?'

'Actually, Frank is going to his in-laws. But they said they would drop by sometime in the evening.'

'Oh, so just the two of us, then.'

'Well, actually I have a friend coming over for dinner.'

'A man friend by any chance?'

Bernie's mother laughed. A dry smoker's laugh even though she hadn't touched a cigarette in over a decade. 'I want you to meet him, sweetheart. He is really looking forward to meeting you and Frank. He does yoga. Can you believe I met the only guy in Coniston who is a fully stretched out yogi?' She laughed again. Bernie couldn't help but think back to that afternoon in the attic. The day she cried for her father. When the wasps came out of the dark to torment her. Then her thoughts drifted towards Clara and the hospital. She wondered what she would be doing tomorrow. How she would be feeling not able to see her children on Christmas morning. She shut it out again and came back to the land of the living. 'I look forward to meeting him,' Bernie said.

'We'll have turkey and all the trimmings, and plenty of plonk!'

Bernie couldn't have the conversation about not drinking now.

'I'll see you tomorrow, mum,' she said, and waited for her mother to say the same. They both hung up together. The lights from outside shut off and the darkness crept its way back inside the cottage. She turned off the tv where the carollers were marching up towards the altar with lit candles held aloft. Hemingway followed Bernie upstairs.

She went to bed thinking of her article for *The Herald*. Or, more accurately, of how she was going to tell the world about two crooks. One named O'Hara and one named Bird. She smiled as she drifted off to a pleasant sleep.

5

Eastview ward was shut down for the night. It was officially Christmas, as Marice had already said a couple of times, not realising the moment wasn't now to be feeling in a festive mood. They both had a job to do and that was to film the woman in the basement. If she was still alive, that was. Whatever they would see down there they would capture it on the mobile anyway. Clara told Marice to keep quiet as she pushed the button for the basement lift to take them both down. Kath Jennings had been washing dishes in the kitchen while they had crept towards the corner of the hallway and past the dining room double doors to the lift. They both felt like thieves in the dead of night. Both waiting for the truth to out itself. Just the two of them with no idea what was coming. Clara realised that she had been holding her breath and she let it fall out of her mouth, took a few deep ones in and fixed her eyes on the little number flashing above the door. It said B and then it came to a halt rather abruptly. She couldn't remember that happening the first time she came down alone. But that was when she was on her meds. Maybe it just drowns out the real world a little too much. Maybe you just don't notice things the same. She took one final breath in and out before the doors opened up and then the darkness swamped them both, engulfed them like they were fish in a deep and black ocean and it felt terrifying.

Clara told Marcie to hold up the mobile with the flashlight turned on. She pointed it straight ahead with a shaking hand. She told Marcie to shush. She thought she heard something up ahead. 'Maybe it's just rats rattling around,' said Clara.

'Is that supposed to settle me?' Marcie said, with a shiver in her voice.

'Keep moving and start to film. We don't know if there are people down here or not, but they may be just around the corner or something.'

'People?'

'Well, if Mary is down here then somebody obviously knows and they could be here too.'

'You mean Pillman?'

Clara didn't answer. But she gave Marcie a look that said she was hoping he wouldn't be here too. A look that said *don't worry I'm utterly terrified too*. But she walked on ahead of her friend until she needed the light in her step. Then she took the mobile off Marcie without asking and lit up the concrete below their feet.

'This is where she was,' said Clara as she neared the ominous door marked MORGUE. 'Shush. Keep quiet.' Clara held a finger to her mouth and got the mobile ready, out in front of her, still shaking a little. She was ready. Marcie had gone a little ashen in the face, her eyes as wide as canyons as she looked at her friend, both horrified and charged, like a bolt of electricity was running through her.

Clara leant her ear to the door but couldn't make out what the noise was. The dust was covering the small pane of glass on the heavy-duty door so she couldn't see through to the other side. She knew that she must open it to uncover the mystery. The mystery of a phantom patient who prowled the corridors at night, who left messages on windows for her to see. And it did seem like it was only her, only Clara and Clara alone. That made it all the more personal to her now, in the darkness, in the realms of nightmares.

'I'm going in,' she said to Marcie. But when she turned to see her friend, turned to see that she still had her back, Marcie was already walking in the other direction, away from Clara and the door marked MORGUE.

'What are you doing?' Clara asked. 'I thought you were coming with.'

Clara shone the flashlight at her friend's face, lighting up the worry frowns and the twisted mouth that spelled fear. Marcie began to stammer. Clara started to whisper, afraid that if she spoke too loudly then the woman on the other side of the door may well vanish into thin air. She didn't want to make a racket in case she scared her off. But there was definitely somebody on the other side. Clara could feel it. 'She's in there, Marcie. I can hear it. I can hear her moving, I can hear the wheels of the chair.' Clara crept silently to her friend, took her by the arm and told her that it was going to be okay. 'She is a prisoner down here,' Clara said. 'She wants to be saved just like us. Just like us, Marcie.'

Marcie continued to back off, tears forming in her large beautiful eyes. 'It's okay,' Clara repeated.

'I'm scared, Clara,' Marcie said.

'I know. I am too. But it's going to be okay. Look, we have a camera so we can film it all. We're not going to become her, Marcie.'

Marcie straightened up and rubbed her eyes with her sleeve. 'Take the mobile if you want,' Clara said. She handed it to her friend. Marcie was hesitant at first but with a little persistence and persuasion she took the mobile in her hands and held it out at arms-length, as though the bogeyman would be kept at bay by doing so. She held the mobile like it was a crucifix warding off a vampire, but she would have preferred a stake. Together they moved back to the door, Clara with her arms linking with Marcie's, and both of them breathing hard. 'I'm going to open the door,' Clara said in a barely audible whisper.

'Be careful,' said Marcie. Then Clara did open the door, slowly, and with the adrenaline running through her veins, she stopped dead in the haunting sallow light of the morgue. She was horrified at what she saw.

'Sharne?' Clara said. She looked through the screen of the mobile phone to see Sharne Williams, who was always complaining about feeling so tired, sitting in the wheelchair, her eyes rolled upwards so that only the whites were visible, and her breath spilling out of her mouth in big gasping clouds. Marcie was jacked up against the brick wall, her eyes barely in their sockets. But Clara couldn't see her friend now, all she saw was Sharne seemingly having a fit.

Clara switched off the mobile and rushed towards Sharne. 'Sharne! Sharne! Can you hear me?' Clara knelt at Sharne's feet, which were bare and dirty from the hard floor. 'Sharne!' Clara screamed as loud as she could, hoping that she would snap out of it and look her in the eyes and tell her just what was happening. She wished she could just tell her what has been going on ever since she walked in to Waterside House. 'It's me, Sharne, it's Clara.' Clara grabbed her by the shoulders and shook her. She shook hard feeling the terror in her shaky hands. Marcie was stupefied. She looked on in horror, hoping that at any minute she was going to wake up in her warm bed and start the ward festivities. But this was happening. This was real.

'Sharne!' Clara screamed, letting go of all the frustration and the torment she had endured from her husband, from Francis Bird, and now this confusion at seeing a fellow patient in a catatonic state, in a fit. 'Marcie help me,' she shouted back at the dumbstruck Marcie, who was slowly inching her way back out of the morgue, back to the safety of her hospital bed. 'Marcie!' Clara shouted again. This time it had an effect. Marcie began to move. As she neared the horror under the pale glow of artificial basement light, she saw something on Sharne's neck. 'Look, Clara,' she said. She pointed. Clara looked at the neck, where there was a mark, stretching down the right side, from her earlobe all the way to her shirt collar. 'And look here,' Marcie said, pointing to a spot on her arm where the sleeve had ridden up under Clara's grip. Clara pulled the sleeve up further to see that it was ink. Now Sharne was rolling her head side to side and her tongue was protruding from her mouth. Clara took Sharne's arm and twisted it slightly (hoping that Sharne might just break out of this spell) and read the words that she had read all those weeks ago in the bathroom. It said: get out or you'll die in here. 'Sharne!' Clara screamed over and over, still scared to death of what was happening, but also out of anger. The anger that was always there under the surface, waiting. And here it was, spewing out of her like vomit. Then just like that, just like a magician's trick when it's time to stop the magic, Sharne looked straight at Clara and said weakly, 'Has she gone?'

Clara smiled, pulled Sharne close to her body and said, 'It's gone. Whatever it is it's gone. She hugged Sharne before she could say anything more.

CHAPTER 30

Present day

1

Bernie hadn't laughed like this in a long time, and she even passed on the prosecco that her mother brought out before the big Christmas dinner. She had to deny several times that she was 'probably' pregnant, her mother half-joked. It would be impossible anyway, she almost said, for you need a man for that to occur and there hadn't been anybody for a while. There was no man for Bernie, but Robert Moss seemed genuinely fine for Bernie's mother. He made the effort with his small talk – not the usual how's work, how's the cat and didn't your mother say you were living out in the woods? It wasn't that kind of small talk. He talked about how hard she must find it being suddenly teetotal, about how life can be tough on your own – but that she was in no way going without – and she agreed with all of that. He talked about holidays with his son (who was about Bernie's age), about the impact of Brexit, about old pop music and his love of literature – Evelyn Waugh being one of his favourites – and how Hemingway was a delightful name for a cat. The man was charming without being a terrible cliché, and he was kind – she could see it in his eyes, which dazzled when he smiled. Bernie's mother had found a good one.

Robert Moss refilled Margaret Waller's glass and they all shared a laugh when he zipped the bottle quickly over Bernie's unused one. But the guilt came on then. It came in a rush like a huge overbearing tidal wave that would drown everything in its path. No plate of good food, or hearty conversation with loved ones (and new found ones) could prevent it. Margaret knew when her daughter was going to that place, just as she did that afternoon up in the attic all those years ago. The damn wasps. Only now there were no wasps and Margaret found it desperately hard to ascertain just why Bernie went off like this. Bernie hung her head, stared down to the napkin resting on her lap. Margaret put her hand over Bernie's, and smiled one of her great comforting motherly smiles at her, hoping that her very best effort would be enough. But it could never be enough, perhaps one day way back there, or one day miles ahead, she hoped. But not today. 'What is it, Bernie?' Margaret asked.

'I know I shouldn't be thinking about work stuff today, but I can't help it,' said Bernie. Margaret waited. *Don't be a smother mother*, she said to herself. *She just needs a little space*, she added. Bernie appreciated that, almost hearing those words aloud, and she knew it was being said in her mother's mind. At least Frank wasn't here to butt in at the worst moment and talk all over her. 'It's just that. . . I can't shake this awful feeling of guilt. It's wretched. It usually comes at night, in the silence. But right now, I'm incapable of enjoying a nice family dinner because Clara is locked away in Waterside House without her children for company. She has nobody to comfort her, and that swine Francis Bird. . .' Bernie had to cut off, the lump in her throat was growing, the eyes were watering. Margaret looked at Robert, and he placed a hand on her shoulder before he got up to leave the table. 'I'll give you girls some alone time,' he said. As he left he leant his warm, gentle hand to Margaret's shoulder, which she took in hers and without thought kissed the flesh.

'You can tell me anything, Bernie. You know that, right?'

'Thanks mum. I mean that.'

'What are you thanking me for?'

For just being here. I know how hard it must have been after dad left. But I'm glad you've found someone. You deserve to be happy.' Margaret squeezed Bernie's hands and smiled beautifully. It lit up the room and made it seem a happy one. Bernie could remember when it wasn't much like that. The endless fights, the arguing, the vitriol.

As she thought about Francis Bird the night came back to her. The rainy night in Vienna. The awful and endless one. But she held her tongue. At least she would for a little while longer. Anyway, how and where could she possibly have begun? But she did want to talk about Clara. 'I have to get her out of there,' Bernie said. 'She's been to hell in that place and now we know all about her husband it just makes it all the more sickening.'

'What about the doctor?' Margaret said. 'This Francis Bird chap?'

'He only wants what is best for himself. He signed as a witness to hand over lasting power of attorney to William O'Hara. He won't want the bad publicity.'

'But he can't keep her in there for ever, can he?' Margaret said with bewilderment.

'No. But he insists on saying she still needs the treatment. At least until Dr Slinger has given his second opinion.'

'And how long is that, dear?'

'At least until way after the holidays. It stinks, doesn't it?'

'It sure does. But there must be a way. There must be something that can be done.'

'Maybe there is,' said Bernie, looking off into the darkening skyline. Only candles now provided the light on the dining room table, flickering in some unseen winter breath.

'Maybe there is,' said Bernie again, with a little more sureness than before.

'Where are you going?' asked Margaret as she watched Bernie leaving the room urgently.

'You'll see soon enough,' said Bernie, passing a smiling Robert in the hallway and feeling strangely alive. She picked up her mother's landline, thinking it was better coming from an unknown number. She dialled and waited as the hum rattled on. Then she heard the voice, as steely and cold as ever.

'Francis,' Bernie said. 'We need to discuss one thing. It can't wait any longer.'

2

'You wouldn't,' Francis said. There was a touch of horror in his voice, as though he were afraid that if she did then the whole universe may come undone, revealing itself to be nothing more than an unstable dream. The threat was there and it was real. Bernie would reveal everything she knew.

'Try me,' said Bernie. Her voice was flat, dead, serious. It didn't need any more explanation. She would do what she never felt she could until now: tell her readers about Francis Bird and that rainy, blood-soaked night in Vienna. She had dared him, pushed him into perhaps saying something like *okay go ahead, print your story let's see where it gets you. Let's see who they believe. A doctor or some journo hack trying to make a few quid.*

She needn't have worried. Then came the great sense of relief. It was pure relief when Francis said, 'I want your word that this goes no further.'

'Release Clara,' said Bernie, 'and it'll be swept under the carpet for all time.' Even though the guilt came on, guilt for that poor young woman in that hotel room, the one she never got to ask if she was ok, never got to check on her, ask if she still had nightmares – this nameless woman who may not be alive right now – even though the guilt was swimming down her throat, it seemed like a decent trade-off: one girl for another. One life.

'I'll release her,' said Francis. 'After the holidays.'

'That won't do. It's no holiday for Clara, so why do you get one?'

'Bernie this is going too far.'

Bernie went red hot in an instant. She didn't even realise that her mother was listening, stood at the mouth of the doorway under the hallway arch. That was until Robert ushered her away, telling her that her daughter needed her privacy.

'The article is written, Francis. I just need an excuse to stop avoiding pressing that send button, and maybe my boss gets the story. Maybe by tomorrow morning the police will be at the door.' Francis half sighed and half exhaled in exasperation, as though he were on death row and the executioner had just asked him for his final words. 'I think you are bluffing. You wouldn't want the world to know either.'

'She couldn't have been more than twenty-three, and her eyes were sad that night. But she was unaware that the doctor wanted his fun. She was helpless and vulnerable,' said Bernie reading from her imaginary article. Francis didn't know. But he could not hear any more.

'I'll call Slinger. Tell him there's no need for a second opinion. I'm releasing Clara in the morning. Now give me your word.'

'I already did.'

Bernie hung up and turned to her reflection in the mirror, the tinsel hanging down the sides, the candle light both magnetic and funereal. She cried. It was over. It was finally all over and she watched the tears streaming down her face, hanging off her chin like icicles. Clara was coming home.

3

David called out for his father. The room was cold and stubbornly listless, as though winter had swallowed its paint and wood and spat out an unforgiving scene on which a young boy might see his nightmares come true. It was a room in which he used to play. A room that had once brought joy into his life. Now he sat cross-legged in the darkness. His mouth was dry and his stomach hurt. He couldn't remember the last time he ate. Maybe it was yesterday. It seemed a long time. He called out for his father, but he heard only the echo of his own voice bouncing back from the recessed spot lights. 'Daddy!' he cried. His voice feeble, breaking at the ends like a frayed rope with too much pull. There had been no presents to open. There was no tree in the house. No tinsel. No turkey in the oven. The day was falling into night and the house was a ghost on the street. He wrapped a torn blanket around his shoulders. It was the very one that his mother used to cover him with when he was feeling unwell and had to stay home. When he used to watch her paint, or cook, or garden. He thought of her now. The trembling started. The eyes teared up, his dimpled cheeks moist and thin. He sat there like this for what felt like hours. But it couldn't have been more than ten minutes when the door opened and Bill stood in the gleam of a car headlight passing through the street, beaming in on him through a frosted window.

'Go to bed,' he said. He said it with a calm deadness that frightened David. He pulled the blanket up around his ears and shook his head. 'I won't say it again,' Bill said. The menace was palpable. Bill looked at his son, then to the flash of another headlight outside the window – the dinner guests of neighbours making their merry way home – and he waited for the howl of a wind that beat at the window to subside. He wanted to hurt somebody. He really wanted to exorcise some of that hatred that lodged inside him. The hatred that he had for Francis Bird, the hatred that he had for the world. He was hurting like a lovelorn teenager, as lonely as a tearaway kite yet still he had this anger boiling within, an anger that David didn't want to see. He wouldn't wait to find out what his father may do if he disobeyed him another time and so he got up and ran out of the door, the blanket flying behind him like a cape. He ran up the stairs two at a time and came to rest at his sister's door. He peered in through the crack and saw that she was writing at her desk. Then he started to wail, uncontrollably and desperately, until she ran to the door and pulled him inside.

When she had calmed him down, wiped his eyes free of tears and warmed him up with her duvet, Rita told her little brother that she was going to get her mother back. That's why she was writing. She was writing the mummy camp and soon – when she had the correct address from Mrs Hanratty down at the library (Mrs Hanratty knew everywhere) – she would post her letter and mum would come straight back home to look after them. David read the letter slowly and added one line: I love you, so if you love me you'll come home. It was a simple young boy's line but Rita let him have it. Besides, it really just said all that there was to say.

They turned out the light and got into bed. 'Is it still Christmas?' David asked.

'If you want it to be,' said Rita. She lay on her side facing the gap in the curtains where the moon rippled through. 'Next year I'm going to ask Santa for just one thing,' David said.

'What's that?'

'That wherever we are, we are warm and we love each other.'

They both fell asleep before they could have heard Bill downstairs. A drunk Bill who couldn't understand why Marlene had left him. Who couldn't see why Francis Bird had gone back on his word. Who couldn't know that at that moment Dr Slinger was answering the telephone in his usual jovial way.

4

Steven Slinger finished his drink and removed his reading glasses. He looked rather longingly at the Christmas tree leaning against the wall, crooked and tired after the base had busted last year when he moved it from one corner to another. Lord knows he should have thrown it out years ago and replaced it with one of those fancy pre lit ones they sold down at Carlson's All Seasons store on the complex three miles out of town. But the memory of his wife hanging the ornaments while drinking a highball full of port was too great to destroy. Those were the things left behind and he cherished them for all they were worth. The cancer had ripped both their worlds apart. Providing second opinions had appealed to him in the wake of it, perhaps some romantic notion of giving hope to the hopeless was what he needed. Slinger's sister had kept him on the rails – providing meals, cleaning the house, helping to sort through clothes and jewellery and countless painful memories. They were good memories largely, they had led a healthy and happy life together, but there were some moments he just didn't have the stomach to face alone.

He walked into the kitchen carrying his empty lowball glass in his hand. He wanted coffee, and strong coffee at that. He thought of that old joke again; it came often to him and he liked that, about his wife and the way she liked her coffee the way she liked her men: weak and full of sugar. A smile gently parted his lips and his eyes danced like bright blue jewels before tearing up. He had eyes like the ocean, his wife said, but only when she was fond of him. He always knew that she would not make it through the summer. She passed away on their bed in the June heat just days before her fifty-eighth birthday. He had planned something grand, a gesture that he knew would probably be the last. He had an idea to take her back to the bench outside Sacred Heart (the church where they got wed) to relive that first kiss. Yellow freesias and purple tulips in hand, he had the idea of a table being set up – with the help of father Carrigan – and a bottle of his favourite wine that you only get in the bespoke merchants out on Brook Street. It was going to be a great celebration, and perhaps the perfect send off. But it never happened. Instead, Slinger's wife fell asleep two nights before. It crushed him and it still does whenever he tastes that vintage.

He was reading the Gerry Poverly case notes in the fading light, a slim candle glowing on the table. Each flicker the thought of her came and he felt, as he often does, that she was right there with him, probably telling him to clear away some of the dishes and place the tea towel on the correct hook, not on the oven door. The morning had been spent with his sister, as it has these past few years, but she always liked to give him the space he wants. It helps, she knew. It helps him to find her again in the silence, in the cloak of night. But he had other ideas tonight. Sometimes his focus would be in and out, but now he could only throw himself into Gerry Poverly from The Oakfield Unit – just seventeen miles down the road from here. Poverly had died in his room, found choked on a mash of white pills foaming from his mouth like a deadly shot of poison. Poverly had behaved what Dr Bacon deemed 'erratically' in the days leading up to his sad and untimely death. The case notes said enough for Slinger to believe that Poverly and Bacon just didn't see eye to eye. Perhaps Bacon misunderstood Poverly. Perhaps that was the one stain on his copy book. Poverly had been on The Oakfield Unit for seven years. Seven very long years. Slinger only knew that a man like Poverly was led to his death by hands that never cared for him, not truly. Poverly was not going to happen again, Slinger vowed. And it was the Sara Foggin case that was going to see to it that Clara O'Hara would not be another victim. Not another sad case to be filed away for years while the doctors bickered about who had done what, and about who was to blame, really. Sara Foggin was going to set Clara free. He only wished that Poverly was alive to see it. Just as these thoughts swam through his mind the telephone began to ring. That sound alone made Slinger smile. He didn't know why, maybe he just needed a reminder that life goes on.

5

Francis Bird said his name like he was a prisoner on roll call. Singer just laughed. It was the kind of laugh that was mixed with a bit of *what the fuck?*

'On Christmas day?' Slinger said, bewildered. But he had not lost his humour, and he imagined his wife up there on a cloud saying just that. The moment he laughed like that was the moment he knew he would always remember this day until the day he died, or the day when dementia finally took him as it had his dear father. He sat in the lustrous glow of the candle, smiling generously as the anguish on the other end of the line came through loud and clear, like a meteorite crashing through the cosmos. It was days and moments like this that served as a reminder of just why he went into the second opinion game. That and the pleasure of releasing pain from troubled eyes. From himself too. 'Let me speak first, please,' said Slinger. He was met with silence which he took for yes. 'I've been reading a few old case files. Stuff from a few years back, you know, just the stuff that people may have forgotten about.' When he said people, he had hoped that Francis would take it personally. 'Did you ever hear about the Sara Foggin case?' Slinger asked. Francis could only sigh. More anguish coming in bursts of hot air.

'It's all terribly coincidental, I'm afraid,' said Slinger.

'How so?' asked Francis.

'Sara had bouts of anxiety attacks on The Oakfield Unit. So much that they gave her an awful sickness – vomiting, temperature – you name it, poor Sara had it.'

'I don't know where you're going with this, Steve, but I think I should probably interject here and tell you that —'

'Wait a minute,' Slinger said. He really wanted his moment before Francis could jump the gun and do what he felt needed to be done.

'After a couple of interviews Sara opened up and said that her attacks rarely came in the morning, or even in the afternoon. It was always at night. Always in the darkness. She also told me that she got the most intrusive cramps that came with the anxiety. I went home one day and read everything I could about her symptoms. Her treatment and everything the doctor had written.'

'Go on, Steven.'

'Sara had an allergic reaction to her medication. Simple as that.'

'And Clara?' Francis asked. 'What does Sara Foggin have to do with my patient?'

'Well, now you've asked, Clara is unwell because she is taking something that she has no business taking. She is a well woman and it is her medication that is making her unwell. It was obvious by the lack of attacks pre-meds. And her symptoms seem inconclusive enough for me not to analyse any other way. There, I've said it. She's allergic to the damn stuff. It could even cause some serious after effects that we don't want to be responsible for, so in the interest of the patient I will be recommending that all treatment ceases immediately. There is no other reason I can see to be carrying on housing her, and believe me, I've given this faceless woman a generous amount of time. But hopefully she won't be faceless much more.

'That's some good work, Steve, but you've come to the party too late. Clara will be released tomorrow into the care of Bernie Waller.'

Slinger laughed, warm and gentle and he knew that his wife was up there marvelling at his ocean blue eyes. 'That's all I wanted to hear,

Francis,' said Slinger. 'You've done the right thing. It's not easy to admit to your mistakes, I know that better than most. Your copybook is still fine, you know.'

'Take care, Steve.'

'Merry Christmas.'

Francis hung up first. He took off his glasses and wiped them with the tail of his shirt. Behind him he could hear the sound of laughter, from the kitchen where his niece and sister were sharing stories over wine and cigarettes. The only time his sister smoked was after dinner.

He was glad that he didn't have to divulge the real shadiness of what went on with the O'Hara woman. Then he thought that Slinger would probably not have to wait so soon, given Bernie's closeness to the case, her closeness to Clara. She would most definitely write the truth. But thankfully nothing about Vienna.

The music came through then, a song that reminded him of his mother and father. A song that Francis knew they would love to hear. It seemed like Christmas was the time for absences to be felt the most. 'Come and get some wine,' his sister shouted, oblivious. Francis smiled and turned to face the music. He was getting good at doing so, his father might have joked.

CHAPTER 31

Present day

1

The mist had Waterside House surrounded. An eerie Boxing Day glow was setting in with the bite of a fresh frost. Clara opened her curtains to the sight of a pair of crows perched in the branches of the winter-shredded oak tree. The scene outside remained as ghostly as it had been these past few months. The light seemed to never arrive. The cold that washed off the skin of knuckles, made them bleed in the icy air was still present. One of the crows flew off leaving its mate alone. It cawed into the grey sky – that stitched blanket above a solemn hospital roof. It sounded puny. It sounded like a cry to hang on to the world that was, not the one that was coming. It was as though there was a thread between Clara and the outside, and it was becoming more and more stretched. Clara only thought of her children. Why she hadn't been able to get through yesterday on the phone was a mystery. Or not so much of a mystery when she actually ran it through her mind in the cold light of day. She wanted to wish them a merry Christmas but all she got was the engaged beeps. Bill most likely. Or that whore of a girlfriend of his. Maybe she had taken the phone off the hook. Bitch. But she would not get mad no matter how much they wanted her to, no, she wouldn't lose herself. Not now. Not ever.

She finished dressing and a knock came on the door. She hesitated. Said, 'who is it?' and readied herself for more of Marcie's words of wisdom. But it wasn't Marcie. 'It's Kath. I've got someone here to see you.'

Clara walked over to the door, bare feet pattering on wood, collecting the debris on the soles. She opened the door and Bernie was standing in the hallway, a huge grin on her face. It was the first time Clara had seen such an expression. It was open, honest and beautiful. 'I've got some news,' said Kath. Bernie couldn't hold back. She couldn't bear it any longer. 'You're coming home!' Bernie said, dangling her car keys in front of her as though she were attempting hypnosis in one of those corny films she liked to watch on Sunday mornings. Clara very nearly fainted. It was as close to a blackout she had ever had. Only this time there was nobody to tell her what devilment she had been up to. There was no Bill.

It took Clara a few moments to get over the shock.

'I can't believe it!' said Clara. 'I'm really coming home?' she asked, bewildered.

'Come on, let's get packed and you can say your goodbyes,' said Kath, eager to crack on, just like she always was. It was then that Clara nearly broke down in tears. It had been a long few months. 'I'll be waiting in the office,' said Bernie.

It took Clara two minutes to gather her things. She was overcome, unable to speak, so much emotion running through her that she almost took the hangers from the wardrobe. But there was a crumb of guilt that swam inside her also, for why was she getting out when others – Marcie and Garnet – were not? But Clara also knew that her children needed her, and she them.

Bernie explained it in the car. Clara was to be released into Bernie's care. She could take her children if that's what they wanted and leave the authorities to investigate the matter.

'I still can't believe it,' said Clara. 'Dr Bird just caved like that? After everything that he said I thought. . . well, it's just that he practically swore an oath that I would be here a good while yet. It doesn't seem real.'

'One day I'll tell you and you're not going to believe it all,' said Bernie. 'But right now, let's just enjoy the moment.'

Bernie switched on the radio.

'Do you think Sharne will be okay?'

'Sharne? What's anything got to do with her?'

'Oh, you don't know do you?'

'Know what?'

As Clara thought about what had happened down in the basement, she pondered whether Sharne would indeed become herself again, without the old woman guiding her, without Mary Dunn. Had she really been the old woman on all those occasions? The writing on the mirror, the window, the urine on the chair, the newspaper clippings? It all seemed unreal now.

'It's a long story. One day I'll tell you and you're not going to believe it,' said Clara, grinning.

'You could at least tease me a little with the beginnings of a story.'

'It was poor little Sharne all along,' said Clara. 'As for Mary, I dunno. Maybe she is out there somewhere, maybe she isn't. All I know is that we've hit a brick wall. But her spirit lives on inside Waterside House, that we do know.'

2

Bill began to run the water and stared deep into the tub. The day after Christmas had always been a lazy one in the O'Hara household, even back in Bill's childhood. *Take it easy* was the advice passed on, and Bill made sure to keep up with tradition. But on this cold, listless morning Bill felt bereft. He plunged his hands into the steaming water, gritted his teeth against the rush of feeling, against the pain. He thought only of Marlene and her sudden vanishing act. The flit that had brought him so much agony. It felt like the dream was over, and it was, for Francis Bird had seen to that. Since she left Bill had simply slept through the pain. The telephone had been taken off the hook, as he sensed that Clara would be calling, and he certainly knew that she had. Call it husband's intuition, for once. He also knew that she would be coming home sooner than he had planned all those months ago. It was true, especially if Bird had his way. Lord knows he had an axe to grind. Bird wasn't a man to be made a fool of, he got that straight away from the first time they met in the flesh on that rainy afternoon in October. Perhaps he could talk Clara round. Perhaps he could talk them all round. That was perhaps the last shred of hope he had been clinging to in recent days. The one brightness in this piece of shit that had become his life. He once thought of himself as a celebrated author, certainly locally in any case. There was interest in America once. This in turn made him think of Macdonald, their cat that had to be sacrificed for the greater good. For Marlene. Now it was crashing down all around him. He snatched his hand away from the water and turned off the tap. His knuckles were blistered. He heard the noise then. The wailing from downstairs. A child's wailing. His anger rose. All those times his little David and Rita had acted up when Marlene was around. Pushing her away. Coming between the two of them just like their mother. He grabbed a towel off the heater and rubbed his hands dry. 'You're gonna get it,' he said as he left the bathroom, steam plastered over his spectacles.

3

Clara looked into the wing mirror again, still not knowing whether to smile or grimace at the sight of her freshly shaved head. It was a little uneven but she forgave herself for that. After all, she did have bigger things on her mind. She could still taste the acrid remains of instant ward coffee on her tongue. The one that came wrapped in silver foil, just in case anyone with notions of self-harm got their hands on a piece of cut glass from the jar. It was history now – the silver foil, the pills, that mysterious haunting episode involving poor Sharne. She thought about her goodbye earlier. Telling Sharne that she would be okay, funny but true, now that Clara O'Hara (the girl with the orange head band and a psycho for a husband) was out of the picture. Still, it remained a mystery. But she vowed before she left the girls that she would be in touch with news. Marcie had told Garnet all about the night they found their friend sitting in the wheelchair belonging to a woman who had seemingly vanished. Her eyes will forever be in Clara's memory, those grey, watery eyes that were someone else's. Clara was sure that with Bernie's help they could track down someone who knew Mary. Someone who might just have the answers they were looking for. Where was she? But all that could wait. For now, she had a battle to win.

She looked to Bernie and still could hardly believe what had happened to her these last few months. But she knew that it had started much earlier than last October just gone.

Bernie slowed the car down to a stop, pulled up behind a livestock truck carrying sheep. She wound down the window on her side. The air had a bite in it and the smell from the animals was intense. They looked at each other for a moment. Bernie was unsure of what to say. She wondered what there was left to say. 'I'm sorry we didn't spot it sooner,' Bernie eventually said.

'It's nothing on you,' said Clara. 'You've been a great friend to me, Bernie. In fact, if it wasn't for you, I'd like to bet I'd still be in there come next Christmas. Still none the wiser.'

'What are you going to do?'

'I know what I'd like to do but that'd get me locked up quicker than a cat lapping chain lightning. And I doubt that I would get out so soon.'

'You need some space and time.'

'I need my kids, and then possibly my mother, if I can stand to tell her the truth.'

'I'm always here for you, Clara.'

Bernie pressed her heel to the pedal and they were moving again. Clara lost herself in the grass and the hills and in the mountains that surrounded them. The snow drifts sat on the tops and reminded her of icing on her favourite cake. As a young girl she often placed a cherry on the tops of those mountains when they were snow-capped, just in her imagination, but now it was there breathing along in the passenger seat with her. It seemed that all she had done in recent months was stare out the window. She imagined this moment a hundred times but none came close to how she actually felt right now. It was supposed to be a celebration, her freedom that she longed for, but the stone in her stomach felt a million miles away from that. The one that was in her throat too. As they neared home her throat closed up completely. Bernie slowed. 'Are you alright?'

'I used to have blackouts. Bill always tried to make sure everything was okay. He used to tell me what happened, what I had done. I could never remember any of it.'

'Because it wasn't true,' said Bernie.

'It's hard to think that the person you love could betray you in such a way that it destroys everything. It's like a hurricane.'

'You never deserved it.'

'Oh, he'll be punished. He'll be an outcast once your article is written. He'll be ruined. No publisher in the world will touch him.'

'Shall I take you home?'

'Take me home, Bernie.'

Soon they approached the quaint street, something that was a little more alien to Clara now. It looked the same on one level, but on another the sky was strangely artificial. It screamed of falsehood that was hard to ignore. There were dogwalkers on the other side, the same as they had always been, the same lampposts alight at the end of the road. But none of it was right.

4

Bill kicked off his writing slippers, left them by the bathroom sink. He opened the door and stepped out onto the narrow slip of hallway. He heard the wailing coming from below, louder now, unruly. It was a child's wailing. It got under his skin like a bad itch. Just like it did to his father, and his father before that. A long line of short fuses, ready and waiting to blow at any moment. He took to the steps, slowly, methodically as a surgeon might place a pair of latex gloves over their hands before a careful bit of scalpel work. It wasn't surgery that was in Bill's mind, but something else. Something bad. He reached the bottom of the stairs, turned to the closed door of the playroom, gazed down to the kitchen. The recessed spotlights flickered above him, saying *no, don't do it.* Rita was making toast, barely reaching the counter, the smell of burning bread sickly. Bill watched her for a moment, wondered where his childhood had gone. It wasn't supposed to be like this. Once upon a time he was on his way to becoming a celebrated author, a person that people would look up to and say things like *that's William O'Hara, the writer. Isn't he talented, I wish I had his skills.* But nobody had said anything like that in a long time. He used to get compliments and an ego massage from well-wishers, from small time editors but not in so long that he felt redundant, a complete fraud.

David's hollering brought him back to the real world – the real shitty piece of crap world that was his now. He flung the playroom door open, fury pasting his mouth into a twisted smile, eyes burning in their sockets. 'I'll give you something to cry about,' he said, marching wickedly to his son. He pulled David to his feet, the crying wilting in the face of madness. 'I'll teach you to be so insolent.' He took his son by the collar, dragged him to the stairs, the first one creaking under foot. He shoved the boy up the steps, before turning back and darting to the kitchen door. He closed the door with a snap, pulled a chair up to the handle, wedged the door shut. Now they wouldn't be disturbed. Rita screamed, muffled against the wood grain. The handle was jimmied but the chair remained where it was. She was locked inside. 'Get up those stairs!' Bill shouted. The terror in David's eyes did little to abate the ferocity, the horror in Bill's.

'Where is she?' Bill said. 'Where is Marlene?' he took David by the arms. 'You need to tell me where she is now!'

'You're hurting me,' David said.

'Where is she!' Bill shouted. The screams were still coming from the kitchen.

'She's a moody old witch!' David said. 'She's a moody old witch and I hate her!'

Bill, without another second of thought, picked up his son, carried him to the landing, just as he might if he were putting his child to bed. Only bedtime was a long way off.

David could sense the heat of the water, somehow, almost as if he were pre-empting what was going to happen. Bath time.

'I've had it with you kids,' Bill said. 'Now you're going to be sorry.'

'But I didn't do anything,' David said. The thought of biting his father on the arm crossed his mind, but he shook it free. He was in trouble for something, don't make it worse. 'I didn't do anything, Daddy.'

Bill kicked the door wide open, steam perfuming the walls, clouding the mirror. 'I feel like I'm drowning. I'm drowning,' Bill said. 'Now you can drown too.'

He dropped David head first into the water, held him there with the strong grip of his hand, dug the nails into the back of David's neck. David kicked, lashed out with his legs, shouted under the water, his cry muffled. He couldn't breathe.

5

Clara stared up at the bathroom window. Around them there was silence. The light was on and the blind was still up which seemed a little strange, but neither she nor Bernie mentioned it to one another. Bernie switched off the engine and felt the relief that her tank of junk had made the journey. Every time she hit the pedal in recent days she wasn't sure if it would be the last time. They shared a long silence, could've lasted minutes, maybe just mere moments. But in that silence many things were being said, things that neither of them could verbalise right now. Bernie couldn't hide her worry and Clara was struggling to disguise her anger. Clara looked down at the red on her thighs, and up to Bernie's beautiful eyes. She had drawn blood with the edges of her fingernails. Her skin below the dress matched the claret in her face as blood rushed and boiled. 'Are you sure you don't want me to come in with you?' Bernie asked.

Clara undid her seatbelt, took a look in the mirror, saw someone staring back that she didn't instantly recognise. The eyes looked the same, the same scar on her nose looking like a comet blazing through the sky, but that hair was alien. Just like the street a moment ago. It just looked different. Perhaps the absence of Clara's gaze had given everything around her that foreign look. It would take time, she figured. 'No, Bernie. Like I said, I need to face him alone.'

Clara slammed the car door and saw that Bernie was mouthing something at her. Clara stopped in her tracks, took another look at the bathroom window and its absence of shadow, and waited as Bernie wound down the window.

6

David was losing air. His body fading in the choke. Bill continued to push his head down, further into the water, lips peeled back in a terrible, horrifying snarl, and he listened to the water gurgle as David's breath hit it hard, again and again. Bill cursed the women in his past, all of them, at least all the ones he could remember. He thought of his mother and wondered why she had stayed so long in a loveless marriage. Why she had consistently turned a blind eye to his father's affairs. He cursed those women too. The whores who had sucked cock enough times to get a loyalty card at Cocksuckers 'R' Us, and then flounced in front of the father of the church, sat on men's laps for fun, his father's lap, his loser of a father's lap and then laughed at his dear mother. He saw David move below him, his legs kicking and flailing, trying to kick him off. Bill pressed his knee to the small of his boy's back, into the back of his knee and saw him buckle under the pressure. Bill had him trapped.

7

Clara moved a little closer to the open window where Bernie was saying something she couldn't quite hear. 'I just wanted to tell you that I think you're the most brave, amazing, sincere woman I've met,' said Bernie with a huge smile.'

Clara gushed with awkwardness, a little embarrassed at the compliments. She brushed her fingers over her ears, forgetting that the hair was no longer there to be tucked behind the lobes. 'Thanks,' she said, shyly. Her eyes squinted in the light as she gazed up to the bathroom window. 'I think Marcie might tell us to go and get a room or something if she could hear us talking this way,' Clara said.

'I want you to be the first one to read my article,' said Bernie.

'I'd be honoured.'

'It may need a little input from you though.'

'Just say the word.'

'I was kind of hoping we could go through it together one night over a bottle of wine.'

'And spoil your hard work getting sober?'

'I think I'm okay now. I just needed to get my head clear, sort my priorities sort of thing.'

'It's going to be good us living together for a while,' said Clara, feeling her freedom for the first time since that rainy day in October. 'You can stay as long as you need,' said Bernie. She looked up at the window where the light flickered in the winter skyline. She felt some sort of queer dread that was unexplained, perhaps she was picking up on Clara's vibes, she thought. Better not add to it. 'I think I'll go and feed poor Hemingway, then I'll make up your room, okay?'

'Sure.'

'I'll be back very soon.'

Bernie started the engine, saw the road ahead and thought of those weather reports of snow this afternoon. She hoped she would make it back in time. She pulled up the window and was glad that the chill would soon be gone. Then she pulled away as Clara watched her getting smaller and smaller.

8

David was about to lose consciousness. He was drifting into the great unknown, his body trembling, his legs losing strength. His arms went limp, not struggling anymore, not fighting, not able to lift, to beat against the beast. His legs buckled, the rigidity lost and he fell further toward the darkness. The water splashed up out of the bath and fell onto Bill's socks, causing the white to turn dark. David had gone. He had fallen into the ultimate blackout.

9

The house looked the same. The street had. Her eyes in the wing mirror had, but then again, it had all changed. She noticed the nails in the wall where her art had once hung. The living room was dark, all curtains closed. The playroom was dead. No tepee, no chairs. She was on her way through the house when she heard a noise coming from upstairs. Instead of going to the kitchen she turned to face the sound. The sound of her husband.

Clara gripped the banister hard, held on for dear life, as though if she were to let go then she might fall down, curl up, become dead meat. She passed the window on the staircase, open and letting the chill blow in through the house. A few months ago she would have joked about living in the drifts of a cold, airy barn. Just the way Bill liked it. Heat never played a part in a good book, he said. It had to be icy for his head to deliver to the page. Ice cold.

Clara stood at the top of the stairs, breathless. It may as well have been the Old Man for all the strength it had taken her. To the right was Rita's bedroom. David's next to that. But the noise was coming from the semi-closed door of the bathroom immediately to her left.

'Bill?' Clara said. 'Bill, I'm home.'

Then came the banging from downstairs. An awful, loud, hard banging that shook fear into her. It was coming from the kitchen. *Why didn't I go in there?* Clara asked herself. The voice was Rita's. A shout so loud it would have woken the dead. Clara was about to step back, go back down, go to her daughter. But she saw the shadows under the door. Shadows of Bill. 'Rita!' Clara shouted. 'Wait!'

Clara burst in to the bathroom, almost slipped on the damp that spread out across the linoleum. Bill held David in the water head first, never looked at his wife, never heard her screaming. David's neck was sore, blood red with pressure, with the grip of his father's hands. His legs motionless, body limp. 'David!' Clara shouted. She grabbed a hold of Bill, tried to wrestle her son free. He knocked her backwards. The light overhead flickered again. Clara's screams bounced off the tiles. Still the noise from downstairs, from the kitchen where Rita banged furiously against the door. 'Let him go!' Clara shouted, a hurt cry, weak and sorry. She was sorry for letting him destroy everything. Sorry for believing him.

Bill held on to the boy. Stared deep down into the ripples of the water. Stared until he saw something that stopped him dead.

A woman's face. A wrinkled, bruised face that just appeared in the water.

Grey eyes. Bony cheeks. Long unwashed hair, lank and lifeless. Bill let go of the boy, backed up sharp. David fell limply to the ground.

Clara never heard anything else. It was drowned out by what she was seeing. She didn't hear the cries from downstairs, now getting closer and closer. The footsteps that drew ever nearer. She only saw the unthinkable, just as Bill did. A hand that rose from the water. Liver spots, broken and hungry nails chipped, bloodied and dark with muck. Bill cried out, turned to run, slipped on the damp, fell backwards. There was a sickening thud from behind Clara. Clara forced her body to move, even though she was stricken. Even though she was frightened. She rushed to David, held his head in her arms, told him to wake up now. He was a lifeless doll.

She cried out, heart racing, heart sinking, head burning with the will for her son to breathe. Then a voice, familiar, haunting in those fatal seconds. She looked to the door where Bernie was standing, Rita by her side, tears streaming, mobile phone in her hand.

'Call an ambulance!' Clara shouted. 'He's not breathing,' she said through a well of tears. She cupped David in her arms. The first flakes of snow fell against the window. Bernie shouted down the phone for them to hurry. Time was passing by and nobody was here to bring the boy back to life. They both waited for a siren that seemed to take as long as the night is dark. Finally, it came and the power left them all for those few minutes.

CHAPTER 32

Two weeks ago

Stuart Pillman ran his bony hands over the four-day stubble on his cheeks. The once bright blue eyes were now glassy and tired. The nose hair was hanging down like icicles off a roof gutter. He could still see his father in those eyes, but it never hurt him, not anymore. That had faded into a dull ache years ago. He picked up the cold razor and began to scrape off the hair, the grey sides hacked off as if they were squatters being turfed out of his derelict home. Falling to the dirty basin with another flick of his wrist. The old song came back to him as it often did in these lean years. In the brooding winter light, as if daylight had abandoned him for several years, leaving him an endless cycle of black, he sang the song his mother used to sing. The last song that Mary Dunn heard before she . . .

Stuart groped at the sagging flesh on his smooth, clean-shaven face. He couldn't remember when age had come for him. It seemed to have always been this way. But of course, it hadn't. He had been young once. He was still sure of that; he just couldn't say when. Perhaps age had taken him the day when he left her in the morgue, or the day he went back to find her still flat on her stomach, still bloody and bruised. But still breathing.

When he thought of Mary in the immediate aftermath, it made him happy. He was glad that mother had finally got what she deserved. But it wasn't mother, it was just some old lady in a wheelchair who was in the wrong place at the wrong time. This is what brought him down, the fact that he had hurt someone he didn't even know. It wasn't mother and the guilt was eating at him. He felt it now like he'd been feeling it for years. But that guilt had turned to hatred. He hated himself. He hated the cold, callous world and all of its misery and bullshit. He hated the runners in the morning fog, the shoppers who took up all the space on the pavement, the prams and buggies and dog leads and dog shit and puddles of rainwater. He heated the recycling once a week, the tv dinners that went ding at four-thirty, he hated the overgrown weeds in his small garden, he hated the sound of people's voices. He hated everything because everything reminded him of her.

He sighed heavily and turned out the light. He made his way down the staircase, passing mother's room that was locked. It had been locked for years. Never did he open it, never. He checked the mail that had been dumped on the floor underneath the letterbox. He didn't care much for these new postal workers. They were loud and rude and they bever said *hello*, not anymore. But who did?

He opened one of the letters. He knew it would seem strange. But fuck them, they can all screw off. Guess the reasons why. They can guess all day long. He didn't know why he was opening it, perhaps it was that old curiosity gene he inherited from . . . no, he mustn't think that. He wasn't one of those. He didn't like children in any way, he didn't like anything to do with them. And he never got an erection. Not with Mary, not with his mother. He certainly wasn't one of those. He despised them. Father was, though. He must have been. For when he came in the . . . he paused to let this thought trail off. A local councillor's newsletter, a charity collection sack, and an offer to buy faster broadband for only nineteen-ninety-nine a month. He had no use for broadband. He never liked the idea anyway. All those flashing lights, all the wires. He hated wires. The ones they put inside you warping your mind, the ones they put down your throat because you can't stop throwing up in the morning. He was sick of that too: the endless vomit. The doctor reckons he could have a hernia, and his stomach is being stretched as a result. But Stuart knows he just wants to stick his dick in his arse. They were all like that. Pretending to be one thing, doing another. All the post went in the trash.

He took an envelope from the kitchen drawer, placed it down on the table, took one more look at the mould on the ceiling and on the wall. How long had it been this way? It seemed forever. He thought his runny nose was just hay fever, until it never went away, even in the depths of winter. It was the damn mould. Mother would have kicked up a fuss about it. About the mould, the mess, the damp, the state of things. About the whole damn world. The way that things simply were. Mother always kicked up a fuss.

He picked up the note he he'd written this morning and read the top line again: *There is something I need to tell you, and you're not going to like it.*

It made him feel good to read it, not fully knowing why. It had a strange power that made him like himself, if only for a moment, then it dissipated like everything did these days. It fell to the curb and laid down ready to die. He slipped the note inside the envelope. 'Fucking sickness,' he said to an empty room. 'I'm sick of this fucking sickness. Mum, I'm sick.'

He placed the envelope on the kitchen counter, wrote his name on the front – in tired penmanship. It had never been that pleasant to look at anyway. He placed the dining room chair in the centre of the kitchen, under the hard wood beam. 'That's right, mum,' he said. He took the three-strand laid rope in his hands and began to finger it through, feeling the coarse texture, the wonderful way it smelled, of oil and petroleum. He only knew one knot – the bowline. He laid the rope across his left hand, the free end hanging down limp and lifeless. He formed a small loop and brought the free end up to and through the eye from the under side. He wrapped the line around the standing line and then back down through the loop and tightened the knot pulling on the free end while holding the standing line. It was done. The rope was then hooked over the wood beam in the small nest of the kitchen. Then it was all done, forever.

His head went through the loop, he closed his eyes and stood listlessly on the chair. These were the final moments, the last breath, the ending his sorry existence demanded. He closed his eyes, rocked on the chair, back and forth, left and right. The wood creaked. The rope heaved. The light flickered. He rocked and swayed and finally the chair toppled to the floor. But something was wrong. He wasn't dead.

The knot had been too weak. Instead of nothingness, there was a daft, endless light still piercing his eyes. The suicide hadn't come to fruition. He laughed, shook his head, held the broken noose up to the light, frayed end mockingly fragrant. 'Well, that didn't work,' he said. 'But don't worry, I'm not a quitter.' Smiling, he picked up the sharp carving knife on the counter, took it to his throat and in one sweep he sprayed the whites of the cupboards, the counter, the refrigerator, crimson. He sank to the ground.

As he bled, he thought of Mary Dunn and her last moments on that lonely morgue bed. He thought of the way her body gave in, her chest heaving until it could take no more breaths. But his final thought was the way his mother smiled at him when he told her that it was all going to be over very soon. And then it was.

CHAPTER 33

Present day

It was cold and grey on the outskirts of Waterside House. A crowd had quickly gathered by the fence, the one that meant you can't get near the water. Yellow police tape flapped in the wind. A strong icy January blast that made Detective Cunnings turn up the collars on his worn-out winter coat. The same one that his wife donated to Oxfam three weeks ago, only to find it returned to its place in the wardrobe days after. He had a knack for finding things out, he said to her. Now he was fishing for something else. Dredging the waters of Coniston on a note left in one of the bloodiest scenes he had come across in all his years on the job. Suicides weren't usually like that. Someone usually just took a box of pills, washed them down with Jack Daniels, or they waded into deep waters and said a silent goodbye. This had been a bloodbath. Tried to hang himself but the knot was too weak and too badly made. When that had gone wrong, he sliced through his throat with a carving knife, spraying the kitchen white goods in the process. He'd bled out on the kitchen floor, a note resting on the counter with one name on the envelope: Stuart Pillman.

The note was a confession. Not your average 'goodbye world.' In the note he'd named a woman, a patient of Waterside House. Her name was Mary Dunn – class of '88.

Cunnings walked a little further down the line of yellow tape, the yellow scream of horror. He turned and faced the top floor of The Old Forge where faces white as snow stared down. He remembered a line from the note which just wouldn't leave him alone: *she was always blue, and so I beat her blue to match.*

There was no apology, no remorse. But why write the note in the first place? Why now? why confess now?

Another part of the note: *I drowned her in the water outside the grounds. She was always so quiet, I often wondered why. I guess some folks just are what they are.*

The note went on like this, as though he were engaged in a generic conversation with his reader, just a little chat over coffee – so nonchalant, so wicked. *I packed her with bricks so she wouldn't float. The wheelchair I had to leave behind. Actually, to tell you the truth, I'd forgotten about the damn wheelchair, that wretched thing, and by the time I realised she was going down fast!*

Cunnings swallowed hard, felt the acid slide down his throat. Just when he had visions of his morning coffee reappearing, there was a shout from one of the officers wading through the icy water. 'They've got something,' said Cunnings, not caring that only he could hear. He could feel the excitement, the horror, the anticipation building up inside. It was the moment he'd been dreading. 'They've fucking got something,' he said.

He rushed over to the small boat and the waders. He heard the crows in the oaks above and behind him and wondered if that dreadful caw ever got under the skin of the patients. It must. There was pointing from the windows up in The Old Forge. Rubberneckers. But Cunnings didn't care, for once. He simply waited for what felt like an eternity before he cupped his mouth, gasped and then, when a body was pulled up from the water, he said, 'he was telling the truth.' But he hadn't doubted that, nobody would invent such horror, but he kind of wished that he had. 'He was telling the fucking truth.'

The body had been scavenged, but there was no doubt in Cunnings's mind that it was her. It was Mary. He made the sign of the cross, waited for the next load of bones to be dredged up. 'That poor woman,' he said to Katie Grey – his new*ish* partner who'd arrived in time to give him his third coffee of the day. He took it, not knowing if he could keep it down. 'Are you sure it's her?' asked Katie. 'Could be—'

'Oh, it's her,' Cunnings said, cutting across Katie. 'I know it's her. I have that feeling.'

'Sure it's not an elaborate hoax?'

'As sure as anything.'

'She has no family,' Grey said.

'No.'

'Nor any justice.'

'At least it ate him up in the end,' said Cunnings, remembering another line from the note: *I can't stand to touch myself anymore. All I see are cripples. All I can hear are crows. Those shit-eating crows.*

'We need to wait for forensics,' said Grey.

'We will,' said Cunnings. 'But I know it's our girl. He told us so, didn't he?'

'I suppose he did. Do you think there are any more?'

'I think so. I think he killed his mother too.'

'Jeez, what is wrong with some people?' Grey said.

'Takes all kinds, I suppose.'

They watched as more of Mary came into the light. Watched as onlookers pointed down to the horror. They watched as people shook their heads and made the sign of the cross.

Cunnings stared over the discovery lying on the boat, above the flurry of waders and depressed onlookers, into the darkening skyline where it might just break at any moment and shower them in hard rain. He closed his eyes and listened to the dull, aching tones of those 'shit-eating' crows. He wondered what truths they carried. If they ever saw anything of kindness or solicitude from people. If they too were sick.

EPILOGUE

'At first, I used to close the curtains for privacy. But then I realised that I kind of like the darkness. It feels safer, somehow. And no one can watch me. Rita says that it makes me morbid. She's probably right about that. It started when David was in the hospital. I suppose I never really got over the fright he caused us all. I think that's the real reason. I just feel safer knowing the dark is always there.'

Dr Hawthorn watched on as Clara took her eyes to the wonderful winter sunlight streaming through the window. The ground below their second-floor room was frozen, hard and unforgiving. 'Maybe the dark is how you manifest things. Maybe it is your crutch for now,' said Dr Hawthorn.

There were a million things that Clara had wanted to say, but she knew that she couldn't. She couldn't say how she had watched Sharne roll back her eyes and took on the spirit of an elderly woman hell bent on being discovered at the bottom of the waters. She couldn't quite articulate everything.

'I couldn't attend his funeral,' she said. 'I just couldn't.'

'Your husband—'

'Ex-husband.'

Clara took some water. Couldn't talk about what she had seen in the bathroom tub, the face, the hand, the spirit and (somehow) the body of Mary, the way Bill fell back to the edge of the basin, that awful thud, and the blood that followed.

'How do you feel about Bill's death now?' Dr Hawthorn asked. She had to ask it.

'I'm just glad he never wore his writing slippers that day. I always told him he would catch his death in those sport socks.'

'And your son? How is David?'

'He still suffers with his asthma, which is another thing he gets these days. Plenty of fresh air, they said. But I am starting to see signs of his old self returning. Bernie helps.'

'Good.'

Clara thought about that moment again, like she did a hundred times a day. What If Bernie hadn't decided to turn the car around and come back for her, knowing that she might need some moral support? What if?

'Bill's death has been the one blessing I needed, and I'm refusing to apologise for feeling that way.'

'It's perfectly understandable. He was your monster.'

'No, he was his own monster. I just got carried along like a wave.'

'How is your sleep these days?'

'It's hit and miss.'

'Well, I suppose if anybody was in your shoes they might have a little trouble getting their eight hours.'

'Try two and you're getting close.'

'And there is more change for you now. The name for instance.'

'It was a stupid combo anyway, Clara O'Hara. I always laughed it off, but now I don't see the funny side. Only the tragedy. I'll be Clara Fernsby for a while. Maybe forever.'

'It must be nice living in Bernadine's cottage out in the woods for a while?'

'I's peaceful. But I'm making plans. In the summer me and the children are moving to Cornwall. My mother and father have room for us there. At least until I can figure out what to do next.'

'The house still has memories?'

'Nightmares.'

'And the vanishing of Mary Dunn?' Dr Hawthorn asked.

'At least she is in peace now. I hear Sharne is doing very well too. She is out into supported living. I'm pleased for her. It must have been hard believing that the mother you killed so viciously with a claw hammer was asking you to do things. Things like go down to the basement every night and sit in that chair. Or haunt me, for that matter. She thought it was her mother, she thought she was making amends.'

Dr Hawthorn smiled. It was a sad sort of smile, mouth and heart. She checked her watch and Clara began to stand. She didn't need to be told it was time up anymore. The two of them stood to leave through the door. A door that did not have a porthole. A normal door to a normal place outside. Clara tucked the hair that was growing behind her ears and left the room.

Outside there was a freshness in the Cumbrian air. The smell of animals rang down from the hilltops, lay at her nose in an early Spring fashion. It was becoming the season of the lambs. It would be the fear of death that would eventually destroy them.

Clara opened the car door and sat down. Bernie Waller didn't need to ask her how it went. She could already tell it had done some good. She also didn't need think about the land of dead air. She doesn't think anything is in the land of dead air anymore. Not since her article was published, and the comments section of the online *Herald* went crazy. It was simply out of her mind for good, she hoped. And whenever the darkness did threaten her, she smiled and thought of Clara Fernsby and the ordeal she had gone through to get to the other side. Where Bernie was standing, free of ghosts.

They motored onwards, the windows half way down so that the ring from the animals found its way inside. Clara leant on the window with her elbows, felt the wind at her ears, the speed rushing through her short hair. She looked to the heavens, through a patch of smouldering cloud, looking like it was just passing through – a vagrant with a sense of unbelonging. She saw a murder of crows flying through the skyline. It was then that she knew whenever she heard the crows crying, she would think of Waterside House and the girls that she had left behind. 'Goodnight Vienna,' Bernie said with a crooked smile.

The End

Printed in Poland
by Amazon Fulfillment
Poland Sp. z o.o., Wrocław

25862944R00170